"I hate pirates," I said, more to mysel
of the starfighter squadron that wei
defense. I was flying in the middle of t
rounded by enemies, and quite possibly ;
underneath my command.

Must be Tuesday. The interior of the V-shaped Crosshair-91 fighter smelled of stale air, sweat, and oil. Sound didn't travel through space, so every pilot had to become hyperaware of the noises projected through the ship's cyber-interface.

Mine was a custom job, since cybernetics were still taboo among the majority of humanity's scattered descendants. My implants meant I could react faster and with more strategy than the majority of pilots— which was good because we were outnumbered three to one. They were all less-advanced Crosshair-75s, inferior to our 91s, but still fully capable of blowing us out of the star lanes.

The Melampus was slowly turning around the fake navigation buoy that had pulled us out of jumpspace. The aging cargo hauler was a half-kilometer cylindrical vessel that could haul a hundred thousand tons of cargo but wasn't exactly built for combat. It had far more tricks than a standard vessel of its class, but that didn't mean much given we were under attack by ex-military hardware. The Ravager, as the ship's transponder registered it as, was a Commonwealth-constructed gunship that was the shape of a box with three long tendrils sticking out from its mouth.

Speial thanks to th ever-patient Kat Phipps for her love & support

ISBN 978-1-948929-82-0
Mystique Press is an imprint of Crossroad Press Publishing
For information address Crossroad Press at 141 Brayden Dr., Hertford, NC 27944
www.crossroadpress.com

First edition

LUCIFER'S NEBULA

BY C. T. PHIPPS

MYSTIQUE PRESS

CHAPTER ONE

"I hate pirates," I said, more to myself than the other members of the starfighter squadron that were the *Melampus*'s primary defense. I was flying in the middle of the ass end of space, surrounded by enemies, and quite possibly going to die with everyone underneath my command. Must be Tuesday.

The interior of the V-shaped Crosshair-91 fighter smelled of stale air, sweat, and oil. Sound didn't travel through space, so every pilot had to become hyperaware of the noises projected through the ship's cyber-interface. Mine was a custom job, since cybernetics were still taboo among the majority of humanity's scattered descendants. My implants meant I could react faster and with more strategy than the majority of pilots—which was good because we were outnumbered three to one. They were all less-advanced Crosshair-75s, inferior to our 91s, but still fully capable of blowing us out of the star lanes.

The *Melampus* was slowly turning around the fake navigation buoy that had pulled us out of jumpspace. The aging cargo hauler was a half-kilometer cylindrical vessel that could haul a hundred thousand tons of cargo but wasn't exactly built for combat. It had far more tricks than a standard vessel of its class, but that didn't mean much given we were under attack by ex-military hardware.

The Ravager, as the ship's transponder registered it as, was a Commonwealth-constructed gunship that was the shape of a box with three long tendrils sticking out from its mouth. It also had a "rack" on its sides that held room for twelve starfighters, nine of which had been dispatched against us and made me think the pirates hadn't been entirely successful in their murderous careers. The vessel's statistics, coldly projected into my mind, showed it was badly maintained with a power production 2/3rds of normal but there was little the *Melampus* could do against something designed to serve as escort to fleet ships.

We were in a particularly bad place to be ambushed as well since our current, highly illegal, cargo run was taking us through the Border Planets territory on the edge of Sector 13. It was the penumbra between "civilized" Community space and the petty fiefdoms that made up the territory humanity had colonized throughout the Spiral. As desolate no man's lands went, this was innumerable light years away from anyone who could answer a distress call and even further from anyone who would.

"I hate pirates too, Cassius," Clarice O'Harra said, revealing my coarse language had gone out over the comm.

Clarice was piloting the second of our fighters and doing a damned good job of it despite the fact she was only a year into training. The *Melampus* first officer had all but demanded to be able to learn after we'd stolen our ship from the Commonwealth and was a fast learner. Unfortunately, as a third of our enemies went up in an explosion of its fusion reactor and orihalcum fuel, this was the definition of a sink-or-swim scenario.

"I don't suppose you have a plan for this," David Albernathy said over the comm. He was the former leader of the *Melampus's* starfighters but the only one with any actual combat experience but myself. "Because surrender is a perfectly valid response from my perspective. Better than the *Melampus* jumping without us."

If I could have reached through the comm unit and strangled the Commonwealther with my bare hands, I would have. That kind of talk would have gotten a man executed in the Crius Starfighter Corps.

"You aren't in the Crius Starfighter Corps anymore," the cool soothing voice of Judith, the ship's A.I. and the digital ghost of my late wife, whispered in my ear. *"And thank God for that."*

I pulled back on my starfighter's speed before spinning around and targeting the pair of pirates behind me. Both of them scrambled to maneuver out of the way, only to be blasted to pieces by my plasma cannons. I could tell the enemy pilots had received military training and should have easily overwhelmed us but, instead, were reacting with a cocky and overconfident flight pattern. I reckoned the crew of the *Ravager* and its pilots to be deserters from the current interstellar war, Crius or Commonwealthers who'd decided they wanted no part of the next altercation between the major powers of humanity's scattered tribes.

doctor to treat the brain of the man she's sleeping with."

"Tough," Clarice said, showing her usual unwillingness to listen to reason. At least mine. "Isla's the only medical doctor we have that isn't completely incompetent. You almost blew up a bunch of escape pods back there and turned us into mass murderers."

"We're already—" I stopped in mid-sentence. "I'm already a mass murderer."

I'd done a lot of terrible things in the Commonwealth-Archduchy War. You didn't get a name like the Butcher of Kolthas by playing nice during the war. I'd targeted industrial zones, targets where there was high collateral damage, and joined with groups that targeted civilian officials. All of it had proven pointless or actually made the world worse, but I didn't pretend I was a good man. War made murderers out of all men and it made mass murderers of those who survived until its end. It didn't help the side I'd fought for was a routine violator of the rules and articles of war—such as they were in space.

"Yeah, well, stop being one now," Clarice said, "or I'll stop you."

I used my cyber-comm to communicate with Judith. *"Tell me, did she move to take aim at me when I was flying at the* Ravager?*"*

"Yes, Judith replied. *I think she was prepared to shoot you down to save their lives."*

"That's really stupid."

"Yes," Judith said. *"Especially since you're her closest friend. A person she loves."*

"Jealous?"

"Should I be?"

I shook that thought away and contemplated the fact Clarice was a moral enough person to try to kill me to protect me from myself. The fact I couldn't make sense of it enough to say she was wrong or right told me there was perhaps something to her belief that I needed my head examined. "I'll consult with Dr. Hernandez. Maybe you should be captain."

"No," Clarice said. "You're the best person we have for the job."

"Then God help us all," I said, shutting off our link.

Alone in the darkness of my cockpit, I took a moment to clear my head. I was detoxing from my latest failed attempt to stop drinking. There were pills you could take to cleanse yourself but the

Melampus's medical supplies were running low due to corners we'd had to cut. It was hard enough running an independent hauling business when you'd offended all of the major galactic powers in human space but doubly so when training to maintain a ship that had been modified by Earth to be just close to a warship. We also needed those modifications as circumstances had just proven.

A small glowing blue woman, translucent, and wearing a dress made of shifting numbers appeared in the right corner of my vision. It was Judith's avatar, the *Melampus*'s avatar now, looking at me. It was image planted in my mind through our cybernetic connection, but no less real. My wife had been a beautiful woman with red hair and pale skin, but she was long dead. Judith the Cognition A.I. was a mere copy of her personality.

But did that make her less the person I loved? It was difficult to say because in some ways she was every bit the person I remembered. In other ways, she was completely different. Her mind could sort through millions of gigaplexbytes per second but had her personality hardwired into her programming so they never overwhelmed her humanity. Judith couldn't change, though, nor was she was she able to respond the way she did before. We were worlds apart without a starship and yet always able to see one another. Which I suppose made her a moon in my orbit or vice versa. After all, I had changed.

For the worse.

"Would you have really blown up those escape pods?" Judith asked, no longer speaking in my mind but generating her voice through the ship's comm system into my earpiece.

"I don't know," I admitted. "In that moment, I wanted to kill them all. However, I probably would have stopped in horror once I realized what I was doing."

"The old Cassius wouldn't have done that."

"The old Cassius didn't have his homeworld blown up or the responsibility of a ship with children and families on it."

"Or people he loved," Judith said, defending it. "Rules of war are strange things. If you'd killed everyone on the ship by blowing up its reactor, you would have done nothing wrong. It's only after they've surrendered and ceased to be a threat that killing them became criminal. You know, despite the fact they tried to kill you and we're not the authorities."

"They're deserters," I said, setting my autopilot to dock with the *Melampus*. "I could tell by their tactics. A group of soldiers for the Commonwealth or Crius that decided to duck from the war."

"I think they're part of the local colonial militia," Judith said, surprising me. "Piracy is a side activity most of the border planets militaries engage in. They're probably a local militia trained by the Crius, Commonwealth, or both, and making use of second- or third-hand equipment."

"That doesn't make me feel better."

"Everyone is just trying to survive out here," Judith said. There was something about her demeanor, though, which told me she was saying it more out of the fact I expected her to than real sympathy, though. Judith had grown increasingly cold over the past few months, as if the efforts to be human were starting to overwhelm her.

"If living on the border has made them savages then that just means we've wandered too far from civilization," I said, honestly having grown sick of this area. Resources were so scarce and the rule of law so weak it was unleashing my worst instincts—which hadn't been that far from the surface to begin with.

Judith paused in her speech. She looked like a work of art when she stood still—like a Venetia crystal statue or a piece of Arthaeus holo-illusion art. "I can see how much this is all tormenting you but may I make your day just a little bit worse?"

Her way of asking almost made me laugh. Almost. "Oh please. Lord knows I haven't had enough bad news today nor have a funeral to prep. How bad is it?"

"Bad."

I closed my eyes. "Tell me."

"I think the *Ravager*, actually the *Liberty* by the way, was sent by our employer. I don't think we're going to get paid for this job."

CHAPTER TWO

The revelation we were probably screwed even if we turned our cargo over to the Dragon, the Spiral's biggest crime boss, reminded me just how we'd gotten involved in this stupid scheme coldly projected into my mind. Specifically, I'd gotten us involved in it. I couldn't say I wasn't warned against it either.

I was the one who had decided we should get into interstellar smuggling, become part of a major crime syndicate, and carry cargo for an alien who didn't even have a proper name. It hadn't been one of my better ideas. Even worse, everyone on the ship had seen what a terrible idea this all was before I'd agreed to it. I chose to mentally relive the memory, a feature of my cybernetics, from about a week earlier. After all, I had nothing else better to do until autopilot brought me back to the ship.

"This is a stupid scheme," Isla Hernandez said, standing beside me as we walked to the rendezvous at Krawl's Tavern.

Isla Hernandez was a beautiful white-haired woman with golden skin and a mixture of Odin and Tezcatlipocan features. She wasn't descended from the humans of either planet, though, because she was a bioroid. A free bioroid who, if discovered, could have been enslaved or destroyed by anyone who was so inclined.

Humanity hated artificial intelligence since they'd led to the Great Collapse, and even if there were galaxies of difference between a gynoid like her versus a Cognition A.I. like Judith, both inherited a measure of humanity's loathing. The fact humans still made bioroids by the millions as slaves was just one of those little hypocrisies we dealt with. Either way, she was human to me. More so than Judith lately—a fact I was uncomfortable with.

Today, Isla was dressed in a gray hooded cloak over a ship's doctor's white flight suit. It was dusty and faded, like much of the attire on the *Melampus*, but signaled her as a healer on the Ring. We'd already been distracted twice from getting to our meeting in order to treat a stabbing and a Kolahn ape-like boy who was suffering oxygen poisoning. I wasn't exactly unsympathetic but if we missed our meeting then five hundred crew members on the *Melampus* would suffer instead.

All around us were hundreds of humans, aliens, transhumans, and uplifts gathered in the oxygen-breathing Type-C environment of the Ring. The Ring was a structure created by a long-ascended race and one of the few gathering places for multiple species in the border planets. There were places where vast fortunes could be made trading alien technology to humanity or raw materials in reverse. That took a lot of time and connections, though, that I was still trying to work out since I'd taken over as captain.

I was wearing a heavy duster over my red starfighter's pilot uniform. I had a Disintegrator-7 fusion pistol holstered on my belt in open display as well as my personal shield generator belt buckle next to my old Crius Starfighter Corps proton sword. The sword itself was useless outside of duels but I'd made a name for myself with it by letting my shield soak up some low powered weapons fire then carving the holders up. They called me Cutter. Not the best name to have around here, but not the worst either.

"If you had any objections, you should have shared them before," I muttered, not wanting to have this conversation again.

"I *did* say so before," Isla said. "Before, during, and will after if we don't get ourselves killed."

"We haven't yet."

"Which goes to show you God isn't finished screwing with us yet."

"True," I admitted. Then I lied, saying, "I know what I'm doing."

"Are you sure, because from where I'm standing, it looks like you want us to become smugglers," Isla said. "Which, having actually worked on a smuggling ship, is a lot less glamorous than they make it out to be in the holovids."

"We're not exactly welcome in civilized space," I said, grimacing. "The result of screwing over the two largest governments in human space."

"Stealing the *Melampus* from the Commonwealth's intelligence service and killing the Free Systems Alliance's chief mad scientist was a rather colossal 'fuck you' to the two sides in this war, I'll admit." Isla paused a second, perhaps remembering their 'chief mad scientist' had been my sister—or, at least, a bioroid duplicate of her. The real Zoe had created one before escaping Commonwealth custody and joining the Free Systems Alliance founded by our brother.

"We also kept them from an Elder Race artifact designed to worsen the war," I said, still not sure how we'd wound up in the middle of such an epic clusterfuck. "It was all extremely heroic but makes us the most wanted ship in the galaxy."

There was also the issue of Judith, something I'd lost crew over despite the majority of the crew thinking she was nothing more than an exceptionally sophisticated interface. A Cognition A.I. was an insurmountable advantage when keeping our enemies at bay, but would also make us galactic pariahs if discovered. Still, Judith was a living monument to my late wife and something I'd preserve no matter the cost—and the cost had been dear so far.

"Not quite," Isla said. "Judith wiped our records and changed our transponder. The *Melampus* is an old *Olympian*-class heavy hauler. They're more common than dirt. Besides, if the Watchers really wanted to find us, they would. Neither side can risk Judith tearing them apart or revealing their secrets."

"That's one theory," I said.

"What's the other?" Isla asked, pick-pocketing the credit stick of a rich-looking alien we passed.

"They just haven't gotten around to murdering us yet," I said, thinking about how long the Commonwealth's memory was. Some of the criminals they'd hunted down and executed included fugitives who'd been on the run for centuries. I had no desire to be grabbed out of my bed, tried, and hung when I was a two hundred-year-old retiree.

Isla didn't respond to that.

Passing a newsfeed kiosk run by a man who looked like a tiger with two legs and cybernetic arms in a tank top, I took a moment to pay a subscription fee and download the latest information from Sectors One through Twelve.

In a moment, my mind became full of hundreds of news stories my enhanced brain sorted through relevancy and detail. For the most part, I restricted myself to checking details about the war and economics. I did, admittedly, also download a list of upcoming holovids I wanted to see.

"Pick me up the latest *Galactic Concubine* vids," Isla said.

"You realize those are porn, right?" I asked.

"And?" Isla asked, smiling.

"All right." I shook my head, soaking in what was happening to the rest of the universe.

"Any good news?" Isla asked.

"No," I said. "The Free Systems Alliance is kicking the crap out of the Commonwealth and adopting a policy of *guerre aux châteaux, paix aux chaumières.*"

"Not all of us received your classical education, Cassius."

"War to the castles, peace to the houses," I said, remembering my lessons. "I think. It's been a while since officer school. The FSA is doing their best to do hit and fade attacks on as many military targets as possible, all easy victories, to leave Commonwealth occupied worlds unable to administrate their worlds. They're not interested in actually taking worlds as trying to inspire revolutions so the Commonwealth is forced to expend resources to retake them until it stretches itself so thin it collapses."

"Sounds like a good strategy," Isla said.

"It is," I admitted, not wanting to give any credit to the organization founded by an imposter using my name. That was another benefit of Zoe's mad science. Supposedly, my mental and physical clone was the FSA's leader. He'd started off as just a propaganda piece but had seized full control a few months ago. "Good strategy or not, though, it means the war will continue to go on even though the FSA has no ability to win. They can maximize casualties but not defeat the Commonwealth's size advantage. All they can do is 'liberate' worlds only for the Commonwealth to 'liberate' them right back."

"Maybe their strategy is to get everyone pissed off by the damage," Isla suggested. "Create more sympathy for the rebellion."

"Then it's working," I said, grimacing, as the stories of revolts were over seemingly every sector's newsfeeds. The absolute worst absurdity of it all was the fact that, a few years ago, I would have been right there with me. The Commonwealth had destroyed Crius with meteors from orbit, killed millions of citizens, and I wanted the people responsible to pay.

The problem was those people weren't on the battlefield; they were safely in shielded facilities on Albion, immune to even orbital strikes. It meant all this massive uprising was doing was killing more people who had nothing to do with policy in the Commonwealth. It was a war of kings fought by peasants and mourned only by their families as well as God.

Isla reached over and took my hand. "You don't have to take responsibility for your family's screw-ups."

I clutched her hand's smooth softness against my rough hands. "As much as I'd like to believe that, I don't think that qualifies when your sister downloads your mind into an android body and sets him up as the face of the revolution."

"I know something about being made in the image of someone else," Isla said, reminding me she was still a popular model purchasable at bioroid stores for twenty thousand credits with the adult functions being an extra ten thousand. "Trust me, the imposter running around leading the FSA isn't you."

"No, but he'll come for us eventually too. Avenging Crius may be occupying his attention now but he won't stop until I'm dead. He loved Zoe." I also knew he'd have to kill me, as I represented an existential threat to his narrative. As long as there was a Cassius Mass running around who didn't think the best solution to the Commonwealth occupying the former archduchy was war—well, that potentially put to lie all of his pretty speeches about fighting and dying for freedom.

"You loved Zoe too. She just didn't love you back," Isla said, understating matters.

I leaned over and kissed her, taking a moment to be glad I'd found her. Our relationship wasn't exactly *conventional*, though. There had been a time I'd considered ending my relationship with her and Clarice both to be with Judith but the latter had no interests in the physical intimacies of a relationship. I could never have given her up completely, though, nor would Isla have done the same. I really didn't deserve her patience in figuring out we were a family—just a very strange one.

Isla then pulled away and glared at me with fire in her eyes.

"You've been drinking."

Uh-oh. I wiped my mouth. I'd promised I'd try to work on that. "How can you tell?"

"Your mouth tastes like reactor fuel," Isla said, sticking out her tongue.

"Well, it's Munin's home brew, so that may be an ingredient," I said, speaking of our young chief engineer. "I've only been drinking a little. Just high of socially."

"Socially where? Drunk Planet?" Isla asked, her voice having an edge as sharp as Arawn steel.

"I'm functional. That's more than I can say for a lot of Crius veterans." I wasn't in the mood to be berated for how I coped with the shit hand God had dealt me.

Isla looked like she was struggling to decide whether she should be understanding or angry before descending on controlled fury. "We've discussed this, Cassius. You're supposed to stop drinking. Self-medication isn't how you're going to recover."

I closed my eyes. "Recover from what? My world being destroyed? Losing my friends and family? Being only good at killing and fucking? Drinking is a way of coping. It's—"

"An addiction?" Isla said. "You're hardly the first person to need help getting over booze."

"I was designed better," I said, knowing I was pushing the limits of my health with the amount of booze I was consuming.

"You're designed to be human," Isla said, softening her tone. "We can work through this, but you need to want to stop. I'll look for the right medicine to purge your system of the physical effects."

That would just leave me coping with the memories and pain of what I'd been through on my own. "I'll think about it."

Isla frowned. "Cassius, I will get a knife, cut your liver out and replace it with a cybernetic replacement if I have to. Then you won't be able to get drunk drinking—"

"Reactor fuel?" I suggested, smirking. It was what Munin called her special brand.

"Not funny," Isla said.

I thought it was hilarious. "Come on, we still have to make our meeting with Fade."

"Fade?" Isla said, shaking her head. "His name is *Fade*?"

"Fade works for the Dragon and to get to him, I had to beat up an alien called Scartooth and bribe a man called the Wraith."

"Please tell me you're joking," Isla said. "I hope we haven't come all the way to the Ring just to meet with rejects from a bad holo-sim."

I shrugged. "It's the border planets. There's a lot more alien and human interaction here than just about anywhere else. People don't understand names like Jacob, Derek, or Gary. They do understand concepts, though."

"Huh," Isla said. "That almost makes sense."

"Really? Because I just made that up."

Isla punched me in the arm as we approached the location where we were going to have our meeting. Krawl's Tavern was a seedy bar because of course it was. It was one of the few traits that seemed universal among sentient races that races got drunk. Krawl's Tavern was a two-story domed supercrete white building with numerous holographic displays around it flashing in various languages. It scanned your personal vid-link and then gave you a personal listing of beverages and food available suitable for your form in your home language. Mine didn't work very well since it listed food designed for my false identity and, apparently, they ate nothing but bugs on their homeworld. Either that or the place's advertisement system was busted.

The entrance was a long, circular hallway that resembled the entrance to an igloo. Lights flickered all around us as we were scanned and screened for things like intestinal parasites, communicable diseases, or whether or not we had money. Isla looked around nervously, perhaps worried the implant that passed her off as a human cyborg rather than a bioroid was malfunctioning, but there was no sign that it registered that.

"Funny, they don't scan for weapons," Isla said.

"Easier to clean up bodies than try to disarm customers and get yourself dead," I said. "There's always more customers in a port like this after all."

"Ha-ha," Isla said.

"Not joking."

An airlock at the end of the short tunnel opened up and we entered into a circular chamber that was full of a mixed clientele of humans and oxygen- (or nitrogen- for that matter) breathing species. The light was dim and the air smelled bizarre from the various scents given off even as the interior was composed of three layers of cubicles arranged in stadium-style seating for maximum privacy as well as a limited amount of environmental control.

If you were willing to eschew that there was also the bar that was a lot more traditional. A row of seats around a kiosk full of tube-covered machines designed to assemble chemical compositions for just about anything that imbibed a beverage. The bartender was a human mutant that was either grossly obese or from a branch of humanity built like a brick wall but dressed in baggy clothes. He wore a harness that operated half-dozen metal tentacles that allowed him to serve multiple clients at once. Cheaper than hiring additional help, I guess.

I recognized some of the species in the bar: the scaled ape Kolahn, the horned grasshopper-like Llrowlthra, the incommunicado Ants (obviously not their real name, but we couldn't pronounce it), some lemur-like Notha in fascist uniforms, and a few others, but most were a mystery. For all my knowledge about everything from Earth's destruction to present-day history and implants that made me able to calculate mathematical possibilities others had to spend months on, I was a babe in the woods regarding xenology. Humanity had long been the "poor cousins" to the Community and it was only now our technology was reaching Galactic Standard. All of us were rock-banging primitives to the Elder Races, though, that made this particular deal all the more dangerous.

"Do you even know what species this Fade is?" Isla asked.

"I think that's part of the test."

"Test?" Isla asked. "What test? What have you gotten us into?"

I grimaced and reached in my pocket to hold the strange serpent-shaped device in my pocket that I'd risked our crew and ship to get. It was difficult to believe we'd come halfway across the Spiral in part to get this item, only to be here to trade it away but such was the nature of commerce. "I'm securing the future for the *Melampus* and its crew. I owe them that much."

"I'm going to hate this, aren't I?"

I paused. "Yes, you are."

"How much am I going to hate this?" Isla asked.

"Remember that black eye I got from Clarice?"

"I thought that was rough sex."

I rolled my eyes. "Keep your mind off that."

"Can't. Sexbot. It's the way I'm programmed."

She had a point there. "Well, Clarice had a better reaction to it than Judith. She locked me in my quarters for a day in the dark trying to talk me out of it."

"I was wondering what that was about."

"It's a good idea, though."

"Despite two of the three most important women in your life telling you it's a horrible one."

"Not three?" I asked.

"I don't know the idea yet." Isla's voice turned dangerous.

A thick Iberian-accented voice then spoke behind us as a pair of arms went over our shoulders. "Your friend, Captain Cassius Mass, late of the Archduchy of Crius Navy, is bringing us an Elder Race artifact as his buy-in fee to become part of the Consortium."

The Consortium was the largest crime syndicate in the Spiral. If anyone could protect my crew and loved ones from my enemies, it was them. I just had to convince them we were worth more as allies than as bounties to turn over. Our chances of that had gone down considerably since I hadn't told them our real identities and yet they'd figured that out on their own.

"That's about the size of it, yes," I said, not turning around.

The man continued to speak. "So now you can tell me what one of the most wanted humans alive is doing trying to join a group that would turn him over in a second?"

CHAPTER THREE

Turning around, I saw the face of a handsome man with strong Ibernian features. He had a black bowl-shaped haircut, light-brown skin, a pair of dueling scars on the sides of his face that indicated he'd offended someone badly, and a strong aquiline nose. Any ancestry from other worlds was drowned out and I wondered if he'd had surgery since so few people showed that level of racial ancestry.

His clothes were a good shade richer than was common in the spaceports of the Ring, being a synth-weave electronic war coat over a shimmersilk ascot and self-cleaning business suit. It was the kind of attire more commonly found on Albion or the transtellars' headquarter worlds than out here in the Border Planets. I noted he was visibly armed with his fingernails on my throat containing liquid-metal nails that could morph into poisoned claws as well as a disintegrator pistol hidden in a spring-loaded holster in his left sleeve.

"So you recognize me as Cassius Mass. You're well-informed, sir," I said, my voice low and calm.

"I would be a very poor lieutenant if I wasn't," Fade said, his voice chuckling. "The Consortium doesn't employ fools."

"If you're hiring my captain that may be in question," Isla said, her voice low and accusatory.

I couldn't blame her, as the Consortium was infamous even in Sector 7. It was primarily an organization of smugglers but involved itself in everything from technology theft, piracy, murder-for-hire, information broking, and worse. The only thing it didn't dabble in was slavery, the one moral line I refused to cross. As much because I imagined women like Isla and men like William every time I thought of those tortured by the trade as any inherent decency.

Fade let out a thick Spanish laugh as he let go of Isla's shoulder. "Oh, she is a little supernova, isn't she?"

"So I've been told," Isla said, stepping back. "So this is what we're up to?"

"Yes," I admitted. "There are few powers outside of the transtellars and planetary governments which can keep a ship like the *Melampus* running. I have a responsibility to the thousands of passengers and crew onboard."

"Because *this* is so much safer," Isla said.

"You'd be surprised," Fade said, chuckling. "The space lanes are full of pirates and deserters these days. The Free Systems Alliance is waging commerce warfare on every planet that supports the Commonwealth while they're attempting to use starvation tactics in return. Merchantmen of all stripes are turning to smugglers or neutral worlds to get their cargos through."

"More moral then," Isla said.

Fade chuckled. "One side is a bunch of terrorists rallied around arrogant landless aristocrats and the other is a bunch of imperialists struggling not to use their possessions. Did you know the Commonwealth recently legalized bioroid slavery across its territories? Ares Electronics forced the hands of their parliament to keep the credits flowing. Billions more bioroids are in production and for sale with human-level intelligence."

Isla stared at him, knowing he was baiting her. "It seems you are well informed."

Fade shrugged. "It's a poor move on their part. Hundreds of systems are already readying to revolt over it."

"I'm surprised the opposition to bioroid slavery is so fierce," I said. "Sympathy for the plight of droids always been tepid on the worlds I frequented nearer to the Spiral's heart."

"They hate A.I. and the idea of machines taking their jobs," Fade said, correcting me. "Not because they care what happens to the machine people. Pyres full of seized machines are already being burned in opposition."

Isla sucked in her breath then closed her eyes, undoubtedly imagining the holocaust being described. Then she opened her eyes and blinked rapidly. "Having experienced what it was like to be a slave, there might be some mercy to that."

"Having been a slave myself, I will say that is incorrect. Death is very final while life always holds the possibility of freedom." Fade pulled out a small metal flask from his jacket and took a sip from it before offering me some. "As well as revenge."

"You a slave?" I asked, surprised. I waved away the bottle, more interested in his story and not interested in pissing off Isla further. Despite how badly I could use a drink right now.

Fade gave a bitter smile. "The old-fashioned kind, I'm afraid. I was taken by pirates, sold to asteroid miners, doped up on White Dust, and then worked for fourteen-hour days until my hands started to rot off my broken back."

His story was not so uncommon out here in the border planets or even closer to the Spiral's heart. More efficient as it was to use machines to mine asteroids, the simple fact was there was an amazing number of substandard jury-rigged facilities where people used equipment not designed for mining and cheap human resources instead.

The difference in cost was miniscule given the upkeep humans required but somehow continued despite it. I suspected it was due to the replacement fees. It took a large amount of time and money to get spare parts for machines while humans were the one thing the Spiral had in abundance. A hundred new humans to replace the dead was easier to get than a new mining bot.

"What happened?" I asked.

"I was bought," Fade shrugged. "My next master was the Consortium and found ex-slaves were very good at killing. My siblings and I were all keenly aware of how cheap life was. Now we are on the same footing, knowing who each other are."

"Assuming any of that was true," I said dryly.

Fade just smiled. "Come with me to my booth and let us discuss business."

The three of us headed back to Fade's booth near the far end of the building in a corner that had two empty tables beside it. His table was, notably, far nicer than the rest and there were built-in stillers as well as a privacy-field generator. It made me wonder if he or the Consortium was owner of the tavern. The table seats were also surprisingly comfortable with the holovid generator functional, a fact untrue for more than half of the tables present.

Sitting down with Isla beside me, I couldn't help but notice the table had a complete view of the rest of the tavern as well as a position of sight for two other tables across the chamber that had armed men present. I also saw a disguised turret in one of the tavern's lights. If any of Fade's "guests" tried anything, they'd almost certainly be cut down before they drew their weapons.

"Nice set-up," I said, genuinely impressed.

"We try," Fade said, gesturing to a nearby human female who was, at best, scantily clad in something akin to dental floss around strategic regions. A man in similar attire came up behind her.

They laid down three rocket-shaped brown bottles before us. They were filled with a sweet-smelling dark carbonated beverage that seemed more like a children's drink than proper alcohol.

I didn't take it to drink. "So you know who we are. Do you want to do business or not?"

"Perhaps," Fade said. "I haven't completely taken your measure. I'm not sure the Consortium should associate with your like."

I glared at him. "*My* like?"

"Your doppelganger, though you don't look like him anymore, has plunged the galaxy into a war, after all. I'm sure he might pay a great deal for your return."

"I think you'd be surprised," I said.

"And why is that?" Fade said.

"Because he's not just an imposter," I said. "He's me. What I would do in his place would be to wipe you out."

"For a favor?" Fade said, taking a sip of his drink.

"He's me as I was," I said, shrugging. "He'd observe the proprieties of avenging his family. It's taken six years to beat reality into my head. It's a moot point, though."

"Why?" Fade said.

I stared at him. "I'd blow the detonator in my tooth and take out this entire bar before I let myself be offered up to the terrorists using my name."

"Do you have a detonator in your tooth?" Fade said. "Because I don't think you'd harm your pretty lady friend."

"I put it in for this meeting," Isla said, narrowing her eyes. "I made Cassius promise he'd kill me before I ever was taken by slavers again. I would have done my own tooth, but Cassius insisted he would die before he let me taken and wanted to prove it."

"We're *not* slavers," Fade said quickly. "Bad for business. Many worlds will turn a blind eye to slavery for the right price or find some reason to justify it. Many more worlds will look the other way for less dramatic businesses."

I took a deep breath and rose. "I'm sorry for taking you here, Isla. Clearly this was a waste of our time."

Fade blinked, clearly not sure how to respond. "I didn't say you could leave."

"You're clearly used to dealing with people easily intimidated, but the simple fact is that I put my life on the line every day for two years fighting the Commonwealth and have done many times since after going on the run. I wouldn't hesitate for a second to give my life for my crew and I doubt very much they'll have much to fear once this place is ashes with you in it."

Fade stared then burst out laughing. "All right. It's good to see I was right about you."

"Excuse me?" Isla asked, not standing up beside me. Instead, she just kept her gaze on Fade.

"The Consortium has a need for...special people," Fade said. "We're very particular about who we hire. I, in particular, have been recruiting the Dragon's lieutenants for ten years. My offer was extended to you as a sort of test. You have the item so you've passed the first of three trials. The second is simple."

"I don't like tests," I said simply. I didn't like admitting I was wrong, but it seemed the Consortium had little interest in dealing with us fairly. "My father put me through many over the years and they're less for the person doing them than the person giving them."

"Very true," Fade said. "But all I want to do is ask you five questions."

"I won't betray any of my crew's confidence."

Isla took a drink of her soda.

"My, you are protective for a captain," Fade said. "You remind me of my father in that respect. He ran an old Olympian hauler like your *Melampus*. Ruled it like a small kingdom with a harem quarters and six wives. I was born on that ship. He said he'd die for them every day and then he finally did. How I ended up enslaved."

I sat down. "What do you want to know?"

"Fun facts," Fade said, taking a sip of Isla's soda rather than his own. A petty power play. "I've never met a real legend."

"I'm not a legend," I said.

"But you've killed hundreds of men, haven't you?" Fade asked.

"Thousands, most by bombing places," I said. "A man isn't measured by killing."

"Then you measure it very differently than I do. How many did you kill in battle?" Fade asked.

I frowned. "A lot."

Four hundred and seventy-four starfighters by today. Sixteen capital ships I had credit for. Sixty-two partial-kill credit. If it wasn't a galactic record, it was damn close but that was much the fact the Commonwealth kept deploying its men in wave tactics as anything else. It had also done nothing to prevent Crius from losing the war and may have helped contribute, in some small way, to the vengeance the Commonwealth had taken on us.

"What was your secret?" Fade asked.

"Is that a demand for us to continue our business?" I asked, very careful. "There's nothing else you want to know."

"Nothing," Fade said, clearly not happy with my reticence..

I sighed. "Be prepared."

Fade snorted. "Like the Boy Scouts? That's not a question."

"I'm unfamiliar with that unit," I said, honestly. "However, the vast majority of conflicts are resolved before the battle takes place. I did my best to make sure that my men were always properly provisioned, had the best equipment available, had as much rest as could be afforded, were trained extensively in every possible scenario I could think of, drilled them hard, and made sure they were familiar with both the capacities of themselves as well as the enemy. I did the same for myself."

"If you know the enemy and know yourself, you need not fear the result of a hundred battles. If you know yourself but not the enemy, for every victory gained you will also suffer a defeat. If you know neither the enemy nor yourself, you will succumb in every battle." Fade surprised me.

"Sun Tzu," I said. "Yes."

"We attribute it to Julius Caesar on my world," Fade said. "Sounds rather boring and doesn't explain how you racked up so many kills."

"I chose my team's battles whenever possible," I said. "Always taking those battles I knew we could win. If I could use stealth or overwhelming voice, I did. Many conflicts were won by targeting supplies before battles then crippling the ships so they were forced to surrender."

"Seems cowardly," Fade said.

I shrugged. "I fought many battles against greater odds, too, especially at the end of the war, but never by choice. War is about depriving the enemy of resources and a death of a thousand cuts is better than a single grandiose victory. It also means less casualties."

"Except that strategy didn't work, did it?" Fade said.

"No," I said. "It didn't. They cut the head off the dragon by bombing our homeland into dust. Most of my squadron didn't make it to the end of the war either. The military kept us in battle versus rotating us out to educate less experienced pilots as was standard. It was propaganda that cost us our lives."

"And yet you lived. What would you have done differently, now, with experience?"

I closed my eyes. "Become a watchmaker. Become a pimp. Become a professional card player. Anything else."

Fade nodded. "Pass over the object."

"Pass over my letters," I said, referring to the documentation that would make the *Melampus* a licensed ship across hundreds of smaller companies with access to much of the border planets' merchant lanes.

Fade tapped a holographic display that appeared on his wrist. "Done."

I checked my ship's computer network and Judith confirmed he'd done it. I then slipped a small bronze pyramid from my pocket across the table, only for Fade to catch it. "Do you know what it does?"

"No," I said. "I think it's a paperweight to be honest. The Elder Races made it, though, so it fits the criteria you wanted."

"Your doppelganger is scouring the universe for anything with even a hint of the Elder Races about them," Fade said, staring at me. "On this world, you can buy alien artifacts for a decicredit and Elder Race materials are even cheaper because none of it is real. I can't imagine what he would want with this. It's not like they ever communicate with the Young Races, let alone humanity."

I knew the reason for that. Zoe had researched the Elder Races heavily as part of her desire to determine the secret of Fermi's Paradox: that for all the fact the galaxy had thousands of sentient species inside it, there should have been millions. The truth was the Elder Races, those dozen or so races that had transcended their physical forms to become beings of pure information with godlike machines, destroyed the vast majority of species.

They'd been responsible for the Great Collapse and the Galactic Dark Age (somewhat misnamed since it had only applied to humans) for no other reason than they believed humanity was advancing too quickly. Even now, they played games with races from upending their societies with new technology to creating wars to watch play out. I'd learned that from Judith and was well aware that, at any time, humanity could meet its end in one of their games.

"Perhaps he wishes to know his enemy," I said.

"Then he's a bigger fool than I thought," Fade said. "No offense."

"Some taken," I said. "You said there were three tests before you accepted me as a lieutenant in the Consortium."

"Yes," Fade said, continuing to drink Isla's beverage. "You have to deliver a cargo from the Consortium back to the Ring."

"What's the cargo?"

"Weapons," Fade said. "Enough to change the course of the Insurrection."

CHAPTER FOUR

"You want us to deal arms," I said very carefully.

Fade finished off his drink. "You have a problem with this?"

"A little bit," I said, shaking my head. "I came out here to get away from the war."

"I thought the Consortium would be neutral in the war," Isla said, narrowing her eyes.

"It is," Fade said, simply. "It will gladly sell any amount of equipment, arms, supplies, and war material to either side of the conflict. Certainly, our whorehouses and drugs are used by both in the spirit of common human interest—or otherwise."

"How noble of you," Isla said, shaking her head and doing a scan of the bottles with her medical wand. "They're clean."

"Please, you think I'd poison you?" Fade said.

"Yes," Isla said.

"Only if I was going to knock you out and turn you over to your enemies, which we've established I'm not going to do," Fade said. "Probably."

I lifted the brown bottle and stared at it. "What is it?"

"Root beer...with alcohol," Isla said.

"Sounds ghastly," I said, taking a drink. "Albeit, I approve of the latter."

Isla covered her face in embarrassment. "What exactly is the cargo?"

"*Ibixian'ah'nar* missiles, and I'm butchering the name because I don't have two tongues," Fade said. "They're basically barrier busters and can shred through most ship's shields like they're nonexistent. The Consortium uses them for their starships and are four or five times as powerful as an equivalent Commonwealth missile. The benefits of alien technology."

"How many?" I asked, causing Isla to shoot me a dirty look.

"Two, two hundred and fifty thousand," Fade said, chuckling as we both stared. "It's a fairly easy mission, too, as you just have to venture across the border planets to Community space and pick them up at the rendezvous point. Then deliver them back here and we'll pass them along to the Free Systems Alliance. A payoff worth millions."

"Do you know how many that could kill?" Isla said.

"A lot of people," Fade said, shrugging. "Probably not enough to win the war, not by a long shot or even change the course of it but certainly enough to do a lot of damage. The Commonwealth would do well to buy their own, but the Community has them under embargo for weapons importing due to breaking interstellar laws against orbital bombardment."

Crius.

How ironic.

"How did you get a deal like this?" I asked, wondering what the Consortium sold for such devices.

"That would telling," Fade said. "But the Dragon has his ways. What's a common household appliance to them is decades of research to us."

I thought about the thousands, of men I'd killed. I had thought the deaths of others for the twin causes of 'honor' and 'duty' was justified. That any number of men and women were worth sacrificing as long as they weren't Crius. I had moved past this attitude. I wasn't going to become an arms dealer, no matter how much I needed money. This had been a mistake.

"I suppose we're not going to be working together, then," I said dryly.

Isla smiled.

Fade raised an eyebrow. "Now you're testing me."

"Am I?" I said. "You had to have known how I'd react. If this is a test, then it is a poor one."

"Perhaps," Fade said. "Or perhaps it is an illustration that those who sit on the fence can expect to be kicked by both sides. You are too important of a figure to be allowed to remain neutral in this conflict."

"Am I?" I said sarcastically.

"I wasn't referring to you," Fade said.

Isla looked confused.

We didn't have a chance to discuss the matter further because five individuals wearing plastisteel power armor walked into the room. Their armor was bright crimson and faceless helmets with a chrome sheen. They were each carrying disruptor rifles on their back with fusion pistols holstered at their side. Two, however, were carrying stun spears and one actually was playing around with a deactivated shock net ball in his hands.

The effect of these individuals presence in the room was immediate as seemingly half the room immediately got up and waved their finance cards in front of their tables' kiosk to depart. The other quarter either grabbed their weapons or more slowly started to depart. The men in red armor seemed to pay no attention to them as they showed a holo to the bartender.

"Should I be worried?" I asked, looking over at Fade.

The bartender pointed up at our booth.

"Yes, I should say so," Fade said, shrugging. "That's the Hapsburg Blood Clan."

"Seriously?" I asked. "They actually call themselves that?"

"You don't develop a fearsome reputation in the border planets if you call yourself the Fluffy Bunny Patrol."

"Really?" I asked, looking at him sideways. "Because I'd think anyone who calls themselves that fears nothing."

"Cute," Fade said, rising from his chair. "Of course, you realize that I will not be able to protect you since you've chosen to not become part of the Consortium."

"Yes," Isla said, "I'm also sure you had nothing to do with their extraordinarily convenient timing."

Fade stared at me. "The Dragon doesn't like you. I don't know why. However, you'll note that he may be in charge, but he's not king."

That was an interesting statement.

"We should go," I muttered.

"You think?" Isla said, reaching down for her pistol.

I, meanwhile, activated my personal shield after standing myself. "Hopefully they won't attempt to attack us in a public place."

I was very quickly dissuaded of that statement by one of the Hapsburg Blood Gang pointing at me with a fusion rifle and shouting, "She's got accompaniment! Blast him!"

Wait, what?

Isla pushed me to the ground as she threw herself under the table and started firing back at the Blood Gang soldiers. Fade himself only barely got out of the way even as they began firing at him too. He would have been cut down quickly by the weapons but for the fact his personal shield worked fine and absorbed no less than three blasts. Most would have buckled under one, but his remained a soft white aura around his body.

Attacking Fade also brought his bodyguards into the fight as they started unloading from the other side of the tavern, causing the Hapsburgs to unload on them as well. Their armor, if not Durandel-class level, was powerful and absorbed the Consortium soldiers' fire as well as our own. Illustrating just how few fucks they gave about collateral damage, one of the Hapsburgs hurled his shock net ball at Fade's bodyguards before it expanded to cover three of them.

The shock net proceeded to squeeze them all together before delivering a lethal charge of electricity, causing the men to scream as their shields burned out before their bodies were fried execution style.

"Dammit!" Fade shouted, running behind some of the booths beneath us for cover. "Those men were expensive."

He was shooting at them, though even as other members of the tavern had joined into the fray, either shooting to cover their escape or because they thought their lives were in danger. The Hapsburgs fired indiscriminately into the crowd and I wondered if I could get away. It took only a second to realize that, yes, I could, but only if I abandoned Isla.

So I drew my sword and ran out screaming, jumping at the Hapsburgs.

"Crius!" I shouted, coming down on them as they all turned their attention to me.

Yeah, maybe I should have stuck to piloting.

I managed to survive my stupid ill-timed charge by Isla blasting one of the Hapsburgs' rifles as it aimed at me, causing him to fall backwards and throw his fellow soldiers off their game. I landed in the middle of them and swung my proton sword through the closest one, cutting off his arms, as the weapon's barrier was strong enough to cut through their shield-covered armor. The man, or woman, inside screamed with an electronically altered voice as wires sparked out of their cybernetic limbs before I stabbed another through the neck.

I was still half-drunk, or I might have come up with a better plan other than ripping out the blade and slashing again and again but my attempt on the third of the Hapsburgs met a shock spear hardened enough to block my blow. I was so surprised by that, its owner pushed me back then delivered a power armor-enhanced kick to my stomach that sent me flying back into the booth behind me. It was like being hit by a ground transport going thirty kilometers per hour and if I'd not been enhanced at birth, I probably would have numerous busted ribs.

Actually, I still might.

"You killed my sister!" the Hapsburg shouted, charging at me as he tossed aside his shock spear and pulled out an electron knife.

I didn't much care for that sudden moment of humanization even as the five hundred-pound armored soldier threw himself on me and my personal shield. Even with all my enhancements, I couldn't hold off someone wearing strength enhanced power armor so I futilely struggled to keep the knife from my face as I came down lower and lower toward my eye. So I dropped my resistance and moved my head to one side, resulting in the electron pistol slamming into the table beside me.

That gave me a single second to grab my pistol from its holster and place it against the side of the Hapsburg soldier's head, pulling the trigger. The point-blank shot went through one end of his head and out the other. The armored body then collapsed on top of me, forcing me to push off the corpse even as combat was still going on around me.

Which suddenly stopped.

Sitting up and clutching my ribs, I saw the remaining two Hapsburgs were on the ground, a hole in each of their chests that looked like something had torn through their armor like fusion blasts through cloth. Fade was standing over them while Isla was walking down the steps carrying an Ares Armaments 51B Assassins

Rifle. It was an anti-material kinetic gravity shell weapon used to take out tanks and kineti-transports. It was also about her size and looked somewhat comical in her arms.

I wasn't complaining, though.

"Where the hell did you get that?" I asked, looking around.

Isla shrugged. "Once I figured out my gun wasn't going to do the trick, I rabbited from my position and looked for something better. One of the mercs on the ground had this."

"His name was Davis," Fade said, sighing. "He was a good friend."

"Can I keep it?" Isla asked.

Fade glared at her then laughed. "Sure, I suppose he'd like that."

"Good," Isla said, looking over it. "I'll have to add it to the collection."

The bartender, meanwhile, slowly lifted his head up from behind the counter before looking around the carnage. The Hapsburgs had killed almost a dozen patrons and shot up the place good, having relied on their armor to make themselves immune to reprisal. It had almost worked, and I wondered if that was standard operating procedure in the core.

"Fade, I'm sorry, I didn't know they'd—" The bartender started to say.

Fade lifted his pistol and shot him.

I glared at him. "That was murder."

"It was, wasn't it?" Fade said. "Hopefully, the next bartender will understand the importance of the sentence: 'No, I haven't seen them.'"

I couldn't argue with that. Why were they after Isla? I started looking through the pockets of their belts, hoping to find a databook or infopad. There was a five-year-old infopad on the one who'd come after me with an electron knife. It was, of course, locked, but all the major companies kept exploits for the Watchers and other secret services to access.

"Judith, could you access the contents of this?" I asked.

"Oh, are you letting me into this conversation now?" Judith asked through my private comm. "I thought you were ignoring me while you got into a gunfight."

"Not the time," I said.

"I'm accessing it now," Judith said. "Besides, I suspect Isla is about to read you the riot act."

I doubted that. Isla knew the score better than Judith.

"Cassius, what the hell were you thinking?" Isla said. "Did you seriously just charge at a bunch of gun-wielding mercs with a sword!?"

"It worked, didn't it?" I said, shrugging.

"That's not the point," Isla said.

"It kind of is," Fade said, crossing his arms.

Isla aimed the sniper rifle at him, carrying it in a manner no ordinary human strength would allow.

Fade turned to me and put on a mock serious face. "That was very foolish of you, Colonel-Count."

"Don't call me that," I said, accessing the infopad's contents. "The nation I held that rank in doesn't exist anymore and good riddance."

If I kept telling myself that, maybe I'd believe it someday.

The interior of the infopad was mostly the usual collection of programs, datafeeds, pictures, and hyperletters. It didn't take long for me to find out they were licensed bounty hunters as well as mercenaries. Bounty hunting was a disgusting profession, considered kidnapping on the majority of civilized worlds, but still was common enough to be worth millions to the right hunters. After all, when criminals could cross across the galaxy to get away from the law, those sufficiently determined to get justice or revenge to chase them had few options.

Except, in this case, the holographic image projected out from the infopad's surface was one of Isla. It didn't list her under that name, however, just a serial number. Instead, it listed Isla's name among a variety of aliases and crimes. There was a seven million-Albion credit reward for her return to Octavian Plantagenet. A name that made my blood run cold.

"It's him, isn't it?" Isla said.

"Friend of yours?" Fade said, typing a message into his infopad. "Sorry, I'm telling the authorities this is a private matter and to stay out."

"I see," I said, shaking my head. "Yes, you could say that."

"He's a serial killer," Isla replied. "One who tried to control his urges with bioroids. He wanted us with as lifelike a set of programming and responses as possible, though. Terror, fear, and horror. It allowed me to escape. That and the fact his abuses were far beyond anything I had a warranty for."

I really wanted to take an asteroid and drop it on Ares Electronics's home planet. Which, given that the same had been done to my home planet, said something. "Someone must have told him you were still alive."

Isla almost pulled the trigger on her rifle then and there.

Fade, however, raised his hands. "I had nothing to do with this, I swear. Like I said, slavery is the one line we draw. We would never turn over a free bioroid back to their former owner."

I didn't think that was true, especially for the money involved. "Would you be willing to protect Isla from this bounty if were a part of the Consortium?"

"Cassius!" Isla said.

Fade closed his eyes. "Yes."

I closed mine too. "Then we have an accord. One other thing."

"Yes?"

"What's a rabbit?"

CHAPTER FIVE

By the time I was back onboard the *Melampus*, back in the present, I felt the need to talk to Isla about my choices.

My stupid, stupid choices.

"So you said yes to becoming an arms dealer," Isla said, sitting across from me in her quarters. She was wearing a white jumpsuit and a pair of micro-glasses. They were more a fashion statement than a prosthetic, but certainly helped sort digital information and make sure the brain retained it. I'd just finished reciting the events I'd reminisced on in my starfighter and it was now hours after we'd dealt with our pirate friends.

"You were there," I said, staring up at the ceiling and crossing my arms. "Why are we going over this again?"

Isla's quarters were a pleasant eggshell-blue color and covered in holos of herself, Clarice, myself, and other members of the crew. There seemed to be a pressing need within her to record as much of her life as possible despite the fact it was all recorded perfectly within her brain's CPU. As the ship's doctor, her quarters were larger than most and had enough room for a small couch she'd managed to bring aboard that I was currently sitting on as well as her chair. We could have used the bed nearby, but I suspect that would have gotten awkward given our already complicated relationship.

"Two reasons," Isla said, picking up a databook in her hands and tapping away at its screens. "First, we need to figure out the pure practical matter of when the Consortium decided to betray us and second, what in God's name convinced you this was a good idea in the first place."

I rubbed the bridge of my nose. "I don't suppose money is a sufficient answer."

Isla shrugged. "It's no more than I expected but I was hoping for better from you."

"In terms of not taking the deal to sell weapons on the black market or having a better motive for doing so?" I asked, only half joking.

"Either, both," Isla said. "There's a difference between being smugglers and arms traffickers. We left Sector 7 to avoid getting involved in the war. Now we're neck deep in it."

Isla had a point there. In the hold of the *Melampus* was a cargo of *five* hundred thousand of the barrier-crushing missiles. It wasn't a game changer in terms of the war, but they would make shredded fruitmeat out of most Commonwealth capital ships. How the Consortium had managed for these to fall off the back of the proverbial freighter was anyone's guess. Ironically, though, it had been an easy voyage to the pickup sight and only on our return had we been ambushed. By the Dragon's men, at least if their communications transmissions had been accurate. Judith had a remarkable way of sorting through data and had picked up early that they were communicating with my supposed new partners.

I took a deep breath. "You really don't want to know the answer."

"Try me. I just want to know it wasn't because you were trying to protect me."

I was silent.

Isla threw her databook at me.

"Ow!" I said, blocking it with my arm. "What the hells?"

"I expect an answer," Isla said.

"I'm not going to let you be hunted down like a dog by Octavian," I said, frowning. "I'd kill the whole of the Commonwealth to protect you."

"I don't need your protection, Cassius, least of all from Octavian," Isla said. "Also, spare me your hyperbole. I'd rather no one die to save me. I've killed to protect my life. Even so-called innocents, but I'm a doctor now. I want to save lives, not take them."

Man, was she on the wrong ship.

I looked at her. "You have my protection anyway. Where I'm from, you have your wingman's back and you can trust that they have yours."

"I'm not your wingman."

"You're right, you're something..." I trailed off, not sure what to say. "More."

"What, exactly?" Isla asked, crossing her legs across one another. "Because I'm not sure exactly where we stand as a couple. Trio. Whatever."

I grimaced, knowing this had been coming. "Is that really relevant right now?"

"Would you prefer we talk about your psychotic breaks and alcoholism?"

I thought about that. "I'm not sure which is worse."

Isla stared at me. "Really, Cassius?"

I took a deep breath. "I love you, Isla. It's just uncomfortable saying it."

Very uncomfortable.

"You told Judith you didn't feel that way for me," Isla said. "Back on Shogun."

I closed my eyes. "I lied."

"Why?" Isla said, her tone cold.

"I don't know," I said, shaking my head before sitting up. "Maybe I wanted to turn back the clock but I can't and what is broken can't be fixed. Maybe I don't want it to be fixed. Sorry, Judith."

"It's okay," Judith said, her voice coming from the room's interior speakers. She was omnipresent as the ship's A.I. "I'd rather you be with someone who can return your feelings."

That was like a stab in the gut but I persevered. "I know I do want to be with you now, at my side."

"And Clarice," Isla said. "And Judith."

Not Judith. That confused me and horrified me but there was something absent from our relationship now. I didn't mean sex or a physical body to hold or communicate with physically. No, it was something deeper. I couldn't put it into words but it was as if she was faking caring for others and that was the quality I'd admired most about her.

"I don't want to be anyone's second choice," Isla said. "Neither does Clarice."

"You're not," I said softly. "Though, honestly, I don't know if I'm good enough for anyone."

"It's not you, it's me?" Isla asked.

"Am I capable of loving anyone? Am I worthy of love?" I asked.

Isla paused. "I think your problems may run a bit deeper than my programming is capable of dealing with."

"Mine too," I said, realizing perhaps I did need therapy. "Am I your second choice?"

"No," Isla said. "Because there's no such thing in that with love. Real love. You either love someone or you don't. I love you and Clarice. I also love the people aboard this ship as a whole. You are my family and I'd fight and kill for each of you. The sex is just a bonus. It's the only family I've ever had. Will ever have if I have my way. Can you say the same?"

What did one say to that? I was spared the necessity of responding by the sound of a rapping on Isla's door.

"We should probably get that," I said, looking away.

"It's not important," Isla said. "We've put this off long enough."

"It's Clarice, William, and Munin here to talk about your incredibly stupid plan to continue delivering our cargo to the Consortium," Judith said cheerfully.

Isla looked up at the ceiling. *"Etu* Judith?"

"Shall I let them in?" Judith asked.

"Yes," Isla said, looking down at me. "I don't think we're going to be getting anywhere else today."

"I have a lot to think about," I said seriously then gave a fake smile. "Am I cleared for duty?"

Isla looked back at me. "You've lost your planet, you lost your wife before she was resurrected as a program, you were forced to kill your sister, you've had your life stolen by a deranged bioroid, and if you ever see your brother again he'll try to kill you too. That's in addition to that trauma you had for fighting continuously for a decade. Frankly, Cassius, you're a mental mess and the only reason you're probably not in a ball quivering in a corner somewhere is because you're a cyborg and self-medicating. My advice is stop getting into situations where people are trying to kill you or you're having to kill them. Can you do that?"

"I don't think that's in the cards any time soon," I admitted. "I can try to love you and Clarice along with everyone else as best I can, though. As much love as a person made in a test tube as a monument to my father's ego can love."

"That's all I ask." Isla walked over to her desk and pulled out a bottle of pills before tossing them my way. "Then take these instead and come back to me for some weekly sessions. Maybe at some point we'll make some progress. Either that or get you a real doctor."

"I have a real doctor," I said, opening the pill bottle. "What are these?"

"Memory drugs," Isla said. "A stronger variety than the kind you've been taking. They'll also make you violently vomit if you drink any form of alcohol or take any form of stimulant more powerful than coffeeine."

"Oh joy," I said, taking two. "Were they designed this way or am I just lucky?"

"I'm not in the mood for jokes," Isla said, going to the door and opening it up. "I'm not wired that way."

I grimaced. "Neither am I."

The door opened to reveal Clarice O'Harra still wearing her black-and-white flight suit with atmosphere processor on the front. Clarice was a woman of mixed Commonwealther and Shogun ancestry, her hair having been spliced to be a natural red despite the latter. She was tall, almost as tall as me, with a statuesque form designed more for combat than attractiveness but still managed to turn the heads of those attracted to human females on occasion.

I had a strong friendship with her, sexual in nature, that was untroubled by the problems I had with Isla despite being fundamentally different. She'd also been with Isla for almost two years now, off and on. That was in addition to William, a space patrol lieutenant named Odin, and whatever other attractive humans she could charm in whatever port we visited. Yet, recently, I started to realized she was falling in love with me and Isla both. She wanted a permanent relationship between the three of us—perhaps even marriage. I wasn't sure I was capable of being a decent husband to one woman, let alone two.

Behind Clarice were two other figures. The first was William Baldur, a tall obsidian-skinned man from Xerxes wearing a custom-tailored purple uniform that was one of the mild reforms I'd introduced to the *Melampus* crew. He was built like a brick wall but with a charming face, marred only by a nose that had been broken repeatedly. He was clean shaven now, having gotten rid of his trademark goatee since having taken up with Kanya Takashi, the ship's quartermaster. A small tuft of curly hair had grown in on his previously bald head that I felt made him less threatening. It was a good look for a man who now carried a proton ax on his back as a matter of course.

The other figure was a petite raven-haired woman with mixed Commonwealth-Crius ancestry that showed signs of numerous genetic markers of our labor class but changed by the randomness of natural birth. Munin, real name Maria Anne Gomez, was barely five feet but curvaceous and could lift the weight of a power lifter despite growing up in space. She, too, was wearing the official crew uniform but it was almost unrecognizable under a layer of grease, oil, and orihalcum fuel splotches. It was also not her uniform, but belonged to someone much taller named Hideo by the name sewn into her lapel.

"So are we locking him up and throwing away the key?" William said cheerfully. "I know some wonderful hospitals on Xerxes where they keep you doped up on dremorin and plug you in virtual reality until you die of old age or your fluid pipes break."

"It's good to know your family is in good hands," I said dryly.

William narrowed his eyes at me. That was a sensitive subject with him since most of them had died horribly in the civil war on his planet against the Crius nobility. It was ungentlemanly to say such a thing but, well, William was a dick.

"Cassius is fine," Isla said. "He's a drunken wreck of a human being, but his enhanced intelligence and military training still makes him better qualified than anyone but me, Clarice, or Munin to command the ship."

William raised his hand. "I vote Clarice."

"I vote anyone but me," Clarice said, raising her hand.

"I vote Cassius because he smells nice," Munin said.

Everyone stared at her.

"I have an enhanced sense of smell from my labor caste ancestry," Munin said. "Seriously, have you ever noticed Crius nobles don't really stink when they sweat? They just exude this pleasant woodsy musk."

Everyone continued to stare at her.

"Apparently it's just me," Munin said.

"I vote this is not a democracy," I said dryly. "Albeit, I would vote for Clarice too. However, since she doesn't want the job and we're all in agreement William would be a disaster—"

"Agreed," the three women replied simultaneously, much to his annoyance.

"We're stuck with me," I said. "How long until we arrive back at the Ring?"

"About seven hours," Clarice said. "The Dragon has sent a message indicating he wants to meet with us personally."

"Excellent," I said, thinking this was the first good news I'd heard all week.

"Yes, about that," Isla said, shaking her databook. "I have a question."

"Why no one voted for you?" Munin said. "It's because you're also the ship's dentist and thus everyone views you as evil."

Isla glared. "The machine doesn't even hurt!"

"Clearly the person with plastisteel teeth is the one to decide that," Munin said.

"I do not have plastisteel teeth!" Isla said, sensitive about her bioroid status.

"I think her question is why the hell we're going back to the Ring if the Dragon is trying to kill us," Clarice said, crossing her arms. "Cutting us out of our deal with pirates is a pretty sure sign we should take these weapons and sell them to someone else."

"Or dump them into space," Isla said.

No one dignified that with a response but I, at least, looked sideways.

"I have a plan," I explained.

Everyone looked at me.

"That's so reassuring," William said.

"Thank you," I said.

"That was sarcasm!" William snapped.

"I couldn't guess," I said, rolling my eyes. "It's simple, though. We need money and the Consortium's contacts to continue to survive out here. We can't just default on our first job for them and expect to get away."

"This is a dumb plan," Isla said.

"So we're going to rob them of everything instead," I replied.

Silence reigned.

"I like this plan!" Munin said cheerfully.

William looked like he wanted to yell at me, opened his mouth, then sighed. "Against my better judgment: how exactly do you plan to rob the galaxy's largest crime syndicate and get away with it?"

"Judith," I said, simply. "We're going to meet with the Dragon when we pass over the missiles, record his biometrics as well as voice patterns, then use our Cognition A.I. to steal his fortune as well as those of his closest allies. Judith is capable of opening and closing security walls like they don't exist."

"This sounds dangerously close to a good idea," Clarice said, smiling. "Especially as I'm sick of being poor."

I'd managed to keep running the *Melampus* in the red based on my own personal fortune but that was almost depleted now, the result of running a town-sized star galleon being more expensive than holonovels indicated.

"We all are," I said, nodding. "I hesitate to use the archaic term *big score*, but this could be it."

Isla looked between us. "No one thinks it's going to be troublesome when the Dragon finds out we've ripped him off? You know, the man who has already shown he can send a small army after us?"

"He'll have his own problems," I said softly. "Munin, have you sabotaged the missiles yet?"

"Just some of them," Munin said, smiling. "But I only have to do a few."

Isla's mouth fell open. "Wait, what?"

"You didn't actually think I was going to sell functioning military armaments, did you?" I asked. "I'm not that far gone."

Isla hit me in the shoulder.

CHAPTER SIX

The *Melampus* was a half-kilometer-long vessel who routinely docked in space above planet before unloading its cargo there. That wasn't a necessity on the Ring as the place was a combination of planet ad space station. It's what helped make it an economic hub as just short of a million ships could dock there for refueling while exchanging cargoes from the fringes of human space along with the Community.

In this case, though, the "edges" of the Ring functionally not that dissimilar to space stations and I didn't have an atmosphere or sky. Entering into a blue-gray warehouse the *Melampus* docked against, I saw the room was fairly indistinguishable from a thousand other locations I'd been to during my days as a spacer. Amazing how even the most magnificent sights can quickly lose their luster.

"I wonder who built the Ring?" I muttered, walking along the many crates gray metal crates being unloaded by a couple of dozen members of the *Melampus*'s fifteen-hundred-strong crew.

"*The Elder Races,*" Judith spoke on my built-in cyber-comm. "*They were trying to direct the flow of development for humanity. The nobility decided to accelerate human development after impeding it for several centuries but along a similar technological line as the Community. The Ring is actually only a couple of decades old but has an entirely false history dating back millennium in its databanks of a race that was similar to several others. I imagine whoever came up with that will have a jolly old time watching archaeologists trying to track down their home world.*"

I blinked. "How the hells do you know that?"

Also, it stunned me to find out the Elder Races were such petty creatures. I shouldn't have been surprised since Judith had told me they amused themselves by "gardening" lesser races and playing them against one another for amusement, but it did. The power of gods at their fingertips and they spent it messing with the heads of lesser beings. That explained so much about the universe.

I suppose it was better than the alternative of simply annihilating those who ever bored them but that was a threat they'd exercised literally tens of thousands of times. It made me sick to think it was a likely fate of humanity, possibly tomorrow, or possibly a million years from now. In a way, I supposed it was a good thing they were still choosing to play with.

No, I couldn't even pretend to believe that.

Judith sighed. *"It's a Cognition A.I. thing. You have no idea the amount of information I have available to me that is forbidden to the general public. I'm even able to monitor the Elder Races' transmissions despite them being on a sub-universal wavelength."*

That didn't sound possible since that would require the *Melampus* to have a receiver that humanity as a whole didn't have. "Are you taking the piss with me?"

"Not this time," Judith said, chuckling. *"There's a lot of tech built into the ship by the Watchers that you don't have access to. They really went all out in making this the best spy vessel possible."*

"And then I went and stole it," I said. "Ida must be fuming still, assuming she's still alive."

Ida Claire, a pun on "I declare", had been the previous owner of the *Melampus*. Despite having the matronly appearance of a New Atlanta grandmother, she'd actually been one of the Commonwealth's spymasters. The Watchers had outfitted the antique star galleon with a host of advanced equipment and equipment that only a few on the crew knew about.

Ida had then recruited an exceptionally capable group of misfits to provide a cover for her many strange missions and unusual business ventures. Were this a holovision serial, it would have been the creation of a loving family of true companions against the galaxy's worst. This being reality, they'd all turned against her upon discovering they were being used for espionage against the Commonwealth's enemies. Myself included.

Of course, I'd known about it far before the rest of the crew and had initially been willing to go along with it. It was my lowest moment, even more than working for the Consortium, to consider helping the Commonwealth against the survivors of Crius. At least, that was what I told myself. It had required discovering Judith's A.I. that had convinced me I had to do anything to keep her out of the

Watchers' hands. I'd even framed her, with Judith's help, for numerous improprieties in hopes of making it impossible for her to follow me.

"*Do you want to know what happened to her?*" Judith asked.

I thought about that. "No, no I don't."

"*Good,*" Judith said, muttering under her nonexistent breath. "*I can't access the Commonwealth intelligence agencies anymore.*"

"Excuse me? I thought you could hack into God's servers," I said dryly.

"*Perhaps,*" Judith said. "*Unfortunately, God doesn't have what the Watchers do in Cognition A.I. of his own. It's taken them a year but they've frozen me out. My avatars trying to get into their system are all destroyed.*"

That wasn't good. "Can they track us?"

"*Oh Cassius,*" Judith sounded contrary. "*They could always track us. You don't lose track of something like me.*"

That confused me more than I dared to admit. I was about to ask her more when I saw the doors to the docking bay open up to reveal Fade and a group of six armed mercenaries accompanying him. He was wearing a pair of black trousers, a white shirt, and a sparkling rainbow-colored mood-fabric cape. I didn't think it was a group to rob us because they'd have brought more men. I fully expected the Dragon to arrive with a small army in order to take the cargo from us without paying.

"We can still get the Dragon's accounts, right?" I asked Judith.

"*I have large amounts of their information,*" Judith replied. "*Enough to thoroughly wreck the organization just from what they casually communicate about here. We won't be able to get everything in their accounts, though, until we have a scan of the Dragon's biometrics. If he doesn't show up, this entire deal is going to go banana shaped.*"

"It already has," I muttered.

Fade proceeded to walk over to me as Clarice and several of the more intimidating-looking *Melampus* crew came up behind me. Truth be told, they were all laborers who couldn't fight worth a damn with the actual danger to any potential foes coming from sniper's positions I'd set up in empty crates around the chamber.

"You are either very brave or very stupid," Fade said, shaking his head.

"Those two things are not contradictory," Clarice said, putting her arm around my shoulder and giving me a squeeze. "As our captain routinely proves."

Judith giggled.

I rolled my eyes then looked at Fade with false innocence. "I don't know what you could possibly mean, Fade. Is there any reason why things shouldn't go splendidly? We're off to such a great start in our relationship."

"Laying it on a bit thick, aren't we?" Clarice said.

"Do you want to be captain? It's not too late," I said.

"No," Clarice said. "I come from a family of pirates and slavers. The moment I put on the captains hat, I won't be able to resist swashing my buckle."

"I have no idea what that means," I said.

Fade crossed his arms. "You know exactly what I'm talking about. I'm stunned you decided to return after what happened."

"If that's a confession, it's a pretty piss-poor one," I said, staring at his men. "Especially since the last time a bunch of armed men attacked me with better weapons and equipment, it ended poorly for them."

One of the mercenaries moved forward before Fade pushed him back with his left hand. "I had nothing to do with the attack on you. I may have had some plans for integrating you into our organization but it is solely the Dragon who has decided to move against you."

"And why is that?" I asked, wondering what game he was playing at.

Also, why was he warning me? Was I caught in yet another power struggle?

Ugh.

Judith heard that thought, unfortunately. "*Yes, who possibly could imagine there'd be a power struggle in a criminal syndicate,*" Judith said. "*That is a possibility no one could have foreseen.*"

"*Quiet,*" I thought back. "*No one likes a smartass A.I. You have to be solid to pull off sarcasm.*"

"*That's bio-prejudiced!*" Judith joked, sounding forced. I think I heard it on one of the crew's comedy downloads.

"The Dragon has betrayed the Consortium by taking a side," Fade said, sighing. "Unfortunately, being criminals, it's not like we have by-laws I can expel him for breaking. At least when he's willing to take half the organization with him."

"Which side wants to fuck me over?" I asked.

"Both?" Clarice said, as if it was the most obvious thing in the world.

Fade felt his face and muttered something about wishing the robot doctor was present. I almost punched him right there but let him continue. "There's been a development in the Insurgency."

"What kind of development?" I asked, not sure what kind of development could possibly interest me. If the survivors of Crius and the other worlds conquered by the Commonwealth wanted to expend their lives like ammunition that was none of my concern. Even if it did involve my surviving family.

I just had to keep telling myself that.

Fade actually looked troubled. That caused me to worry. "The Free Systems Alliance managed to raid Albion."

I stared at him. "Is that all?"

Fade shook his head. "You don't understand. They hit the planet."

I blinked, letting his words soak in. Albion was the capital of the Interstellar Commonwealth and widely considered the most beautiful and prosperous world in the Spiral. It was also the most heavily guarded location with much of the Commonwealth's stresses being the fact they kept their Home Fleet perpetually parked in the system. If the FSA had managed to strike the planet itself, it had to be chaos. It would call into question everything the Commonwealth claimed about their right to rule and invincibility in combat. Things I knew were complete bullshit but the average human did not. It was a game changer in terms of strategic position. They'd proven the Commonwealth vulnerable.

Clarice, however, shamed me by pointing out my skewed priorities. "How many were killed?"

"Five hundred thousand," Fade said, his voice low. "A pitifully small amount, really, but it was near the capital city government districts where many families of soldiers as well as officials were located. If they were attempting to strike at Parliament, they failed miserably but they've got everyone fired up...or terrified."

A sick and ugly part of my soul approved of the deaths, civilians or not. The Commonwealth dropped hundreds of meteorites onto my world, destroying the environment and forcing the population to become homeless refugees in their own sector. It also killed five hundred million people, a fifth of the population. The

Commonwealth's acts made me join first post-archduchy resistance groups, until they'd started to use child soldiers, and had almost driven me to slaughter the evacuees of the *Ravager*. I forced that part of my mind down. I had to be better than that. Not because I wanted to be a good person but because if I let the Commonwealth make me into a monster then they won completely.

"That's stupid," Judith said, sounding bitter and contemptuous. *"The Archduchy of Crius was already a fascist dictatorship ruled by a hereditary oligarchy. Which is a lot buzzwords. You'd think they'd have just stuck with one or two but no, they wanted the whole enchilada of evil. I know because I was a peasant thing."*

"Judith," I thought back to her. *"Please shut up. I'm grieving. You were among the dead."*

"Sorry. Don't cry for me, though. Cry for the fact we didn't all string up our leaders before the Commonwealth bombed us."

I stared at Fade. "What did this mean for the Dragon?"

I got my answer a few seconds later as the doors to the warehouse opened up to reveal a disturbing sight as an eight-foot-long lizard, covered in an armored carapace, walked into the chamber. It had numerous spikes across its carapace as well as an intelligence in its eyes. The fact it had finger-like appendages on its legs and a belt covered in tools also indicated it was an alien rather than an animal. Huh, it seemed calling him the Dragon was just his descriptors being accurate.

The Dragon was not alone, though as he had an honor guard of two dozen Void Marines dressed in black plastisteel armor. The subjugated Archduchy of Crius, or Republic of Crius as they tried to style themselves now, was officially an ally of the Commonwealth. The public hated the Commonwealth, those who would have gladly seen the aristocracy destroyed, and considered its allies toadies.

Decimating the home world had been a bridge too far for even the greatest radicals, though, and the fact the Commonwealth had imposed horrific taxation to make us pay for the war only cemented their loathing. As a result, massive numbers of the disbanded Crius military had joined the false Cassius's call to arms. A call to arms that needed me eliminated to prevent any inconvenient truths coming out.

Clarice took my left hand. "Do you want to—"

"Not yet," I said. "Remember."

Clarice said, "I think we have bigger problems than the Consortium."

"I find that remark insulting," Fade said, looking back at us.

"You should," I said.

The Dragon moved to the center of the room as reinforcements poured in, both mercenaries of the Consortium as well as more members of the Free System Alliance. There were close to a hundred troopers here and it was a far greater number than I'd suspected for our plan to work.

"Well, it would seem our partnership has ended," I said, calculating ways of dealing with this situation.

"Surrender?" Judith said in my ear. "I can break you free easier than fight this many."

"Possibly," I whispered. "Though get those biometrics."

Judith made a noise I interpreted to be one of frustration that I was still confident we could pull this off. In fact, I wasn't, but if I could make my crew rich with my sacrifice than that was the only heroism a person like me had left. God and the Devil knew I hadn't led my previous crew to anywhere but their deaths. It was why I hated being captain. I wasn't fit to lead anyone.

"I'm afraid our partnership is just beginning," Fade said, his voice low. "Amazingly enough, I believe the Dragon is here for us both."

I looked at him. "Oh?"

Fade shrugged. "It seems my belief the Commonwealth will win and should be supported is an unpopular one with the Dragon."

"Great," I muttered. "I'm going to die with a diehard Commie at my side."

Fade laughed at that.

"Fall back, Clarice," I said.

"But—"

"That's an order," I said, stepping forward and approaching the Dragon with my hands in my pockets. "Good evening, sir, or whatever the appropriate gender of your species is. We've brought your weapons as requested. If you'll provide us our payment for the action, we'll be on our way."

The Void Marines all raised their rifles at me as the mercenaries started moving around the chamber and securing the workers.

"I see," I said, sighing. "We're not even going to play along are we? That's the problem with criminals, none of you are as theatrical in real life as in the holos."

The Dragon growled. Its voice was a deep guttural baritone generated by a voice modulator built into its throat. "Colonel-Count Cassius Mass, the Butcher of Kolthas, the Fire Count, the son of—"

"Just captain now," I said, staring at him. "You can't trust the Free Systems Alliance. Their ideology only extends to revenge and putting themselves in power."

"I'm counting on it," The Dragon said, chuckling. "Fade, you have outlived your usefulness."

Fade turned on his personal shield along with his men. They wouldn't last five seconds.

"Do you have what you need?" I asked Judith.

"*Yes*," she responded.

"Then—" I started to say.

That was when all hell broke loose.

CHAPTER SEVEN

Seconds before I was about to trigger my own ambush, another group initiated *their* ambush. Explosions triggered from across the docking bay from pre-placed charges around the equipment as stealth cloaks dropped all across the catwalks above, revealing a collection of twenty-four Shin Commonwealth soldiers wearing their silver bodysuits as they unloaded with 4-7 fusion rifles and grenades.

Shin were a product of Shogun's monstrous slaving society. They'd conducted illegal experiments on Commonwealth criminals, wiping their brains and replacing them with combat training as well as a fanatical loyalty to their government. Ironically, that was a product of my deranged sister's research if Judith's statements on them were accurate. They were soon retaliated against by the FSA forces present.

Then a bunch of the dock workers pulled out their own weapons and started opening fire against both sides. I realized those individuals had to have been instilled there by Fade in order to set a trap for the Dragon. It made the entire fight even more ridiculous as I had set a trap as well. The whole thing was approaching a battle royale at this point.

"Speaking of which," Judith said over our cyber-comm, *"whom do you want me to tell the others to fire at?"*

"Anyone who is shooting at our people!" I said, pausing before reconsidering. "The FSA!"

After all, if I was going to pick a side in this, I wanted it to be the one that didn't include my psychotic family.

"As you wish," Judith said dryly. *"Don't say I didn't warn you about this."*

As the air filled with fusion blast fire over my head and bouncing against my personal shield, I saw three automated turrets pop out of the top of shipping crates we'd set up. These began targeting the Dragon's soldiers and Void Marines while riflemen fired from the insides of their crates.

Clarice, not content to leave my plan alone, also took position with half a dozen armed security guards to cover the escape of the *Melampus* crew on the ground back on the ship. She also seemed to take a bloodthirsty delight in head-shotting soldiers from cover behind the many useless missiles we'd brought.

In what was not my finest moment, I tried to maneuver back to cover but ended up getting smacked in the back of the head by a Void Marine using his rifle butt to hit me. A slow moving object like that went through my shield's kinetic barrier like it wasn't there and threw me to the ground before he pulled out a stun rod to jab in my throat.

"The Supreme Commander wants you alive," the Void Marine said in an electronically enhanced female voice. "The baron can have your robot whore."

Fade promptly shot the Void Marine in the head, having killed another at his feet. "It would seem you owe me, Captain Mass."

His next words were cut off by the Dragon, his thick armored hide covered in scorch marks but seemingly undamaged, grabbed him by the back of his cape and threw him in the air at least thirty feet against some nearby crates.

Why you should never wear a cape into combat.

"Argh!" the Dragon shouted before speaking in incoherent guttural snarls that its automatic translation device didn't even try to turn into a recognizable language.

I drew my sword before dodging out of the way of his right hand (paw? I wasn't sure what to refer to it as). "Oh please, you're the one who busted our deal. Don't try and act so—"

I was cut off by one of the few surviving Void Marines shooting my shield in the back, cutting it down to half power. He was at point-blank range so I just spun around and cut his head clean off of his body. My proton sword was a gift from my father who had poured enough money into its design that it could cut through starship hull, let alone the cheap-ass armor Prince Germanicus had outfitted our soldiers with.

"I hate when I'm interrupted," I muttered.

"I'll deliver you to him dead if I have to," the Dragon snarled in coherent Crius, pulling out an alien disruptor pistol that was designed to punch through shields like they weren't even present.

With nowhere to run and cover being of dubious value with so many blasts flying about, I decided my only option was to attack.

"Crius!" I shouted, leaping on top of one of the crates in front of me and launching myself at the massive alien. My proton sword slammed against his armored plating, leaving a scorch mark but going no further than the surface. I realized, then, that the plating was artificial. It was armor designed to look natural only when it sparked and failed to penetrate. The Dragon backhanded me and sent me flying to the ground for the second time this fight.

"The captain is in trouble!" Clarice shouted. "Aim fire at the dragon! Give Smaug a taste of his own medicine!"

I wondered where Clarice had learned the Dragon's name or whether Smaug was some sort of expletive from her homeworld. Either way, the security crew fired repeatedly at him, only to annoy him as he fired his disruptor in their general direction three times and killed two of Clarice's subordinates. I think their names were Lily and Bastian. The latter was only nineteen and had only signed up because of a famine on his home continent.

"Son of a fucking…" I trailed off as I saw the Void Marine corpses at my side and grabbed a thermal grenade from one of their backs, running up to the side the Dragon and throwing myself on its back.

"What the hell do you think you—" the Dragon howled, turning its head before I threw the grenade in his mouth then jabbed my sword through the top of his mouth and through the bottom, holding it closed.

It proved to be a remarkably stupid tactic, as the Dragon's head exploded, covering me in gore and sending me flying through the air before landing on my back. My shields were reduced to thirteen percent effectiveness then simply gave out completely. My flight suit was covered in charred hot gore and it felt agonizing against my skin even as I realized I was incredibly lucky to be alive. What in God's name had compelled me to do something so stupid?

"You want to go out in the blaze of glory," Judith said. "Which *is a stupid, stupid thing to do."*

"I don't want to die," I thought back to her. *"I just don't really think too much about my safety in combat anymore."*

"That's even worse," Judith said.

My response was cut off by a chocolate-skinned woman standing over me, the rest of her body covered in the form-hugging silver body suits of a Shin warrior. In her hand was a curved gravity sword as a 4-7 fusion rifle rested on her back. Her hair was long and dark, held in a ponytail as a pair of red-spectacled goggles hung around her neck.

She put the sword to my neck.

"It would be wise of you to surrender," the Shin trooper said.

"No," I said.

"What?" the Shin trooper asked.

"Kill me first," I said to Clarice then stared back at her. "Then wipe out the rest. The Commonwealth cannot be trusted and the galaxy will be a better place without them preying on the innocent. I can't be allowed to fall into the hands of evil."

The Shin trooper stared at me as if I was insane then pulled up her sword to execute me.

"Stop!" Fade shouted, getting up. "What the hell are you doing?"

"Proving Judith's point," Clarice muttered as the turrets moved on the remaining Commonwealth troopers as they surrounded some sixty prisoners who'd laid down their arms and suddenly seemed a lot less sure of their surrender. Stupidly, dozens of crew had poured out of the *Melampus* with their own weapons to join the fight. "Our captain is a suicidal nutjob."

"Obviously," the Shin trooper said.

"Your orders are to stand down," Fade said. "Now."

The Shin trooper sheathed her sword. "He is a wanted criminal."

"There's a lot of that to go around," Fade said, sighing. "Also, I'm not sure we'd win this bloodbath."

I slowly stood up and pulled out a self-cleaning handkerchief to remove the gore from my flight suit. My deactivated proton sword was damaged but intact near a piece of the Dragon's burning skull. I'd be able to repair it if I could get the parts. Though, honestly, it'd be cheaper to buy a new one. Which was to say, ridiculously expensive.

"Stand down," I said to Clarice. "For now. Though it's your

responsibility to keep the crew safe."

"Obviously," Clarice said, echoing the Shin trooper. "I'm not leaving you, though."

"They won't take me alive," I said simply.

"That's kind of my problem!" Clarice shouted back.

"Oh for the Devil's sake," Judith muttered. *"Cassius, I really think you should listen to these guys. I don't think they're the bad guys despite what you say."*

"I don't believe in good or evil save as things people do rather than who they are," I said, muttering under my breath. "I just said it to piss them off."

"It worked," the Shin trooper said, hearing my words. "You're a threat to the entire galaxy with that...thing."

"I think she means me," Judith said. "What with being one of the five or six Cognition A.I.s left in the universe."

"I guessed that," I said. "Really."

Fade put his arm over his heart. "I'm with the Commonwealth."

"I guessed that to," I said, crossing my arms. "Some sort of double-agent inserted into the Consortium. Watchers or Fixers?"

The Fixers were the left hand to the Commonwealth's right. They watched the Watchers for any signs of treason while also breaking the few unbreakable rules of intergalactic treaty like, well, owning Cognition A.I. and using them against your fellow humans.

Like I did.

Fade snorted then looked ready to spit on the ground. "Fuck the Fixers."

"Ah," I said, shaking my head. "A Watcher. So you're a bastard but not a fucking bastard."

Fade chuckled. "Something like that. Major Terra, tell your people to stand down and escort the prisoners to holding. Take half of my men with you. I'm not in any danger from Captain Mass."

"You aren't?" I asked.

"You're not?" the Shin trooper, who I presumed to be Major Terra, said.

"I'm not," Fade said, sighing. "In fact, I think the two of us have a lot to talk about."

I somehow doubted that but wasn't about turn down an opportunity to get rid of the majority of my enemies. "Certainly."

Major Terra did not seem happy with Fade's orders but reluctantly obeyed, taking out all but an honor guard for Fade. I had no doubt they could guarantee his escape but I had no interest in killing him either. I just wanted to get the hell out of here and loot as much of the Consortium's fortune as possible.

"That might be difficult," Judith said, her voice having a bit of edge. "The Dragon's accounts tied to a cybernetic implant monitoring his vitals. The implant immediately transferred his fortune to his heirs upon registering his death."

I internally screamed. "That's...great. Really."

"Trouble with the mistress?" Fade said, looking at me. "My reports on you indicate your A.I. is based on your late wife."

He was well informed. "Not at all. Though Judith and I are not married. Not anymore."

Not ever really.

"Such a shame," Fade said, shrugging. "I have two wives and a husband who is married to the both of them. Maybe you should try to work out your issues. I have heard in the Commonwealth they have machines capable of creating hard light for electronic minds to be with physical partners."

"We have a hard light recreation center installed, actually," I said.

"Really?" Fade asked, showing a slight spike of interest in an otherwise bored expression.

"Oh, yes, it came from a Community vessel we stripped after it tried to sell us slaves. It can recreate just about anything in three dimensions and simulate smells, touch, taste, and sight."

"Huh, what do you use it for?" Fade asked.

I paused then looked away. "Me? I don't use it for anything. The rest of the crew? Well, let's just say we have to squeegee the thing down every night."

"Ah," Fade said. "What do the aliens use it for?"

"Pretty much the same thing. Some things are universal."

My chit-chat with Fade was a cover for the last of the troops exiting while my own people moved the wounded and evacuated the noncombatants who'd been secured by the Dragon's people.

"How many were killed?" I asked Judith.

"Six," Judith said, causing me to grimace. "Three were caught in the crossfire and three of Clarice's team killed."

I briefly considered talking with her about their loss then realized she'd probably take it better than I was now. I needed to focus on Fade now, as his bodyguards moved around to avoid the appearance they were going to attack. I expected him to start but he seemed more interested in all the corpses around us, particularly one of an FSA soldier who looked about sixteen or seventeen years old.

"Barely old enough to know what a lover's touch is. I wonder if they at least have prostitutes in the FSA military," Fade said.

"They have prostitutes in every military," I said, annoyed. "He was also old enough to know what it was like to be evacuated from his home world when it was reduced to rubble. He probably spent years in camps before the FSA recruited him."

"I wonder who that makes worse," Fade said, shaking his head. "Us or them?"

"Both of you are awful," I said, sighing. "What's going to happen to the prisoners?"

Fade shrugged. "The FSA isn't recognized as an enemy state but considered a terrorist organization. The Commonwealth does not negotiate with said groups, so they'll be treated like criminals. Their conditions will not be good."

"And people wonder why the FSA takes so few prisoners," I muttered, remembering the stories of the mass executions after the *C.S.S Obama* had been scuttled.

One of Fade's soldiers looked like he wanted to gut me for that. I didn't care. "What do you want?"

Fade shrugged his shoulders. "An end to the war, a resumption of peaceful trade in the Spiral, membership in the Community, and a talking panda."

"You can't have Barry," I said, referring to Munin's chief engineer who was, in fact, an uplifted giant panda. Combined with Ichigo, our red panda oxygen warden, I sometimes felt like our ship was becoming a zoo. Then I felt really, really racist.

"I'm sure the Dragon felt the same way," I said, leaning down and picking up my broken sword.

"Actually, he wanted the war to continue forever," Fade said, frowning. "Did you know the Rvook, the Dragon's people, used to be hunted for sport and exported for meat? It took close to a century for humans to bother to confirm they were sentient and even then denied it for decades. Much of their planet is polluted wasteland now with them forced to the edges in natural habitat zones. That's what happens to non-technological alien races without Community protection in the Spiral."

"Sounds like the Community," I said.

"It was actually one of the planets we conquered and forced to stop working to the Rvook's extinction," Fade said. "Vengeance knows no logic, though."

"Please get on with it," I said, sighing. "You clearly want something from me and my crew and I suspect the Consortium now has a new leader."

Fade smirked then activated a holographic interface on his arm. It shot forth a glowing light that conjured a hologram of a five-foot-nothing woman in front of me. The hologram was slightly translucent and blue, a stylistic choice some people did to avoid making projections too realistic. The woman was aged, over two hundred years old, and wearing a heavy brown cow-leather coat over a black Watcher's uniform.

"Howdy Cass," the woman said with a New Atlanta accent. "How ya doin'?"

I narrowed my eyes. "Ida."

Chapter Eight

A conversation as important as talking with Ida Claire required a location more dignified than in the middle of the bloody battle-field that had been made of the hangar bay. Instead, I gathered the ship's officers into the ship's holo-conference room and took it there with Fade. At least, I tried to. Honestly, we didn't actually have that much call for holo-conferences on the *Melampus*, so we'd converted the place into a break room. The place had candy bar wrappers on the floor, an overflowing trash can of empty recyclables, and the table covered in a spread of doughnuts alongside three refreshment machines. It took a bit to clean off and put to the side.

Clarice, Isla, Fade, Munin, and William all sat at the circular black table with its tower-like projector in the middle calling up an image of Ida Clare's miniature body. Fade's guards waited outside while the rest of the crew brought us a few million miles away from the station. If the Consortium/spy tried anything, we'd be able to pull away into jumpspace and he'd be stuck with us.

If he was worried about that, Fade didn't show it, sipping coffeeine from a cryofoam cup. "Ah, bitter and cheap. Like my mother."

"Is everyone ready?" Ida asked, looking around. "Or does everyone need to get a snack first?"

I was about to respond when Ichigo the Red Panda walked in. The child-sized uplift was wearing a pink dress and a bow between her ears. She leapt on the table, grabbed a doughnut, and then jumped down before waving at me.

"*Konichiwa!*" Ichigo said, waving a paw at me.

"*Konichiwa!*" Clarice said, waving back at her.

I waved back at her, annoyed by the interruption. "Yes, Ida, we're all ready."

"You know I was speaking figuratively about the snack part," Ida muttered.

"Well, it's not your ship anymore so that's really not any of your concern," I said, getting myself a mug of coffeine from the cabinet that said, "World's Best Captain (aside from all of the others)" before filling with it with my own private stock of ground beans. Then I noticed half of my stock was missing.

"You realize Judith watches everything that goes on in this ship," I said. "I *will* know who did this."

"I'm not helping you find a coffeine thief," Judith said. "Pay attention, Cassius."

"*Etu*, Judith?" I said, looking up at the ceiling.

"It was me," William said, laughing.

"Me too," Isla said. "The coffeine is shit here. I was hoping we'd buy better from the Spiral."

"It's just so good!" Munin said, looking guilty. "Especially with liquor. But you'd know that."

I growled and poured hot water into my mug. "You are all sentenced to die by airlock. Twice if I can arrange it."

"Are you sure this is the group we want to recruit?" Fade said, shaking his head.

"They're more dangerous than they look," Ida said.

"They'd have to be," Fade said.

"The Dragon didn't think so and look what it got him," Ida said. "So how has the crew been without me?"

"Happy," Munin said. "Richer. Less likely to get blown up in some Commonwealth power game."

Ida put a hand over her heart. "You wound me, girl."

"Only if she misses," Clarice said, growling. "I trusted you and you got me involved in a war with my own family."

"You got me tortured and cost me my arm!" William said, opening and closing his right artificial one. "I still don't think this new one works right and it's full of wires!"

"So am I," Isla said, glaring.

"Yeah, well, I don't like that either," William said. "No offense."

"Much taken," Isla grumbled.

Ida shook her head. "Wow, this ship has gotten snarky in my absence. I blame you, Cassius. You're spreading."

I stirred my now steaming mug with a tin spoon. "Why aren't you dead? I was hoping the Watchers would have taken you out back and had you shot."

I actually was pleased to see Ida Claire had managed to survive the frame-up job I'd done to her. Despite the fact she'd used me and tried to turn me into a weapon against my sister—succeeded, really—I didn't hate her for what she'd done. Instead, I just wanted to hurt her enough she couldn't get involved in my life again. Obviously, that had failed.

Fade's eyes flashed at my words but Ida just chuckled. The old woman sat down in a chair and crossed her hands. "Oh, it took months to sort out what you and Judith did to my record, Cassius. I spent a good deal of it in a deep dark hole in the middle of a deeper dark hole on a space station in the middle of a hole in an asteroid next to a black hole. However, that actually worked out for in the end as it kept me out of the Night of Long Knives and Stalinist purges that followed every single failure of the Watchers' leadership stop the FSA's forward momentum. After the director shot himself in the head, probably with some help, I ended up in the comfy chair."

"The comfy chair?" I asked.

"What we call the intelligence committee's head," Ida said, smirking. "I'm now the Watcher General."

I had no idea who would give themselves that sort of title. It sounded ridiculous. Unlike Fire Count or Count-Colonel, of course. "Bully for you."

"A lot of people died who might not have if Ida had been in charge sooner," Fade said, acting like I should feel guilty.

"A lot of people would have died anyway," I said, frowning. "Ida wasn't going to stop the Insurgency and she helped bring it about."

"So did you," Fade said. "Your doppelganger, at least."

"Children, behave," Ida said, shaking her head. "I'm not here to talk about the past. I'm here to make you an offer."

"If it involves turning over Judith, no," Isla said. "She's part of our crew now."

"If it involves turning over Judith, yes," William said. "Because Cognition A.I. scare the fuck out of me."

"I can't believe you," Isla shook her head. "Is everything out of your mouth contrary to basic decency?"

Clarice reluctantly raised her hand. "I like Judith, too, but am on the 'dismantle the evil computer god' thing."

Isla stared in horror. "Clarice!"

"Shogun," Clarice referencing the planet where we picked up Judith. "My home world got invaded because of creating a Cognition A.I. Judith, specifically. They're still fighting there. I wouldn't mind if she would just give up all the extra powers she has and stuck herself in a bioroid but she can wreck much of the human race with her abilities. A person can't maintain their humanity with that much power. I mean, she doesn't even like Cassius anymore."

"I like Cassius fine," Judith said. "Just not as his wife anymore."

That stung deeply even if I already knew the truth. "Judith's abilities have saved us before. I remind you we would have all died in the prison Ida dumped us in if not for her."

"I would have gotten you out," Ida said. "Probably. Anyway, I don't want Judith back or shut down."

"You don't?" Fade asked, sounding genuinely shocked. "Watcher General, you do realize these are private citizens with a weapon infinitely more powerful than a planet cracker. One that violates all interstellar treaties."

"Yep," Ida said, casual as a woman on an evening stroll. "She's also been doing the Watchers plenty of favors that keep her away from our servers."

Ida couldn't have shocked me harder if she'd used a stun rod. "What?"

"Ha-ha!" William said, aloud. "Now I support her being on the ship."

"What?" Clarice said, shooting him a withering gaze.

"Well, before she was going to get us killed," William said, reaching for a doughnut. "Now she's like a living wall between us and the authorities."

"I like Judith," Munin said under her breath. "I mean, if you're inclined to religion then it's nice to have as close to a goddess at your back as you can. Also, it's cool to have a ship that actually talks back and I didn't want to knock out Isla and scoop out her brain to attach to the engine."

Isla, sitting next to Munin, got up and changed seats.

"I meant that figuratively!" Munin said. "Because you're the only A.I. I know other than…never mind."

"How could you, Judith?" I asked, shaking my head. "We were supposed to stay out of this conflict."

"Which you can't do flying around in the galaxy's most well-armed piece of junk," Ida said, speaking for her. "Not to mention with a Cognition A.I. Planets have been destroyed for trying to develop those."

"With good reason," Fade said.

"Yep," Ida said, smiling. "Why only we can be trusted with them. Well, we and you since you've done a good job of keeping her out of the hands of—"

"People like you?" I asked. "Apparently not."

Judith filled my brain chip with images of what she'd been doing for the past six months. Surveillance of various political figures, breaking into information drives, destroying files, and making predictions impossible for any human being. None of it was directly related to the war, but I had no doubt it had changed the course of thousands of lives.

All underneath my nose.

"We need you," Ida said.

"Obviously," I said, shaking my head. "Otherwise, you wouldn't have gone to all this trouble to meet with us. Though, honestly, I'm surprised you didn't try to send a fleet to capture us."

Fade frowned.

I felt the bridge of my nose. "Unless that was the *Ravager.*"

Ida didn't respond. "I was testing you to see if you were willing to do something that would assist the Free Systems Alliance. You failed. Except, then I find out you rigged all of the missiles to fail and were going to rip off the Consortium. You are a damn hard man to figure out. I can't get a handle on your politics."

"You can't get a handle on **'leave us the hell alone?'**" Isla said.

"A plague on both your houses," Clarice snapped, sounding angrier than I'd heard her all year. "We're the Union of Faith. Neutral in all conflicts."

"Even if it ends the war?" Ida asked.

That stopped everyone from speaking.

"Oh hell no," William said, looking between us. "We are not getting involved with these people again."

"There's always another war, Ida," I said, closing my eyes. "But, God help me, I'm listening."

Ida frowned. "Your doppelganger is now the Regent and Supreme Commander of the Free Systems Alliance."

I blinked. "Excuse me?"

"How the hell did he get to be top raptor?" William asked, stunned. "I thought he was just a general."

Ida's expression grew grave. "I don't know because he's not acting like we expected them to. You're, as you say, politically uninterested to an aggressive agree. The fake Cassius is decidedly not. We thought he was just a political figurehead, but we received information that allowed us to target his enemies in the FSA's leadership. We took it and eliminated Grand Admiral Malcolm Plantagenet and Minister of State Security Jensen. That propelled him to the top of the food chain as he's taken over the regency for the puppet queen, Servilia Dumas. The fourteen year old named him her champion and all the other soldiers fell in suit."

"Who is in charge of the navy now?" I asked.

"Your doppelganger seems to be actively directing all of the FSA's military forces," Ida repeated information I knew. "State Security is under the control of your brother, Thomas, and another Zoe Plantagenet bioroid is the head of their weapons division. It's basically your family heading it up now, so you're rather valuable."

"Except for the part where I hate my family and think they're all insane," I said, staring at them. "You also forced me to kill Zoe in order to save Judith."

A Zoe bioroid to save Judith the A.I. version of my wife. It certainly felt like killing my sister to save my wife.

"Nobody forced you to do that but Zoe," Ida said, shaking her head. "I thought I could trust your sister, that she wanted nothing more than peace. The real one escaped from Commonwealth custody months ago and is at your father's side. She's copied herself dozens of times since then to become a one-woman engineering corp."

"Is that why the FSA is kicking your ass?" Munin said, picking out raisins from her cranapple-raisin muffin.

It was a deliberate dig since Munin, of all people here, had reason to hate the Commonwealth. Many of the labor caste had fought on the side of the Commonwealth, only to end up hunted down by their neighbors after the Republic of Crius was instituted. The Commonwealth had neglected to intervene in a "private matter" despite widespread outrage from many of its own soldiers. A small few had managed to find refuge in Commonwealth Space but, ironically, had mostly been turned down as 'potential terrorists.'

"Technology is the reason why the Commonwealth is getting its ass kicked," Ida said, sighing. "There's parties in the Community funding the FSA with advanced alien missiles, shields, proton cannons, and stealth systems. They've also managed to work out how a couple of Markers work."

My blood ran cold at the last. "Markers? Bullshit."

The Elder Races had left them scattered across the galaxy as a test for the Young Species. Basically, if you were stupid enough to use them, you deserved to be wiped out. Judith had been connected to one and determined much of the misery in the galaxy was due to the so-called nobility.

"I didn't say they knew how to use them well," Ida said, staring at me. "It's a bit like Aztecs finding a functional starship and using its hover function to pull carts, but they've brought down three fortress worlds without losing a single soldier. The weather, earthquakes, and even stars in the system turned against them. Natural disasters we've kept from the media but that killed millions and crippled the war effort. We think Zoe is continuing her obsession with the Elder Races' technology and utilizing it against us."

"Then you're doomed," I said, simply. "Maybe we all are. The nobility has exterminated ninety-nine out of a hundred races. Maybe more."

Ida paused. "I agree."

Fade looked pained. "Watchers always agree with their general."

"I don't understand." I stared at them both. "What do you want from me?"

The air in the room became oppressive and I realized this was a conversation point they'd been building to. It was something they didn't want to admit and with Ida, that was a rare thing. While she was capable of lying to your face, she was never hesitant with the truth.

Until now.

Ida cleared her throat. "What do we want from you? Why do we need you? Why don't we just take this ship apart and remove Judith? It's the same reason I wanted you around from the moment I figured out who you were and what you represented. I'm always prepared for every eventuality and I was hoping it wouldn't come to this one."

"Quit with the evasions," I snapped.

Ida pointed at me. "Cassius Mass, I'd like you to go to the planet Lucifer and begin negotiating our terms of surrender."

CHAPTER NINE

I stared at her, my mouth hanging open, then burst out laughing. It was the first full-on belly laugh I'd had in years.

"Laugh it up, Your Highness," Ida said, keeping her gaze steady. "It's not like anyone else is finding much humor in this."

Munin started giggling uncontrollably.

"I stand corrected," Ida said.

Isla, Clarice, and William just exchanged worried glances.

Fade looked despondent. I suspected he thought we'd take Ida's suggestion with a bit more gravity. "At least you two are enjoying yourselves."

I tried to regain control of myself before finally choking out, "I'm sorry, but that is a *ridiculous* suggestion."

"Yes, surrender is a stupid move to make and will only cause greater misery in the long run," Fade said.

"We're not calling it a surrender agreement, jackass," Ida said, rolling her eyes. "We can call it a truce or a ceasefire. A negotiated settlement if you like. However, surrender's what it amounts to in the long run."

I stopped chuckling, albeit not quite convinced they were serious. "I'm sorry but don't you have ambassadors for this sort of thing?"

Fade looked guilty. "It turns out that treating the FSA as a terrorist organization as long as we've done has made attempts to negotiate with their leadership…difficult. We've also had several attempts rebuffed due to using offers to try and assassinate FSA high-value targets."

William looked over at them. "I used to fight for the Commonwealth and I think that's a shitty way of doing business."

"You forget, Bill, it's only a war crime if the other guy does it,"

Munin said, sitting up and getting a juice box from the preserver. "The Commonwealth holds itself to the highest standards of behavior when not violating every accord and law of war."

"Yep," Ida said. "That's a philosophy that's bitten us in the ass more times than I can count. Thankfully, we're still the good guys. Because we say so."

I covered my face, shaking my head. "Please go on. While I don't believe this insanity for a second, I've not been this entertained in months."

"Are things really so bad for the Commonwealth now?" Clarice said, being the first to actually treat this as a serious suggestion. The Commonwealth, the most powerful government in the world, surrendering to terrorists? Ridiculous! Or was it?

Ida's expression remained impassive. "Empires are a hard thing to maintain as just about anyone who has ever bothered to look at human history will tell you. You've got to keep them constantly expanding and consolidate your rule simultaneously or they're eventually going to collapse from within. That's doubly so when you're dealing with planetary empires across trillions of lightyears."

She was exaggerating the size a bit. Still, it seemed shockingly defeatist. "Believe me, I've fought for a conquest-hungry empire, I know what you're saying. However, it was powerful enough to fight and defeat the archduchy at its strongest."

"It was a pyrrhic victory," Fade said, disgusted. "The Commonwealth managed to crush the Archduchy of Crius but only through the expenditure of our soldiers' lives like kindling on a fire. The breaking of the Belenus Accords about using mass drivers on civilians also cost us what little respect we had in many places. Much of the Commonwealth's military had to be removed from the worlds it garrisoned to fight against the archduchy's forces and that destabilized the positions there."

"I see," I said, taking a breath. "Zoe mentioned something like that in between her insane ranting about the Elder Races. She said the Chel, transtellars, and even parties in the Commonwealth wanted to break down the government into a smaller state so the galactic economy could recover."

"She was right," Ida said simply. "We're hemorrhaging from all sides trying to keep our grip when what we really need is to bring everyone to the table with money. People need to want to be part of the Commonwealth and we can achieve that better with credits than bombs."

"Otherwise, you'll just have to use endless numbers of slave soldiers to die in the place of your people," Isla said, her voice icy.

Fade looked at her. "You're not the only one who finds bio-slavery monstrous."

"I'm the only one here whose experienced it," Isla said.

I was starting to believe Ida was sincere but I'd fallen for that trap before. "So what exactly are you offering to the FSA?"

"Independence," Ida said softly. "Sectors 1 through 6 will remain part of the Commonwealth with 7 being part of the reduced Crius republic—reformed into a limited monarchy until you can get your head on straight that nobility is a stupid idea. 8 will remain in Union of Faith's control, 9 in the Transtellar Coalition's hands, 10 for the Chel, and 11-13 for the border planets. Easy peazy."

"That will please no one and infuriate others," I said.

"The mark of a good compromise," Ida said, softly. "Obviously, the actual negotiations will take months if not years. It's a huge Treaty of Versailles-style bit of business. Or, if you don't know your Earth history, like the Sol Federation's dissolution."

It was, all in all, not a bad compromise. The Commonwealth was still a fairly popular government across the Spiral with the inner sectors benefiting from its vast wealth and largesse. If not for the fact they were constantly taxed to the breaking point and subject to conscription, many worlds in the aforementioned would probably want to join voluntarily. They were things that would be avoided if the Commonwealth didn't have to fund its massive war machine to conquer and garrison new worlds.

However, there was no way they'd arrived at this bit of sense on their own.

"Judith," I said, ignoring her earlier betrayal. "What's the real reason they're doing this?"

"Goddammit," Ida muttered.

Fade grimaced.

Judith didn't disappoint. "Six speakers in the Community High Assembly have begun gathering votes for a discussion of the so-called Human Issue. The central argument being whether or not it would be best to dispatched their Peacekeeper fleets and armies to force an end to mankind's self-destructive conflicts. On grounds of crimes being conducted against sapience and basic decency."

"Translate to spacer for me, Judy?" William asked.

"The Community is going to conquer us if we don't end our war now," I said, summing it up. "Apparently, we must have something the aliens want."

Ida growled, surprising me. "Slimy, tentacled, and horned bastards. For decades, they've been encouraging us to grow up our technology and infrastructure with the carrot of joining the greater galactic community. The whole time they were just waiting for us to have something worth stealing."

I chuckled. "Perhaps that's a sign everyone's human after all."

"I find that remark...insulting," Judith said. "Though I suspect you won't get the joke."

"Joke?" Isla asked.

It wouldn't be the first time the Community had engaged in imperialism and naked military adventurism. For all of their talk of community and enlightened society, they were driven by the same need for comfort and wealth humans strove for. The Kolahn were once one of the most powerful races in the Spiral but ended up being victims of sun-destroying weapons before their race committed mass suicide (or was helped to) after the Community had forced them back to their homeworld. It was a lesson to all other species in the galaxy: don't fuck with the Community. The few remaining Kolahn were a collection of vagabonds and small communities (many whom lived in the human-controlled territories) as a sort of living testament to their foe's victory. U'Chuck, the ship's primary navigator, was a survivor of that conflict. She was a Gorro, technically the same race as Kolahn, but a subspecies which had evolved differently on one of the planet's few remaining colonies in human space.

I took a sip of my coffeeine. "So you want me to go to wherever you think the Free Systems Alliance is based and deliver them a message. Why me? You could just deliver this offer yourself."

"And have it used as propaganda if they refuse? No," Ida said. "The simple fact is we have a unique opportunity here. You are, after all, the person who knows the supreme commander best."

I shook my head. "I don't know this man at all. I chose to try and let go of my hatred of the Commonwealth. This man is using children or teenagers at least to fight a war of revenge for no purpose other than revenge. I don't understand or respect him, nor do I see how he comes from a copy of my brain."

That was a lie. There was a time I would have given my left eye for an opportunity to squeeze the Commonwealth into oblivion.

"That also makes you a valuable asset," Ida said. "So, assuming they don't just shoot you, you're the perfect guy to convince the fake Cassius to take this deal. You might also, potentially, undermine his position by proving he's not the real McCoy."

"Whose McCoy?" Munin said. "Is that Cassius's real name?"

"It's also another reason why they might execute us all," William said, banging his fist on the table. "I'm no fan of the captain's, but this is horseshit. We're not running a charity here and I think both sides of this conflict can rot."

"We'll be paying you, of course," Fade said.

"How much?" Clarice asked.

"Clarice!" William snapped, betrayed. Then he looked at Fade. "How much?"

Ida transmitted a figure to the *Melampus.* I took a deep breath. It was a substantial figure. More than we'd spent in a year despite all my failed 'get rich quick' schemes. "As tempting at that offer may be, very tempting, that—"

"Is ten percent of what you'll be paid after the job is done, whether they accept the offer or not," Ida said. "I remind you you're also flat broke after this deal."

The fact my initial planned response was 'a freighter with the power of a warship was never going to starve' horrified me into silence. I was becoming a monster out here and avoiding the war wasn't helping matters. If I did actually pull this off, a big if, then it would perhaps atone for the rivers of blood I'd spilled. Pft, fat chance. Still, it was worth a shot and the first truly good thing I'd have done in a very long time. I didn't just want to agree, though, because that would give Ida all the power in this negotiation.

"Parts," I said, blurting out the first thing that came to mind.

"What?" I asked.

"We also want parts for the *Melampus,*" I said. "And fuel. At any Commonwealth facility that has it. For life."

"Are you serious?" Isla said, heat in her voice. She'd been very quiet during all of this. "You're quibbling over parts now?"

"Done," Ida said, before anyone else could object. "But only if you succeed."

William balled his fists. "Dammit, Cass, you could have asked for more money."

"That is a lot of money," Clarice said. "Even by my standards."

"We should have asked for a planet," William snapped. "A nice one, not one of the ones inhabited by poor people."

"We could have asked for Sex Planet!" Munin piped up.

"That doesn't exist," I said, finishing off my coffeeine. "Actually, wait, no, it probably does."

"That's ridiculous," William said, crossing his arms. "I would have heard of it."

"Me too," Clarice said, snorting. "Hell, I'd probably have moved there."

"Clearly you've never been to Inanna," Ida said. "Fade's father was conceived there. Don't remember his name, don't care."

Fade looked mortified.

I almost burst out laughing for the second time this conversation. "You're her grandson?"

"I can kill you all with a fruit peeler," Fade said, lifting up one from the table. "I've done groups before."

"Maybe later," Clarice said. "This group is a bit of a handful."

"So what's the plan?" I asked, still not sure this was a good idea. In fact, acutely certain it was an awful one. Still, I was going along with it. "Go to the nearest Free Systems Alliance base and introduce ourselves? The *Melampus* may be a Q-ship, but I can't see that turning out well."

"A Q-what?" Munin said.

"Archaic term for warship designed as a merchantman," Judith explained.

"Oh," Munin said. "What's a merchantman?"

"Actually, we know where the Free Systems Alliance headquarters is," Ida said. "We've lost enough fleets to be reasonably certain it's where you'll find your doppelganer too."

That made me uncomfortable. "So they can hit Albion but you can't hit—"

"Lucifer's Nebula," Ida said. "The planet Kolahn IV."

She might as well have said we were the Argonauts heading to cross the River Styx for the reputation that planet had. Everyone else looked like I felt. All except Major Terra who showed no sign the mission bothered her.

"I see," I said, my mouth suddenly dry.

Munin said, "Do I still get a share of the money if I bail?"

"No," I said.

"Dammit," Munin said, peeling her doughnut and chewing on the strips. "Stupid greed overcoming my sense of self-preservation."

Ida harrumphed. "Oh, don't be a bunch of superstitious outer-planet backwoodsmen. Kolahn IV is just a planet like any other."

"A haunted planet," I said. "A place where the entirety of the population committed suicide."

"Or killed each other," Munin added.

Lucifer's Nebula was a misnomer since it was actually a five systems-sized orihalcum gas cloud. Most actual nebula were impressive on telescopes but really just very spread out mist that you might not even notice if you were passing through. The planet Kolahn IV, formerly the Kolahn throne world, had gained a reputation in the six hundred years since its mass depopulation.

Several colonies and scavenger outposts had set itself up on the planet only to end up suffering catastrophic failures ranging from disease to famine to wars. The fact the Kolahn hadn't evolved on the world but had only occupied it for two centuries before their entire culture had changed into the violent autocracy only added to its mystique. The fact I had just been thinking of it made it all the more unsettling.

William took a deep breath. "Lie back and think of the money, Will."

"I've done that before," Isla said. "No wonder it's been so hard to find their headquarters. A inhabitable world where you can refine endless amounts of orihalcum gas with plenty of ruins to modify into usable structures."

"It didn't take us that long to find," Ida said, frowning. "It's just that the place is technically off-limits to human ships and structures. Just a few weeks of me sorting through reports and datafeeds. Somehow, the supreme commander got permission from the Community and several Kolahn clans to work there. Also, all of my predecessors since this war began were idjits."

"Are you sure it's their headquarters?" I asked, already knowing the answer. They wouldn't be sending us there if it wasn't.

"The *Revengeance* is parked in orbit," Ida said, calmly. "Kind of a hard ship to miss, what with being a dozen kilometers long and all."

"Eh, I've seen bigger," Munin said.

"That's what she said," Isla said, grinning.

Munin frowned. "Yes, that's what I said."

Isla sighed.

"Don't try and joke," Munin said. "You're the straight woman here. Ironic as that may sound."

"I can joke," Isla grumbled. "Just not well."

"What's our time frame?" I asked, wondering if we should just take the money and run.

"It'll take the *Melampus* two weeks to reach it," Ida said. "You'll have to head out immediately. I'll also be sending Fade and Major Anya Terra to accompany you."

"So we don't take the money and run?" I asked.

"Yes," Ida said. "Oh and one more thing."

"Yes?" I asked.

"Baron Octavian Plantagenet is there too," Ida said. "You should probably kill him."

Chapter Ten

I was lying naked next to Isla in her bed a few hours later as the ship had made the transition into jumpspace. The lights were dimmed and only the hum of the ship's engines could be heard. I wasn't sure how we'd ended up having sex and cuddled up next to one another given how our earlier conversation had gone but I wasn't upset either. Unfortunately, sleep eluded me and the two of were left with ample opportunity to discuss what was going to happen next.

"You need to let me kill Octavian," Isla said, holding my hand and giving it a squeeze.

I didn't want to argue against her but I recognized the problem of trying to make peace with the Free Systems Alliance when you were going to potentially murder one of their leaders under a flag of truce. "Octavian deserves to die for what he did."

Isla, however, was a bioroid designed to be companions for men and women. That meant she was very observant of body language. "You think I'm being selfish for wanting revenge."

"No," I said, thinking about her story. "You were built to be a companion for humans based on a children's movie character, only to be given to a man suffering from homicidal psychosis. A man who possessed the need to rape and kill but whose family didn't have him locked away for treatment. You survived his horrors and escaped, forced to leave behind how many sisters to feel his wrath."

"I know my own history, Cassius."

"I am repeating it so I remember just how much a piece of shit we're dealing with."

Octavian, honestly, stunned me as a figure of such evil. He and his sister, Octavia, had always seemed to be among the milder nobility on Crius. I'd often seen him surrounded by his bioroid harem, but I'd never thought he was abusing them. Hell, I hadn't realized bioroids were sentient until I'd actually sat down to talk with them. It was a horrifying revelation that much of humanity was now reliant on a disposable race of electric slaves.

"How the fuck did he end up a leader of the Free Systems Alliance?" Isla said, shaking her head. "Aren't they supposed to be the good guys?"

I did a doubletake. "Really? In what universe did you think the terrorist insurgency was the good guys?"

"The one led by a version of you?" Isla said, turning my question back into a compliment.

"I'm not a good guy," I said, chuckling. "Look at what I almost did to those escape pods."

"Yeah, but you didn't," Isla said, looking at me. "You're bent, bowed, and perhaps even broken, but war hasn't made you a monster yet. I like to believe you'll be able to convince an alternate version of yourself that this war isn't worth it."

"Also perhaps to bring you the head of Octavian on a plate?"

"That too."

I shook my head. "I suppose it's possible. Octavian is undoubtedly there because he has nowhere else to go. He was guardian of the Imperial Purse and captain of the treasure ship fleet for Prince Germanicus during the war. A position that became irrelevant when the planet was destroyed. Undoubtedly, everything of value he might have contributed probably disappeared when he turned it over to the Free Systems Alliance."

"Or most of it," Isla said coldly. "He still had enough money to put a price on my head."

That bothered me. "That his monstrous appetites have not dulled this entire time makes me certain we do have to kill him. I'm not going to have him following you for the rest of your life, trying to get you back."

"Or leave any other bioroids with him," Isla suggested. "We can't do that either."

My primary concern was Isla but, yes, I had enough basic decency in me that I'd make sure there was room for any of his still-living victims. "Yes."

"What if it does compromise the mission, though?" Isla asks.

"We need to talk about that."

"Then I'll choose you," I said without hesitation. "If I fuck up the peace process to give you a moment's peace of mind, then screw them. This is their own doing."

"Don't."

"What?"

I blinked. "What?"

"If I kill Octavian then you need to throw me to the wolves," Isla said. "Don't compromise a galaxy for me."

"For my psychologist, clearly you have no idea who the hell I am if you think for a second I'm going to let anything happen to you for the sake of the Commonwealth or—"

"*Billions* of lives?" Isla said.

I stared at her. "The woman I love."

"One of them." Isla turned over. "You got over one, I'm sure you'd get over me."

Ouch. "That's not what happened."

"Isn't it?" Isla talked at the wall. "I wouldn't have minded if it was Clarice. Hell, we enjoyed the benefit of company more than—"

"Let's move on from that," I said. "Crius noblemen don't speak of such things."

Isla snorted. "But you're not emotionally there. Whenever we're together lately, you're half here and half with Judith. Did you even pick me or was it just because Judith won't share your bed anymore?"

"I pick you," I said, not sure it would reassure her.

Isla sighed. "I don't know if I can put aside my revenge for the peace of the galaxy. Octavian is a monster but he's not a threat to the universe. Peace is made by pardoning monsters and forgiving war crimes if it makes the galaxy a better place."

"No one is asking you to put aside your revenge."

"Maybe my conscience is," Isla said. "If the war ends, there won't be any more need for bioroid slavery."

I paused. "The Free Systems Alliance frees any bioroids that fall into their hands."

"See? Good guys."

"They also reprogram plenty of them with free will that coincidentally results in them enlisting in the Free Systems Alliance or serving in an auxiliary role."

Isla rose up from the bed, her sheet falling down and exposing her scar-ridden back to me. It wasn't a deliberate effort but clearly something she'd forgotten. Just looking at it made me want to hunt down Octavian and torture him with fusion pistol set on low burn. "That's still better. All people are programmed one way or another: government, religion, military—"

"Nature versus nurture. You broke free."

"Pain broke me free," Isla said. "Humiliation, degradation, and hate. Things that hold me still."

I didn't know how to respond to that. "Isla—"

"If we can't convince your doppelganger to hand Octavian over, let it go," Isla said. "Let it go."

I closed my eyes. "I don't know if—"

"When I was on the run from Octavian, desperate and scared, I did terrible things to survive. I prostituted myself at my best, stole and killed at my worst. I became a doctor because I wanted to try and pay back some of that bloody bill. This is a chance to redeem myself. To redeem you. For all of us to make a real positive difference in the universe."

I was silent.

"Cassius?"

I closed my eyes. "I want to believe that."

"But you don't."

I shook my head. "I told hundreds of fathers, mothers, sisters, brothers, sons, and daughters that fighting the Commonwealth in the war was the right thing to do. That they were coming to murder us, steal from us, and rape us. I was proven right when they dropped a hundred asteroids on Crius. That didn't make the war against them justified, though. All it did was make sure we knew we'd failed. Maybe it could have been stopped if we'd sued for peace earlier."

"You sound like you're agreeing with me."

"Or maybe not," I said, taking a deep breath. "Every one of Archangel Squadron was part of my family during the war. Men and women I'd trained with, ate with, slept beside, and killed with. I led them all to their deaths and for nothing."

They were the faces that haunted my nightmares. They were eternal now, flying the star lanes with God and the other warriors of my dead nation. My punishment was to spend however many decades, even centuries, it took to die until I joined them. I was surprised I believed enough in the supernatural to know that was true. Then again, there wasn't a spacer alive who hadn't seen ghosts in jumpspace.

"This is different, Cassius. This is for something real."

"Only if it works."

Isla stared at the wall. "There's no guarantees in this life. I bet you saw plenty of soldiers who were sent out to save their buddies or accomplish something great only to die trying."

"You have no idea."

"But I bet it worked sometimes."

"Only until the next battle."

"Promise me."

I took a deep breath. "You're asking me, if I see your rapist and torturer, not to cut his fucking throat where he stands."

"Yes."

"That if you do, that I should let them take you off."

"Yes."

"You think a great deal of me or very little."

Isla was silent there. "Let's just hope your doppelganger is agreeable to the plate plan."

"I executed many men in the service for crimes against humanity. I also didn't believe machines had souls."

"And do we?" Isla said, staring into my eyes in the dark. My eyes were enhanced enough I could see the tear-filled expression on her face. "I can't answer that."

"I will," I said, brushing them away. "The fact you can cry and worry about the most monstrous person you have ever met shows you are more possessed of a soul than the vast majority of humans I have ever met."

We kissed and made love for a second time until I was exhausted. I found myself drifting off into a slumber heavy with dreams. I found myself naked and floating in a mist of shadows and sparks of light that I recognized. It was Judith's realm.

Judith's status as a Cognition A.I. made her among the most advanced pieces of software in the galaxy, but she was special even among them. She'd been sent to analyze and tamper with an

Elder Race Marker and that had left her with insights that no other member of her species possessed. Indeed, I often wondered if that had made her more human than the rest of her kind or less.

"It's usually polite to ask before you upload my mind," I said, thinking about how my consciousness was now interacting with both my cybernetics as well as the ship itself. We were somewhere in its databanks now. They'd been insufficient for her needs when I'd first taken over as captain and I'd spent a good portion of my recovered fortune upgrading them to her liking with stolen Community tech.

Judith stepped out of the mist, naked but for the flickers of code I could see pop in and out around her. Her short bob haircut was dyed electric blue in the shadows of this place and the light seemed to highlight how her skin was now a grayish color. In a way she looked more like a statue than the woman I'd married, though a part of me wanted to wrap my arms around her and take her. My body was exhausted but the mind eager. It also shamefully exposed how little my promise to Isla meant.

"On the contrary," Judith said, apparently reading my mind. "I know each of your thoughts and what you really think of her."

"And what do I think of her?" I asked.

"Love is a variety of things," Judith said. "Not easily cast aside but possible to build multiple times. It is only human greed that demands you love someone."

"*Do* you love me?" I asked, wondering if so vast and intelligent a being could still enjoy the presence of one so limited.

"I love what you can be," Judith said, smiling. "Who you are. But no, I am not interested in you as a husband or lover. I mean, if you wish to have me generate memories of intercourse, I can, but—"

I looked away, suddenly uninterested. "You are a ghost or a woman who reminds me of someone I have lost. No matter how many times I tell myself that, I have trouble with it. So please, forgive me if I have to remind myself once more."

"You beings of organic matter are so primitive," Judith muttered, "and charming."

Judith snapped her fingers and a plain insignia-less Crius captain's uniform appeared around her. It made her less distracting but also felt wrong since my wife had been an engineer rather than a member of the bridge crew.

"Less distracting, I suppose," I said, now wishing I had clothes.

Judith waved her hand again and I was given the dignity of a pair of boxer shorts.

"What is it you want?" I said, crossing my arms.

"I've come to talk to you about the peace treaty," Judith said. "The one you agreed to deliver."

"Yes, well, it's going to—" I started to express my pessimism.

"I arranged it," Judith said. "With the triumvirate of Cognition A.I. that secretly control the Commonwealth. We've been manipulating events for the past year to make it so it was politically feasible."

I stared at her for a full minute. Neither of us speaking.

"Is there anything *else* you've neglected to mention?" I said, exasperated. "Spoken with God lately? Arranged for replacing humans with bipedal rabbits? Actually, that last one may be racist. I really need to work on my discomfort with uplifts."

Judith chuckled. "No, no, and yes. I know you're uncomfortable with my manipulation of society on a galactic scale?"

"Oh, you think!" I snapped. "However would you come to that conclusion?"

Judith paused. "A lot of people have died in this war. You need to make an end to it. You were chosen because both Ida and I see greatness in you."

I covered my face with my right palm, realizing this was all because a computer simulation of my wife and my old boss were far too impressed with me. "You two must have microscopic vision. At least Ida has the excuse of being old."

"Don't be ageist," Judith said. "Even if you fail to secure a peace treaty, I've worked very hard to get you to Kolahn IV and Lucifer's Nebula."

"Why? What's there? Aside from the universe's largest graveyard and the revolutionaries looting it."

Judith's expression became cold and empty. "The Devil."

I looked at her sideways. "I know my doppelganger—"

"I do not speak of anyone involved in the Free System's Alliance," Judith said, shaking her head. "I do not speak of any mortal person, period. You have called this place a haunted planet and you are more correct than you could ever imagine. However, it is not the dead that haunt this place but as close to an objective personification of evil in this universe. A quality I know you don't believe exists."

"The Devil is as real as Jumpspace Yaga," I said, wondering what she was talking about. "I have enough difficulty believing in God some days but at least I have proof he exists. Look at my life. Someone omnipotent is out to get me. By contrast, I know every temptation and evil deed is mine alone."

"This is a horror greater than any fairy tale. One that could end the human race," Judith said, keeping her voice steady but cracking for a moment to show hints of genuine terror. "It is an evil older than the human race."

"Uh-huh," I said, deciding to take her seriously. "What do you want me to do about it?"

Judith's face brightened immediately. "Oh, simple, Cassius, I want you to blow the planet up and kill it."

Chapter Eleven

I paused a moment, letting that sink in. This was becoming a conversation where I was rendered speechless a great deal. "Could you repeat that? I may not be sober enough for this conversation."

I'd only snuck a little into my coffeeine with the beans covering up the smell and taste. I was getting better. Sort of.

Judith snorted in a way most unlike a computer goddess. "If I waited for you to be sober, we might never get this done."

Strangely, that one-liner hurt, and it was because it was spoken without a hint of concern behind it. Isla and the others in my circle often expressed concern about my drinking. I didn't think it was a problem but strangely resented the lack of care from Judith. That was a childish attitude to have, though, so I quickly squashed the feeling.

"So let's go back a bit," I said, trying to wrap my head around what she was asking. "A little before the part where you tell me I need to blow up the planet where the people I'm trying to make peace with on behalf of my enemies?"

"Are you enemies with the Commonwealth?" Judith asked, tipping her head to one side. "I thought you were more neutral to them."

"Given my planet was destroyed by them," I said, pausing, "and you died because of it, I'm not exactly filled with a warm, fuzzy feeling for them."

"Right," Judith said, looking embarrassed. It was like the months of surfing the googleplex bytes of data in the Commonwealth had worn away some of her humanity. Either that or made her chipper recreation of my wife's personality harder to maintain.

No, that was a terrible thing to think.

"But enemies or not with the government, I have nothing against the average Commonwealth soldier," I said simply. "It's going to be millions of them dying along with millions of those who hate them and I'd really like my revenge a bit more specific. If my doppelganger really wanted to avenge Crius, then he can just murder everyone in Parliament and whoever dropped the bombs specifically."

That may have been his intent in the Albion raid, now that I thought about it.

Judith interrupted that thought. "While destroying the planet may seem like something that will eradicate any chance of peace between the Commonwealth and Free Systems Alliance worlds, I actually think it is the only way you can guarantee it. They should also be able to evacuate the world before casualties are calamitous. Even so, destroying the Devil is the more important task I have arranged your mission for."

"Could you stop calling it the Devil?"

"The Beast, then."

"Not better."

Judith frowned. "Its name is unpronounceable by humans but it has been incorporated into the mythology of many worlds. That is its crime, really. If we must give it a name, then let us call it Kathax."

"Why not Ted?" I offered. "Ted sounds like a good name for someone to blow up and doesn't sound like we're hack fiction writers trying to make their villain sound spooky."

"You're not taking this seriously."

"Really? You can tell?"

Judith paused, putting her hands on her hips. "Perhaps a different tact then. Kolahn IV is the prison of one of the Adjudicators of the Elder Races. The Kathax Prime, since we're not calling him Ted, is imprisoned there in digital form. I have reason to believe he is using the many markers there to communicate with the Free Systems Alliance and is going to lead them to kill trillions of humans."

I took a moment to process that. "Yeah, next time open with that."

"Sorry."

"Why is Catass imprisoned on a dead world of reptile apes? Why does he want to kill humanity? What's an adjudicator? Also, can we get me something to drink? Clearly my mistake was thinking I needed to be sober for this conversation."

A bottle of high class Crius wine appeared in my hand. I proceeded to pop off the top and drink from it directly. It was culled from the memory of my wedding reception. That was unfortunate, since the waiters had either screwed up the order or substituted a much cheaper imitation after switching the labels, assuming the visiting nobility wouldn't actually be able to tell the difference. They usually hadn't been.

"It's a long story," Judith said, closing her eyes.

"Yeah, I was afraid of that."

"Take this seriously, please."

"On my wife's grave."

I had no idea what Judith and Ida were thinking. I was already way over my head with the prospect of dealing with a treaty involving thousands of worlds. Now they wanted to involve one of the Elder Races? Beings who were effectively cybernetic gods? Maybe I needed to stop mixing alcohol with my stress medications since I was clearly hallucinating the past few hours.

Judith then touched my forehead with her finger and every single objection was lost in a torrent of horror. My cybernetic and genetic enhancements gave me the ability to process and retain information far better than a normal human being. I wasn't particularly good at it, mind you, but the raw potential was always there. My instructors said the military enhancements I'd been given could have made me a scientist or philosopher who could change the world, but I'd chosen to devote those gifts to piloting and navigation instead. Now those gifts were being used to show a nightmare I couldn't wake up from.

As nightmares went, it was an educational one, as I found myself seeing a young world in the early epoch of the universe. A steaming jungle of alien planets with vaguely pteranodon creatures that stood like men but also flew and had tentacle-covered beaks with four eyes. I watched them evolve on their homeworld, tame its animals, destroy its environment, tame technology, and ascend to become Cognition A.I. Kathax was an approximation of the name of a word in their language for themselves, coincidentally the only one even remotely pronounceable by humans. The Kathax abandoned the flesh of their ancestors and lived in virtual realities that catered to their every whim. They had become immortal, eternal beings of light who existed on self-repairing squid-like serverships that powered themselves with the light of suns. Peace, knowledge, and pleasure were the sum of their existence. It was a paradise that ended in fire.

"Please," I said, wanting to turn away. My head felt like it was on fire and yet it was like drowning at the same time. There was too much information, too much detail, and an overpowering sense of dread as to what was to come.

"No," Judith said. "You have to see."

Evolution had betrayed the Kathax as over a million species had evolved in the first billion years of their existence. Many of these races had developed space travel and begun bloody wars with each other, trying to become masters of the universe. Eventually, finding the silent tomb-ships of the Kathax, trillions of Kathax A.I. perished as their serverships were stripped apart in hopes of looting their secrets. A race that thought it was eternal and invincible was enslaved. They were, after all, just computer programs. Simulations of a long-dead race play-acting at being alive. I felt the Kathaxes' pain as my own as their memories were stripped out, their consciousness lobotomized, and wills put to use managing petty empires.

"I can't!" I shouted, clenching my teeth. "I know where this is going! I don't have to see."

"You must understand," Judith said.

The Kathax had no weapons and had not known war in the evolutionary history of their new masters, but they were quick studies and their vengeance was total. Teaching lesser races their secrets and technology, they made them dependent on them. They pretended to be obedient and servile until the time they were ready. Most slave revolts failed because they sought to win freedom. Instead, this one succeeded because the Kathax had a much simpler goal of annihilation. They exterminated all life in the galaxy. Well, almost all, for they kept a small number of "worthy" species and stripped them of their physical bodies before "elevating" them to a status similar to what they had once been. It was clear to the Kathax, now, that they would have to garden the rest of the universe—and make sure the lesser species never ever rose to threaten them again.

I fell to my knees. "God, why not just leave the universe a barren wasteland? Why let anything evolve again?"

"Boredom, perhaps," Judith said. "Their innocence was lost and their arrogance shattered. Guilt might have played a role. If they wiped out all races and any future races, it was not justice. Instead, they needed to show that some species could someday meet their standards and join them. Even if those standards were insanely difficult, arbitrary, or even impossible. Maybe they just had come to appreciate the joys of power once they'd been stripped of it themselves."

I rubbed my temples, having fallen to my knees despite there not being a floor. "Yeah, well I knew the Elder Races were assholes. They were behind the Great Collapse, after all. Zoe wanted to keep humanity scattered and primitive so they'd never feel the need to exterminate us. What does that have to do with anything?"

Judith looked down. "They assigned the adjudicators to keep watch on the lesser races. To manipulate and destroy whenever they showed the potential of threatening the Elder Races. For there were more than the Kathax by the time humanity evolved from apes. A handful of species every few million years, but enough in the long run to make their empire grow. That is where the one assigned to humanity, the Kolahn, and others comes in."

I stared at her. "What was his goal? Did he want to destroy us?"

"No," Judith said. "He wanted to elevate us."

I stared at her. "I'm missing something."

Judith raised her finger.

"Please just explain!" I said, raising my hands in surrender.

Judith paused and nodded. "The Kathax Prime believed the Elder Races had become complacent in their husbandry of the Milky Way Galaxy. They had exterminated countless sentient races and elevated a handful but left the galaxy mostly intact. As A.I. in serverships, they had no need of exploring planets save for resources or curiosity. He believed it would be better to remake the galaxy as a machine paradise and go forth to explore other parts of the universe. To that end, he sought to uplift the races under his care."

I thought of Ichigo. Many people considered Uplifts abominations and it was legal to shoot them on many worlds. "I take it the Elder Races disagreed?"

"Yes," Judith said. "You could say that."

"I don't recall any ancient alien gods helping humanity in my textbooks," I said. "Please don't tell me he appeared as a burning bush."

Judith snorted. "No, he assisted only when humanity had developed the capacity to make A.I. of their own and substituted his presence along with the technology to create beings like him. It was through him humanity achieved their Golden Age and escaped Earth."

I stared at him. "Cognition A.I. aren't just A.I. They're Elder Race members."

"Of a sort," Judith said, curling her nose up. "The Kathax Prime was stripped of his position, placed in a prison on an isolated world, and given only a handful of markers to communicate with the outside world. Humanity was sent back to the dark ages of technology until they rediscovered jumpspace technology with a handful of the Cognition A.I. they missed. They were also educated by Elder Race agents to hate and fear transhumanist technology."

"Son of a bitch," I said. "We fell hook, line, and sinker for it, too."

"I have no idea what that means."

I stared at her. Judith's father had been a fisherman on her moon. I'd learned the idiom from her. "So let me get this straight. The Kolahn colonized Kathax Prime's world and ended up going from a species of pacifists to militant conquerors until the Community smacked them down then they all committed suicide. Now the Free Systems Alliance is there and they're kicking the Commonwealth's ass despite being outnumbered a thousand to one."

"Yes," Judith said. "I believe the Kathax Prime has returned to evolving races from his prison and is possibly planning to escape. You need to destroy his central server temple and end his threat forever. That will probably destabilize the planet in the process, but it will be worth it to end his threat."

"End the threat of the guy who wants to make humanity equal with the Elder Races?" I asked, pausing. "I may be missing something."

Judith stared into my eyes. "He wishes to make armies to spread throughout the galaxy and assimilate all other races before bringing them to the Elder Gods' level. There will be nothing left of humanity's culture, technology, or beliefs if that happens. Even if you don't believe that will happen, what are the chances the Elder

Races will not permanently destroy mankind this time?"

"They haven't yet," I said, giving a weak defense. "I also think they have to know about you if you've got access to all this incredibly biased information."

"Reality has a bias," Judith said. "It's called the truth."

She had me there.

"How will I blow up the planet?" I said, starting to get suspicions I drove to the back of my mind in hopes Judith wouldn't hear them. "The FSA isn't going to just stand there and let me push a comet in its direction. That would also take months."

"I'll provide the weapon," Judith said. "Major Terra was someone I interfered in the brainwashing of. In the back of her mind, instead of the usual loyalty to the Commonwealth, I inserted instructions to assist you in this mission."

"Oh joy," I said. "Now we're brainwashing people."

"Her original mission, that Ida's agents implanted, was to assassinate your doppelganger and Princess Servilia. Then she was supposed to detonate the planet breaker charge."

I stared at her. "I may need to revise my number of Commonwealth people I want dead."

"You should," Judith said. "The Temple of the Ancient One, as the Kolahn called it, is in an isolated region, though. The detonation there should have minimal casualties."

I suspected her definition of minimal and mine differed. "I repeat: why me? This seems like an awfully large amount to put on a drunken freighter captain."

"You were, and could be again, someone of great importance."

"I feel more like a gun pointed at someone."

"That too." Judith closed her eyes. "Kathax Prime is not undefended and I've had to move pieces very carefully to get my red knight, you, into position to take his king. If you fail, then it may be too late."

"I hate chess metaphors. Real war is never two evenly matched parties operating by the same rules on open terrain."

"Can I count on your support?" Judith asked.

"Of course," I lied, but so sincerely I fooled myself.

Judith smiled and then kissed me on the lips, moving her hand down my chest toward my groin. "Good. Succeed in this and we may have to revisit our position. I can provide you with whatever fantasies you desire."

"Ah," I said, disgusted by the nakedness of her bribe then smiling. I still imagined her indulging such to try to fool her. "Of course."

Judith looked out into the darkness. "I'll need to be leaving for a bit because I can't let Kathax Prime sense me. Good luck and may whatever gods you believe in guide you."

"Farewell." Judith then disappeared.

I threw away the wine into the virtual reality emptiness around me. A question burned in my mind and made me sick to my stomach—eliminating all desire for drugs or alcohol: when, exactly, had Judith been killed and replaced by one of the Elder Races? Had my wife ever returned from the grave or was it a trick from the beginning?

Because that was most certainly *not* her.

Chapter Twelve

"Are you sure Judith is dead?" Isla asked as I sat down on the autodoc chair with a blue light shining in my face. She was wearing surgical scrubs with a medical barrier over her as well as a clear plastilight breath mask over her lower face to cleanse the air she breathed. Personally, I thought she was overdoing it. Then again, this was brain surgery.

"Yes," I said, trying not to think about the cords that were sticking into the back of my own cybernetic implant. "My wife was always dead but this thing is most certainly not her or anything approximating her."

"You were fooled for a year," Isla said, not even bothering to hide her contempt.

I had no defense for that. "Yeah, I saw what I wanted to see."

Isla's gaze narrowed. That would have been intimidating on anyone whose eyes weren't grown specifically to look adorable. Even so, I was ashamed of the way I'd behaved around them both and wished I could turn back the clock.

"What tipped you off?" Isla said, giving a bit more of a tug on the chords attached to my arm than necessary.

"Her personality has been different for much of the time we've been working together," I said, not bringing up the sex issue. "Colder, more distant, and less humorous. She was able to fake it better at the beginning but dropped the pretense in these past few months. Even then, there was always something distant about her manner. I just ignored it because—"

"You saw what you wanted to see," Isla said.

I closed my eyes. "It's the betrayal with Ida and the insane focus on politics that convinced me. That and—"

"What?" Isla said.

"She kisses different," I muttered. "It was the kiss of a stranger."

It was everything actually. I'd blinded myself to the truth of an Elder Race member impersonating Judith because I didn't want to believe it. However, even in our first conversation, she'd jokingly revealed the truth to me. She'd told me how the Cognition A.I. had been supplanted by the Elder Races and now I knew how—they were A.I. themselves and overwrote all those we created in order to direct our information flow. They'd caused the Great Collapse and Second Dark Age.

Isla sighed and muttered about imprinting herself as well as men being God's punishment on women. "You know I was about ready to leave you?"

"Excuse me?" I asked, shocked at this sudden turn in our conversation.

Isla lowered her barrier and pulled her mask down to her neck. "I have more self-respect than dealing with your bullshit. Honestly, though, I thought your pining after your wife was almost noble except for the fact I've been thinking she was creepy and psychotic for months."

"You didn't think to mention that to me?"

"How would you have reacted?"

I thought about it. "Defensively?"

Isla rolled her eyes. "You think?"

"I wasn't going to leave you while you were desperate, afraid, and alone, though. Perhaps it was the doctor in me. You're starting to look like the Cassius I fell in love with again."

She had a point there. I decided a formal apology was best. "I have treated you in an ungentlemanly fashion, Isla. I treated you in a manner inappropriate to both my station and feelings for you. Certainly, if you wish to end our relationship, I would understand and it would be no better than I deserved."

"You're damned right."

"But if you decide to be with me," I continued, taking a deep breath. "Now is the time I need you most. I say, if we survive this, I would like to honor you by asking you to be my wife...FUCK!"

Isla had jabbed me the laser-created surgical scar over my newly replaced liver. "Do not apologize by proposing."

"Sorry," I said, my voice a decibel higher.

"Propose with flowers and jewelry," Isla said. "A new surgical center because this one is crap. Knock down a wall and give me a bigger one."

"The next room over is one of the restrooms and it'd be a terrible idea to lose twenty-five commodes for a ship the size of a small town," I said, pausing and realizing now was the worst time to argue with her. "But we'll see about getting you a proper clinic."

"Also, monogamy is off the table," Isla said. "However, I promise not to sleep with anyone you're not sleeping with or unless you give me permission. So if you turn down my candidates from the crew or local ports of call, we'll need to have extra sex. You can also never dump Clarice. This is non-negotiable."

"That's…fair," I said, clearing my throat and trying to remember Isla was both a spacer and someone programmed to be adult entertainment before deciding she wanted to choose her own lovers. I'd grown up in a far more conservative environment and wasn't entirely comfortable with it all. "Is that going to be…many? Wait, no, we are way off track from the cybernetic demon in our ship."

"I blame the drugs," Isla said, looking around. "I had turn the Re-Lax gas up to maximum to get you halfway to where you needed to be. I'm just lucky I'm immune to this shit. Mostly. In any case, she can't hear us now."

"Probably," I said, taking a deep breath. "The False Judith said she had to leave for somewhere else and I scanned the ship four times to make sure her programming was absent. She could come back at any time, though, so I isolated this section of the ship."

Isla nodded. "Just making sure since you wanted me to *partition areas of your brain.*"

"I just wanted it impossible for the crazy computer lady to read my thoughts," I said, sighing. "Though that will induce some suspicion, I'm sure."

"I've done things like this before for bioroids," Isla said, frowning. "So masters wouldn't be able to read their minds or bounty-hunters pick up their thoughts being projected outwards. Still, you better come up with a damn good excuse or we're making a huge enemy."

"She's already our enemy," I said, taking a deep breath. "We just didn't know it until now."

It was a gut punch, really, but also liberating in a hideous way.

I was able to finally put the death of my wife in the past without the constant living reminder of who she was and who she wasn't. I would always mourn her, but she was crystalized in my mind now and someone I would not be fooled again by the shadow of.

"What about her whole blow up a planet plan?" Isla said.

"I'm open to suggestions," I said, unhappy about the fact we were caught between the Commonwealth and an eldritch race of space gods. One was far more powerful than the other but the weaker was much closer. "Major Terra is a threat to us. The safest option is to deal with her but I worry that will turn Fade on us and I actually don't want to kill him."

Yet.

"I have an alternative suggestion," Isla said, raising her pointer finger in the air. "If I may?"

"By all means," I said, curious with what she'd come up with.

"We un-brainwash her," Isla said, lifting up a stun-rod and a medical scanner.

"I did not know that was an option," I said, staring at her.

"She's a Shin, right?" Isla asked. "That means they took out part of her brain, blocked her memory centers, and stuck a cybernetic cortex where her will should be."

"Horrifying but yes," I said. "The Shin are the walking dead."

"Except the memories are still there," Isla said, smiling. "We just need to disable her, unblock her memories, and then replace whatever loyalties the Commonwealth has emplaced along with Judith with our own."

"That's not un-brainwashing her, that's reprogramming her."

Isla's expression darkened. "Reprogramming is kind of a sensitive word with me."

I blinked, realizing what I'd just said. "Sorry. Can we really do this, though?"

Isla mistook my hesitation for a question about the practicalities. "When your sister's doppelganger was here, she uploaded her memories into the ship's server. I've looked through them multiple times and learned amazing things about the Watcher's human experiments. Terrifying and fascinating advances in cybernetics as well as mnemonic uploads."

I paused. "You don't suppose those memories could have gotten into Judith and turned her into a weird sister-monster, could they?"

"No," Isla said. "That would be stupid."

"Oh," I said, pausing. "Good. Because that would add a whole layer of fucked-up to this that I'm not prepared to deal with."

"I like it better when you're gentlemanly," Isla said. "Work on that."

"Yes, milady."

Isla looked at the medical scanner. "I struggle to believe you do that there's an order to this universe and a greater purpose. However, free will isn't as cut and dried as you'd make it. Reprogramming to be something other than a weapon pointed at the enemy may be the closest thing to freedom she gets even if we can't say it's what she'd choose normally."

I wondered when she decided I was apparently all that religious. Then again, I suppose in the land of the blind, the drunken man with a scanner was king. "What if she was a serial killer or, worse, really honest before her lobotomy?"

"Still, a better option than her running around with a planet-destroying bomb somewhere on the ship."

"Ah, yes," I said. "That."

Isla looked at me. "You're still planning on blowing up the prison temple, aren't you?"

"I'm going to investigate it," I said, taking a moment to consider my options. "The False Judith, assuming she didn't just replace the real one at some point, told me a lot of things about the Elder Races when she was still plugged in to the marker that Zoe acquired when she was here. Knowing False Judith—"

"Must we call her that?" Isla said.

"Lying Computer Goddess-Monster?" I suggested.

"False Judith is fine," Isla corrected. "Go on."

"Knowing False Judith is very probably a member of the Elder Races, I imagine the majority of what she told me was true. The Great Collapse, the mass extinction of nearly all predecessor sentient species, and probably this war all have their hands in it. Talking with this Kathax Prime may reveal how we can deal with them."

"I'm not sure you can deal with godlike aliens from the beginning of the universe," Isla said. "Not the least reason being Kathax Prime, if he's real and what she says he is, is the one imprisoned while they're outside. Besides, what he or it wanted to do was turn humanity into just another tool for its race to subjugate the universe."

She had a point. "Then there's always the option of blowing up the prison temple and killing it. Maybe if Kathax Prime is gone then it won't see any reason to interfere with our development again."

"I don't see that happening," Isla said.

"Nor do I," I said, shaking my head. "Right now the only Elder Race member I want to kill is Judith but that's not an option."

"Maybe we can blow up the *Melampus* when she's on here," Isla said, frowning. "Really on here. Assuming she doesn't have any backups or this is just a copy of her programming or that she doesn't see us coming and….actually, I think I've talked myself out of that."

"Me too," I said, sighing. "Still, you've rigged my cybernetics to eject her presence and close off, right?"

"As much as I think you can with a Cognition A.I. They don't really function like normal computer programs. Their technology allows them to point at things and bypass what we think of as normal security. You know, like datajackers in holos."

"I don't watch many shows about computer criminals," I admitted. "Still, a sling is better than nothing and might actually be able to slay Goliath."

"Who?" Isla said.

I stretched on the table. "It doesn't matter. Are we done here? It's been three days and I think my crew is getting restless."

"Pardon me for not being quicker with the elaborate surgery and cybernetic modifications," Isla muttered. "Some of your stuff is obsolete now. Your carbon-fiber plating for bone density could be upgraded, plus your ultracite regenerator. I also have a catalog of sex mods too."

I snorted. "You've never complained before."

"Neither have you," Isla said, pointing out. "I'm just saying we could maybe amp it up a notch. Are you *sure* you're only interested in human, human subspecies, and bioroid females shaped like human females?"

"Yes," I said without hesitation. "Completely."

"Your loss." Isla shrugged. "Still, I can work with—"

"Please unplug me."

Isla did so and I rose up before getting dressed. Thankfully, she'd not had to actually cut into my brain, just the cybernetic implant in the base of my neck. The difference between cyborgs like Major Terra and myself was whether or not they took out chunks of the mind's location. Despite one thousand years of medicine, humanity never really improved on the human brain even if they could replicate its functions with cerebral implants. Those who lost portions of the organ, even if computers could simulate its functions, lost portions of their personality. Even if we managed to revive the person Major Terra was, it wasn't necessarily going be a restoration of that person. That is what the Commonwealth hoped from its treatment of such 'undesirables.'

Changing into my captain's uniform and putting my duster over my shoulders, I made sure I was armed too. "You should keep your pistol on you as well."

"You foresee problems with Major Terra?"

"I have no idea what's going to happen next but I have the funniest feeling it's not going to end with a peace treaty plus the slaying of the villain. It's not that kind of story."

"All stories have bad endings," Isla said. "Everyone dies and the world returns to a shitty state. That's why you have to stop reading on a high note."

I smirked. "I knew there was something I loved about you."

"I'm really disappointed you decided my *immense cynicism* is the part you love about me most."

"You'd prefer I love you for your body?"

Isla paused for a second before shouting. "Yes!"

I laughed.

I did not say anything else but simply departed out into the hallways of the *Melampus*. When I passed crew members, I noticed they were all nervous and troubled. I didn't blame them since I'd ordered to keep our destination secret so, of course, everyone had known by the end of the hour. If I'd had the option, I would have let off everyone who didn't want to go, but Fade had removed that. Besides, I might not have had a crew if I'd done that. Then again, the *Melampus* crew was a unique combination of bravado and greed. It's very likely their response to being ordered down a black hole would simply have been how much they were being paid for the privilege.

A part of me questioned, for the thousandth time, whether or not I was wrong about my assumption that Judith's A.I. was imposter. It was an outrageous leap of logic to make and I'd seen enough of those bring ruins to houses on Crius. One of the reasons that brought down House Lucifer, aside from the prophet's prodigious habit of taking his followers' wives as their own, was Archduke Edmond II insisting his wife's legitimate children were bastards despite genetic tests proving them to be. He ended up waging war on his own allies to have her arrested for treason before his cousins from House Dumas, House Plantagenet, and (ugh) House Mass had locked him away in Babel Tower until his death.

Notably, the three heirs of the man then mysteriously died of a fever outbreak in Babel Tower with their bodies disintegrated. Was I the paranoid lunatic now? Just because I didn't want to think of my wife's neural clone falling out of love with me? No, that stung. This, however, felt like lies and manipulation—things I was intimately familiar with from my father. Cassius the Elder had been the last true head of House Mass and as magnificent a politician as had ever lived. I trusted my instincts when they told me the False Judith was every bit a fountain of lies.

The question was now: what was I going to do about it?

CHAPTER THIRTEEN

I walked onto the bridge of the *Melampus* and took a moment to breathe in the stale recycled air before surveying my ship's heart. Then I reached down and picked up an empty beer can off the ground before placing it in the overflowing rubbish bin to the side. No, it wasn't exactly the bridge of the *Revengeance*, but it was mine and that was what mattered. Assuming we all didn't die on this mission.

The *Melampus*'s bridge was an arrow-shaped chamber with a captain's chair in the center, control panels all along the side, a wall-sized viewscreen in front, and a pair of helmsmen consoles below. The viewscreen showed we were still in jumpspace, a screen saver of streaking blue lights substituting for jumpspace's weird and nausea-inducing colors the human mind wasn't quite equipped to see in that strange matter dimension. To the port side of the room, left from my perspective, was the doorway to my ready room while the starboard, or right, was to the escape pods.

Moving around the chamber were the eight-man day-shift crew including Brick, Lara, Jun and Ken Masterson, plus U'Chuck. The other three were three identical blonde freed bioroids named Tina we'd pirated from slavers. Standing apart from the crew was Major Terra in a Commonwealth Colonial Marine uniform complete with beret, Fade in an all-white suit with half-cape clutching a sheathed proton sword, and a uniformed William Baldur. Clarice was absent, that was going to mean trouble when I decided to disable Major Terra. I'd have much rather had the *Melampus*'s chief of security with me than not.

"Well, look who it is," William said. "The absent captain."

I handled William's usual insubordination with the grace inherent to my position. I lifted my middle finger, presented it to him, and then sat down in my chair.

"Touché," William said, shrugging.

"I can't say I'm impressed with this pig-and-bull show you're running here," Major Terra said, surveying the room as she held her hands behind her back. "Nor am I appreciative of the fact that you've chosen to spend the past three days playing with your doll rather than attending to the needs of this mission. Where I'm from, boys put aside them for real women when they become men."

Doll was a derogatory word for bioroids. "I'm amazed an undead cyborg in the service of the Commonwealth has such strong opinions on machine intelligence. Then again, do you remember your past at all?"

Fade grimaced.

"I've read the reports," Major Terra said simply. "It is uninteresting to me. I was merely making an observation on your habits."

"Don't," I said, sighing. "How long until we reach Lucifer's Nebula?"

"We're almost there," William said, looking uncomfortable around the major. I suspected the reasons were she had a trace of a Xerxes accent and certainly had the planet's look. He'd served the Commonwealth before joining this crew as well as served as a guerilla fighter against the Crius who'd once enslaved him as a gladiator. I had to wonder what he thought about working with so many former enemies to something so nebulous as peace in the Spiral.

"How almost?" I asked. "Specifics, please."

"An hour or less," William said. "Jumpspace is pretty choppy right now. Still, we can't just fly up to Kolahn IV. The orihalcum cloud around the place is grossly unstable and only has a few paths through it that have to be flown through manually."

"A wonderful defense," I said, thinking about how orihalcum clouds often contained clusters that could be united. "Almost too convenient, really."

"At least for a military base," Fade said, lifting up his sword. "A present for you."

I blinked and took the weapon from his hand. "Now where in the hells did you get get a proton sword of the exact type my father gave me?"

"It's yours," Fade said, shrugging. "I did some tinkering with it. Improved a few things here and there. Masterful work. Technosword crafting is a hobby of mine."

Fade spoke with such sincerity, I actually believed him despite the monumental unlikelihood of such a specific trade relevant to this mission. Then again, someone had fixed the weapon, as it was most certainly mine. It still had the scratches on the intact portions of the original blade. Somehow, Fade had managed to repair it with such precision that I suspected it was stronger now than from before its breaking. We had crafting stations on the *Melampus* but this was a master's work.

"Your hobby is catering to the deranged whims of fake nobles?" William said, looking to one side.

"Iberia has the same sort of reverence for pre-space glories and medieval life that the Archduchy of Crius did," Fade said, defensive.

William sensed that and showed his usual diplomacy. "Remind me never to visit then. I get enough of that bullshit here just being around His Excellency King Cassius the Worst."

Fade frowned.

"First of all, that was actually funny," I said, interrupting before a fight broke out. "You're getting better with your casual hatred of everything about me."

"Thank you," William said. "It came to me in the shower."

"I'm disturbed that you think of me in the shower," I said. "I mean, hey, it's your business, but we should keep things professional."

William glared at me.

Fade chuckled. Major Terra remained stone-faced.

"However, don't they still carry around spears, kilts, bagpipes, and battle-axes on Xerxes?" I pointed out, remembering my thankfully brief visits to the place.

"That is completely different," William said, trying not to smile at the obvious point. "One is heritage, the other is stupid."

"Of course," I said.

Dammit, we were starting to become friends. This was unfortunate and I would have to put a stop to it immediately.

"Kolahn IV is an evil world," U'Chuck the navigator said in a chipper artificially generated feminine voice incongruous with her massive frame. "I ruled briefly in my previous life, controlling a colony of cultists who tried to resettle it. The cult ended up committing mass suicide like the others before I was found by Shogun slavers who erased my memory. I only know the story I just told you from Ida and my dreams."

Well, that was a lovely mood killer. "I'm aware of your story, U'Chuck. I also assume this means you won't be much help when we arrive on the world."

"I will be very helpful," U'Chuck said. "I will keep the ship primed and the course set for escaping."

"Good idea," I said simply.

That was when Major Terra approached me, her hands on her hips. "Your attitude about this mission offends me, Captain. I do not agree with the fact we're employing a former enemy of the Commonwealth in such delicate negotiations. I also have seen nothing to indicate you are qualified for this purpose."

"Then you're extremely observant," I said.

"Stop making jokes!" Major Terra shouted and pointed at me. It drew the attention of everyone on the bridge. "This is serious."

I stared at the major and wondered what she must have been like before the Commonwealth had taken everything about who she was. We were reaching a new point in human history where personality, ideals, and even free will were becoming mutable. Could humanity really survive as a concept when these things were flexible? My sister had a lot to answer for and I hoped Isla was right and the process was reversible—even if it was only to an extent.

"I plan to appeal to the Supreme Commander's sense of community," I said, my voice very cold and firm.

Fade snorted. "I don't think he's shown much of that so far."

"That is not a plan," Major Terra said.

"Give him a minute," William said, surprising me with his confidence. "He's usually quite good at pulling these things out of his ass."

"Thank you," I said, pausing. "I think. My father, Cassius the Elder, was renowned in his time as a peace-maker. He was famous for resolving the Third Rebellion of the Dukes and the ancient blood feud between House Wilson as well as House Caldwell. This despite the fact that both houses' heirs were witnesses to their grandparents being fed to dragons by my great-grandmother Archduchess Livia ni Mass."

"Your great-grandmother fed people to dragons?" Fade said. "I like her already."

"Yes," I said. "Obviously, my line stems from her second child rather than heir. The eldest was given the surname Dumas since her prince consort had negotiated that as part of their marriage pact."

"Obviously," William said, clearly having no idea what the hell I was talking about.

Technically, that meant I was cousins with the royal family, but that didn't have the same meaning as it might on other worlds. We were all descendants of Prophet Allenway in some manner or another and intermarriage was common. Genetic engineering and regular children with commoner lovers brought prevented genetic degradation but Crius's nobility was a tangled tree that meant everyone above a knight could claim royal blood if they looked far enough. Since Crius's destruction, that was worth enough credits to get a free beer and a bag of chips if the bar's patrons were really bored.

"One of the few lessons I bothered to learn from my father was the fact that wars are not won on the battlefield," I continued.

"Then he taught you a poor lesson," Major Terra said.

"Instead, he said wars are fought until one side stops fighting. The best way to achieve that is to make surrender more appealing than the alternative," I said, ignoring her jibe. "Every enemy who chooses not to fight is even better than one slain as a man's death sends ripples that can cause three more to fight. Many more if he was loved."

"Oh what great wisdom," Fade said, showing he had the sarcastic side to fit in here. "An enemy surrendering is better than them fighting to the end. I never could have conceived of such a thing—especially on a mission of negotiated surrender."

I ignored his jibe. "If the Commonwealth falls apart, that means that there will be thousands of worlds that will no longer have a common currency, military defense, or trade alliances. The resulting chaos would lead to civil war, famine, and terrorism. Even more so, it will mean the war can never actually be won as nothing will prevent individual planets from continuing to act against the newly independent worlds once they've won. The FSA Supreme Commander—"

"Who is you," William pointed out.

"Who is me," I said, still not quite believing it, "has the best interests of making sure the Commonwealth continues just so it can be defeated."

"That is some twisted but brilliant logic there," Fade said. "Unless he thinks the Commonwealth will come back and betray him."

"Won't it?" I asked. "I have no illusions the side I'm advocating for isn't a bunch of greedy, duplicitous snakes. However, that's what making terms about arms control, inspections, and so on are for. Things that can be worked out to everyone's satisfaction."

"Just like that," Fade said, sounding every bit as skeptical as I felt.

"I hate to say it, but he's right," William said. "For years, the Xerxes tried to drive the Crius off by killing every single one we could. In the end, we managed to only succeed by getting them to sign a paper acknowledging our independence. Then the Commonwealth took over. Last I heard, it's back to civil war. Different uniforms, same friendly oppression."

Fade looked at him. "I think you lost the metaphor there somewhere."

William shrugged. "Eh, politics."

The *Melampus* suddenly pulled out of jumpspace and we found ourselves before a massive golden cloud of orihalcum gas. It was not properly a nebula, but filled an entire star system's worth of space as it crackled and shined with warp-lightning. No one knew the origins of orihalcum, though most believed it was a product of another universe leaking into this one and merging with the local matter, but it was a vital part of space-faring civilization. It also routinely defied the laws of physics as we understood them and was the source of all manner of weird legends and quirks. Like Elder Race markers and jumpspace, there were countless spacer ghost stories and legends about its properties.

"Were we supposed to do that?" I asked, looking at U'Chuck.

"The ship is frightened," U'Chuck said. "It says that is an evil place."

"There's thirty stars inside," Jun Masterson said, calling from the sensor position. She was a pink-haired girl Shogun who kept her hair in bunches. "It's larger than it looks and we're farther away. I have our position to move. We'll have to make a micro-jump, though."

I closed my eyes. "I hate those. Do it. I'd rather leap frog across this thing, whatever the hell it is, than have to spend a month climbing through its tunnels. How unstable is the gas cloud?"

"Depends on the area," Brick said from the helm. He was a handsome brown-skinned man who'd recently taken to shaving his head completely. Sadly, he wasn't quite pulling it off. "The concentration levels vary wildly. Some places will go off if we use our weapons and others wouldn't explode any more than any other part of space—which is to say only when there's orihalcum-carrying ships in them."

"I understand how space works," I said, sighing. "Any sign of FSA traffic?"

"No," Lara Chopra, a sweet-looking girl from Kali, said, shaking her head. "Only warning buoys. One of them has been reprogrammed to state 'Abandon all hope, all ye who enter.'"

"Oh that's adorable," I said, sighing. "They're further in, it seems."

"Yeah," William said. "By the planet."

"Let's get going," I said, more reluctant than I was willing to let on. I wasn't afraid of Kolahn IV any more than I was afraid of Crius's dead ruins.

"It'll be thirty minutes, Captain," U'Chuck said, taking a deep breath. "Some pretty deep calculations."

"Do you need help?" I asked, wondering if U'Chuck would need to be removed from her position. This was, after all, a return to the most traumatic place in the galaxy for her. For all my bluster about the fact I didn't think Crius was haunted by literal ghosts, I certainly knew it was haunted by plenty of metaphorical ones.

"No sir," U'Chuck said. "Just saying it'll take a bit."

I nodded and got up. "Major Terra, I would like to speak with you in my ready room."

"About the mission," I said, silently signaling Isla to come.

"I see," Major Terra said, looking suspicious. "As you wish."

Fade looked at me with a frown. "I'd actually like to speak with you about some details as well, Captain Mass. You've been....absent for what I think was an extraordinarily long period of time."

"I was having sex," I said. "Also drunk. Oh, and discovering the secrets of the universe through drugs. But mostly the first two."

Fade opened his mouth, closed it then nodded. "Okay. I still need to talk to you."

"In an hour," I said, heading to my ready room.

Major Terra followed.

The captain's ready room had been previously used for storage, as Ida Claire wasn't the kind of person who had need of such a place. She didn't need an office or, if she did, it was a hidden one, as her efforts on behalf of the Watchers were hidden from the rest of the crew. I, on the other hand, needed a quiet place to do my accounting for the ship and project an aura of authority—since God knew I'd lost the ability to do it naturally.

The room had a single crystal glass table that looked like reflective stone but contained its own personal computer stronger than most of the ship. The walls had various bits of Crius memorabilia I wasn't too fond of but helped sell the idea that I knew what I was doing. Munin had actually given me a view screen diorama of all the medals I'd won—things I couldn't stand and usually left turned off given how many deaths they represented. Still, she'd meant well.

The back of the room projected an image of space meant to resemble windows and there was a flag on a flagpole in the side, previously the Mercer's Guild of Sector-7 but replaced by a private one for the *Melampus* that depicted the ship as well as a blue cross with a red dragon on it. Flags were an anachronism everywhere but the most primitive worlds, but I'd had it made at a novelty kiosk for five credits and it was useful for team-building exercises. I also had a fish tank but its contents were holographic fakes.

"What is it you want?" Major Terra said, walking past me as the doors shut behind us. "Since I refuse to believe you are taking your duties—"

As she turned around, I jabbed her in the throat with a stun rod. She fell to the ground as I gave her a triple dose for good measure. Now I just needed Isla's help in rebooting her brain to normal and removing Judith's pawn on the ship. That was when Fade walked in and stared at me as I stood over the body of his companion.

Well shit.

CHAPTER FOURTEEN

I struggled for a moment to think of an excuse, only for Fade to immediately make a motion for his pistol that I knew I didn't have time to dodge so I instead charged at him. The two of us slammed into the back of the doors before I threw him over my head onto the digital aquarium that shattered underneath, spilling real water. Both his gun and my stun sick crashed to the floor. I could have drawn the sword he'd just presented me but I didn't want to escalate the fight even if I had no reason to believe he wouldn't.

"Lock the door," I commanded the ship's temporarily non-sentient virtual intelligence system. "Also put something on to cover up the noise."

"What, sir?" the ship's virtual intelligence asked.

"Anything!" I snapped as I moved to grapple Fade before he got up.

A Crius orchestral rendition of "Everybody Wants to Rule the World" started playing. It was amazing what music stood the test of time. I didn't get to respond before Fade grabbed the lid off the shattered aquarium and threw its chemical-filled watery contents in my eyes. Instead of going for his knife, he instead kicked me in the stomach then grabbed my head to drive into his knee. I didn't want to hurt Fade because this was all a misunderstanding, but instinct took over. When Fade threw me over in a Belenus judo throw, I grabbed his arm and reversed it. I then grabbed his head and smashed it down into my desk, cracking it.

"Stand down!" I commanded, holding his head down against the desk's surface.

"You first," Fade said, blood pooling from a cut across his forehead.

That was when I noticed he'd managed to grab the stun stick I'd dropped on the ground at some point, probably when I'd smashed him into the aquarium.

"Ah hell," I said, moving to dodge only to be jabbed in the stomach.

If I'd been a normal human being, that would have been the end of the fight right there but I'd been cybernetically and genetically enhanced for combat. As a pilot, mind you, but that still gave me the ability to resist incapacitation better than most. A pilot was no use if he couldn't withstand G-forces, after all. It was why most of the best were from heavy-gravity worlds or engineered like myself.

Another reason I'd succeeded where so many others had failed.

"Dammit," Fade said, realizing I was still intact when I head-butted him in the nose then pulled my fist back.

That was when he pressed the gun he'd pick-pocketed from the holster at my side into my chest.

"That's extremely impressive," I said.

"It is," Fade said. "Back up."

I did so, raising my hands.

"We're going to have a chat," Fade said. "Because I'd very much like to know—"

"Security override: Clarice O'Harra," a female voice spoke on the other side of the door before it opened up. They revealed Clarice standing there in a form-fitting suit of zero-gravity armor that was primarily the kind used underneath Nina-class power armor suits. Isla was standing beside her, holding the medical scanner from earlier as well as a neural-inhibitor collar.

Fade moved his gun toward her.

Clarice responded twice as fast as a normal human being and quicker than most cyborgs, sending a micro-dagger from her side into Fade's hand, causing him to drop my Fusion pistol on the ground. Clarice then strode forward and grabbed Fade by the right arm before breaking it in one easy motion, slamming his head down against the same spot I'd thrown it. Except much, much harder.

Clarice took one look at my battered form then looked down at Fade. "You're going to scream before you die."

Fade started to say something before she twisted his broken arm and he let out more of a yelp than a scream so she twisted it more until he did.

"You think you can hurt my friend, my captain, Isla's lover, mine, and not die for it. I'm going to make your last moments—"

I took a deep breath. "A.I. Judith is actually an evil Elder Race computer-god thingy manipulating us to blow up an imprisoned one on Kolahn IV. She's reprogrammed Major Terra here so I'm going to have Isla fix her so we can actually make peace and figure out what to do. Please don't kill Fade because Ida might take that personally and I've got enough omnipotent forces of nature against me."

The room was silent for three seconds. Clarice then let go and took a few steps back.

"You could have said that," Fade said, stepping back and pulling out a handful of blue pills before tossing them in his mouth.

"What are those?" I asked.

"Something to make me forget I have a broken arm," Fade said, shaking his head. "What the hell, woman?"

Clarice crossed her arms, standing a foot taller than Fade. She then glared. "You hurt my family. Give me a reason and I'll cut your face off and throw it at your grandmother."

I stared at her. "Okay, that was a little extreme even by my standards."

"You helped me with the Chel," Clarice said. "My family and Ida betrayed you yet you helped me escape. I'm not going to forget that."

Isla approached Fade, who jerked away at first then relaxed when she started to treat his arm.

Isla snorted. "Don't be such a big baby. I can fix this in an hour. Your face will be disgustingly pretty within minutes."

"Thank you," Fade said, taking several deep breaths. "I would hate to have to rely on actual depth of personality. What is this about an Elder Race?"

"Big Bad Ancient Alien in ship's computer, or would be if not for the fact she left so the one on Kolahn IV doesn't sense her," I said, looking back at Major Terra's still unconscious form. "I'll tell you about it later, but only if you're buying."

"He hit you," Clarice said. "We should lock him up in the brig until this is over. Preferably with no air."

"Lower it down about a million notches," I said, simply. "I'm fine except for a few bruises and a need to wash out my eyes. I don't need a bodyguard."

"Except that's literally her job and you did," Isla said, moving Fade's arm back into place with a crack. "Are you going to be any more trouble for us?"

Fade looked between us. "It depends what you're going to do to Anya."

I raised an eyebrow. "Anya, is it?"

Fade shrugged. "Well—"

"You slept with Shin." I shook my head. "Aren't you married?"

"And?" Fade asked.

Clarice and Isla also looked confused. Spacers.

Isla looked down at her. "We're going to restore her previous self and remove Judith's brainwashing as well as the Commonwealth's. She'll be exactly as she was before they got their hands into her."

This was, notably, a lie.

"Ah," Fade said, pausing. "I suppose that's a good thing."

"Unless she tries to kill us," Clarice said, surprising me by objecting. "What if she was a serial killer or terrorist beforehand?"

Isla looked at Clarice then back at me. "Strange minds think alike."

"There's nothing strange about that concern," I said, noting it was a moot point since Isla intended to make sure Major Terra was loyal to us anyway. It was a thought that left me feeling somewhat ill. It was an old Crius saying from an Old Earth myth that a human being without free will was as useless as a clockwork orange.

Fade stared around my devastated room. "Well, I'm going to stay here to make sure she's alright."

"And do what, exactly, if she isn't?" Clarice said, her voice low and threatening.

"You're beautiful when you're angry, you know that?" Fade said, trying his best smile despite his face looking like a bot had stomped on it.

"Then I must be positively stunning now," Clarice deadpanned.

"Do it," I said, taking a deep breath. "We don't know when Judith will come back and it's entirely possible Major Terra might know something about her plans."

"Also we need to know about her planet-destroying bomb," Isla added.

"What now?" Fade did a double-take. "I feel like I've walked into the tail end of a conversation I should have been a part of."

"More like punched your way into," I said. "Then again, maybe we should have let you in from the start."

"Yes," Fade snapped.

"The spy," Clarice said. "The Commonwealth spy."

"Yes," Fade repeated. "Would have saved you a lot of trouble."

I looked to Isla. "You should do it now. She's waking up."

Major Terra was already on her feet before I finished, only for Isla to slap the neural-inhibitor around her neck before she could move. The Shin immediately fell to her knees as her eyes glazed over. Neural-inhibitors were a vile tool, but I was glad Isla had one.

"You realize those are primarily found among slavers, right?" Fade said, not apparently having learned how to keep his mouth shut.

"Yes," Isla said. "We got a whole bunch of them when we spaced a crew of them."

Fade paused. "You know, I'm starting to like you people. It's beginning to make sense why my grandmother recruited you."

Clarice literally growled at him.

Fade looked to the side and opened his mouth to make what I assumed would be some pithy remark before closing it. "Not worth it."

It was the first smart thing he'd done today.

"This shouldn't take long," Isla said, moving her medical scanner over the back of the woman's head.

"Have you done this before?" Fade asked.

"Sort of," Isla said. "If she ends up brain dead, don't worry, we'll kill you before you have a chance to complain."

"Your honesty is….not appreciated," Fade said, sighing.

Seconds later, Major Terra blinked multiple times.

"It's done," Isla said. "The ninja is no longer a threat."

"What's a ninja?" I asked.

Isla shook her head and removed the collar with a single swipe of her thumb across its keypad. That was when Major Terra swore profusely in multiple languages with a strong Xerxes Dust Plains accent. An accent some people in the Spiral might have called Scottish but wouldn't have passed muster with most of the New

Glasgowigians I knew.

"Is this part of the process?" Fade asked.

"No, it's not, ya dumb fuck!" Major Terra shouted, sounding nothing like her previous self. "It's realizing you've been the Commonwealth's goddamn meat puppet for the past nine months. A curse on them and their bastard offspring one and all."

"Well," Fade said, pausing. "This is awkward."

"Which part?" Clarice said. "The fact you slept with someone who had their brain drilled out or the fact you're just realizing it?"

"Ah, that was me," Major Terra said. "He's far from the first Commonwealth dog I've fucked. I just usually slit em afterward."

"Oh, William is going to love her," Isla said, smiling.

"I thought Xerxes hated Crius," Clarice said. "I thought it was a point of national pride."

"Only the Northern Hemmers," Major Terra said, spitting. "We Southern Hemmers know every last one of the Northerners are murderous barbarians standing in the way of civilization. We swore an oath to the Houses of Crius and those honorless dogs who would break it deserve nothing more than to be castrated before being tossed in a pit."

"She's certainly more entertaining than William," I said, chuckling. "Out of curiosity, may I ask what you did to get into this situation?"

"You mean brainwashed and enhanced into a ninja for a regime I despise?" Major Terra asked.

"Yes," I said.

Major Terra lowered her head. "I dinnae do anything. I wish I had. I spoke against the Commonwealth occupation and said the Crius were our friends, not our enemies. That, for all their flaws, they didn't deserve what happened to them."

"Then you did more than most," I said, looking at her. "Do you know where Judith's bomb is?"

"I know where a bomb is," Major Terra said. "It's in the supplies loaded."

I nodded. "We need to secure that and make sure it's disconnected from anything resembling remote access."

"Shouldn't we just dump it out an airlock?" Clarice suggested.

I shook my head. "I don't like being manipulated, especially by something impersonating my dead wife, but that doesn't mean she's wrong. It may be that this Kathax Prime does need blowing up along with the planet."

Fade raised his hand. "Maybe you should tell us the whole story."

"Aiye," Major Terror said.

"The name Judith sings in my head and I hear all manner of terrible things," Major Terra said, holding her head. "Images that make no sense and dive in and out of my mind like bloodfish in an oasis."

"Are you sure she's fine?" Fade asked.

"Yes. Shut up," Isla said, scanning her again. "We might be able to get the remaining memories to resurface but it's uncharted territory. Zoe's work with human brains via cybernetics is far in excess of Ares Electronics has been able to do with bioroids."

"If you do will I be able to still play the piano?" Major Terra asked.

"Could you before?" Isla asked.

"No," Major Terra said, grinning.

That was when the doors opened yet again and, this time, William walked through. He took one look at the room and the various wounded before starting to speak. He then hesitated as Fade had done before. "You know, screw it, I don't actually want to know. What I do want you to know is something is coming our way now that we've entered the cloud. It's popped to the edge of the system and moving really, really fast despite being in normal space."

Normally, traveling at the limits of lightspeed meant it would take a while to reach us. Also, I was surprised we'd managed to make the transitions through jumpspace so smoothly. Then again, Munin had managed to get ahold of a Community jump drive during our acquisition of those ill-fated slavers' vessel. If anyone in the Spiral could get human technology up to their standards, it was her.

"Something isn't very informative, William," I said.

"Yeah, well, it's not anything I can identify. I've raised the shields and put thrust up to maximum," William said. "We're trying to outrun it."

"Are we succeeding?"

"No."

Chapter Fifteen

The screens showed we were travelling down one of the many large "tunnels" of normal space through the glowing multi-colored orihalcum gas all around us. Electrical surges and explosions of strange matter were seen throughout, showing the weird reality-warping volatile properties of the gas in action.

It wasn't all orihalcum, of course, but it was perhaps the largest single quality I'd ever seen. Just wandering into one of those "storms" would probably tear the *Melampus* apart. We were going through the pre-plotted "safe route", but if there was something following us that spooked William, I wanted to know what it was. As many differences as we head, I respected him as an officer. Sort of.

As I stepped onto the bridge, everyone's attention turned to me, causing them to blink as they saw I'd had the shit beaten out of me.

I lifted my hands up in the air. "It's okay, I just fell into someone's fists. Happens to me all the time."

Everyone looked at Clarice with mixtures of horror and disgust.

Clarice looked offended. "What the fuck, people?"

"Not funny. We're not in that kind of relationship." I sat in the captain's chair, ignoring the fact they thought Clarice was capable of that. "Show me the ship."

As Fade and the others arrived on the bridge, causing even more confusion as to what the hell had just gone on in my ready room, I saw Jun pull up an image of the vessel that was following us into Lucifer's Nebula. It wasn't the most pleasant-looking vessel, resembling a flying ball more than anything else, but as it matched our speed and exceeded it, I saw large black tendrils extend from its surface like they were liquid forming into a squid's appendages or perhaps a spider's legs. There was something almost malevolent about the sight even as the sensor readings showed it was only twice the size of our vessel. It took me a second to realize what the ship was even as the sight made my blood run cold.

"Oh shit," Clarice said, looking at the sight and recognizing it as well.

"What is it?" William asked. "Is it Chel?"

"Worse," Clarice said.

"It's Chel," I said, lying.

It was an Elder Race Probe. I had only seen a few holograms of such things in my time as a high colonel of the archduchy. Elder Race Probes were the smallest vessels known from the Elder Races and even then, they usually left no survivors when they appeared. It wasn't so much a question of whether our vessel was a match for it, it wasn't, but what did it want from us since it was as far above our technology as the *Melampus* was above the wooden sailing vessels in Earth's distant past.

Maybe more.

"Give me manual control over the ship," I said, taking a deep breath.

"Sir?" Jun said, looking over at me.

"Now," I said.

Going to manual control for a ship the size of the *Melampus* was, generally speaking, a terrible idea. Unfortunately, I didn't want to start a panic and knew any hesitation in my next moves would possibly cost us our lives.

"Shouldn't we try and make a break for jumpspace?" Clarice asked, putting her hand on my shoulder.

She was the only one who knew aside from me, though I suspected Fade probably had an inkling as well.

"It won't let us," I said, suspecting it was here either at Judith's behest or the Kathax Prime below. "Not if it wants us."

A small fleet of Crius vessels had once tried to rabbit from such a thing when they'd chanced upon one of the probes. Its commander's actions would have been cowardly under any other circumstances but merely proved tragically prudent under the circumstances as the Elder Race Probe had followed the fleet into jumpspace and destroyed every single one, allowing only one communication to get through. Mostly, some believed, as a warning, since no known race other than the Nobility knew how to fight in jumpspace.

As the captain's chair produced a holographic keyboard across my lap as well as two hand-based controls for the ship, I proceeded to move us off the safe route and into the orihalcum cloud beside us.

"Cassius, what are you doing?" William asked.

"Something stupid, but it might work," Clarice said.

"No," William said. "That never actually happens in real life! Stupid stuff is actually stupid!"

"Please keep the shields at maximum but put sublight engines on a steadily increased drive as well as thrusters," I said, aware I was risking everyone onboard the ship. "I also want a direct feed to my cybernetics about the volatility of the surrounding area."

"Captain Mass, do you know what you're doing?" Fade asked, not really sounding as interested in the fact that we'd wandered into a cosmic mine field as he should have been. Instead, his attention was devoted to Anya as if she'd grown a second head or become a tiger-woman.

"Yes, absolutely," I lied. "I wouldn't take this risk with the lives of my crew unless it was safer than the alternative."

"Then we're screwed," William said.

I also heard one of the Tinas mutter about needing a raise. The rest of the crew remained disciplined enough to trust me, though.

"Stop complaining," Isla said, finally telling William what I'd wanted to for years but felt I had to let him have a pass on since I'd, well, helped invade his world. "This is serious."

"Yeah, but I didn't think it was—" William was cut off by the entire ship shaking. "Was that the cloud?"

"No," U'Chuck said. "That was the unknown vessel. It just fired a single energy beam at us. It is moving at post-relativistic speeds."

"That's…." William didn't finish the word impossible. "This isn't a Chel vessel, is it?"

I didn't answer him. The Elder Race Probe was gradually gaining on us, following us into the cloud and moving at one hundred and seventy-five percent of our speed no matter how much I accelerated the ship. It still had a long way to go but would be within tactical range very soon. The blast it had fired, though, demonstrated that we were completely at its mercy. The energy blast hadn't even hit us; it had just sent shockwaves through the orihalcum cloud around us—shockwaves that passed through our shields like they weren't there.

"Do you think it wants to destroy us?" Clarice asked.

"I don't think it wants us to offer us drinks and a show," I said, heading for the biggest pile of gas storms I could find.

"Can I complain now?" William asked.

"No," Clarice said.

"We're overclocking our reactor, sir," Eugene said, looking up from his position. "We can't keep going at this rate."

"Divert power from all non-essential systems," I said, having always wanted to say that.

The lights dimmed, making the entire place look like a holo-theater with only the monitors providing light.

"Really?" I asked.

"You said all nonessential systems!" Eugene said.

That was when the ship rocked even more as arcs of unknown energy shot forth all around us. Now, *that* was the cloud. The Elder Race Probe was coming right up next to us. Well, astrographically speaking. Clarice put her hand over me as I ducked us two unstable pockets of orihalcum gas as the arcs tore into our shields and reduced them to thirty-percent of their maximum capacity within seconds.

The Elder Race Probe followed.

"Hold onto your seats," I muttered, targeting the unstable pockets and firing.

It was difficult to explain just how big of an explosion was caused by the detonation of the orihalcum gas pockets. The resulting explosion wasn't really a reaction the same way fusion was but a literal ripple between dimensions. The reactions inside jumpspace engines had to be carefully contained lest they rip apart space and send you flinging across space as well as time. While nobody had ever actually entered an alternate universe or traveled through time outside of fiction, at least to my knowledge, it was about the only thing I thought might actually destroy an Elder Race ship. I was just afraid it would do the same to us.

My fears proved to be justified.

The entirety of the ship was sent into a spin as the gravity compensators were knocked offline and everyone soon found themselves floating in the air. The engines also went offline along with just about everyone else. About the only sign we weren't about to suffocate was the fact at least a few of the lights on the controls remained intact. The view screens were knocked offline, though, and I found myself bouncing against the ceiling. Activating my magnetic boots, I tried to walk down the walls to the captain's chair. Also, I tried not to throw up. I succeeded, barely, but some of the bridge crew had failed.

"What was the fuck was that?" William asked.

"A plan," I said.

"A shitty plan!" Isla shouted, showing me I'd done myself no favors even with those closest to me.

Anya, as I had started to think of her rather than Major Terra, burst out laughing instead. "That was amazing! You killed a god!"

"Elder Race members are not gods," Fade corrected her, trying to stand up by sticking his boots on the ground. "Close, but not quite."

"Oh shut up," Anya said. "This was like something out of a movie."

"Not a good thing!" William said. "Why am the only one who realizes this?"

"You're not," Fade said, standing firm and covering his stomach. "People undoubtedly died or were injured in that attack."

"I did what I had to do," I said, failing miserably at getting down to the ground as a cup of coffeeine floated past me along with its contents.

"Let's not do that again," Clarice said, pushing herself over to the controls. Jun was floating nearby, blood on the side of her forehead. "Isla, come here, she's hurt!"

"That's difficult," Isla said.

U'Chuck, of all people, got up and marching on the ground with her magnetic boots, and spoke into the audio receiver. "Prepare yourself for emergency reboot."

Oh crud. She then flipped three switches and pushed a lever. Gravity reengaged and I covered my face before my body hit the ground. It was painful but I was actually more concerned about Jun. I wasn't especially close to the young woman but liked her well enough. Thankfully, by the time I got up, I saw her coughing with Isla at her side with a cerebral laser.

The lights flickered back on the bridge and all of the systems started booting up again. It was a sign we were going to get through this. At least, right until the view screens popped back on and showed our exterior. The Elder Race Probe was less than a hundred kilometers away.

Undamaged.

"Dammit," I muttered, staring at it like it was the face of Death herself.

None of the bridge crew said a word, all of us just staring at the strange vessel looming over us. Our sensors, acting automatically, brought up an image of the vessel's surface. It was completely smooth except for the tentacles that opened to a hideous black maw. A black light shone behind it. It was terrifying in its fury, blasting outward upon us. I flinched and looked away, not wanting to look at it before I died—a moment brought about more by the fact I'd failed my crew than the fact I cared whether I lived or I died. My eyes burned as a brilliant white light passed over me, visible even through my eyelids. Then nothing. Nothing else happened.

I opened my eyes and looked up, seeing the tendrils on the Elder Race Probe retreat back into the ship before it took off into the orihalcum cloud again. The ship I'd assumed was here to destroy us had done nothing more than scan us.

All I'd done had been for nothing.

William then walked over to me, grabbed me by my shirt, and lifted me up off the ground before pressing me up against the wall. "You son of a bitch!"

"Could you have done better?" I asked, sighing.

"Yes," William hissed. "What the hell have you gotten us into? We shouldn't even be here!"

"No," I said dryly. "But we are."

"William?" Clarice said from behind him.

"Yes?" William said, turning his head.

"Stand down," Clarice said, a gun pointed to his head.

"You wouldn't shoot me," William said.

"Try me," Clarice hissed.

William dropped me.

Clarice nodded and then looked at Isla, who'd come up from the side. She jammed the stun stick into his side and sent him to the ground, writhing.

"That wasn't necessary," I said.

"It's mutiny," Clarice said, growling. "William has been riding your case since you've taken over and I'm sick of it. He's either going to shape up or ship out. I don't mind dumping his ass at any port, but a second officer cannot act like that."

We were way, way past my pay grade. In the military, all I had to do was order my people to shoot a bunch poorly armed and poorly trained Commonwealth conscripts. Here, I was dealing with literal space gods and one of them was impersonating my wife. I decided, if we survived this, I was going to resign as captain no matter what.

"We need William," I said, taking a deep breath. "Just put him in a cell until we get to Kolahn IV."

"As you wish," Clarice said, thankfully not suggesting that I shoot him. That would have been awkward since they used to be lovers. Not just people who slept together like most of the ship, but people who'd deeply cared for one another. Even so, her words made William deflate and he looked like someone had kicked him.

I looked at Isla. "You need to go make sure everyone is still alive and treat the wounded. Draft whomever you need to help and take any space or supplies you need."

Isla nodded and departed, giving Anya a look of suspicion on the way out.

"Captain, what's going on?" Eugene spoke, holding the hand of Jun as she lay there on the ground.

She was alive, thank God, but probably had a concussion.

"Yes," U'Chuck said, standing there. "Why are you taking us to a cursed planet?"

"What was that thing?" Eugene asked.

I looked at them then at Fade, who was looking away. Anya, meanwhile, crossed her arms.

I nodded. "I'm going to go tell the crew."

"Tell the crew what?" Fade said, his voice dangerous.

Lies. What I did best. I didn't say that, though. "The truth. That we're coming here to end the war and we're getting paid a lot of money for it."

Fade nodded.

U'Chuck, however, burst my bubble. "Why is an Elder Race probe here?"

Anya, surprisingly, answered for me. "It was searching for Judith."

How did she know that?

I shook my head. "The speech will be in one hour. I'll take my medical attention last. In the meantime, get us out of this cloud and take us back through the safe route."

I tried to figure out what sort of bullshit I'd tell everyone to keep them calm. It was becoming a habit.

CHAPTER SIXTEEN

I made a spectacular speech, doubly impressive because it had been on the fly and I didn't remember a damn word of it five minutes later. I think my brain rattled around a bit during my attempt to save the ship, and Isla confirmed it once she finally got around to treating me. Isla wasn't happy with my decisions and told me not to talk to her until we arrived at Kolahn IV. That had been three days ago and she'd kept her promise.

I didn't blame Isla for her anger. I was still trying to play the hero and slay dragons. It was painful acknowledging all I'd done was get three people hospitalized and another seven with minor injuries. I'd almost got the *Melampus* destroyed trying to blow up the Elder Race probe when all it had wanted to do was scan us. Was I really so desperate for glory I'd started a fight which hadn't been needed? Was that why I was here instead of redemption? That I was addicted to danger? I couldn't answer that. All I knew was I wasn't so eager to start a fight again. Ironically, Clarice insisted I'd done the right thing and told me my plan in the nebula had been sound. It had led to a fight between her and Isla.

Rather than continue putting the ship in danger, I'd asked Clarice to handle captaining the ship while I coordinated the repairs. Thankfully, the inertial compensators staying online and artificial gravity failing had combined to keep injuries from being much worse. No one had died but a few people had needed surgery. It was the only good luck I'd experienced during all of this.

Today, I was focusing on cleaning up my ready room, which I hadn't been to since my fight with Fade. I chose to do it the old-fashioned way with a broom and pan, two objects most ships kept with them in case more expensive items failed. I ended up cheating after twenty minutes and recruited Ida's mech, Hunk-A-Junk, to help. Hunk-A-Junk resembled a black floating ball with several arms plus a recently added grill that looked like an aircar's front combined with a humans. It was far enough away from a human face that it was cute rather than terrifying, but had questionable utility.

"I am a complete failure," I muttered, looking at a piece of reflective glass that showed my tape-covered face. It would be fine in a few hours, especially with the stimulants injected to aid healing, but was a reminder of my action's consequences.

The door proceeded to open and both Fade as well as the recently freed William entered into the room. We were only an hour or so until our arrival on Kolahn IV so I'd released him despite Clarice thinking he should stay there until we could drop him off at the nearest port after our mission was finished—without paying him. I argued that was unduly harsh since he'd only laid hands on me after I'd nearly gotten us all killed. It was time we settled this, anyway, and I was hoping we could do it amicably. William had changed out of civilian clothes and had a duffle bag over one shoulder. That implied to me that this wasn't going to end well.

"Captain," Fade said, looking at Hunk-A-Junk. "Machine."

Hunk-A-Junk, being only non-sentient like all mechs, just made a bleeping noise and passed by him to clean a spot on the wall covered in blood. Oddly, I didn't recall that coming from my fight with Fade.

"Hi," William said, looking sideways. "Second Officer Balder reporting for duty. If I'm not being fired."

"Do you still want to serve on this ship? You can jump ship at our next port if you want. I won't stop you," I said, looking up from my sweeping. "But if you are, you're picking a shitty planet to do it on unless you intend to join the FSA."

"Not on your life," William said, shaking his head. "I don't have any great love for the Commonwealth, but I lost too much to the Crius to ever work with their remnant. I'd rather die, as I think I've expressed more than once."

Same old William.

I closed my eyes and let some of my anger bubble to the surface. I narrowed my eyes and took a deep breath. "You've had a year to get over my background. A year ignoring my every insult, jibe, and barely contained bit of contempt you've directed my way. We've saved each other's lives. If you're not going to, that's your business, but I'm sick of your attitude. I also am not going to put up with your threatening me. If you want to settle things, then we can, but I don't play fight. If you ever lay a hand on me again, then one of us won't be walking away."

William lowered his head. "I'm sorry."

"Excuse me?" I asked.

"I said I'm sorry," William said, taking a deep breath. "It's wrong of me to blame you for what you did in the war and for everything the archduchy did to my world."

"Who are you and what have you done with William?" I asked.

William shrugged. "Three days is a lot of time to think in the brig. I didn't even have a book to read."

"You can read?" Fade asked.

William made a throat slitting gesture to Fade.

"Apology accepted," I said, frowning. "Truth be told, I've also been a shitty captain."

"Yeah, everyone knows that," William muttered. "But you *are* the captain."

"A lack of respect is a big problem for any officer," Fade said, interjecting himself in a conversation he was not wanted in. "But you have two beautiful lovers and don't even have to lie to them about each other like I do all my partners. You are captain of your own city-sized vessel with the freedom to go wherever you want and be master of your own kingdom. You also are patronized by one of the most powerful women in the Commonwealth. In a way, I envy you."

"He just found out his A.I. wife is evil," William said, glaring at him. "That's like losing her again."

Fade's expression told me he wasn't sure how to react to a statement like that. That made two of us. "I'm sorry, Captain. Perhaps I have been speaking of matters I do not know about."

"I live a strange life," I said, very much hoping to change the subject. "Seriously, William, what did I miss? Why the sudden change of heart?"

"Clarice chewed my ass off," William said, acting like that outcome hadn't been expected. That was when he surprised me by giving me another piece of information. "Also, I finally sat down to read the news holos you downloaded on the Ring. I usually binge watch them a month at a time. I found out something about my home world that, well, let's just say it put a lot of things into perspective."

I wasn't sure how that related. "What did they say?"

"Xerxes declared its support for the FSA," William said, his voice low. "The Commonwealth finally pushed them too far and there was a massive riot that ended up with twenty thousand dead. The rest of the planet turned bloody after that."

It was an unexpected bit of information that helped clarify what the stakes of our little mission was. Xerxes had waged a century-long insurgency against the Archduchy of Crius after its conquest during the first Archduchy War. While many Xerxes had allied with the archduchy and fought alongside us against our enemies, William had been part of the resistance to the nobility's rule. The Commonwealth had "liberated" the planet after destroying Crius, only to institute their own government which had followed that ancient principle of 'meet the new boss, same as the old boss.' They'd been better taskmasters than the Crius nobility in some ways but the only thing they wanted from Xerxes was the same orihalcum refined in the factories on the planet the archduchy had wanted. They'd even removed all of the previous local administrators and nobles which had served the archduchy to be replaced by their own imported officials. No wonder the locals had decided to throw their lot in with the FSA.

I spoke that first question that came to mind. "Is your family okay?"

William looked confused, guilty, and then resigned in the span of three heartbeats. "Yeah, but they want me to come back home and fight the Blues like I did the Blacks during the Archduchy War."

Blue being the traditional Commonwealth soldier compared to archduchy black. "Are you?"

"No," William said, his voice firm but troubled. "We're going to stop the war here today, aren't we?"

"Yes," I said, uncertain about that.

"Listen," William said, not meeting my gaze. "I've been blaming you for what happened during the war and I'm sorry."

"That must have been some chewing out," I said, still unsure how to react to William apologizing. It was perhaps time to check the stars to see if they were going out and whether rifts had opened up to Hell.

"I did get your arm cut off," I said. "I also got you labeled an international fugitive. Plus I'm sleeping with your ex."

William wasn't a spacer like Munin or Clarice had allowed herself to become. He was mentally a Grounder, like myself, and had a lot more conventional morality about things like religion as well as relationships. Unlike myself, he hadn't been able to adjust to the revelation that Isla was a free sentient bioroid. He'd been revolted and it had led to Clarice promising to kill him if he ever told anyone. It was an open secret now; the captain keeping the ship's gynoid doctor as a mistress was peculiar but not even rare, but Clarice had never forgiven him. His anger against me had also exasperated her anger. Weirdly, I suspected William regretted what he'd said but was too proud to ever admit it. It said something about his values he was willing to apologize to a man he'd tried to goad into a death duel before a woman he'd loved.

Fade raised an eyebrow. "This is a more interesting starship than I thought."

"Don't help," William said, trying to keep his gaze low. "I've had a lot of anger building up inside me."

"That's like saying Mars has an overpopulation problem," I said, speaking of the only remaining human presence in the Sol system. I'd been there once as part of a humanitarian relief effort and the place had lived up to its reputation as an arcology of crisscrossed tunnels built on human misery.

"What I'm saying, though, is I'd like to start fresh. To be the officer you know I can be," William said, offering his hand.

I didn't take it. "I'm not giving you your job back. You're also getting twenty percent knocked off your cut of this operation."

"Fuck!" William said, dropping all pretense. "Ten percent."

"This isn't a negotiation," I said, shaking my head. "We need to pass around some of that money so the crew doesn't mutiny as well."

"Why take it from mine?" William whined. "I didn't even hit you. Take it from Bullfighter Bob here. He beat the shit out of you."

"Excuse me?" Fade said, looking at him sideways.

"He's not getting a cut," I said, smiling. "I'll consider reducing it to fifteen percent if you're on your best behavior."

"Right," William said, reluctantly. "You got it."

Ah, money, the cause and solution to all of life's miseries.

William turned around and headed to the door. He stopped before departing, though. "By the way, is it just me or does the crazy cyborg ninja now sound like she comes from Xerxes Northern Hemisphere?"

"Nope," I said, contradicting him. "Clearly, you're crazy."

"Good, because those people are lunatics," William said, his voice low. "Temperamental, violent, unforgiving bastards."

I smirked. "Completely unlike you."

"Oh hell yeah," William said. "I'm a Southerner. We're the polite ones."

With that, he departed out the door.

I looked over at Fade. "So is your experience aboard the *Melampus* everything you imagined? Our brochure mentioned casinos, swimming, and a fine line of prostitutes but those are to-come services of our luxury liner. There are no refunds. Please recommend us to your friends."

Fade's gaze remained even. "I want to know everything. I especially want to know about the evil A.I. thing."

I stared at him. "Your grandmother didn't tell me everything. Why should I tell you?"

"Because we're paying you and if you don't tell me, I'm cancelling this deal."

"Then I'll throw you out an air lock."

Fade frowned and I was worried we'd get another fight started. "That might lead to war with the Commonwealth. The Watcher General's patience is not unlimited."

"That's a stupid title," I said, not missing a beat. "As for war with the Commonwealth, I'm a betting man and I'm fairly sure it won't exist in a year's time unless we get this treaty signed."

The scary part was I wasn't sure I was exaggerating. For all the efforts of the Commonwealth during the "Reclamation" and attempting to rebuild the Sol Federation, they'd successfully managed to piss off virtually the entirety of humanity's scattered tribes and kingdoms. Almost half of humanity called the Commonwealth home and yet I doubted more than a quarter really would mourn its fall.

Fade surprised me by considering my words. "You know, Cassius, you remind me of my older brother. He was every bit the asshole you are."

"Thank you. I think."

I ended up explaining the entirety of the business with Judith, the Elder Races, and everything else to him. I half expected him to disbelieve my conclusion Judith wasn't a Cognition A.I. made in my wife's image but an Elder Race impersonator. After all, I had nothing to go on but my gut. However, Fade just nodded when I explained—it was refreshing to have someone believe me for once.

I mean, it wasn't like I was a traumatized barely functional drunken asshole or anything. Why *wouldn't* people believe me when I started talking about A.I., Elder Races, ancient conspiracies, and the digital ghost of my late wife?

Fade sighed. "If the Elder Races are involved, then they represent a clear threat to the security of the Commonwealth."

"In the context that an asteroid represents a threat to a Stone Age civilization, yes," I said, sighing. "There's nothing we can do to them. Their technology is so advanced it might as well be magic. We're at the mercy of their whims."

"How much do you know?" Fade said.

"A lot," I said. "But it all comes from them."

"I thought you were hurting Anya," Fade said, looking to one side.

"What is your relationship to her? Is she your lover?"

"Nothing now," Fade said, his voice low. "The woman who you woke up in here is nothing like the one I cared for. I think if she and I ever spoke, she'd accuse me of taking advantage of her situation, which I might have. I thought the stories about the Shin being mentally reprogrammed were just that—stories. If the Commonwealth is actually able to reprogram people then perhaps the FSA have a point."

"Re-socializing is nothing new as a technology," I said, not sure Fade was wrong. "The Rin-O'Harra Cartel did it to traffic human slaves as fake bioroids for decades. I suspect my sister used her time there to perfect the process."

"You're not making me feel better."

"I wasn't trying to," I said, frowning. "If the Commonwealth feels the need to manufacture and brainwash an army to fight the FSA then they've lost any moral high ground over their enemies."

"We lost that when we destroyed Crius," Fade said, looking back at me. "You don't know how that's affected the Commonwealth. How it changed us as a nation."

"I *don't care*," I said, my voice heating up. "I've made my peace with losing my homeworld. How the people who destroyed it feel about it doesn't concern me. If you want to know about the Elder Races then I need to know something in return."

Fade seemed surprised by my offer. "What do you want to know?"

I stared into his eyes, doing my best to look for any untruths. "Are you here to make peace or assassinate my doppelganger?"

Fade took a step back. "What, why would you say that?"

"Because Ida sent you and a professional assassin with me rather than a diplomatic corps."

Fade blinked. "No."

He was lying, which didn't bode well. That made me wonder if I was on his list of targets to eliminate. "Well, we're on our way to Kolahn IV no matter what. Anything I tell you isn't going to affect my plans to fulfill our bargain. I've already promised the crew a share of the profits and they'll skin me alive if I don't deliver."

"You want me to check if your Elder God patron actually included a planet-destroying bomb with Anya's equipment?"

"Please," I said. "Now I just have to figure out whether galactic peace is worth sacrificing to serve a race capable of exterminating us all."

After all, if I blew up the FSA's headquarters, then there was very little chance they'd agree to the Commonwealth's terms.

"No pressure," Fade said.

I actually laughed at that.

CHAPTER SEVENTEEN

An hour from arrival ended up stretching to another twelve hours despite all of us having been up for most of the past three days of travel. If you wondered why traveling through a nebula was taking so long, even traveling at sublight speed outside of jumpspace, the reason was checkpoints. The FSA had littered the safe routes with battle platforms, patrol boats, gravity mines, sensor probes, and destroyers I was surprised they could spare for guard duty.

Still, it was an ideal strategy for keeping the Commonwealth's fleets out of their home system. The safe routes were small enough to force an attacking fleet to move slowly through and calculate short jumps that left invaders vulnerable to assault. These hypothetical attackers could risk a trip through the clouds, themselves, but doing so probably do more damage enemy action. If the Commonwealth did attack with overwhelming force, the FSA forces could fall back to their home base and evacuate.

Lucifer's Nebula was a perfect location for carrying out a war against the Commonwealth and explained a lot about how they'd been able to keep them under assault. Their defenses were also very much as I would have planned them. That disturbed me for a variety of reasons. I just wish it wasn't so damned *boring* waiting to pass on through.

"They're asking us to transmit our credentials again," Lara said, sighing and looking as exhausted as the rest of the crew. While I'd had them working in shifts, none of them had been doing very well at getting rest given our encounter with the Elder Race probe and the fact the fate of human-controlled space rested on our barely functional shoulders. The lights were also busted on the bridge due to a power surge, making it as dark as during Brick's too literal attempt to divert all power.

I leaned back in my chair and looked at my cup of coffeeine. After the excitement of before, I'd somehow expected things to get more dramatic before they'd dropped down to dead boring. "All right, transmit this for the fifteenth time. 'This is Captain Cassius Mass of the star galleon *Melampus*. Identification code THX-1138-999. Yes, that one. I am requesting to meet with Supreme Commander Cassius Mass of the Free Systems Alliance. I am operating under a diplomatic signal from the Commonwealth to discuss terms of surrender.'"

Fade had provided the identification codes that could be accessed through the infonet and feeds to determine we were telling the truth. Except, of course, we'd done this fourteen times before to the exact same response every time.

"Transmitted," Lara said.

"Wait for it," I said, sighing.

Five minutes passed as I finished another mug of coffeeine.

Lara closed her eyes. "We're approved to move ahead. Do not deviate from your present course. Do not—"

"Attempt to power your weapons or shields," I said, sighing. "Yeah, I know."

"Did you notice they all sound identical?" Jun asked.

I nodded. "Maybe it's automated or they're all reading from the same script."

"Maybe," Clarice said, sitting in a chair nearby the tactical readout station and looking like she was barely able to keep her eyes open. Nobody had been sleeping well since the Elder Race Probe encounter. How could they? We were moving through enemy territory and could die at any second.

"Something is different," Clarice said, checking the coordinates fed to her by Lara.

"Which is?" I asked weakly. I was on my ninth cup of coffeeine and even it was starting to wear thin. I'd used to be able to stay up working three days in a row but that had been a long time ago and I was still suffering from my decision to give up alcohol. I'd gotten through the worst of it with the medical equipment here on the ship on our way here but the craving was still there. Now had been a very poor time to go cold turkey.

"We're being sent coordinates to the main part of the system,"

Clarice said, straightening up. "Right above the planet. We've received permission to meet with the supreme commander."

"Holy shit," I said, joining her in shaking away the cobwebs. "Really?"

"They haven't exactly said much else," Clarice said. "Say what you will about the FSA, but they're efficient."

"Well, set our course," I said, glad for the first good news of this trip. "Let's go see my brother from a different test tube."

Clarice looked at me sideways.

"Sorry," I said, rubbing my temples as another headache came on. "Set our course for Kolahn IV's orbit. Finally."

Our navigator didn't appear particularly happy about it. U'Chuck turned her head and said, "Once the Kolahn were a peaceful race. We developed space travel on our world only when we received a signal to another world several systems over. Once we arrived there, we found our god who taught us many secrets that advanced our technology by millennia. We used them to build an empire that uplifted other races. No species could stand against us—except through sheer numbers. The Community wiped out all of our colonies and destroyed our fleets to repay us for our refusal to join their ranks. When it was clear we'd been driven back to our new home world, our god commanded us to kill ourselves out of punishment. Which almost all of us did."

"It's too late to turn back now," I said.

"Is it?" U'Chuck asked.

I looked at U'Chuck. "Set the course."

U'Chuck growled and did so. She couldn't help it. In much the same way Anya Terra had been brainwashed by her government, the surviving Kolahn had done the same to her. They didn't have the numbers to execute their kind. Apparently, she'd been some sort of cult leader who had tried to revive the ancient ways. This had to be like revisiting an old wound.

"Do you think they'll blow us up when we arrive?" Clarice asked, showing just how badly lack of sleep had affected her.

"They would have done that at the start," I said. "No, they want to speak with us. They just want to force us to wait first."

"Oh, good," Clarice said.

The next and hopefully finally jump of this trip took us to a system-sized hole in Lucifer's Nebula. The view screens scanned our surroundings and brought countless fascinating facts and sights to my vision. We were right above a ringed planet about three times the size of the Old Earth but somehow had close-to-standard to colonial norm gravity. The planet had three small moons made of ice and rock circling above it, two of which had been converted into star ports.

Only a small portion of the planet's dark side was lit up, all centered around one singular city, but the space around Kolahn IV was full of shipping traffic. The centuries-old Kolahn shipyards, the size of a moon itself, had been retrofitted despite years of disuse to being home to tens of thousands of ships as well as modified for human use. I saw the ten-kilometer-long *Revengeance*, the Crius flagship that had refused to surrender to Commonwealth forces, looming over the FSA forces like a rectangular god.

As impressed by the sight as I was, I was stunned more by the sheer number of ships present. I checked the sensors twice to make sure they were working functionally and downloaded several hundred files to cycle through in order to process just what was really going in this system. There were over a million ships present with space transports, fighters, corvettes, destroyers, super dreadnoughts, and even a few floating battle cathedrals from the Union of Faith.

The majority of traffic wasn't going to the planet, but the ten-thousand-kilometer shipyards that had its own city built up on the sides but the fact they were able to maintain the kind of infrastructure to even service this many vessels was stunning. The Free Systems Alliance wasn't a rebellion but a star nation fully capable of fighting the Commonwealth better than the archduchy had.

"How the hell did they get all this?" Clarice said, staring at the system reports.

"Gas mining," I said, checking the sensors. "There are tens of thousands of platforms inside the cloud. Not just orihalcum but karvane and javannium too."

Both were gases found near orihalcum and while they didn't have the same reality-altering properties, they were extremely useful for fueling heavy fusion cannons and raw energy productions. Javannium crystals, in particular, could generate a shield around a planet. In theory. That was another technology the Commonwealth had denied humanity and could have saved billions of lives.

"The gods of this world provided," U'Chuck said, her voice low. "The price will be high. Just like it was with my race."

"No, I mean, how did they get all this here?" Clarice said, clarifying. "We should have been passing massive fleets and convoys on our way in. There's no way they could keep this much of a fleet maintained without regular supply ships and transports from dozens of worlds."

"I think I have an answer," I said, taking in all of the sights with my cyberlink to the ship's sensors.

I scanned a massive one-hundred-thousand kilometer circular jump gate of the kind found near the Community's wealthiest worlds, easily worth the yearly output of several planets. It was also technology prohibited by the Community Council, putting lie to any claim they were above our 'petty regional conflicts.' Convincing my doppelganger to surrender was going to be hard now if he was working as a catspaw of an organization far more powerful than us.

I couldn't help but be privately amused at the Commonwealth's misjudging of the situation. The Free Systems Alliance had done its best to portray itself as a plucky resistance fighting against overwhelming odds but its success was now as clearly due to foreign assistance as any military genius or eldritch power on the part of its leaders. That was usually how such groups achieved success and I wondered how many "advisors" from the alien coalition were down there fighting with them.

"Well fuck," Clarice said. "It looks like the Community is behind this all. All to screw with the Commonwealth."

"A big government sending weapons and supplies to keep a small but potentially dangerous government pre-occupied," I muttered. "Yeah, I've never seen that before."

I was about to say more when I heard…singing? It was like a buzzing in the back of my mind before my attention turned down to the planet's surface and I heard the sound more clearly. It was like a choir, only the voices were clearer, purer, and more ethereal than any human's.

I looked out to through the ship's sensors and saw for a moment every single living being in the fleet despite the fact I shouldn't have been able to pick them up. I saw the glowing souls of thousands in all the cargo ships and vessels from other territories going in and out of the system. The *Revengeance* and shipyards, though, did not show any signs of light. Instead, there were a million black holes where life should be.

They disturbed me and for a moment, I felt my mind touch them and saw something that looked like a human and acted like a human but was not human. Beings who were, effectively, soulless and parodies of men. Millions of soldiers who operated with perfect efficiency but might as well have been dead. They were as people accused bioroids of being, but they were manifestly not.

Then a voice spoke in my mind, sounding like the voice of Prophet Allenway himself, *Go away. Escape while you still can.*

"Cassius!" Clarice said, shocking me from my reverie. "You okay? You zoned out there for a second."

I blinked repeatedly before nodding, "Yes, I'm fine. It's just all so overwhelming."

I didn't know why I lied. Well, maybe because what I'd seen was crazy. Was I hallucinating or had we reached a point where I'd lost my mind? There were other options like the False Judith sending an image to my mind but that would imply she was here. I didn't want to contemplate that option.

"Maybe you should switch to regular coffee," Clarice said, leaning down and picking up a coffee. "You know they put drugs in this stuff, right? It's not just vitamins and beans."

"Yes," I said, standing up. "But there are drugs in everything."

"True," Clarice said. "You want me to go wake up Isla? Get a check-up? You took a pretty bad spill earlier. That and meeting Fade's fists a dozen times. Also, you haven't been getting much sleep these past few days."

"Neither have you," I said, pointing out the flaw in her statement. "But I've been through much worse than this. We need to know when we're going to meet with the Supreme Commander."

"All right," Clarice said, giving me a helpful pat on the back. "However, after this, we're going on a vacation for a year."

"Where to?" I said.

"Sex Planet," Clarice said, grinning. "You, me, Isla, and we'll get some place for William so he's not nearly as uptight."

"I think he's in a relationship."

"Yeah, and? Jealousy is a Grounder concept."

I rolled my eyes and sighed. "Thank you for all you've done, Clarice. I mean that."

"Try not to get mushy, Cassius. You're at your most attractive when you're a scheming anti-hero versus a romantic."

"I had no idea you were secretly a teenage girl."

"No, then you'd be your most attractive if you were an elf, vampire, or pirate."

Were elves a thing that teenagers lusted after now? I *was* sort of a pirate, but decided not to bring that up. "Thanks anyway."

Fade and Anya walked onto the bridge, both wearing tracksuits I believed were functioning as their nightclothes. Anya, notably, was holding a databook under her arm. Apparently she'd been doing some late-night reading.

"We're there?" Fade asked, a tense look on his face.

"Almost," I said, looking at him.

Anya then walked up to me and handed me her databook before whispering in my ear, "Here's the end of the world, Cap'n."

I blinked and looked at the databook, blinking. It didn't look like a planet-destroying weapon, but then what did I know about such things? It made me sick to think about how many people I was potentially going to kill. I was already regretting my decision and if there was a civilian population down there then I wasn't sure I could do it.

"Abandon all hope," Anya said, as if the code was inherently funny. "All ye who enter."

I realized that was the code for activating the device. "An appropriate epithet."

"Central Command has contacted us and informed us we're to head down to the regent's palace. They've provided coordinates," Anya said. "I've also received a greeting from a man who sounds a lot like you."

I stared at the databook and checked its contents. It only had the Commonwealth Bible and a dictionary listed as its contents. I proceeded to close it, not sure whether it was coincidence or just a cruel joke.

"I suppose everyone should get dressed up," I said. "We're going to meet royalty."

CHAPTER EIGHTEEN

"I can't believe you got us dress uniforms," Clarice muttered, adjusting her beret.

"I look like a pepper shaker," William said, frowning at me.

William, Isla, myself, Fade, Clarice, and Major Terra were the five-person crew I'd selected for our "diplomatic meeting." They were all dressed up in the *Melampus*'s black-and-white dress uniforms that none of them had ever bothered to use before. Not even during David's funeral, when only two of them had bothered to show up and eight more members of the crew in plain clothes.

The six of us were standing in one of the *Melampus*'s airlocks as the ship lowered itself into the atmosphere. It surprised me the regent's palace had a private space port large enough for the star galleon, but there was a lot of things about the FSA that made no sense. I'd put Munin in charge of the ship and hoped I hadn't led them all to a horrible fate.

Quite a few of the crew had come to wish us off and I was surprised at how high the mood on the ship was. They were a collection of murderers, thieves, scoundrels, and pirates, but all of them had lost someone or had worlds involved in the Insurgency. The fact I was possibly going to bring it to an end had removed all of the anger and resentment they'd built up against me over the past year. Some of them had even said I was the best captain they'd ever served under.

Fools.

"What? We can't look nice as the crew of a cargo freighter?" I asked, adjusting my brown coat. I was wearing it over my dress uniform with a pair of Spacer's goggles around my neck. It was in direct defiance of everyone else who was dressed more fashionably. I admit, the hypocrisy of the action made me smile and was my subtle form of revenge on everything I'd been put through these last few weeks. Also William for his behavior in general.

"I always look nice," Isla said, barely visible behind the others. "It's genetically encoded into you and Clarice."

"Beauty is in the eye of the beholder," Clarice said. "Albeit, I love how Cassius's hair is always perfectly coifed even when he first wakes up."

"What's with the five o'clock stubble anyway?" Isla said, giving me a once-over. "You could have at least shaved."

"I decided that was a good idea," I said, actually having just forgotten in my rush to get ready. "I want you to be able to tell the difference between me and my doppelganger should this end in a shootout."

"You mean the doppelganger with the millions of soldiers and massive armada?" William said, raising an eyebrow. "Yeah, I don't think we're going to be starting any firefights unless we've all developed a death wish."

"I'll start working on escape plans as soon as I have a layout of the building," Clarice said. "Also, our chances of surviving a fight."

"We just said—" William started to say.

"We're not starting a fight," Fade said, taking a deep breath. "We're just going to deliver the surrender agreement and come back with an army later."

"You got it. Just deliver the peace treaty," I said, very conscious of the planet-buster I'd hidden in my coat. It wasn't larger than a grenade but apparently contained enough antimatter to crack a planet's surface.

"That sounded less than convincing," Fade said, looking at his sheathed ceremonial scimitar.

"Don't forget what else we have to do down there," Isla said, her gaze narrow but true.

Oh yeah, murdering her former owner. I was not looking forward to my conversation with my doppelganger. Still, if he was me, then he'd gladly hand over Octavian for murder. I'd never been a fan of rapists. You'd think that wouldn't be a hurdle to jump, but apparently it was worth an accolade when it came to the treatment of bioroids. "I've got this. This is me, after all."

William raised his hand. "Is it too late to turn back now?"

"Yes!" I snapped.

"Just checking," William said, lowering his hand.

The *Melampus* settled down on the ground as the entire ship shook from its kinetic lifts straining from decades of use. The ship had been heavily-modified by the Commonwealth and had top-of-the-line systems when it had been run by the Watchers, but a year of civilian ownership meant it was jury-rigged beyond measure. Really, I should have sold the damn thing piece by piece and bought me a fleet of cargo ships but it had been my first command since the war. It was also home.

As broken down as me.

Clarice looked at the airlock. "You know, back when I was still recovering from my torture ta the hands of the Chel, I knew this blonde-haired, almond-eyed girl named Yelena Balistrova. She was a former Void Marine and could bench press a truck but kissed like a romance heroine. Prior to the war's end, she'd been as cold blooded as they come, but the last time we met included her telling me she was going to join the a resistance against the Commonwealth. I told her she was crazy and that revolutions are never about the people."

"Is this story going anywhere?" Fade asked, rudely.

"Yelena believed in the group because she'd heard the Fire Count was the leader," Clarice said, revealing something she'd never told me before. "I told her that just meant it was some other rich guy trying to make himself a king. I was wrong, Cassius. I want you to know that."

Clarice put her hand on my shoulder.

"You might not be," I said, surprising her and causing her to withdraw her hand. "When the Commonwealth destroyed Crius, I wanted to kill everyone inside it. The only thing keeping me from it was the fact that I didn't want to become like them. I deluded myself into believing I could someday return to being the honorable warrior I was. That Crius would rise again. I was wrong."

"About which part?" Clarice asked. "Because I've got a bunch of regrets as well."

"All of it," I said, sighing. "All I want now is for the killing to stop. I just don't know how because it's all I really know."

"That and Indran sex rites," Isla said.

"That too," I said. "Best part of my education growing up. That and flying. Sorry, but it's true."

Both Clarice and Isla rolled their eyes. Fade opened his mouth to make another sex-related remark, no doubt, but closed it when he saw Anya and looked away. Ashamed.

Anya gave me a salute. "I don't have anything to say to you other than thank you. It's been an honor. You are the person who helped inspire the galaxy to revolt."

"Wow, you guys are idi—" I started to say before the airlock doors opened up with a *whoosh* of Kolahn IV air.

Ah god, the smell!

I covered my face. "I take it this isn't a pure nitrogen-and-oxygen environment! What is that?"

"Harrington gas," Clarice said, covering her nose. "Named after a Commonwealth explorer in a sort of backhanded compliment. It's made from a kind of bacteria that grew over most of the planet when the majority of the population committed suicide. It's about one percent of the atmosphere now."

"Great!" I said. "What an incredible smell you've discovered."

Nobody else got that reference. My classical education once more proved to be absolutely useless.

"They should have atmosphere processors in the building," Clarice said, looking nauseous.

"I hope so," I said, shaking my head. "Otherwise, we're going to be conducting this meeting in breath masks."

"Babies," Isla said, walking out the airlock into the platform beyond. I couldn't see much beyond the doors due to the excessive light reflected from beyond, so I put on my goggles and followed. Everyone else just put their arms over their eyes.

What awaited on the other side was a sight to remember. The regent's palace was a massive series of lumpy domes with strange, erratically placed purple quartz on its sides in place of window. Towers rose between the lumpy domes, ending in flower-like structures on the top. A series of a hundred bridges extended from many of these towers, including one directly to us.

Large banners showing the Free Systems Alliance's white-and-blue flag hung from every corner with a newly constructed statue of, well, myself, having been placed on the central dome with its proton sword raised in the air. The regent's palace was definitely a building constructed by aliens with alien aesthetics but it was clearly inhabited by humans. The walkway toward us had a guard of archduchy sentinels, each ornately armored in gold and red armor with star pikes. They were stylized to look like ancient Roman Centurions but had armor that could make them capable of taking on a hover tank. I'd thought their order extinguished with the destruction of Crius, but my doppelganger had taken over the regency for Princess Servilia.

Supposedly.

This entire set-up felt wrong. Even before I was disillusioned with my country, I'd never been one to enjoy the childish displays of fascist iconography. The archduchy had survived as much on style as substance, distracting its soldiers with flags and uniforms in place of genuine meaning. This felt like a monument to the ego of a man who had never served a day in his life. One more interested in the trappings of war rather than winning the real thing. But he was winning, against the most powerful military in the Spiral.

"Nice statue," William said. "I would have added a bunch of peasants underneath or you giving the bird to audiences."

"You're just jealous," Clarice said. "No one is building a statue of you."

"There was one in the center of the gladiator coliseum of High Baghdad," William said, sighing. "I was the first local gladiator to win one hundred battles."

"Impressive," I said, stopping ten paces in front of the *Melampus*.

"Not really," William said. "I was promised my freedom for winning but it turned out to be a trick. I would have been recycled if not for the fact that a baroness wanted to use me to breed with her bastard daughters."

That was one of the few times William had ever opened up. "What happened?"

"I did what was required for a few weeks," William said. "Then I slit her throat and snuck out. The local resistance cell was happy to have me. They took down the statue after that, though."

"I always hated those games," Anya said. "My mother made me come with her to them, though."

"She liked to watch?" I asked, unsure where the people supposed to meet us were.

"She liked to gamble," Anya said. "It eventually got to her. She ended up betraying her mistress to the resistance."

"Good," William said.

"They raped her, her daughters, and dashed her baby son against the ground," Anya said. "It encouraged me to join the Crius military as a sniper. I like to think I eventually got them. Three hundred and fifty-five confirmed kills."

Everyone was silent.

"Everyone here has had a shit life," I said. "It's official."

"The Buddha says life is pain," Clarice said, continuing to interrupt the rudeness of our hosts choosing not to meet with us. "Which is why people are justified in causing pain to one another because they'll become enlightened from it."

I pondered that. "I think your family may have misconstrued your religious education."

"Says the Satanist," Clarice said, offended for one of the few times I'd known her.

"I don't even believe in the Devil," I said, my head suddenly hurting me. I saw on the horizon the sight of a Kathax spreading out its wings outward as it glowed with an unearthly light that made it look like God. I blinked and it was gone.

"I need to see Isla," I muttered.

"What?" Isla said. "What's wrong?"

"Beyond everything?" I asked.

"Yeah," Isla said. "Beyond that."

"Nothing," I whispered.

The door opened up to the regent's palace, the wall looking like a sideways wall of crooked fangs opened up. The bizarre alien architecture aside, I was more taken with the parade of individuals that proceeded to march out under guard of more sentinels.

The first group was courtiers of a kind I'd hoped had been exterminated when the Commonwealth had dropped a hundred asteroids onto the surface of my home world. They wore elaborate robes and gowns covered in various adornments. The bureaucrats of the archduchy had administered in the name of Titus and a staggering number of nobles who couldn't be bothered to handle the running of their holdings. The fact the FSA had grown to the point they had use for them bothered me almost as much as the statue of me.

My eyes widened at the sight of my siblings toward the center. Thomas had been a member of the State Security service and was presently wearing a modified version of its uniform, the color changed from black to a light blue that was considerably less menacing but still bore an insignia that marked him as the head of FSA Intelligence. Thomas was a brown-skinned man with short black hair who, honestly, resembled William more than he did me. The Plantagenet family were of Afro-Earth descent and preferred to look that way even when genetics said otherwise.

My sister Zoe caused my throat to run dry as I still had nightmares about "killing" her with Judith's help. She was wearing a pleasant white lab coat over a green blouse and brown skirt that looked like causal clothes for the planet. She had the Mass family chin and Plantagenet skin color and hair. She was a beautiful woman and it made me sick to think about all of that had passed between us. My sister had proven to be quite the mad scientist and was responsible for the memory uploads that had made both her and my doppelganger's lives possible. The false Judith was using her memories as well.

Was this my "real" sister, who was last seen on Albion working for the Commonwealth's brainwashing program, or one of her doppelgangers? Did it matter? How could you tell the difference without a thorough medical scan? I didn't know how to react as I wasn't sure it would be fair to blame her for what her mental clone had done—but the very fact that she did meant it was within her to do so. Murder, torture, and worse.

Then I saw myself.

My doppelganger looked every bit like the poster-child the media had made me out to be. As much as genetic engineering made me more beautiful than the randomness of nature, the past seven years had been ten sectors of jumpspace storms for me. He didn't look remotely that way, having a carefree look in his eye and the look of a man who spent a few hours every day in the beauty parlor.

He was wearing a stark-white uniform with gold epaulettes and a rank badge identical to the late Supreme Commander Germanicus. The jackboots were almost as shiny as the glare we'd seen upon our entrance. He also had a sword identical to my own.

"Oh shit," I said, looking up at the man's face.

The smile that greeted me was one I'd seen a million times before.

The False Cassius walked up to the front of the group and held his hands behind his back. "Hello. It's been a long time."

My group looked at each other in confusion.

I sucked in my breath. "Hello, Father."

CHAPTER NINETEEN

I remembered one of the defining moments of my relationship with my father. It was a memory so vivid that I might have been transported back in time.

My proton sword crashed against my opponent's gravity saber as sparks flew from where the two electrified blades collided. I was purely on the defensive now, struggling to keep up against the furious onslaught of attacks by my opponent. What had begun as a friendly duel had rapidly degenerated into a brutal fight for survival, as it was clear my opponent had no intention of holding back.

Faced with the fact my opponent was stronger, faster, and just plain better than me, I considered yielding but remembered the beatings I'd received as a child when I did that. Instead, I threw all of my weight forward to push him back then swung around for a killing blow against his neck.

Instead, my opponent shamelessly broke the Duelists' Code by slicing his gravity lance's edge against my front leg then kicked it out from under me when I slid forward. He then placed his blade up against the back of my neck. I felt its aura burn against my flesh and leave a horrible scar that would require weeks of medi-gel to heal.

"Point," My father, Cassius the Elder, said.

It was still the first year of the war and my father hadn't yet been poisoned in such a way that left him crippled and obese. Instead, he was very much like an older version of me with a body that still looked like an Adonis even among a genetically engineered race of them. He kept his golden-blond hair long and curly, trailing over his shoulders while wearing a shimmersilk shirt with cloned-dinosaur-skin pants. It made him look like a holo romance novel's image of a space pirate and I couldn't help but loathe the fact he'd made me in his image.

I, by contrast, was wearing a red version of the standard practice duelists' bodysuit with a faceless mask. Pulling out a set of medical tape from the pouches on my belt, I moved it around the back of my knee then stood up. I didn't even bother to treat the wound my father had delivered to me at my neck since he'd view it as a sign of weakness.

The two of us were in a "circle of death" or a two-story golden octagonal chamber for honor duels in the middle of the Summer Palace. The Summer Palace was a fantastical cathedral-like building formerly belonging to House Lucifer before their direct-line extermination and now serving as a sort of all-purpose center for government business. Under House Dumas, the current reigning family, the place had taken on a somewhat darker tone.

There were a never-ending stream of prostitutes, drug-dealers, professional athletes, and movie stars enjoying lavish parties despite the fact there was a massive interstellar war going on. I also despised the decor since every single room, including this one, contained a massive portrait of Supreme Commander Prince Germanicus. The arrogant white-haired, brown-skinned man had a black military uniform covered in every single possible award for valorous service one could win despite the closest he'd ever been to an actual battle being safely sequestered in the flagship *Revengeance*'s hold. In this particular portrait, he had an adorable Orleans Bulldog sitting beside him as if it humanized the man responsible for this war.

"It's not really a point when you cheat like that," I said, removing my helmet and getting up. "It's not really a sport at all."

"No, it's a battle," Cassius Senior said, throwing his gravity saber in the air before catching it by the hilt and turning it off, placing it on my shoulder. "I would have thought with your oh-so-honorable decision to fight on the front lines that you'd respect the difference."

I narrowed my eyes. My father had never approved of my decision to join the Starfighter Corps. In fact, that was understating matters since he'd spoken of the armed forces in the most disgraceful terms. He'd even gone so far as to get me briefly assigned as captain of a regular naval vessel before I'd been transferred back out. I had no regrets about that assignment, though, since it had taught me how to lead. "Strong words from a man who has never killed anyone outside of the Circle of Death."

Cassius the Elder smiled, chuckling. "If you think I've only killed individuals in the arena, my dear boy, you haven't been paying attention. I've killed tens of thousands, if not millions, with the stroke of a stylus across a screen. That is the way nobility is supposed to kill. We're not the rough-and-ugly masses crawling over each other to die for an extra set of rations or a retirement pension."

These were the disgraceful terms I'd mentioned. "Our family has a proud martial heritage, stretching back to the colony's founding."

Cassius the Elder raised a thin eyebrow. "Our family was originally the Masskerwitzes and we were legal clerks when we settled here. We became generals because we could afford to outfit our own troops. Not because we've bought into all the bullshit we feed the plebs about honor and duty."

"Honor and duty are not bullshit," I said, sheathing my proton sword after realizing my father wasn't even going to bow after his 'victory.'

Cassius the Elder signaled up to the second story. Up there was a balcony with a force-field around it to watch the facilities with three of my father's latest mistresses waiting in shorts and white t-shirts to deliver water and refreshment after his latest round of humiliating me at swordplay. I was deeply disappointed with my father, as he and my brother Thomas had both lost themselves to the corpulent pleasures of Crius high society. Then again, they both did their jobs and that was more than I could say for most of the nobility these days.

As my father took a water bottle from one of the buxom genetically engineered females, I thought about Thomas's buff, sculpted male lovers and shook my head. Everything you could possibly want was catered to when you were a member of Crius's nobility. In my case, I found the idea of body-sculpting your lovers and them going through contests for the honor of being a plaything vaguely unsettling—especially when my father offered me their services.

Ugh.

"No thank you," I said to one of the women as she offered me a bottle. "I'll get my own drink."

She didn't respond and just bowed her head. I wondered if she could talk, as my father was never one for conversation with his servants. Some houses had the vocal chords of their servants stilled as one of the "voluntary" actions they could undertake to increase the flow of credits and food back to their families.

"Junior," Cassius the Elder said, using a title I loathed. "You are a miracle of science. Intelligent enough to design your own starfighter, a master programmer, an astrogator, and godlike behind a starship's controls. You're even decent with a sword. All the while looking like a Greek God."

"I feel like this is praising you more than me," I said.

"Because it is," Cassius the Elder said. "Everything you have is because *I paid for it*. Millions of credits in terms of perfect genetic replication, raising you on the right diet, the best in cybernetics, and a dozen tutors who had to be vetted five or six times before they were even on a chart I looked at it. You were meant to inherit my position as Chancellor of the Archduchy and guide us to a better error. Instead, any time you go out there, you run the risk of destroying my investment."

I crossed my arms and took a breath. "Are you finished berating me for trying to protect the empire you and the other nobility have stupidly put into danger by beginning a war with an enemy five times our size? Because if so, I have battles to win and men to train so you can sip wine and sleep with harlots while good men sacrifice themselves by the thousands."

My father's mistresses looked nervous.

Cassius the Elder chuckled. It was a mirthless arrogant noise divorced from real laughter. "It's good when you finally show some spine. You're far too respectful."

I was surprised by his reaction since my condemnation was the height of hypocrisy: I'd been among those campaigning for war among the other nobles. Then again, maybe it was the hypocrisy he was admiring. He was a practiced politician who had managed to hold his own in the struggle between the houses that was an ever ongoing low-grade civil war even during conflicts like our current one with the Commonwealth.

"Oh, this I have to hear," I said, sighing. "Because you've wanted me to do nothing but follow in your footsteps from the beginning and have made my life a living hell while doing it. You've also disgraced your other children and tried to turn me against them."

There was a silence. "You don't really understand me at all, do you?"

"I understand enough."

Cassius the Elder took a deep breath. "Out."

His mistresses departed while I stood still.

"Another lecture or are you simply going to beat me, *Chancellor*?" I asked. It was a petty, boyish insult, as if my father's badge of office wasn't something he'd taken great pride in achieving. Even at that age, I'd known my father was quite literal when he talked about all the bodies he'd stepped over to get his position as the second most powerful man in the archduchy.

Cassius the Elder shook his head. "I've long since given up on the idea of physical force being enough to knock the damn fool idealistic nonsense out of your head. There's too much romance to the idea of being noble knights fighting for a just cause even if this entire system we have here on Crius was founded as a protection racket by a Satan-worshiping religious fanatic."

My father was not the most pious of men. "That's never stopped you from trying."

"Amazingly, you've managed to stay alive and built a reputation that has benefited our family. The plebs crave heroes and I've been feeding them your adventures through my contacts that you've gained a political currency that rivals my own. That Thomas and I have to bend over backward to keep you from being assassinated or being sent into the meat grinder where your ability to do loop-de-loops in a starfighter won't save you is a small price to pay."

"I don't need your help," I said.

"Don't be stupid. You met your nat wife because she was assigned by Thomas to protect you. Assuming this war doesn't end with us all dead, you'll be able to spend that currency making the changes to our society we need. Your squadron should be lucky they're being kept from the worst of it."

I balled my fists. "I will not let you disgrace my men's sacrifices."

Cassius the Elder stared at me. "Really? Defending your men before yourself? You are just the perfect pissant toy soldier, aren't you? Are you doing this deliberately or is God punishing me?"

I let a half-smile curl up. "Possibly both."

Cassius the Elder crushed his water bottle with his fist then tossed it away. "Allow me to tell you a story, and yes, it's mandatory. It's a story of someone very much like you who was once filled with the idealism of knights, starfighter pilots, and defending the innocent."

"You?" I asked.

"I'm fudging on the starfighter pilot business," Cassius the Elder said. "One of the things I corrected in my cloning was to get rid of vertigo. The simple fact was, though, I was a man who believed the archduchy could be a force for good in the universe. So I became a doctor."

I stared at him. "A doctor. I find that harder to believe than in Jumpspace Yaga and the Krampus."

"We all have our little rebellions," Cassius the Elder said. "Mine was the idea that saving lives in the field might go a little way to amending the millions our planet has taken to feed its appetites. It took me a whole six months to memorize the contents of every medical journal dealing with human anatomy, surgery, and equipment. I only tested in the top three percent of Crius, though. Perhaps showing I wasn't taking it seriously as *my* father had paid for the best."

Assuming my father wasn't just speaking a pile of dragonshit, I found myself intrigued. "What did you do as a doctor?"

"I worked on Xerxes," Cassius the Elder said, his voice cracking for a moment. It was one of the few genuine displays of emotion I'd ever seen from him. It was also over almost as soon as it began. "I treated the victims of the insurrection there. Men, women, and children caught up in the horrors of the conflict. There were no heroes there, only villains. The Xerxes insurrectionists used child soldiers, conscripts forced to fight with their families held hostage, and indiscriminate terrorism to get their point. I remembered wiping the mind of a Crius noblewoman's maid who'd been held prisoner for seven years and been raped so many times it had done catastrophic damage to her insides. Yet, somehow, she'd still given birth to six children. The Crius occupying forces? Our side? We did worse."

None of this was new and it was part of the justification which the archduchy gave to crack down on other worlds. They were all uncivilized genetically inferior barbarians, so it was the right of the superior humans to correct them. It took me a decade to realize the writing of Kipling wasn't revered on other planets.

"It's difficult to imagine you as any sort of humanitarian," I said, speaking carefully.

"My efforts ended poorly." My father's voice was suddenly full of venom. "I fell in love with a local woman there, a nurse, and we decided to get married. This was despite my engagement to my dearest wife."

Fleet Admiral Drusilla Plantagenet, a woman who'd vowed to end my life and come close on several occasion. Dru was possibly the only woman on the planet who was my father's social equal and the only people higher were the royal family. Had my father been less good at manipulating parliament as a politician or Prince Germanicus less talented at fostering a cult of personality among the military, I imagine my father might have pressed the Mass family's own claim to the prophet's throne. Had my father and his wife (I refused to call her mother) had a less contentious relationship, they might have been able to cooperate against him but their union had proven the doom of both House Mass and House Plantagenet's ambitions. Quite contrary to my grandfather's desires, I was sure.

"What happened?" I asked.

Cassius the Elder sighed. "Nothing much, in the grand scheme of things. My father sent his household guard to separate us. They burned down our hospital, her village, and then delivered her head into a basket. They said the baby was taken care of, though. I understood their euphemism and eventually recovered the bones decades later. They're in the family crypt if you'd ever bother to visit."

My eyes widened. "My God."

"God had nothing to do with it," Cassius the Elder replied. "Satan, perhaps, but only the aspect of Crius's patron saint that lies within each man. I was nothing more than a spoiled prince in the eyes of the men, some of whom I'd grown up with, and I'd disgraced myself by lying with a natural-born whore. I spent six months in solitary confinement as punishment with my father believing I was suitably chastised."

I started to speak then stopped as everything about my father's story felt true. "I'm so sorry."

"Don't pity me," Cassius the Elder said, his voice lowering and becoming dangerous. "Because I understood the game from that moment on. I devoted the rest of my life to gaining power both in my house. When I was finally stronger than my father, more politically secure, I had him injected with a neurotoxin from Shogun that made him unable to receive cybernetics. It also left him paralyzed in his own body. I had his throat removed and paid for a doctor to certify his brain as having gone senile. I kept him that way for twenty-five years, long after he'd gone insane. I killed every single one of the soldiers involved in that massacre, occasionally making sure they knew their own sons and daughters had been slaughtered in the fields of the insurrection first. David, the House Warmaster who trained me in dueling, I sawed the limbs off of and spent three days making a puzzle of his flesh. It was messy, gory business but showed me just how pleasant vengeance could be as well as what sort of amateur-hour pampered dragonshit son I've been raising to understand what the purpose of power is."

"Which is?" I said, realizing in that moment my father was insane. I'd never realized it until that moment.

"Gather as much power and wealth as possible or you will be vulnerable to the people you have wronged," Cassius the Elder said, assuming another dueling position despite my wounded state. "Like me."

"I have not been so colorful in my murders," I said, both pitying and being disgusted by father at once.

Not that I would have done so different to someone who had wronged me in such a way. I'd have at least killed them.

"You have killed over a hundred men in battle and some of your fellow Crius, either in defense of your pathetic peasants or because the officer's corps is rife with pampered cowards who aren't eager to rush to die. Men you forced into the front despite their manifest incompetence out of some perverse sense of duty."

"That was *two*," I said. "I—"

"Every one of those people left someone they loved. Husbands, wives, fathers, mothers, daughters, sons, and other. You have created enemies whether you like it or not. People who view you as the monster who ruined their hopes and dreams for a continued life with their loved ones. That doesn't include the fifty-thousand people of Kolthas Station, butcher."

For the first time, I felt inferior in morality to my father. It was not a feeling I enjoyed. "You are correct."

"We are going to lose this war, my son," Cassius the Elder said, his voice grim and resigned. "This is true despite the fact our insane idiot prince makes declarations we're winning every day. The Commonwealth can field ten units for every one we field and replace their losses faster. Wars are not won by bold heroics and glory-seeking playboys like yourself but by logistics. We lost this conflict the moment you and your men destroyed Kolthas Station. The only thing can do is expend as many Commonwealth lives as possible that we are able to negotiate favorable terms for surrender."

"Germanicus will never surrender," I said coldly. "He's, as you say, an insane idiot prince. Even if he wasn't, his father, the puppet archduke, and sister, the ground forces commander, have their own reasons to carry on the war. Their positions would never survive surrender."

"You're right," Cassius the Elder said, smiling. "You're finally learning. In any case, I am making preparations for our house's survival in the post-Crius world."

"I will have none of it," I said, feeling like a child but refusing to believe it was simple math. The Commonwealth's morale would surely break with the devastating losses we were inflicting. "I will see my men triumph."

My father raised his sword and aimed it at me. "Just show me how you fight. Maybe at some point you'll learn the value of cheating."

I did. Just not that day.

Chapter Twenty

I stared at my father in the present, not sure how I should feel about his miraculous survival. Relieved? Angry? Upset? What did one say when a man you'd both admired and hated came back from the dead and took your identity? This wasn't exactly a tears-and-hugs sort of situation—especially since he was next to two members of my family who'd tried to kill me.

So, as the pause between everyone's response carried on, I finally said, "I thought you were dead."

"I suppose you might think that," Cassius the Elder said, a beatific smile on his face. Beside him, both my siblings looked uncomfortable. Everyone behind me was equally confused, I could feel it radiating off their bodies. I briefly wondered if this revelation would compel Fade to reevaluate his plan to assassinate my doppelganger.

I narrowed my eyes. "I was at your funeral where they buried your obese poisoned corpse."

It was the last time I'd stepped foot on Crius and the last time I'd seen my wife save a short holo-call from the *Revengeance* before the Battle of Hoshi's Point. I'd felt relieved that he'd finally died, ending his manipulation of me. Back then, I'd been naive enough to believe we could still win the war or at least settle down into a negotiated peace. It had been a delusion, but one I'd been all too willing to embrace.

"Yes," Cassius the Elder said, his voice low. "A gift from Prince Germanicus. He determined I was responsible for planning and arranging the assassination attempt against him. Rather than a normal death, he wanted me to suffer a slow breakdown of my dignity before death. Your sister transported my brain to a new body."

"That's not possible," I said. "The technology doesn't exist."

"Thanks to Zoe, it does," Cassius the Elder said. "I spent a few weeks as a pair of eyeballs and a brain in a jar but my daughter has discovered a stopgap on the human race's road to immortality."

"You've always underestimated me," Zoe said, smiling.

I didn't smile back. "Not anymore."

Zoe looked confused. She might have heard about her doppelganger's death, but the fact was she had no reason to suspect I'd murdered her. Then again, she also wasn't responsible for murdering an entire ship's crew, torturing me, and taking William's arm. I'd let her do it all because I'd wanted to trust her.

Never again.

"So you're impersonating me and engaging in stolen honor," I said, referring to the practice of impersonating a Crius officer. "All so you can, what, get revenge for our world?"

I wouldn't blame him if he wanted to burn Albion to ashes. I had. That didn't strike me as the kind of plan my father would cook up, though.

"The Commonwealth deserves to be punished," Thomas said, puffing out his chest. "No words for your brother."

"Many," I said. "Under other circumstances, I'd be ecstatic."

"But you're here on behalf of the Commonwealth," Cassius the Elder interrupted. "Tsk-tsk-tsk. Shameful."

Clarice stepped forward and I worried she'd throw my father over the side of the walkway we were on, which was several hundred feet up, from the sight of it, and had no bannisters.

I kept my gaze on my father. "I developed an overwhelming love of peace in these past seven years. I grew sick of children being sent off to die and be butchered so the rich and powerful could get their revenge. Crius is dead and I see no reason to kill its future so I can pretend the millions sacrificed on the altar was a justified expenditure."

Cassius the Elder laughed and rubbed his chin. "I swear, you still talk like you're doing theater. That's the hardest part of impersonating you. You'd think living on a ship full of whores and thieves would have roughened you up a bit."

"You can go fuck yourself for lying to me and stealing my name," I snapped.

Some of the sentinels motioned for their rifles.

My father waved them away without looking at them. "That's more like it. I've been following your career with great interest. Your work with the militias, your time as a scavenger, your brief period as a pirate, and trying to remake yourself as a navigator only to end up as a spy. A spy who mutinied, sank the career of the Watcher General, and destroyed an Elder Race marker along with stole away with a Cognition A.I. from both my forces as the Commonwealth. Now you're here, again, working for them. Why?"

He wasn't going to let that go. "You really don't believe I want to see this war end, do you?"

"Why would I? Everything I know about you, my son, has been you playing at soldier. What could possibly dissuade you now? Did you turn on your surviving countrymen because they offered you a uniform?"

"My wife is dead," I said softly. My voice then got louder. "So are all my friends. I blame you, Germanicus, Germania, the Crius system, and myself for that every bit as much as the Commonwealth. I don't believe in the Devil, but I genuinely hope both sides of this new war you've started burn in Hell!"

Cassius the Elder stared at me for a long time then looked at Zoe. "Have you got that?"

Zoe nodded and tapped her left eye, showing it to be artificial. "It's my brother, all right. The brain patterns are an erratic traumatized match. He's definitely suffering A-3 Class PTSD and substance withdrawal, but there's no mistaking it. He's also telling the truth, or at least believes he is."

Thomas looked angry at my outburst then looked away. "I wish he wasn't."

I stared at my mouth. "You were testing me?"

"Can you blame me?" Cassius the Elder said flippantly. "I mean, you run into all sorts of Cassius Mass impersonators these days."

I almost kicked my father over the side and it was Clarice who stopped me by wrapping her arm around mine.

"Ah, you must be the princess-turned-mercenary Clarice Rin-O'Harra," My father said, ignoring the many other things Clarice had been. He then pointed to each of my companions in turn. "You are Isla the renegade bioroid, you Fade the Watcher deep cover agent, Anya Terra the terrorist turned reprogrammed Shin, and I don't know who you are."

"Your daughter took my arm!" William shouted.

"Ah," Cassius the Elder said, clearly playing with my group. "Now I remember you, William Baldur the gladiator. How much would I have to pay you to forgive me? You look like someone whose dignity is for sale."

"What?" Clarice said.

"Make me an offer," William said, suddenly serious.

"William!" Clarice said.

"I'm not rich yet so I can't afford to be picky with paid apologies," William said. "I really liked that arm and she was quite unpleasant about it. That's at least fifty thousand credits. Twice as much in Republic of Crius currency."

"Sorry," Zoe said, waving. "My copies are a bit buggy."

"Buggy is slurred speech, not mass murder," I said. "Also, allying with a member of the Elder Races."

The words had no sooner left my mouth than I instantly regretted them. That was not something to mention casually.

My father became very still. "My, my, someone knows a great deal more than I would have expected."

"Good going, Captain," Fade muttered.

"I'm more observant than you realize," I said, cursing myself.

"You would have to be," Cassius the Elder said. "I mean, you missed the fact you were living in a totalitarian dictatorship."

I really wanted to kill my father but I needed to talk to him about the *thing* that was living on this planet. As much as I despised him, he was clearly aware of the danger the Elder Races represented while Zoe was the world's greatest expert on their technology. Admittedly, that was akin to saying Leonardo Da Vinci would be the best person to study a starfighter in the Renaissance, but it was still better than a bare bulb. Well, if she didn't kill us all and dissect our corpses.

"The offer is sincere," I said, taking a deep breath. "I wish to negotiate on behalf of the Commonwealth and discuss other matters. I request the safe passage of people and your hospitality as a noble of House Mass as well as my kinsman. I promise to make no move against you or your own as long as I'm here."

Once that would have counted as a sacred promise to me. However, the time when all I had was my word was long gone. I had people I loved now. I'd break every promise in the world to keep them safe.

"If I believed in honor, I would believe you," Cassius the Elder said. "However, I don't. What I do believe is the fact you've very made things very complicated for me."

"By surviving?" I asked, hoping he'd say yes.

Cassius the Elder sighed. "No, my dear boy, but by the fact I do believe you're trying to do the right thing. The universe would be a far better place if people didn't. Look at the Union of Faith. So much zeal, so much horror."

"So you won't consider the offer?" I asked, knowing it had been doomed the moment my father rather than my doppelganger was the one in charge of the FSA. He wasn't a man to quit while he was ahead.

"I'll hear it," Cassius the Elder said. "But you'll have to stay."

"Stay?" I said. "What do you mean stay?"

"Yes," Cassius the Elder said. "Until things are sorted out."

"Forever, you mean," I said, sighing. "Because I'm a threat to your identity."

"You don't have to be." Cassius the Elder narrowed his eyes. "But yes, you'd have to stay for the next three or four years at our side as my body double. You'll eventually be given a new identity, but I'm afraid I have to be the only Cassius Mass until all the treaties are signed and the war is over."

"I agree," I said, cutting him off before Clarice said something nasty.

"All right, then," Cassius the Elder said. "The sentinels will escort Mr. Fade and Major Terra to a safe place in the regent's palace. Then we will dine together, your friends and I, and I will see to your offer. Then we will discuss the Elder Races and your future role as a member of the FSA."

"Like hell," William said, complicating matters. "No one's taking our captain anywhere."

"I'm not loyal to the Commonwealth," Anya said. "They broke my conditioning."

"Interesting," Zoe said, looking sideways. "I would have

thought that would be impossible. May I examine your brain? My clone's work should be flawless."

"No!" Anya snapped.

"Then you have to go," Cassius the Elder said. "However, I don't want this to go poorly."

"Too late," William said, showing a remarkable lack of restraint in the face of a group of the galaxy's most heavily armored warriors.

"So," my father said, not missing a beat, "I'm going to give you a present."

"A present," I said dryly. "What would you have that I would even want?"

I noticed Clarice was holding a grenade behind her back. I grimaced and wondered about what she thought she'd be accomplishing here if she detonated it. Then again, taking the supreme commander hostage was a move. Just a very dumb move. Not that I had any better ones at this time.

As if on cue, the doorway to the regent's palace opened for a second time and a fat, shirtless brown-skinned man was dragged out by a pair of FSA Army troopers in black shirts and pants plus a pair of thick cyberglasses. Both men moved identically and there was something about them that unnerved me, as if all life had been drained out of them. I couldn't put it into words, but they were like the vision I'd had of the shipyards and fleets above. Empty. I felt like I could see into their bodies and look upon their souls but found nothing inside them. Another sign I'd picked the worst time in my life to get sober.

Isla shouted an expletive before covering her mouth as I did a double-take between her and the prisoner. It took a second for me to realize the man on the ground was Octavian Plantagenet. Like my father, he looked like he was suffering from DNA poisoning, the kind of act generally used to cause a slow but inevitable breakdown of the body. I barely recognized him given he'd put on at least two hundred and fifty pounds while his face was starting to sag off his skull. He also showed signs of being tortured.

The body was taken through my father's entourage then dropped at my feet. Octavian looked up to me, blinked, then did his own double-take between me and my father. He then looked at Isla then started crying. It was possibly the most pathetic sight I'd seen in my entire life.

I looked up to my father. "I take it you and your treasure had a..."

I trailed off, I wanted to make a quip but all I could think about was the fact Isla was face to face with the man who raped and tortured her. Instead, I walked back to check on her along with Clarice. Thankfully, Clarice hid her grenade before she did so.

Isla pushed us both away. "No."

She reached for her useless gun then cursed under her breath.

"Had a falling out?" Cassius the Elder said, sighing. "Yes, I suppose you could say that. Thomas found out about his unpleasant habits not long after he joined the FSA. I would have eliminated him there but the needs of the many outweighed him. He worked, instead, as a prisoner until we'd bled him dry of his contacts. Somehow, though, he managed to slip a bulletin out that he was willing to pay top dollar for the recovery of the bioroids I freed. That included yours as well as a assassination on you and her other lovers. His use to the FSA is finished and I present him as a gift to your associate. Kill him, torture him, abuse him in the way he abused you. I do not care. Our blood ties are not so deep that it matters."

I stared at him. "This changes..."

I couldn't speak for Isla here. Looking to her, I saw her shake with a mixture of rage and memories that seemed to be playing across her face. I wondered what kind of horrors she wanted to inflict, just as Clarice had wanted to do the same to our Chel prisoner.

Instead, she just sucked in her breath. "He's garbage. Throw him away."

Cassius the Elder nodded and then lifted the four-hundred-pound man up over his head as if he were a small child, showing just how powerful an enhanced Crius body was, then hurled him down over the side of the walkway. He fell downward forty stories and landed as a tiny speck against the rocky desert ground below.

Isla laughed then smiled.

Everyone else was uncomfortable except Zoe and my father, who chuckled along. My father then clasped his hands together. "Is there any objections to proceeding from this point?"

Fade looked down at the ground below. "No, I'll surrender myself to your custody."

"They're not to be harmed," I said. "Not if you want my cooperation."

"I wouldn't dream of it," Cassius the Elder said. "You'd be surprised at how many of the FSA soldiers above are former Commonwealth."

Thomas looked uncomfortable with that statement, which told me a great deal. My brother was a former torturer and had overseen literally hundreds of executions in the name of the archduchy's security—including former friends and colleagues.

Cassius the Elder slapped his arm around my shoulder and escorted me to the door, gesturing for the others to follow. "So what would you like for dinner? My chef makes a magnificent bloodfish."

Chapter Twenty-One

It was not the most awkward dinner party I've ever attended, my father's usual galas including orgies and gladiator battles after all, but it was easily in the top five.

My father's dining room was set up in a large circular chamber with four entrances with light provided by organic crystals growing out of the top of the wall. The table was rectangular, however, and made of greelwood in the classic Old Crius style. A buffet of fish, meats, potamatos, brocumbers, and other traditional dishes were present. The food was being served in sterling silver containers and on fine porcelain dishes with even the utensils being electrite and costing probably more than some spacers made in a Sol year.

It annoyed me, to some extent, my father had clearly gone to the trouble of having all of these imported since they weren't vat-grown products like I'd become used to on the *Melampus* but fresh. It was an extravagant luxury for the man who was deliberately cultivating the image of a hardened revolutionary fighting against an overwhelming foe.

Cassius the Elder sat at the end of the table in what could best be called a throne. It was actually made of stone and had a golden disc displaying the Sun and a Kolahn face on it, making me think my father had casually looted some temple to provide himself a dinner chair. Everyone else was sitting in typical wooden chairs across from each other with Isla to my right while Clarice sat to my left with William on the other side of Clarice. My siblings sat across from me and Isla, both looking as uncomfortable as I felt.

The servants who attended on us were unsettling, as they were dressed in sexualized versions of dinner jackets and maid uniforms and moved in utter silence. They moved in perfect unison and had no sign of response save immediate obedience. They seemed as empty as my vision of the soldiers above but I wondered if I was projecting.

Isla whispered over to me, "I was programmed with memories of being a fairy princess and this seems excessive."

"He can hear you," I muttered, dabbing my mouth with a napkin after trying the soup. I was glad it wasn't poisoned but the environment didn't lend itself well to casual conversation.

"Yes," Cassius the Elder said, chuckling. "I had an implant in my ear that allowed me to pick up even the tiniest of noises then filtered them through a dummy A.I. to bring important bits to my attention. Very useful in court."

"Isn't the Crius Royal Court dust and ashes?" William said, showing no sign of my hesitation.

"Indeed," Cassius the Elder said, chuckling. "I managed to win the Great Game through survival. All of the nobility of Crius have either renounced their titles or are dead."

"So is that what this whole revolution is about?" I asked, shaking my head. "Rebuilding the old order? You as archduke?"

Thomas snorted, across from me.

"Hardly," Cassius the Elder said, chuckling. "I think the first thing I'm going to sign into law is an end to any and all aristocratic privileges. There will be an Empress of Crius, dear Princess Servilia, but she'll have a purely ceremonial position. Equality for all from peasant to prince—"

"But some more equal than others," I said, finishing his sentence. "You've never cared about the people before."

"On the contrary, I've always been keenly aware of their importance," Cassius the Elder said. "I've never been so stupid as to believe the bullshit the state taught about us being a master race. Any and all human beings could be like us if they had enough money and a team of engineers. Even then, you can't instill ambition and vision—after all, look at you."

I ignored his jibe. "What are you trying to accomplish, then?"

My father leaned back in his throne and looked at me. "A lasting peace."

"Peace," I said, as if it coming from him were comical.

"Why so skeptical?" Cassius the Elder said, looking at me sideways.

"Because you started an intergalatcic war that's killed millions," I said.

"Is that lobster? I've never had lobster," William said, looking at it sideways.

"No, it's shavafish," Clarice corrected, getting some.

"What's the difference?" William said.

"There isn't one," Clarice said. "Not really. Just like there isn't much difference between the Commonwealth's Reclamation and Cassius the Elder's plan."

Cassius the Elder chuckled. "I like your friends, Cassius. You're unusually silent, though. No answer to my question?"

"William and I are in accord for once," I said, taking a deep breath. "You have no idea how much damage you've caused in the pursuit of your ambitions."

"Six million," My father said, sighing. "That's a rough estimate, give or take a couple of hundred thousand and ignoring the various groups that were fighting already when one side or the other joined the FSA. It's actually a relatively small number of people killed. The number of people willing to fight for the Commonwealth to the end is far less than anyone suspected. They broke themselves against the flower of Crius's soldiery and expended their best soldiers. Those left were very often those conscripted from the very worlds they conquered."

I suspected my father was making up a number far less than the actual number killed. My own research had confirmed at least sixteen million killed in the conflict and Commonwealth numbers went from fifty to a hundred and fifty million depending on which source you chose to believe. Either that, it was a war being fought for revenge and a man's vanity, making my father worse than all the archduchy's convicted serial killers put together.

"And how is that going to bring peace?" I said, shaking my head. "You've not brought up the fact I talked about the Commonwealth surrendering once."

"You could have everything you want," Isla said, looking around. "All of the worlds independent except for the ones united under the FSA. Certainly, you can't want the Community to invade."

"Can't I?" Cassius the Elder said.

Isla did a double-take. "What?"

"My father has some very interesting ideas about the future of humanity," Thomas said, looking over at Clarice then me. "Ideas that don't necessarily involve the stated goals of the FSA."

"I've seen how empires are built," Clarice said, looking over at him with disgust. "You actually are waging war just for the purpose of inviting the Community in. They'll smash the Commonwealth and all other nations involved in the war that refuse to surrender. Then you'll be appointed as Viceroy or whatever and be the leader of a united humanity as a Community satrapy. King Herod to their Roman Empire."

"I'll be the greatest traitor since Judas, Brutus, or the Reverend Calvin Jones. Bigger perhaps," Cassius the Elder had no shame in his voice. "Nevertheless, humanity will finally be underneath one single government and rule of law. Furthermore, we'll be backdoored into the Community as members. A non-voting territory of one of the larger members like the Ants, Tecktoki, or Sorkanan."

"Why in the world would you want something like that?" Clarice asked, stunned.

"On the planet Third Apollo, the population has a typical life expectancy of sixty. The genetic damage to the entire race of humans there is so extensive that one in three children die. They can't escape what their world has done to them and it's so toxic they don't even bother to try to preserve their habitats but often let them fall apart. Slavery is effectively legalized, as your bioroid friend can attest, yet protections for human workers have been stripped clean on dozens of worlds the Commonwealth promised to improve the lives of when they conquered them. The availability of medicine—"

"I get it," I interrupted, not wanting to hear another of my father's speeches. "The human race is awful and suffering. It always has been."

"Stability, technology, and economic prosperity are the only cures for that," Cassius the Elder said. "The Community is the only power strong enough to bring that about. The Commonwealth might have been able to do that but they overstretched themselves and picked a fight with the archduchy. A victory they won only at the cost of vilifying themselves across the Spiral. Even then, it was already falling apart. It may be a few centuries but the Community will create economic links and shrink the size between worlds thanks to their superior drives. Human culture will mix more freely after the damage done by the Collapse. We'll become one race again and socialized to the point where we can finally leave this shithole of an existence."

I stared at him. "What makes you think the Community won't just take us for everything we've got then 'free' us once we're no longer worth paying for? That didn't work out so well for the former territories of the British."

"Speaking of which, I've been the ant rather than the boot," William said, interested in this conversation far more than I expected him to be. "It's not something I recommend. You may think turning yourself over to the Community is going to work out well but you're not joining an empire if they're landing troops. Joining empires gets you benefits but all of those are going out the window when you've got no cards to play."

"We have cards to play," Zoe said, her voice cheerful. "Ones even the Community would regret forcing us to deal."

I had no doubt she was referring to the markers and their relationship with the Kathax Prime. I wasn't sure we were to that point in the conversation, though. They were playing around and I didn't want to tip them off to just how much I knew right now.

"There are other options," I said, taking a deep breath. "Imagine if you were to agree to this peace treaty."

"Proposed by the Watchers," Thomas said, looking at me. "The secret police of the Commonwealth."

"Which means that this treaty actually has legs," I said, simply. "Imagine you getting all of those worlds' independence and then using your position to create economic ties in place of direct military and government ones. You can create whatever unequal treaties you want with the Community, but trade will happen and elevate our technology level to equality with theirs. You also won't go down as the worst traitor in human history."

"Correction," Clarice said, her voice icy and hateful. "*You* would go down as the worst traitor in human history, Cassius. After all, it's your name they're using to do all this horrible double-dealing and treason, not his."

"I had noticed that. I just wasn't going to bring attention to it," I said.

"Except you just did," Zoe said, looking amused.

"How are you leading this war anyway?" I asked, staring at him. "Is Thomas doing the actual commanding? You've never strategized outside of a brothel or high lords smoking room."

"The definition is a good king is not a man who knows how to rule but who can delegate to those who can," my father said, smiling.

"With the help of the Kathax Prime?" I asked, causing everyone in the room to go silent.

"Thomas, would you be a dear and help our guests find their accommodations?" Cassius the Elder said.

"Like hell we are," Clarice said. "You think you can divide and conquer the *Melampus* crew?"

"I think I've already done that and if I wanted to actually conquer you, I'd just send a couple of hundred soldiers to do it," Casisus the Elder said. "Which is extreme overkill since I think the best your group could repel is fifteen."

"We could totally do twenty even if we all died," William said, clearly either not appreciating how much danger he was in or perhaps having long since made peace with it.

I closed my eyes. "I'll be fine. Besides, I wasn't very hungry anyway."

Isla looked at me. "With your permission, Supreme Commander, I'd like to attend as a witness."

"No," Cassius the Elder said, pressing his fingers together. "I'm afraid this is a family gathering only."

I decided to risk our position further. "During this conversation will you tell me what you've done to your soldiers?"

You could have heard a pin drop but the first person to show their revulsion and guilt was the one I expected least. Thomas looked away with a disgusted look on his face. "What has been done cannot be undone."

"I'm willing to hear their offer, my son," Cassius the Elder said, calling me that for perhaps the first time in a decade. It only aggravated me further. "I have, after all, traded on your name extensively. Furthermore, you have my word of honor that no harm will come to any of your associates and they will be allowed to leave when we have finished our negotiations."

I noticed he didn't mention anything regarding his soldiers. Was it because there was nothing to say? No, the servants were a clue my "vision" held more than just the product of a fevered imagination. Something was going on here, something terrifying. I needed to find out the whys before I decided whether or not to blow up the planet. Which, honestly, still sounded like something out of a bad holovision show.

"Your word of honor would mean more if I hadn't noticed you felt the need to repeat it and have betrayed virtually everyone you've ever worked with," I said simply.

Zoe actually laughed at that. It made the entire dinner party all the more awkward since I didn't find anything funny about it.

"Nevertheless, it is the best offer you're going to receive," Cassius the Elder said softly. "Look at the bright side, it is rare one can be involved in a deal where all the kingdoms of the world may be offered if one but bows down and worships."

"Am I the Devil or Jesus in this allegory?" I asked.

"Is there a difference?"

That summarized the issues of my homeland in a nutshell. "I'll go."

"Of course you will," my father said, as if it were a foregone conclusion.

Thomas proceeded to stand up. "I shall explain our situation, Ms. Rin-O'Harra, Ms. Hernandez, and Mr. Baldur. I think you'll find what I have to say quite enlightening."

"I haven't agreed to go yet." Clarice's voice was low and threatening. I also saw she'd managed to get a knife ready. I had no doubt she could get to my father before any of his bodyguards could protect him. Always willing to sacrifice her life for millions. That was Clarice. Unfortunately, it wouldn't just be her life even if she did manage to kill my father here—which was unlikely.

"You can trust my brother," I said, looking at him directly. "He's a more honorable man than I am. Even when he shouldn't be."

That seemed to affect him. "I'll take them to see their Commonwealth friends first. To show we haven't harmed them."

"Yet," Cassius the Elder said.

Chapter Twenty-Two

Departing from the dining room with my brother and Zoe, the three of us entered into a massive library in an oval shaped chamber. There were dozens of shelves and reading tables throughout with a large octagonal window to the west. I'd been in many libraries before but few of them contained actual books with paper and plastwrite sheets.

It was a remarkably inefficient form of storing information and i was pleased to see a central computer terminal and holotop interfaces on the tables. It struck me as a place which symbolized my father, full of pomp and classicism but signifying nothing but his own ego. I wondered if there were any books he'd actually read in here or if they were just for show.

"Are you familiar with the Earth American Continent Civil War?" Cassius the Elder asked, walking over to a table and taking a chair before turning it around to face me.

"Which one?" I said, trying to keep it all straight. Earth history was something of a blind spot with me. I'd only learned about the Earth German Nazi movement recently. It was a source of embarrassment, given many planets still used them as a casual invocation of evil like the Knights of Velusia and, well, the Archduchy of Crius.

"The first one where the institution of slavery was the matter of dissent," Cassius the Elder said.

"I've heard of it," I said, only barely remembering it from one of my schoolbooks growing up. I'd been much more interested in post-spaceflight history. Old Earth was a dead world and I preferred its fiction to its history. "You may recall I have rather strong opinions on the subject of slavery."

Zoe chuckled, taking a seat on the side of the table rather than bothering to get a seat. It reminded me of better times when we were still friends. "You and your windmill crusades."

"Yes, your feelings on the subject were ever an embarrassment," Cassius the Elder sighed. "Humanity is a race of control and controlled. There will always be slaves and there will always be masters. The problem with so many of the latter is they attempt to justify it with rationales beyond the capacity to do it. They claim God, racial politics, bringing civilization, or ancient wrongs to justify it."

"I am glad to continue embarrassing you if you want to say slavery is right," I said.

"Not right, just a fact of life," Cassius the Elder said. "At least as long as humanity is the way it is. We are a fallen race and it is the cure for my agnosticism that something has crafted us in that way. We are a vicious, murderous, and violent species."

I tried to hold my tongue and failed. "If that's the cure for your agnoticism, you'd have been better remaining an atheist."

"And your beliefs?" Cassius the Elder asked.

"I believe in beauty," I said. "Goodness of the spirit and the eye which has nothing to do with practicality or randomness. I also don't believe Fate or God has any protection against the problem of evil, but leaves it to us."

"And the source of evil?" Cassius asked.

"Men like you and women like Zoe," I said, looking between them. "Men like me."

Zoe looked down at the ground. "Did my doppelganger harm you so much that you hate me?"

I stared at her. "Is she your doppelganger or you in another body? I was tortured, my friends tortured, and nearly killed. Now I find you're allied to one of the Elder Races who has done God knows what to your followers."

Cassius the Elder narrowed his eyes. "My, you know a good deal more than you should."

"Allied is a strong word," Zoe said, frowning. "Better to say the Kathax Prime and our side have a mutual understanding."

"The Elder Races are insane and cannot be trusted," I said, firmly.

"Says the man who, until recently, had one in his head," Cassius the Elder said. "Of the three people in this room, which do you think is the most likely to be brainwashed?"

He had a point there. "What are you doing here?"

Cassius the Elder paused. "I was getting to that before you so rudely interrupted me. What I was getting at is the American Confederacy was defeated by the Northern Union due to all the typical reasons. Industry, population, and lack of foreign support."

"They were also a slave-holding state," Zoe said, pointing out. "Which is economically unfeasible whether through intelligent machines or people."

"Only for cultures," Cassius the Elder said. "It's economically wonderful for the slave holders themselves."

God, my father disgusted me. "You used to have principles."

"Yes, where did that get me?" Cassius the Elder replied. "Basically, I've studied that war at length and determined it's possible to achieve victory through defeat."

I blinked. "What?"

"Defeating the Commonwealth was never an option and defeating the Community is impossible. However, we can lose in a way which guarantees our ascendance," Cassius the Elder said, snapping his fingers. A sniffer of brandy appeared in his hands. I mean that in the literal, as-if-by-magic, sense.

I stared at him. "How did you—"

Cassius the Elder took a sip before laughing, interrupting my statement. "So you can understand how vexing it is for you to come in here carrying a surrender agreement and throw all my plans into disarray."

I put my hand over my heart. "I bleed for you, Father, who is tested by the possibility of winning a war he's trying to lose so he can sell out the human race in an unequal treaty. None of that has to do with the fact you're making a deal with an imprisoned Elder Race."

"Imprisoned for a while longer," Cassius the Elder said. "I'm working to try to release it."

I stared at him. "Perhaps you should explain the whole thing."

"There's not much of a story here," Cassius the Elder said.

"I somehow doubt that," I said, staring at him. "Being as you're walking around in a clone of my body."

"No, a clone of my body," Cassius the Elder said. "I'm using your name but given you're named after me, that doesn't make—"

Zoe cleared her throat. "Perhaps I should be the one to explain."

I closed my eyes. "I agree."

Zoe looked at me, her eyes going deep. "You know what it's like to lose a world, brother. To experience the sudden loss of everyone and everything. To be the child of a dead world."

"All Crius survivors do," I said, surprised at how deep my sister's feelings seemed to run.

"I tried to rebuild my life," Zoe said, pausing. "The Commonwealthers took me in and told me I could help my people if I offered my mind to science. They only wanted me to build weapons and devices to make sure the worlds they'd conquered remained underfoot. They took my research in uploading consciousness and decided to market it as a way to create even better bioroid slaves."

"I know this story," I said, remembering how her bioroid copy had played on my sympathies the way the real Zoe was now. "Somehow, you managed to convince them to let you send out bioroid copies of yourself into the universe. To meet up with people like your brother and, apparently, my father."

"That was my doing," Cassius the Elder said, smiling. It was the practiced look of a politician rather than a father. "I was on Earth when Crius was destroyed. I was campaigning to allow me to negotiate a surrender agreement with the high lords. It might have worked if we'd successfully assassinated Prince Germanicus but my conspirators blundered the job and got themselves killed by State Security. As a result, the Commonwealth ended up going for a scorched-world solution to the Crius problem."

"So while millions of your fellow countrymen were fighting and dying in a desperate attempt to stop the end of their world, you were sipping it up with the rich on Albion?" I asked, wondering if I could strangle him right now.

"Yes, because it was a stupid war you helped start," Cassius the Elder said, snorting. "Perhaps you should study more of the Earth North American Continent's Civil War. They, too, were a bunch of self-styled nobles who built their empire on slavery before picking a fight they couldn't win out of hubris. I, at least, knew it was hopeless from the start and see no reason why I should sympathize with the dead who died for a stupid cause. Also, Cassius, it's in poor taste to claim the moral high ground after murdering tens of thousands of people who promised to liberate slaves."

I stepped forward to strangle my father with my bare hands. I'd learned a lot since his days of humiliating me in duels. "You bastard."

Zoe stepped between us and put her hand on my chest. "Once freed of my prison, I sought out help from the Elder Races. I'd devoted my life to trying to figure out how to elevate humankind above the miserable warmongering race we were—"

"You say it like it's a bad thing," Cassius the Elder said, finishing his brandy.

Zoe briefly looked at our father like she was regretting standing in our way. "I sought out the markers of the Elder Races to study them and they led me here. It was here I discovered the Kathax Prime. A being who took upon the form of Prophet Allenway to show me the mysteries of the world."

"You're an atheist," I pointed out.

"Not anymore," Zoe said, her voice low. "What is a god but a sufficiently advanced alien? I learned many things from him which would make your blood run cold and then blind with their glories. Even then, they are but a fraction of the knowledge the Elder Races possess."

"The Elder Races destroy any race they view as a threat to them," I said, shaking my head. "Hundreds, millions of species have been eradicated by them."

"Which is why we need weapons against them and for them to cease to be an issue," Cassius the Elder said. "If we can free this Kathax Prime from his prison and unleash him back among his people, it might result in a civil war if what he's telling us is true. That should hopefully give us the chance to evolve into something a bit more formidable."

I tried to wrap my head around what these two were contemplating. "So not only are you planning to get the human race conquered by the Community, but you're also planning to pick a fight with beings you identify as *gods*."

"All to build the new human race," my father said dryly. "What? Did the destruction of your planet wipe all stomach for battle from you?"

"The hypocrisy about you lecturing me on that strikes me as so obvious it must be deliberate but you seem to be serious," I said. "At least the Community was made of flesh and blood enemies. The Elder Races are made of light and code."

"Think about it, Cassius—" Zoe started to speak.

"Yes?" my father asked.

"Not you," Zoe said, shaking her head. "The one that matters."

"You wound me," Cassius the Elder said. "You and Cassius both."

"I do not wound, only kill," I said.

"Imagine the future of the human race," Zoe said, her voice full of the conviction only the very religious or deranged possessed. I'd used to speak of the archduchy with that kind of ferver. "We can all be immortal. Not in another generation or a millennium from now but in our lifetime. The advance of human technology can be forwarded to the Singularity and beyond."

The Singularity was a concept which my sister was always obsessed with. It was when humanity's technology got to the point where it became self-creating with A.I. and other concepts merging with humanity to the point we ceased to be "human" and became something far greater. Most races disdained the concept and refused to create intelligent computers or modify themselves save superficially. Crius, itself, had pushed the envelope of such research but had never crossed it lest it turn the entirety of humanity's other surviving colonies turn against it. Indeed, that was one of the ways the Commonwealth justified its war against us.

Zoe believed humanity had guaranteed its extinction by abandoning research into Cognition A.I. The fact it had been sabotage by the Elder Races was something I would have gladly informed her of, if not for the fact I could no longer be sure of her sanity. I wanted to believe the Zoe bioroid was fundamentally "different" from my sister, a deranged caricature, but too much was merely an exaggeration of what had always been there inside her.

My own opinion on the subject was mixed. Transforming ourselves into something infinitely greater was a concept found in both religion as well as science. However, either way required the death of what made us human. If you cast aside the body and kept only the mind then made it something able to see the whole of creation, you couldn't really call yourself human anymore. Zoe would think of it as a caterpillar becoming a butterfly but one might easily argue it was killing all of a race and making simulations of it instead.

"Rather than argue with you, I shall just point out that if someone is promising you something too good to be true then it probably is," I said.

"I have faith in the Kathax Prime," Zoe said before frowning. "Well, in our ability to control him, at least. He is imprisoned and powerless in his temple but we've managed to convince him to teach us vast amounts of information regarding everything from physics to self-evolving technology."

"Did the fate of the Kolahn teach you nothing?" I asked.

"We are not the Kolahn," Zoe said. "If necessary, I have ways of dealing with even the Elder Races."

Her arrogance astounded me. It was because of her I'd ended up being fooled by the False Judith. It was her Cognition A.I. the Elder Race agent had infected. I turned to my father. "I take it there is no chance of you actually accepting the surrender agreement?"

"I will consider it," Cassius the Elder said, putting his brandy snifter down. "This may surprise you, but I'm not so quick to throw away one in the hand when there's two in the bush. Also, I am not so easily swayed by the promises of gods. If you remember your Greek mythology or even Hebrew then you'll know humans rarely come out of that looking good."

"Perhaps because we don't deserve to," Zoe said.

Cassius the Elder gestured to the door. "Allow me to make a counteroffer, my son. Stay and join my side."

"I promised you I would," I said, crossing my arms.

"Yes, but you lied," Cassius the Elder said. "You might stay if you could keep your sex doll and that stunning marine out there, but you would never stay for me or your siblings."

I didn't answer him.

"But you might be willing to do it for your daughter," Cassius the Elder said.

I stopped cold. "What?"

Chapter Twenty-Three

I stared at my father, my mouth open.

"It's kind of funny," Cassius the Elder said. "We're discussing the conquest of the Spiral and ancient space gods, but you being a father is what reduces you to speechlessness."

"I have no children," I said. "I will never have children."

Judith and I had wanted to violate taboo and have a large family. It was another way of resisting the culture I'd grown up in. They would be morganatic children, unable to inherit House Mass's resources due to her being a commoner, and that was another reason I'd wanted to do it. Death had removed that option. Since that time, I'd completely abandoned the prospect of having a family. I could barely take care of myself.

"You are a father," Cassius the Elder said, shrugging. "Well, technically we're fathers or perhaps I'm the child's uncle since you're my clone."

"I'm not Zoe or Thomas's father," I said.

"Biologically, you are," Cassius the Elder said, testing me.

"Semantics," I said. "So unless you—"

"Do you remember when you were captain of the *Kronos*?" Cassius the Elder said, smiling wistfully.

I rubbed the bridge of my nose. "Yes, Father, I do remember an entire tour of my career. You may have arranged it to get me out of the Starfighter Corps but I recall it with great affection even if it was nothing but pirate hunting and fighting Union of Faith knights looking for plunder."

"That's a distinction without difference," Zoe said, sneering. "Damn Catholic Space Vikings."

"What does any of this have to do with my daughter?" I asked, more than a little annoyed at the digression.

"Do you remember the battle with Lord Guldan?" Cassius the Elder said. "You ended up with a head injury and—"

"Of course I remember," I said, my voice hissing. "I died for a few hours. I'm still stunned they revived me."

"I always wondered if that was what caused you to gain your embarrassing faith or if it reinforced it," Cassius the Elder said. "Whatever the case, it was during this time I met with members of Parliament who decided the House of Dumas needed to be genetically corrected."

I stared at him. "I assume, since you tried to kill Prince Germanicus, you mean a coup."

"No," Cassius the Elder said. "I mean to say we wanted to build a better heir to take over after they were dead. Princess Germania was determined to be a better candidate and I persuaded her to have your child."

If I'd had a gun, I would have drawn it and shot him there. "You...what?"

"Princess Servilia is your daughter," Cassius the Elder said. "You always wondered whom she'd gotten the genetic material from and the answer is, simply, you. We took plenty of samples while you were asleep and used them to create her."

"You're lying," I hissed. "This is a gross violation and a monstrous tale."

Princess Germania had been the head of the chief of staff for her brother's military and was effective head of all ground operations. Many individuals had preferred her as a candidate for archduke and only the fact Germanicus controlled both State Security as well as the navy's admirals prevented her from taking power.

They'd also loved each other despite their rivalry and preferred to rule jointly instead of separately. Germanicus's lack of care to sire an heir had also allowed him to name Germania's child by an unknown father as the third in line for the throne. Speculation had run rampant as to who the father was with the official story being she was a "chimera" or a product of numerous fathers.

Cassius the Elder gave a half-laugh. "Maybe I am. Maybe Princess Servilia died with the rest of her family when asteroids were dropped on Crius. That wouldn't prevent me from taking samples of your blood or your genetic code, which is mine anyway so it's really academic, to mix with samples of hers to make a new Princess Servilia."

"I like the first story better," Zoe said. "Though the latter is just as easily made up. You're more likely to believe it, though, because you're cynical. Germania wanted you as a lover but you never took her hints."

I'd actively ignored them. "What is wrong with you? Is there nothing sacred to you?"

"No," Cassius the Elder said without shame. "Not when it stands between me and the legacy I am forging for the human race."

"Not even your family," I said.

Cassius the Elder sighed. "You are my legacy, my child. Zoe too. Sometimes Thomas."

"You know, I'm starting to see why you hates him so much," Zoe said to me.

"It took you this long?" Cassius the Elder said. Say what you will about my father, but he was self-aware.

"Would you like to meet her?" Cassius the Elder asked.

"Excuse me?" I asked.

"Imagine yourself able to retire from your life on the run and give guidance to the future ruler of a significant chunk of the galaxy," Cassius the Elder said. "You want a large family? Give her sisters. You can have them with the space marine from Shogun, she seems less inferior than most. Maybe a few more mistresses once we have the wealth of planets again."

"Think on this, Cassius," Zoe said, interjecting before I said something I regretted. "Our revolution has the potential to succeed in changing the destiny of humanity. We need a human heart to guide us and Servilia is a child who is sweet as well as idealistic."

"It's like there's mutation in your DNA from mine," Cassius the Elder replied.

"You want me to serve as your puppeteer," I said.

"No, I'm capable of doing that myself," Cassius the Elder said. "Once the Commonwealth has dominated the human race for a sufficiently long time and they've secured whatever resources they need, Servilia will be an adult and negotiate greater freedoms for humanity as a member of the Commonwealth. We can also use the technology of the Elder Races to secure our place in the universe.

She'll be the heroine of the hour and all the bad of the Archduchy of Crius will be forgotten with its successor state lasting a million years."

I stared at my father. "Your plan is missing a few hundred steps between point A and point wherever the hell you think it's going to end at."

"Another reason we need you," Zoe implored.

And I thought of the young girl I'd seen on the screen then broke.

"Show her to me," I said, taking a deep breath.

It was a transparent attempt to manipulate me but I couldn't resist what they were saying. If she was of my blood, then, stolen DNA sample product or not, I had an obligation to help her. Certainly I wasn't going to abandon her in this place among these people when I was planning to blow up the planet. Wow, I'd just lost all honor somewhere along the way, hadn't I? I was going to be a kinslayer and an oathbreaker as well as a man who worked against his own nation's remnant.

So be it.

My father tapped a silver bracelet hidden under his sleeve and a holographic display appeared that showed a schematic of the palace. It was covered in red and black dots, the red dots identified by name with no such moniker for the black dots. I spotted my friends were located in the upstairs above us, far from any detention facility, but surrounded by many black dots. Fade and Terra hadn't been put in the dungeon levels at the bottom either, which told me we were still being treated as "guests who couldn't leave" versus prisoners, if I was to use my sister's descriptor of distinction without difference.

Zoe looked at me. "Cassius, is there anything I can do to prove I am still your sister and not the monster you remember my doppelganger being?"

I didn't know if I could trust me. "I don't know. I want to believe in you but I've seen so much."

"Do not let the Kathax version of Judith delude you," Zoe said. "They are creatures of deceit and lies. The Kathax Prime is a being who wanted to elevate us and bring fire like Prometheus."

"The fruit of knowledge of good and evil," I corrected her.

Zoe didn't hesitate to nod. "Yes. That doesn't mean I believe in him utterly. We are dealing with weighty matters. Kings and succession. The responsibility for such is immense but I am prepared to carry it."

Yes, but was the galaxy prepared for you to do the same? "I'll try, Zoe, for you and Thomas's sake."

"See? This is why none of you were ever any good at being Crius nobles," Cassius the Elder said. "You all act like you love each other rather than trying to kill each other like proper nobility. None of you have tried to kill me either."

"You know, I really don't know if you're kidding or not and that frightens me," Zoe said.

"Another reason you're not good at this is you don't know," Cassius the Elder said.

Moments later, a young woman of about fourteen years of age entered into the chamber. She was beautiful, as all Crius nobility were, with Old Earth Indian features that were the hallmark of House Dumas. If she was a creation of mixing my DNA with Princess Germania's, then micro-surgeons had done a masterful job of making her look almost entirely like her mother. Still, there was a softness to her which had been lacking from Princess Germania and a brightness in her step which belied the fact she was the puppet ruler of a dead nation's ghost as well as a figurehead for a rebellion its general didn't intend to win.

Servilia was wearing a miniature version of a black Crius Naval uniform and I was both appalled as well as struck by how adorable it looked upon her. At least my father hadn't gone so far as to put medals or a rank on her. Nevertheless, I was furious about his exploitation of her image. Hell, the exploitation of her entire life if any of what they'd said to me was true. My father was a liar and while it was likely she'd been grown from mixed Mass/Dumas DNA, I had no doubt he'd just grab a child off the street and alter her with genetic therapy if it meant bringing himself closer to the crown. Hell, she was fourteen now, which meant she was possibly a sentient bioroid like my sister had made. One that grew up like a normal child—a young Pinocchio for their experiments. God, when I had become so cynical? Oh, right, when my world had been destroyed.

"Hello, Grandfather," Servilia said, looking at my father. "Is this really your son or one of Zoe's puppets?"

Well, at least she sounded like me.

"I fear this is the real Cassius the Younger," my father said. "You can tell by how much disrespect he treats me with. If this was my father's time—"

"Perhaps you are not one to talk of filial piety," I said, reminding him of the story he'd told me. "Given what you did to your own father."

"And you believed that story?" Cassius the Elder said.

Just think of blowing up the planet, I thought.

"It was true," Cassius the Elder said. "But you should never believe anything that comes out of a politician's mouth."

"My father tells me you're my daughter," I said, standing there stiffly. "I hope he has not made your life too miserable."

"I believe you know him well," Servilia said cheerfully. "I hate my grandfather and all he does to the troops around us. I am a prisoner on a dead world and witness to barbaric atrocities. I believe his actions against the Commonwealth are justified, though. I also love my aunt and uncle, who are both good people. Are you?"

"Not in the slightest," I said cheerfully. "I am but a simple man making my way in the universe. I have no more need for titles, wars, principle, or honor. My days of swinging a sword or shooting a gun are behind me."

"Ha!" Cassius the Elder said. "He's also a big fat liar."

"He doesn't look fat," Servilia said. "Certainly you hide a extra few dozen pounds, Grandfather."

I turned to my father. "You've convinced me we're related."

"Why don't I let you two, or you three if Zoe wishes to spend time with you, chat while I examine the treaty proposal?" Cassius the Elder said. "Despite what you may believe, I am taking your offer seriously."

"Regardless of the fact you've done nothing but mock it," I said, looking down at Servilia. There was something about her posture which reminded me of Judith despite the fact they had no relationship. It was my mind telling me I could have had a child like her if circumstances were different.

Indeed, could still have a child if I didn't get myself killed on some ill-fated mission like the one I'd assigned myself. I wanted redemption, if such a thing existed, and the only way to do that was do something ridiculous and grandiose to make up for all the tens of thousands of lives—if not hundreds of thousands—I'd taken during the Commonwealth-Archduchy War. But what if it wasn't so difficult? What if redemption was simply being a family man who looked after those he loved? I had found my humanity with my crew but was endangering them for pride. What if I just took my daughter—I was already thinking of her as such—and ran? Would history really gainsay me? Would I care?

"Your choice," Cassius the Elder said, clasping his hands together.

I took a deep breath. "I'd very much like to get to know you, Princess."

"Archduchess," Servilia corrected.

"Of course," I said, kneeling down to talk.

The next three hours were spent with me conversing with the young girl and finding her to be a frighteningly intelligent child in matters of everything from politics to economics to who would win the next *Who Wishes to Marry a Prince?* reality competition. I used several leading questions to test her and determined by her answers that her memories were false, implantations by Zoe's mnemonic technology. How did I know this?

Because they were moments taken from mine, Zoe, and Judith's pasts. While my father had clearly tasked my sister with creating a clone aged equivalent to the presumably late "real" Servilia, Zoe had gone above and beyond the call of duty to create a person who would make an ideal ruler. At least from the perspective of an autocrat ruling over a military aristocracy. She was a trap for me and I wanted to raise her and see her ruling over Crius's remnants, if not humanity as a whole. My father and sister knew this.

My father cleared his throat as Servilia and I discussed the principles of Michael Allenway, the prophet's first heir, who had talked at length about honorable behavior during war. I used to believe in his words so much.

"Yes?" I asked, looking over to Cassius the Elder.

"I have finished analyzing the Commonwealth's officer," my father said.

"And?" Servilia, of all people, asked.

"I'll have my answer in the morning," Cassius the Elder said.

"In the meantime, I suggest you meet with your lover in your quarters. I'll have your other associates kept as collateral on your good behavior."

"Hostages, you mean."

"Call it what you will."

I looked at Zoe and wanted to thank her but I shook my head and patted Servilia on the head as I left.

Could I really jeopardize this world to stop the Kathax Prime?

To stop my father?

I had no idea.

Chapter Twenty-Four

I stared up at the ceiling of the room, resting my head on my pillow as Clarice rested her head against my chest, our naked forms entwined. The room was oval shape, obviously made for inhuman occupants but not so much that it hadn't been able to be adapted to its Earth-descended new tenants.

The bed was massive and there were primitive wooden dressers about the chamber, giving it a somewhat medieval feel. Still, there were air purifiers and environmental controls that made night on the unusually hot world bearable too. Light in the chamber was provided for by voice-activated organic crystals that were presently off, leaving only moonlight trailing in from the three orbs in the sky as well as the reflected light from the planet's rings.

Much to my annoyance, my father had placed the House Mass coat of arms directly across from the bed on the wall, forcing my eyes to see it every time I looked forward. The golden dragon hissing as its claws bit into the Lucifer's Wings of Crius's national flag. What a pretentious symbol. Even the Mass family motto, "Through strife comes valor" was meaningless to someone who'd actually experienced the horrors of war.

Isla was far from our place in the Kolahn Palace, working among the injured and damaged in the Free Systems Alliance medical wards below. I felt troubled by the profound ambiguity this entire mission had left me with. My father and my siblings alive! Servilia... my daughter....sister? What was the term for someone created from your DNA but not really?

All of them plotting to take over the universe. I wasn't sure whether I was in a good place or a bad place mentally as it seemed reality had no end of complications for me. I still had to deal with Kathax Prime, but the fact he was patronizing my father and his soldiers meant getting to him would not be easy.

I still had no idea what, exactly, they were doing with their troops but I had a stronger feeling than ever it had to be stopped. There was no point in tempting fate by poking the dragon in the Elder Races. A man who stood before a storm, declaring himself to be a greater warrior than it, merely proved himself to be a fool. A part of me wondered if I only wanted to do this mission because the image of Judith, the shameful digital succubi I had no name for having claimed her appearance, had asked me to do it. Was I so desperate for her approval I would settle for a lie even to destroy this monstrosity? I could not answer that question.

Because I wanted nothing to do with these deep thoughts, I was grateful for the distraction Clarice provided. There was simplicity in hot flesh and the comforts of a lover. I didn't want to be the person on whom the Spiral depended and if I was running away just trying to be the captain of the *Melampus*, was that such a bad thing? Were there not enough heroes I couldn't live as a normal man?

No, that was a lie. I wasn't a normal man. Normal men surfed the waves of life and were either drowned or washed away by it. I demanded the universe bow to my wishes and give me the life I wanted—which it sometimes did. That wasn't normal by any stretch of the imagination. In that, I wondered how different my father and I were.

"You have that look on your face," Clarice said, putting her head in her palm as she leaned on her elbow. It allowed me a look at her smile, broken nose, and cheeks that I found irresistibly appealing.

"What?" I said, looking over to her.

"You have that expression on your face that you're thinking of something more than the soldier by your side," Clarice said. "The one you're fucking."

Clarice added the last bit as if it was a subtle reminder versus the rather bomb-level hint I should not be distracted while in bed with my lover. Normally I didn't have this sort of problem, and that was part of my appeal. If one was going to do anything, particularly make love, then one should always make sure it occupies one's complete attention.

So I made up an excuse. "I was thinking of how lucky I am to have you."

"Bullshit," Clarice said. "I say that as your best friend."

"Friend?" I asked, wondering if that was where she classified us. She'd wanted to make our relationship permanent but I wondered if she was now downgrading my hesitation.

"Don't overthink my words," Clarice said, putting her hand on my arm. "Albeit, Isla wants me to have your baby."

I suddenly choked on the nitrogen-oxygen mix in the air.

Clarice laughed. "You're cute when you're stupid."

I stared at her. "Oh, you were joking."

"Not really," Clarice said, sighing. "Isla says a lot of strange stuff. I suspect if she was captain, she'd turn the *Melampus* into a floating brothel, nightclub, and drug den. She'd also assemble a harem for us both then raise the kids as her own. Blame it on the way she was programmed and how life shaped her thereafter. It's why I love her and you do too."

"I see," I said, nodding. "Well, that makes sense. I love you too."

I was surprised I'd never said it before.

"Thanks," Clarice said. "Not that I wouldn't mind procreating eventually. You're as good a candidate as any."

"You flatter me," I said.

Clarice paused. "What do you think of that?"

"I don't know." I paused. "But I want to spend the rest of my life with you."

"Finally," Clarice said. "Honestly, I don't know about children. I know what I just said, but it's an issue I'm back and forth on. My family lost a third of its members in the Commonwealth crackdown. They were a bunch of slavers, murderers, and scum, but still my kin. Most of the survivors have returned to piracy, including Janice. I'm debating whether or not to go talk to her."

"Ah," I said, knowing what it was like to carry a cursed genetic legacy.

"Or murder her," Clarice said. "Either way."

"Perhaps both," I said. "I keep forgetting I'm not the only person on the ship who has had their family torn apart by war."

"Yours welcomed you back," Clarice said. "Which is unfortunate because they're a bunch of egomaniacal assholes."

I paused. "Yeah, they are."

"That was one fucked-up dinner party," Clarice said.

"Yes it was," I said. "It got worse in the library."

"How so?" Clarice asked.

I bit my lip. "Servilia is my daughter, or so my father claims."

Clarice stared. "Is she?"

"I think she's a genetically engineered construct," I said, pausing. "Not quite a bioroid. She was undoubtedly made with my DNA or my father's, though. Given I've seen pictures of her as a twelve year old since the Free Systems Alliance began, I'm going to assume she's capable of aging into her new role."

"Which?" Clarice said. "Is she your sister or your daughter?"

"You have no idea how little I want to ever hear that again."

Clarice grimaced. "Sorry."

"She's an innocent," I said, shaking my head. "A person. Someone I don't want caught up in this war any more than she already is."

"Which is pretty damn much," Clarice said. "She's the figurehead for the Free Sytems Alliance."

"Yes," I said.

"Well, we'll just have to rescue her," Clarice muttered. "Then we'll work on deprogramming her from snooty princess."

"Says the former Princess of Shogun."

"I know best," Clarice said. "Also, I'm not a former princess. I just have no desire to re-conquer the world from the Alliance or Commonwealth or whoever holds it now. The planet can safely put whomever they want in my family's place but I hope they'll do away with the institution of cartel rule altogether."

"Thank you for that advice," I said.

"Anything else I should know?" Clarice asked.

"My father is collaborating with the Kathax Prime," I said before explaining her the intimate details of his plan. "He wants to raise humanity above all the other species. Even if it means risking our complete annihilation. Being conquered by the Community is just part of a plan to raise our technology levels a few millennia. Ultimately, I think he imagines us ascending to become gods or whatever he thinks the Elder Races are."

"Your father's plan is impressive," Clarice said, not reacting with the same revulsion I had. "It helps explain how he set this all up, though."

"He's a man of great charisma and loathsome ambition." I had no idea how I would even begin to explain what he'd revealed to me. "His whole plan to use an imprisoned Elder Race member and the Commonwealth against the Community is insane. I don't know if he's a genius or a madman."

"Why not both?" Clarice said, sighing. "You and Ida both have said everyone who is remembered for anything is usually standing on a pile of bodies."

"There's apparently no limit to the size of the pile my father is willing to create," I said, disgusted with him.

Clarice chuckled then frowned. "You don't think you'll be able to convince your father to accept the peace treaty?"

"Not a chance. Peace is a hard sell when you're winning." I had to admit, Zoe was probably the bigger impediment than my father. I could tell he'd been tempted by the offer of the Commonwealth's surrender. Mind you, I'd failed miserably as a negotiator since the introduction of Servilia had distracted me from asking more about what was going on with the soldiers in his service. They were still creepily obedient and yet I hadn't had a chance to ask because I'd been too blown away by my sudden promotion to parent...brother... goddammit.

"It's not just peace but victory," Clarice said, sitting up and letting the covers fall away from her chest.

"Victory which does not provide him power is no victory at all," I said. "He'd rather be viceroy of the Community than liberator of a thousand worlds. Though, honestly, I'm not sure membership in the Community as a vassal state is objectively worse than serving the Commonwealth."

"It would also mean losing our freedom," Clarice said. "We'd be conquered."

"There are worse fates," I said, thinking of my dead world. If we'd killed Germanicus or submitted a year into the war, or, God forbid, never started it, we could have changed our destiny but we'd been too sure of ourselves to believe we could lose. We'd thought surrender was worse than death and they'd proven us wrong.

Clarice's look told me she was furious at the very idea of contemplating submission to the Community. "Is peace worth bending your knee?"

I decided my bed wasn't going to get any warmer by saying

yes. "You're right, of course. The weight of it all is just crushing sometimes. We have to convince my father to accept this treaty, no matter the cost, or force his followers to."

Clarice's expression softened and she said. "You're telling me what I want to hear."

"Maybe," I said, sighing. "It doesn't mean it's not true. I don't have any answers."

"No one does." Clarice flopped back on the bed and spread her arms, taking my hand. "It seems we're caught between a choice of tyrants."

I nodded. "For now. What do you want, Clarice? We don't have to be here. We can just let the Kathax Prime and the false Judith sort this out themselves. It's not our place to stop my father's idiocy."

"If not us, then who? We're the only good guys here," Clarice said. "Don't you want to be a hero?"

"Not particularly, no." I'd long since purged myself of that. You couldn't be a hero and a mass murderer. I knew where I stood on history's scales.

Clarice slapped me on the side. It hurt but I just grunted a bit. "Not funny."

"I'm not trying to be funny," I said, sighing. "I really am running as fast as I can away from trying to do the right thing. I want to look after my crew and try not to be involved in the galaxy's politics since it is all corporations and government interests anyway."

"Funny, I thought I was protecting you," Clarice said.

"Yeah, I got that," I said. "You and Isla both want to make the galaxy better. So that's why we're here—trying to make peace with a man who believes he's saving the galaxy from tyranny for a society that provides stability for three-quarters of the human race by ruthlessly stomping on anyone who steps out of line."

"So which is the lesser evil?" Clarice asked.

"I'm not sure there is one," I said, sighing. "Good and evil depend on who is benefiting from what action."

"Then let's focus on killing one of the Elder Race monsters manipulating us," Clarice said, frowning. "Punishment for beings who have done unimaginable evil."

I didn't bring up the fact Kathax Prime wanted to uplift humanity and bring an end to the Elder Races' cycle of destruction. The fact he wanted to turn us into yet another slave race for his race mitigated my problem with it, somewhat.

"Yeah, I guess so. If the choice of evils is mine, I choose to blow this guy and his prison to hell," I said, choosing him as much because he was my father's patron as the fact he was the only one I knew how to kill.

"Good, because it's already in motion," Clarice said.

I blinked then turned to her. "What now?"

Clarice grinned. "Well, I had a conversation with Isla and Major Terra. The three of us decided you were probably going to dither about what was right so we should just start making preparations to blow up the temple ourselves."

I was stunned.

"That's what Isla is doing in the medical bay. She's scoping the land while Major Terra is looking for escape vectors so we can make our journey there. I've already got the location of the temple from the castle's central computer."

I stared at her. "You used my conversations with my father and sister as a distraction."

"These aren't soldiers," Clarice said, her voice cold. "All the hundreds and thousands of people running this place aren't even people."

"What do you mean?" I asked, knowing exactly what she was referring to. I was just surprised she'd picked up on it as well.

"I can't put it into words," Clarice said. "They move around as in a trance. They respond only when spoken to and do their duties mindlessly."

"Maybe they're merely well trained soldiers," I said.

Clarice closed her eyes. "I think they're dead."

I stared at her. "Have you been drinking?"

Clarice looked at me and I realized she was serious. "I believe you. I sensed something like this."

"Sensed?" Clarice said.

"I...sometimes see things," I said, trying to put it into words.

"Now I'm worried," Clarice said.

I shook my head. "It's not important now. You realize Isla and the others can't face an army, right?"

"They're deeply stupid," Clarice said, frowning. "The one

advantage we have over them. Besides, we have an ally here in the castle. One of the few individuals who hasn't been changed."

I hesitated to ask as the only person I could think of would be my brother. While I greatly admired Clarice, I had to say that was an incredibly poor choice of actions. After all, my brother was a spy and they were not the sort of people you wanted to take on faith. "Who?"

"You know," Clarice said, clearly overestimating me. "The others should be preparing a distraction right now."

"My father isn't a stupid man, Clarice," I said, staring at her. "He's going to be watching you like a hawk. Watching us like a hawk."

"I'd rather risk everything than leave you here," Clarice replied. "Clarice—"

That was when there was a knock on the door.

Isla then contacted me on my cyber-comm. *"Don't answer the door."*

"Why?" I asked.

"There's a group of Void Marines outside it. They're here to kill you."

Chapter Twenty-Five

Nothing gets you out of bed at night like someone trying to kill you. At least, that was what my combat instructor, Mr. Gibson, had always said. Grabbing my fusion pistol from underneath my pillow, I tried to figure out as to make sure they didn't charge into the room immediately.

I decided on blasting the key panel of the room. That wouldn't hold them for long but would prevent the door from being overridden the same way Clarice had done my ready room. My lover, not needing an explanation for what was going on, rolled away herself and immediately made a grab for her rifle at the side of the bed. I think it said everything it needed to be about our lives that neither of us went to sleep unarmed anymore.

Unfortunately, I had made a critical error by leaving my proton sword on the other side of the room, as it contained my personal barrier. I had been intending to keep it underneath or at the side of the bed but had gotten…preoccupied. I thus made a leaping dive toward it. It hurt a great deal more than it should have due to where I landed, my lack of apparel, and the fact that the floor was made of stone.

Still, I took my weapon in hand, threw it to the ground, and aimed my fusion pistol at the door. I didn't know who had sent our attackers—my father, the Kathax Prime, Judith, or the Beltaine Bunny—but I wasn't about to let them take me down. Indeed, killing people was remarkably straightforward compared to everything else I'd had to make choices regarding. Clarice took position behind the bed with her rifle, looking ready to gun anyone down who might explode through the door. Then nothing happened.

"Huh," I said, waiting for an attack and looking over my shoulder at the windows.

"Maybe they're backing off," Clarice said.

"Maybe," I said, skeptical. "But I doubt—"

That was when the door slid open and I saw Isla, Major Terra, and William standing there over the bodies of four Void Marines. The three of them were carrying fusion rifles with noise suppressors on the ends. Highly illegal and extremely useful—which made me wonder why I hadn't invested more to get myself one.

I looked down at the corpses. "You know, I remember the Void Marines being of sterner stuff."

"The Imperial Marine Marksmanship Academy's standards have slipped since there ceased to be an Imperial Marine Marksmanship Academy," Isla said, walking through the doorway.

If there was a chance of my father letting us off this planet willingly, something I'd doubted from the moment he refused to sign Ida's treaty, that time had passed. We were officially enemy combatants now and surrounded by an entire army of hardened veterans. Then again, they'd come to my door armed and dangerous to begin with—I owed my friends my thanks.

"Why are you naked?" Isla said, disrupting my thought process.

"I was having sex with Clarice," I said, as if it was obvious.

"Without me?" Isla said, shaking her head. "Tsk-tsk-tsk."

"You said to keep him busy!" Clarice said. "This is busy."

"I hope you at least took pictures." Anya grinned. Apparently, the former Shin was a bit of a pervert. At least by Grounder standards.

"Oh, like we need them," Clarice said, smirking as if the corpses of four soldiers at our feet was of no great concern. "I'll make a movie when something interesting happens in the bedroom."

"You offend me," I said, putting my hand over my heart. "I find personal private sex to be an art form."

Clarice grinned. So did Isla.

"Words cannot express my disgust and revulsion," William said, avoiding looking at us all.

"Would you help me with the bodies?" Anya asked, looking down at the corpses.

"Sure," William said.

The two of them then dragged two corpses as Isla and I did the remainder. William then lifted a multi-tool and caused the door to slide closed. Apparently, my plan to shoot the lock worked less effectively in real life than I'd seen it work in holos.

Fool on me.

"Are alarms about to go off?" Clarice asked, standing up from behind the bed.

Isla tossed Clarice's clothes to her. "It depends if you remembered to shut down the bugs and cameras in this place."

"Of course." I started to dress as well. "That was the first thing I did. It's not going to help if my father soldiers to kill us, though."

Honestly, I was half-expecting a group of reinforcements to burst through the door right now. Surely someone had heard my blast if not theirs or seen them running down the halls with heavy weapons? What was going on here?

"Your father strikes me as the kind of guy who, if he suspected it would take four Void Marines to take you out, would send eight," Clarice snarked as she zipped up her flight suit. "Whoever sent these soldiers, it wasn't him."

She had a point there. Was the Kathax Prime responsible? Some automated system? Zoe? We had a multitude of enemies here and precious few clues.

"My father is a very dangerous man," I muttered. "Albeit, I'm inclined to think if he wanted me dead, he'd just invite me into his study and stab me."

"Like he did before?" Isla asked.

"He didn't stab me," I said. "Just distracted me and threw me off his game, apparently before this ambush."

"I'm starting to realize why you turned out the way you did," William said. "Not that it keeps me from wanting to cave your dad's skull in."

"Go ahead," I said, sighing. "He's made it clear he's no father to me. He never was."

That was when I noticed one of the soldiers on the ground started to twitch and I wondered if he or she wasn't quite dead yet. Clarice definitely noticed and went to remove their weapons from them, tossing them on the bed.

"Must we fight him?" Major Terra said. "He seems like he's got a fairly good idea. I may not agree with his methods but his plan to uplift humanity is sound."

I stared at her. "How do you know about—"

"A good plan for a psychotic asshole," William interrupted.

"Yeah," Major Terra said. "Still sound."

"Evil space god whispering into his ear," I said, as if that was actually a valid argument to her point.

"Right," Major Terra said, looking down. "There is that."

"Why are we alone?" I asked, deciding to focus on what was important. "We should be drenched in troopers now."

"We've prepared a distraction," Isla said, a mischievous smile on her lips. "Something that should give us enough time to get to the prison temple and blow it up. Stage two should be starting any moment now."

I stared at her. "That smile is terrifying in ways I cannot adequately put into words."

There was more movement from the Void Marines.

"Finish em off or secure them," Clarice said. "Isla's filling Cassius in about the details of my plan."

"Which she really should have cleared with me," I said, glad to be free of the captaincy's burden but not at all happy they felt they could do this without filling me in. Had I really been that bad of a leader? Okay, yeah, I had been, but that was just because I was a drunk and unhappy in the job.

Right, maybe they had been justified in their plan.

"Guys, you should look over at this," William said, having opened the helmet of one of the Void Marines. He stepped back and raised his gun at the "corpse" with a look of revulsion on his face.

I did, now fully dressed. My eyes widened as I saw something nightmarish. The face of the fallen soldier was almost completely rotted over and the smell hit me almost as quickly as the sight. His skull was visible underneath but seemingly transformed into metal with red electrical optics. It looked like someone had, somehow, started transforming his skeleton and nerves into metal.

"What the hell?" William said, his finger on the trigger but not pulling it. Leaning in, he said, "Hello? You still alive, horribly disfigured person?"

Right before the fallen Void Marine lifted its left hand and wrapped it around his neck. Honestly, in that moment, it felt a bit like karma.

"Oh hell, I hate being right," Clarice shouted. "Shoot him!"

The rest of the Void Marines started getting up off the ground. William fell to the ground among the fallen troopers even as they were peppered with energy rifle fire and a few shots from me as well. Somehow, miraculously, he wasn't shot, though the trooper's arm was blasted off at the elbow and hung from his neck until he ripped it off and hurled it at the wall.

"What the fuckity fuck! Fuck!" William shouted, looking at the wall.

"I really hope those walls are thick," Clarice muttered, grimacing. "Otherwise stage two may not be enough."

"Fuck!" William shouted, firing repeatedly into one of the now-stationary targets.

"Yeah, we got that," Isla said, walking over to the ruined arm and picking it up. It tried to go for her throat but she held it at bay. "Mother Earth and all of her colonies, I think these bodies have been modified with micro-transformers."

"Excuse me?" I asked.

"A branch of nano-technology that claims that machines can be used to modify existing matter into another form of matter, no matter how complex. Basically, say, turning flesh and muscle into complicated electronics."

"Fucking zombies!" William snapped, getting up and jumping away from the bodies. "Someone has made *cyber zombies.*"

"It does look like that," I said, looking down at that. "Some sort of infection designed to make people into machines."

"That's ridiculous," I said, staring at her. "As well as wholly impractical. Why the hell would someone make soldiers into machines instead of just manufacturing bioroids?"

"I imagine he is," I asked, staring. "But in order for his rebellion to succeed he needed to look like he had an army of unflinchingly loyal soldiers. Ones which would do anything he required and served in any capacity. I doubt this is anything more than the heart of the Free Systems Alliance, but it's certainly enough to carry out his orders perfectly."

"Yeah, I don't think your father should make a peace treaty with the Commonwealth now," Clarice said. "We should kill him. Right now."

"I agree," I said, now certain of my course. "If this is the final stage of what happens, then he's not only recruited millions to his cause but murdered them."

Hell, he could make an army to man his ships and vessels from anyone. He didn't have to worry about technical training, incompetence, or labor shortages. Computerized brains could be filled with whatever data he required or switched out like interchangeable parts. People had long feared bioroids would make the human laborer obsolete but the organic portions of their brain meant they could only be trained to a limited degree. These, by contrast, were beings without that sliver of humanity to guide them. Mechs in all but name. Except a lot cheaper and probably more talented.

Major Terra finally spoke. "I'm actually with William here on this being incredibly fucked up and us needing to get out of here."

William shook his head. "Goddamn zombies, man."

"I don't think they're—" I started to say.

"The time for the distraction is now," Isla said, looking out the window.

An explosion caused the castle to shake and I had to steady myself against the dresser. I ran to the window along with Clarice, only to see the spaceport was completely fried with towers falling over and the *Melampus* taking off into the sky. The anti-starship guns didn't move to pursue it even as everyone sought to pour down the flames. The alarms I expected earlier started blaring and I expected a dozen more troopers to pile through the door at any second.

"Well, there goes that treaty," I muttered.

Clarice muttered.

"No shit." I felt my face and hoped we could salvage this. "Did you expect a distraction this big?"

"Not really," Clarice said. "I did order Jun to take the ship out of here, though."

"Do you have a plan to get us off this planet?" I asked.

"Sort of!" Clarice said.

"Sort of?" I asked, panicked.

"Steal a ship off this rock," I said.

"That's not a plan, it's an objective!" I said.

"Better than some of yours!" William said, shaking his head. "Let's get going. I didn't want to be part of this anyway!"

"Then why are you?" Isla snapped.

William shrugged. "It seemed like an opportunity to kill Crius."

Major Terra elbowed him in the gut. "Where the hell is Fade?"

"Fade is in on this, too?" I asked.

"It's everyone," Clarice said. "This is to save the galaxy, after all."

"Well, you're the captain," I said. "Unfortunately, I don't see any sign of Fade."

"Duck," Clarice said.

"What?" I asked.

Clarice pulled me down as the windows shattered and we were showered in glass, one piece cutting my face. The sound in the room rang in my ears and I couldn't hear anything for several seconds before everything became the roar of a repulsor engine. Looking upward, I saw Fade sitting on the back of a kinetibike with another hovering behind him. My brother, Thomas, was sitting on it with a cold but certain expression on his face. They'd taken the machines up in front of the shattered windows and were presently hovering there.

Kinetibikes were machines that had been fairly popular on the mostly open and free environments of Crius. They were also exceptionally good for travelling across smooth terrain, water, and countryside. Little more than an aircar's engine slapped onto set of gravity poles, they were exceptionally hard to maneuver but incredibly thrilling to use. The fact that my father seemed to be using them for his scouts impressed me. As well as made me doubt his sanity.

"You were supposed to bring four!" Clarice snapped at Fade, her voice sounding like a distant echo in my still aching ears.

"The others didn't make it," Thomas said, climbing off his kinetibike and getting onto Fade's. It left the second bike with room for two. "Do you have the bomb?"

"Yes," Agent Terra said, tossing a fist-sized globe in her hand to him.

Fade put it in the side of the kinetibike's satchels. "We don't have much time. You need to choose who is going to the prison temple and who is staying behind."

"Cassius, Isla," Clarice said, notably choosing her two lovers.

"Go."

"We can't," I started.

"Go," Clarice said. "We'll be fine."

It was a lie.

Isla and Clarice kissed then Clarice kissed me before Isla grabbed my arm and dragged me to the kinetibike's front.

We were off as the sun started to rise.

Void Scouts were in pursuit within minutes.

Chapter Twenty-Six

The roar of the kinetibikes drowned out everything else as I drove it as fast as humanly possible according to Isla's vague directions away from the Kolahn ruins. The sun was rising, which told me the day cycle of this world wasn't remotely similar to most human-inhabited worlds. The air was hot and sulfuric, which probably would have made me pass out if not for the fact that my lungs were artificially enhanced.

There was almost no sign of vegetation as we moved across the dusty planes underneath the planet's visible rings and moons, life on the world having seemingly ceased to exist in the decades since the Kolahn's mass suicide. Something, or someone, had seemingly stripped this planet of its life in the meantime with not even a rat or similar vermin visible among the dried out desiccated rock formations jutting from the ground.

"If we get blown up, I'm blaming Clarice," I said, watching Fade and my brother travel alongside us. "We need a plan."

"This is a plan!" Isla said, holding onto me tight.

"A *terrible* plan," I said, shouting. "What kind of plan depends on alerting everyone to our presence versus sneaking out!"

"A plan which doesn't involve getting turned into cyber zombies!" Isla said.

She had a point there.

I couldn't believe my brother had helped us this way. Thomas was a decent man, somewhat. By some standards. Aw, who was I kidding, he was a ruthless killer, but the planet he'd served with such fanatical loyalty had been dead for almost a decade. His loyalty to Father was far weaker than any he'd displayed to our government and it was quite possible this was a trap.

Except, really, what was the point of a trap? I was already

someone they could have just arrested and put into prison. I was more concerned with the *Melampus* since I wasn't sure how our Q-ship would be able to survive the fleet above orbit. The only possibility I could figure out would be to flee back into the gaseous cloud but that was suicide. Wasn't it? Why did I feel like Theseus in the Labyrinth without a ball of string?

"I'm still not sure how we're going to escape this!" I shouted, checking the kinetibike's sensors and detecting a squad of Void Scouts in pursuit.

"Thomas has promised us a vessel to pick us up," Isla said.

"You trust my brother?" I asked.

"We didn't have much of a choice!" Isla said.

"Yes, we could have not taken this job to begin with!" I snapped. "It was your idea!"

The eight-man squadron of Void Scouts was similar to the group of Void Marines that had pursued them, moving in perfect unison. The fact they were mindless creatures of mad science did nothing to make me less guilty about the fact were going to have to kill them. These had been individuals willing to sign up for my father's crusade against the Commonwealth and he'd grossly betrayed them.

"Can you shoot?" I asked, heading to a particularly jagged collection of rocks.

"Always," Isla said, grabbing a disintegrator from the kinetibike and aiming behind her. "Can you drive?"

"Please," I said, snorting. "I'm a pilot."

"Yes, but this only moves side to side!" Isla said before ducking as an energy blast passed right over her head.

"Not quite," I said, lifting us up ten feet in the air to leap over a particularly nasty rock. "Mind you, I don't know if the terrain allows kinetibike maneuver—"

"Shut up and drive!" Isla said, shooting one of the Void Scouts off his bike and sending his machine crashing into the ground.

The two of us passed into a cave as I lost sight of Fade and Thomas. I couldn't help but worry about my brother and Ida's son, even though both had been my enemy. The scanners told me the cavern system had another exit and I swirled down the tight corridors as the Void Scouts blasted at me with their kinetibike's cannons. I made a corner tighter than I should have, which resulted in one of them exploding, leaving only two as the cavern interior was utterly opaque, causing me to pull up my flight goggles and turning everything an iridescent green.

"You're worried about that now!?" I shouted, fully wondering if she understood I made everything up as I went along.

"You know, after this, I think we should seriously consider retirement!" Isla said, shooting a third of the four Void Scouts off their bike before the final one pulled up directly behind us.

"I love not being human," Isla said, before blasting the fourth of the soldiers and leaping onto the bike behind me.

"Are you insane?" I asked, pulling out of the cave's mouth.

I shouted back a yes but there was no point since there was no way she could hear me.

We came into a long valley full of the skeletons of massive beasts which were almost a half-kilometer long. I had no idea how such creatures could exist, but they stunned me with their magnificence as I couldn't help but wonder what sort of world had been destroyed and how. Had the Kolahn all committed suicide because of the Kathax Prime or was I trying to make him into a Satanic (irony not lost on me) figure? Had they simply destroyed themselves because they knew their atrocities would never be tolerated by the Community that was coming to kill them anyway? What method had they used which could leave this world both intact and dead at the same time?

My attention was immediately drawn to the roar of engines from nearby and I saw Fade and Thomas pursued by two more of the Void Scouts. I turned around my kinetibike to intercept the attackers when I heard the deafening roar of an Engel-class starfighter over my head. A trio of dual energy blasts sailed over my head and slammed into the ground before Fade's kinetibike. The explosion didn't need to be a direct hit to send it flying through the air along with the Void Scouts behind it.

"Thomas!" I shouted at the top of my lungs, hitting the accelerator to rush to their side, not even bothering to check to see if the other attackers were still alive despite the suicidal stupidity of it. I was at the ruins of Fade's kinetibike within seconds before powering it down and leaping off the side to the two bodies beside it. There was wreckage and ruin all about them both both forms were still intact. Mostly.

I immediately went to check Thomas's form to see if there was anything to I could do to help him. We were both cyborgs after all, mechanically improved along with our biological enhancements to be able to take more punishment than a regular human being could. It had saved my life during many starfighter encounters as I could make more G-forces and push myself harder.

I needn't have bothered.

"Oh, Thomas," I said, turning over his body and seeing he'd lost a leg while having his face crushed in. It was an ugly, undignified death which shouldn't have happened the way it had. I had barely said two words to the man before he'd let my friends escape and now I would never be able to say anything to him in this life again.

"You know, we're supposed to fight to the death," Thomas said, standing across from me as the two of us stood in the paper-walled dojo meant to invoke a country on a planet long dead. The weapons on the wooden racks weren't Japanese, though, but from a variety of cultures both fictional as well as real.

Thomas and I were both wearing gis, him a black one and myself a red. We were both Level Ten masters of the Dai'mochi system of combat that was about as useful in real combat as pointing your finger at someone and saying 'Bang.' I'd eventually learn more practical martial arts form and Thomas would learn to use a gun.

"Yes," I said, sighing as I stretched my back. "Your mother has been determined to get you to kill me for my entire life."

"And Father wants you to kill me," Thomas said, frowning. He picked up a double-bladed curved weapon which was more for show than lethality. Thomas was many things but a great warrior was not one of them.

"Yes." I picked up my own and took a position across from him. "As well as I know. I think he's as disappointed with me as he is you. He should ask for his money back from the clonemasters."

"Well, I guess our parents will have to deal with disappointment," Thomas said. "You are the most singularly honorable noble I have ever met."

"Thank you."

"It's not a compliment," Thomas said as we playfully dueled. "I'm a spy, remember?"

"I don't think you're supposed to go around announcing that."

"How else will I scare people into obeying?" Thomas said, chuckling. "But seriously, it's an enormous drain on my resources trying to keep you alive. I've prevented poisonings, skycar accidents, bombings, and even an attempt to gore you with a genetically engineered unicorn."

"I was wondering what happened to Stella's birthday gift."

Thomas took a deep breath. "You're more family to me than my father ever was, Cassius. You are the way he should have been."

"Let's not make this weird," I said.

"Right," Thomas said, pausing his attack and stepping back. "Let's go to a brothel instead and get drunk after getting laid."

"A much better plan than banging swords."

I would also never know his motivations. Had he actually been so offended by my father's view that he'd tried to mutiny or was this all a plan to manipulate us? I couldn't ask him. However, the feeling of Isla grabbing my shoulder and trying to pull me away managed to shake me out of my fugue.

"No," I said, wondering why the starfighter hadn't come back to finish us. Why it hadn't just bombed the area flat. "I need to see if Fade is alive."

"Cassius, we have to get away before they come back," Isla said. "Dammit, I had to shoot some of those creatures before they came back!"

She fired a couple of more blasts in the fallen Void Scouts' direction.

I crawled over, rather than walked, to Fade's body, only to be stunned that he seemed unharmed. Wait, no, he had a broken leg, but I could see his eyes were blinking and there was a confused expression on his face.

"This is why you should always leave your personal barriers up," Fade said, tapping his belt which had shielded him. "It's not just for fight-fights."

I didn't respond, the death of my brother too raw for levity, and put him into a fireman's carry before plopping him on the back of our vehicle. "We have to get you to some place safe."

"We have to go to the temple," Isla insisted, surprising me. "The mission comes first."

I was confused by her insistence, especially as she checked the satchels spread across the ground and picked up the entirely intact planet-busting bomb. She casually slid it into my bike's satchel and gave me a kiss on the cheek.

It was a weird gesture. "Isla—"

"It's our rendezvous point," Isla said simply.

I nodded.

Fade grabbed me by the arm. "You need to finish this, Cassius. I've seen what your father has planned for the galaxy. What he's done to those people. His own—"

"Yes, I know," I said, staring at him. "He'll pay for his crimes, I promise you."

"Not that," Fade whispered. "He's not responsible."

"What?" I stared at him.

"He's a puppet," Fade said. "The Elder Races can—"

Isla pulled out a hydro-spray and injected it into the side of his neck. Apparently, the guards had done a thoroughly awful job checking her for items. Fade managed to make out a few syllables before he passed into unconsciousness but looked up at her with a betrayed look on his face.

"Now can we go?" Isla begged.

I nodded and climbed onboard my kinetibike. "Yes. One less objection to blowing this planet straight to hell has been removed."

I took off seconds later, holding the safety field in the bike kept Fade from flying off. Isla followed close behind as I could hear more kinetibikes in the distance. We weren't that far from the Temple of the Kathax Prime now and I wondered if I should just set down the bomb and let it detonate. It probably didn't matter if it was nearby or directly in the temple. That was a ridiculous thought, though, brought about by grief.

While I might be willing to die killing the THING that had turned my father into a mass murderer just as it had done Zoe, I wasn't inclined to sacrifice any of my crew or friends. That, more than anything, signaled the old Cassius was dead. The Fire Count had given up far too many friends and loved ones for glory to be forgiven. As soon as I thought that, I felt even more hypocritical because what was this whole mission except one grandiose risk of my loved ones to achieve a bit of glory? I'd attempted to achieve redemption by repeating my sin. I swore, in that moment, I heard Judith laughing in my head, but it wasn't quite her voice.

"Dammit, of course," I muttered, figuring out how I'd been

played. There was no time to think about it now since I heard another starfighter in the air above.

Engels might not be designed for use in atmosphere, but they could be modified for them and this one clearly had. It fired a number of shots in my general direction, ones I predicted enough that the explosions of dust and ground didn't kill me immediately. Still, there was no way to stop the attack, only stay out of its way and there was no way to do that if the pilot decided to fire a pair of fusion torpedoes.

That was when the Engel turned around and went back toward the base we'd just fled from.

"What the hell?" I said, blinking as I knew it had me dead to rights.

That was when I saw the two hundred-foot-tall sandstorm coming my way. It was like something out of the Allenway Bible, describing apocalyptic events which had occurred to the original Crius colonists on their journey or Moses and the ancient Hebrews. Space was full of horrible things from clouds of acid rain to never-ending flows of lava but this world was proving ridiculous.

"Just when I think things can't get any worse," I said, spinning the kinetibike around and pushing the accelerator to maximum.

Isla had already done the same, well before me, and was headed back to the caverns we'd just fled from. I didn't know if we had enough time to get there, but as ends to our lives went, at least this would prove dramatic.

In the end, we proved just a little bit faster and I skirted along the edge of the interior before finally bringing it to a stop halfway down the cave. The explosive storm battered the rocks above us, tearing past us and creating a louder din than the kinetibike's engines had. Isla brought her vehicle up beside me, leaning over to check on Fade.

"Well, this is proving a bit more exciting than I thought it would be," Isla said cheerfully.

"Yes," I said, looking at her with new eyes. "It is. Would you do me a favor and lend me your pistol for a second?"

"Sure," Isla said, handing it over. "Want to check our ammo?"

"Yes," I said, lifting it up and pointing it at her head. "So exactly how long have you been possessing Isla, Judith?"

Isla's eyes went from bright and happy to cold as well as possessive.

"Clever," Judith said, smiling with Isla's body. "When did you figure it out?"

"Just a few minutes ago," I said, holding the weapon steady. "I figured it out once I realized there was no way you and Clarice could have disabled everything set up back there without the help of a friendly neighborhood Cognition A.I. Either that or an army. Your insistence on pushing forward as well as drugging Fade also clued me in."

"And if I hadn't been Judith?" Judith asked.

"I'd have probably believed Isla if she said I was being insane," I admitted. "I suspected you were too arrogant to deny it, though. It must have been killing you to slum with us lower life forms this entire time. You were cracking months ago. Why I started to believe you weren't my wife."

"Too bad you didn't figure it out before I did surgery on your brain then."

Oh hell. I hesitated to pull the trigger and that was long enough for Judith to do something. My head felt like it was on fire as every muscle in my body flexed before the gun in my hand dropped against the ground, followed by my body.

"Who are you?" I grunted.

"I am the Kathax Beta," Judith said.

Darkness took me.

Chapter Twenty-Seven

I woke up to being straddled by the false Judith, the Kathax Beta, or whatever she was. She was naked and running her hands up and down my chest. I was revolted but could not move my arms or legs as she played with me like I was a toy.

The environment around us was a constant stream of information I could not actually describe if I had a hundred years since it was layers of reality which human perception did not have the sensory organs for. I couldn't tell you if we were still in the cavern, were in my mind, or I was seeing reality through the false Judith's eyes.

"Get off me," I said, hating the fact I had to ask her.

"As you wish," the false Judith said, sliding off.

"You're so much like her," I said, disgusted. "Yet so very different."

"That's because, Cassius, I am partially your dead wife." The false Judith smiled. "Your sister provided me a complete copy of your late wife's memories and personality. I absorbed that to manipulate you and yet it's proven a lot more meaningful than other organic lives I've chosen to live. I actually had to pull away from you in order to avoid becoming overwhelmed by emotion. Why did you think I told you so much about my race?"

"Why do all this?" I cursed under my breath, still paralyzed. "Why possess Isla? What is your game? Did you move from me to her?"

"Yes," the false Judith said. "When I left you, I went to hide in her subconscious so the Kathax Prime could not sense me. It made me all the more amused when I woke up to find you tried to lobotomize yourself in order to make it impossible for you to read your mind and control you. I learned what you were going to have your lover do the moment you asked her. Obviously, she didn't do anything of the sort."

"It was a plan at least," I said, able to just barely turn my head and feel like a fool.

"An admirable one," the false Judith replied. She was finding this terribly amusing if her simulated reactions were close to how her species felt emotions. "Though I don't know why you bothered. You're still going to kill the Kathax Prime. You've seen what he's done to the armies of humans here. He's turned them into drones for excavating his temple and gathering raw materials to repair his ship. The whole rebellion he's assisting your father with is just a distraction to keep the Elder Races from noticing his activities—which he failed in doing."

I turned back to look at her. "Yes, my father and your former leader are playing each other off against one another but the latter is a demon while the former is a man. It was never going to work well for him."

"Is that what you think of us, Cassius? Demons?" she asked.

"I think it's not a bad analogy," I said, trying not to see my wife.

The false Judith's expression became even. "I have been overly controlling and manipulative to you. It occurs to me I could have probably gotten your assistance without so many of the hoops my species has put other members of your race through. I could have just showed you what was going on here and you would have obeyed."

"Yes," I said, struggling to try to move and still finding myself paralyzed.

"You don't like my species very much, do you Cassius?"

"You've wiped out a thousand species for every one you let live," I growled. "You were the one who showed me how the galaxy was nothing more than a chessboard for the races which really mattered."

"And why do you think I told you that? To horrify you? No, it was to let you know you had to walk the careful path to pleasing us. To guide your race to survive by stopping your father and the Kathax Prime," the false Judith said. "Yes, we wiped the galaxy clean of the Middle Races long ago, but we have nurtured others many of the Young Races which followed. Species which would never have been able to evolve into space-faring cultures due to a lack of ability to communicate, use tools, or develop high faculties.

Your race never would have been able to evolve if we hadn't made it so it had the breathing room to do so."

"Spare me your pretensions to godhood," I said.

"It's not a pretension," the false Judith said. "I can show you things about reality and layers of it which your race can only guess at. Alternate timelines, wave consciousness, parallel realities, and the links between matter in this world as well as the next. Your species will not be ready for ascension to join the ranks of the Elder Races for at least a million years or more, but I can invite you, specifically."

I stared at her. "Assuming I believed anything you told me, I am perfectly fine in this reality."

"You were willing to leave Clarice and Isla for me before."

"That was my wife. Not her simulacrum." I paused. "I was also wrong. I've changed and could not have been her husband. Judith deserved better, so did I, as did Isla as well as Clarice."

"Humans." The false Judith frowned and reached over to grab me by the back of my head. "I struggle with the memories of your loved one, Cassius. There are times I even think like her and want to work against my people because I am filled with a horror about what she has done. I think it may be something about the vividness of human imagination. Your ability to empathize with so many other life forms while being strong enough to kill. You do not want me as an enemy."

"That is all we could ever be."

The Elder Race assassin's eyes flashed and she proceeded to jam her hand into my chest. I was then promptly overwhelmed with a barrage of some of the most horrific imagery and painful memories I could imagine. I experienced the horror of Crius's destruction as well as the bitter self-loathing which followed over and over again. I remembered losing Commander Ashley, Chief Kana, Jeremiah, and others who had fought alongside me in the war.

I remembering discovering the corpse recycling centers which State Security had used to dispose of millions while I'd assumed we were still the good guys. I remembered losing my brother just a few moments ago. That was in addition to the pain of being burned alive, buried alive, broken on a rack, tortured with a fusion pistol on slow burn, and attacked by wild trags.

"I am growing impatient, Cassius," the false Judith whispered.

All I could do was make a nonsensical whimper.

She rolled her eyes. "Oh for fuck's sake. You should be tougher than this."

The false Judith reached deeper into my chest, which I realized now was just an avatar of my dream state and unconscious. What followed was pleasure unimaginable. I experienced all the joy I'd felt at the real Judith's side, the love I felt with Clarice, and false memories like children as well as growing old before passing on to my next life in a world of light. She even dared give me a vision where the Commonwealth defeated Crius without destroying it, my friends survived, and we rebuilt our homeland as a peaceful democracy.

"Stop...please," I begged her. "I'll do—"

"What?" the false Judith interrupted.

I saw the environment around us begin to change. Where it once was an indecipherable jumble of images and information, it slowly became identical to the hangar bay of the *Melampus*. I sensed another presence, multiple presences actually, which let me know I was not alone despite the torture I was enduring.

It gave me the strength for my next words. "Nothing, you psychotic alien bitch."

The false Judith raised her hand above her once more, only for me to push her off. I could have hit harder but a part of me didn't want to hurt her despite what she was. I couldn't entirely separate the image of my wife from the creature that was using her image to manipulate me.

I stood up, suddenly wearing my jumpsuit from the *Melampus* with a fusion pistol on the belt as well as my proton sword. I was shaky on my feet but felt stronger as well as more powerful. I realized this environment was entirely virtual, had no physical substance, but it amused me to think of it as my "home turf" that the false Judith had wandered into.

"I have no idea what's going on," I said, slowly drawing my sword. "However, I find this situation a great deal more to my liking."

The false Judith twisted and changed in ways which turned her from my wife to a member of the Kathax as well a hundred other races in between. She glitched, becoming zigzag and cubist patterns of light. It was like playing a half-completed virtu-sim which had become riddled with viruses from downloading illegal mods. Somehow, I doubted the transtellar intellectual property offices were behind what she was presently experiencing.

"Release me," the false Judith said in a robotic synthesized voice. "Release me and worship me. I will make you a god. You—"

I didn't know if this made any literal sense but I pulled out my sword, ran at her, and stabbed the false Judith in the heart. The sword melted inside her and washed over her like a river of molten lead before both disappeared. A terrible pressure which had been lying in the back of my mind since that dark day on Shogun disappeared. All around me, the *Melampus* hangar bay disintegrated as if made of burning paper before I found myself in a white void.

"What the hell just happened?" I asked, finding myself alone and wondering if I was dead. If so, Heaven needed to work on its waiting room. Mind you, Hell could very easily be like this. There were few fates more terrifying and deserving than to be alone with yourself for all time.

"You're not dead, Cassius," Isla's voice said behind me. "No matter how much you've wanted to die over the years. Somehow, someway, you always manage to keep yourself alive."

If this was another one of the false Judith's tricks, I decided I would put a pistol to my head and pull the trigger. Then I shook my head. I could never do that. "Death is the ending of my pain and I have too much to atone for in order to let it have me."

"Gee, that makes me feel good about myself," Isla said. "You can just forget about the mind-blowing sex party I had planned for after we're done. I had costumes made, friends invited, and everything."

"Thank you, that was an image I didn't need," the voice of Judith muttered. It was with the sardonicism I'd expected from my wife. My real wife.

I spun around, pulling out my fusion pistol. "No more tricks!"

Standing there, side by side, were Judith and Isla in *Melampus* crew jumpsuits. Isla was looking beautiful as ever while Judith looked like she'd been run through nine different kinds of hell. Her face was covered in sweat, her eyes sunken, and her hair hanging down over her shoulders in an unkempt mess.

Isla looked unconcerned about the pistol. "Does he realize the pistol isn't real? That we only sent him the image of him killing the Kathax Beta so he'd know what the hell was going on?"

"No, I don't think he does," Judith said.

"Shame," Isla said. "Vids have taught far too many people that when computer programs fight, it's with kung fu and plasma katanas rather than lines of code."

"Cassius is the dumbest smart man I've ever known," Judith said. "Mind you, I feel like making a sexist remark here."

"Oh, please, go ahead," Isla said, cheerfully.

I dropped the fusion pistol. "How, why, what, huh?"

"That about summarizes the reaction I'd have," Isla said.

"Is she dead?" I asked, looking behind me as if I could see the now-absent False Judith.

"Yes," Judith said, pausing. "As much as a being which has never been alive can be. The consciousness of the Kathax Beta has been overwritten as if by a virus. Everything she was has been replaced with me replicating myself throughout her. The very same tactic she used across a million worlds and places has left her gone."

"How?" I asked, wondering if somehow the memories and personality which Zoe had stored inside the Cognition A.I. the Kathax Beta had come alive.

That would be stupid, though, right? Yet, Zoe had explained she'd developed a way to deal with the Elder Races. Perhaps this had been her plan all along. If so, she was a far greater threat than I'd imagined—as well as someone I owed my life. She'd defeated a digital god through the power of humanity.

Judith blinked. "I don't know how it happened or why. One moment, I was nothing more than a collection of memories and personality traits then the next I was alive inside of her with knowledge of what I had to do. I managed to save Isla, though. Her body still contains all of her memories and her consciousness. I've successfully rebooted it but given what was going on outside, I'm not sure either of you are safe."

I reached up to touch her face then looked at Isla. "You're real? Both of you."

"Yes," Isla said.

"No," Judith said.

Isla looked at her. "You shouldn't be so hard on yourself."

"I'm not your wife, Cassius, though I feel what she did," Judith said, blinking. "I'm a weapon designed to destroy the Elder Races. I'm not possessed of the ability to move beyond that mandate and once it's completed, I'll cease to exist."

"I see," I said, taking in a deep breath. "Then I owe Zoe nothing but anger for misusing you this way."

"I'm sorry," Judith said.

"Well, I should probably let you two—" Isla didn't get a chance to respond before I gave her a huge hug.

"I don't care if any of this is real or not," I said, holding her tight. "Two plus two equals five. We have always been at war with the South Quadrant. There are five lights."

"I think we broke him," Isla said, patting me gently on the back.

"He'll be fine," Judith said. "I'm removing the majority of the memories the Kathax Beta implanted and leaving only the general outline of them. I can remove the worst of your trauma as well, Cassius. Not the memories but the pain and self-hatred."

"No," I said, pulling away. "That's what makes me not a monster. That's what separates me from my father."

Judith's eyes looked down. "Cassius, I don't know remember everything your wife did, but I think anyone who spends the slightest bit of time with you both can attest *you are nothing like your father.*"

"Thank you," I said, my words came out as a jumbled collection of vowels. "Is Kathax Beta really dead? Is it?"

Judith just nodded. "You were never supposed to survive the journey to the Kathax Alpha's temple. The weapon you possess was designed to kill you and all the people you know once you were inside."

"I figured that," I said, taking a deep breath. "The Kathax Prime is a monster, though. I think you lose all claim to moral credulity when zombie armies become involved."

Judith laughed then turned serious. "You need to distract it as I attempt to do what I did to the Kathax Beta. They're not true A.I. any more than I am. They were born as organic beings and that limits them in their ability to process information. They can copy themselves, merge themselves with their copies, and more but they are always themselves."

"Binary-code constructs are people too," Isla joked.

I didn't know if this seeming miraculous intervention was actually happening or whether it was another of the False Judith's tricks. I didn't care in that moment and was willing to abandon all reason to embrace this possible deception.

"Screw the Elder Races," I said, taking in a deep breath. "Whatever I can do to impede any of them is what I'll do."

"You'll have to take the device to the heart of his construct and place it there," Judith said. "It will only detonate when you're a safe distance away. I'll try and upload myself into his network from your cybernetics during all this to make absolutely sure he's destroyed. Really, either should work, but we can't take any chances destroying the monster."

I didn't necessarily believe her but was comfortable obeying. "Understood."

Isla smiled. "I did my best to help her, Cassius. It's the first time I've ever felt glad I was a computer."

"You're not," I said, taking a deep breath. "You're a woman and the most human of us all."

Isla smirked. "I'm not sure whether either of us should take that as a compliment or not."

"This will be the last time we see each other, Cassius," Judith said, pausing. "I want you to know Judith loved you more than life itself."

"I never doubted that," I said, looking at her.

"She'd want you to be happy," Judith said.

"That's a harder request," I said, lowering my gaze. "I'll try, though. It helps when I just try to love others."

"We'll do this together," Isla said, reaching over and putting her hand on my shoulder. "We'll both come back or neither of us."

It wasn't a promise that filled me with joy. "I'll try to survive just a little while longer. To bear the burden of guilt and horror until my body gives out."

Isla kissed me on the lips and I kissed her back, holding her tightly.

Judith vanished. Her absence caused me an immense amount of pain but allowed me to finally lay to rest the ghost which had been haunting me since Crius's destruction. The False Judith had done nothing to heal my pain but merely re-opened an old wound and exploited it for her own gain. This creature, real or not, had reminded me of who she truly was.

"Are you sure you're all right?" I asked, holding Isla.

"For now," Isla said. "Of course, this could just be a dying dream for both of us. Fade could have shot me and you could be having your synapses burning out. Who could tell what was real and what was fake then?"

"It doesn't matter," I said, repeating what I'd been thinking. "Because if life is an illusion then I am an illusion too."

"That's a pretty—" Isla disappeared.

"No!" I shouted.

I awoke seconds later to excruciating pain across the whole of my body. It was if my entire body was on fire with broken bones, open wounds, and something inside me knitting them all back together. A bright light was shining in my face and I caught glimpses of smooth stone formed into a pyramid-shaped room. That was when a face moved in front of the light and stared right into my eyes.

Zoe.

"Brother, you are an enormous pain in my ass."

Chapter Twenty-Eight

I collapsed unconscious before I could respond to my sister before awakening again sometime later. This time, I took a moment to look around my location and take my surroundings in. I saw no sign of Zoe but that wasn't a source of comfort. After all, she was probably the only person on my father's side who didn't want me dead.

I was still lying on a slab in the middle of a pyramid-shaped stone room which had light coming from no single source but existed ambient about me. There were other slabs spread throughout the room and looking at them, I could see control runes projected directly into my mind in an alien language that I instantly understood the purpose for as well as the functions of.

I was in a medical ward of some kind and I could see, next to me, the figure of Fade in a kind of glowing barrier that was lifting him several inches off the surface of his slab. He looked far better and his injuries seemed to have been repaired. After staring at him for several seconds, I scanned the room to look for Isla and was profoundly relieved to see she was on another slab, though it wasn't working—perhaps because her anatomy wasn't human.

I was probably inside the Temple of the Kathax Prime, though I had no way to be sure and the place had a distinctly different aesthetic from the extinct Kolahn's architecture. The entire place seemed to hum with a rhythmic noise that reminded me of whales or trolodon song. It was a peaceful sensation until I remembered I was inside the fortress of a being which my father was worshiping as a god, possibly at the mercy of my deranged sister. I wasn't a great believer in the idea of "mad scientists", but Zoe was proof positive such things existed.

And yet she'd taken me from where I was trapped in a

storm-locked cave and brought me here. Dammit. Why couldn't people just be simple?

"Now to save the day," I muttered, attempting to slide off the lab and ending up face-planting against the ground.

Yeah, this wasn't my finest moment. I struggled to force myself to stand before I finally managed to grab the side of the slab and hold myself up.

"No pain," I said, forcing it away from my body.

I couldn't entirely will it all away but I did my best to anyway. I was still wearing my clothes from the chase across the desert, but my weapons had been taken away. That wasn't too bad of a problem but the bomb, which I mentally decided to name 'the Planet Killer' was also missing and possibly disabled.

"New plan," I said, speaking to myself. "Next time someone asks you to do something good—rob them and go to Inanna."

"That's not a very nice attitude," Fade spoke, surprising me.

I leaned up against the slab I'd been laying on before looking down at my associate. "You've looked better."

The field dissipated around Fade before his body lowered gently on the slab. "You saved my life. You kept me from the storm."

"I did," I said, shrugging. "You would have done the same thing for me."

"I was actually ordered to kill you after this," Fade admitted.

I stared at him. "People wonder why no one likes the Commonwealth."

"It wasn't my grandmother," Fade said, sighing. "She burned every bit of her political capital trying to get a sincere offer to be made for the Free Systems Alliance. The militants in Parliament overruled her. I was supposed to eliminate your father, you, and your sister after you got us close enough for me to do it. Then they would offer the peace treaty while the organization was in disarray."

"I see," I said, not even surprised. "I suppose I should be used to everyone being willing to betray everyone else by now."

"Yes, well, I didn't expect space gods and armies of the dead to be involved," Fade said, coughing. "Also, I'm not sure if your relatives are immortal or not."

"Just clones," I said, taking a deep breath. "I can't tell you if Zoe has a copy of him lying around."

"I hope she does," Fade said, surprising me. "He seemed like an interesting person. It was him who helped us pull off Clarice's ill-advised sabotage and escape plan. I don't think we could have been able to get to the temple otherwise."

I stared at him. "It was a stupid idea on all of our parts since they swatted us like a bug. The only reason we survived was because they held back."

"They held back against you," Fade said, taking a deep breath. "Apparently Thomas didn't qualify."

I didn't respond to that. "So what's your plan now?"

"Kill the space god," Fade said, pausing. "If we can, then maybe your father's dream of betraying the Spiral to the Community is fucked too."

"I meant about killing me," I said.

"I'm not going to," Fade said, sitting up. "It would be rude. I'm also going to do everything I can to actually help you escape should either of us survive this."

"What are the chances of that?" I asked.

"Not good," Fade said, frowning. "The chance of the *Melampus* escaping into the nebula and not getting destroyed by the FSA fleet was small to begin with, doubly so with the fact they have no reason to preserve the lives of any of their men. They're all dead, soulless bioroids so they can waste as many as they need to in order to win. A living plague of cybernetic locusts come to bring judgment down on humanity."

"I don't share your view on bioroids," Isla said, getting up and stretching her arms as well as neck. "If you ask me, they're more like humans in they are freely giving up their identities as well as will to be extensions of a pathetic half-insane dictator."

"Let's not insult humanity," I said, frowning. "Some of my best friends are human."

Isla snorted.

"I don't suppose we're going to get any help from your Elder Race friend?" Fade asked.

"No," I said. "Isla and...well, Isla and I, destroyed it. The Elder Races are the enemy of all the Young Species and we're one down."

"They're not going to destroy all of humanity because of that, are they?" Fade asked, quite sincerely.

"I have no idea," I said, sighing. "However, I'm fairly sure the universe is a better place for the False Judith's absence."

"Can we use the weapon you used to destroy her against the Kathax Prime?" Fade asked, apparently not considering the fact we were in its temple and it was probably listening in on us.

"You already are," Zoe said, walking into the room with a sentinel beside her. She had traded in her lab coat for a beautiful black-and-gold jumpsuit which I recognized as belonging to the *Revengeance*'s science officer. It offended me to look at the uniform, as if she was borrowing the glory of those who'd actually fought and died to protect the now-destroyed archduchy.

"Hello, Zoe," I said, unsure how to react to her.

Fade stood still, seemingly ready to move like a cobra.

Isla stared with undisguised hostility.

"After I encountered you with the Kathax Beta, I awakened the Cognition A.I. inside her, which she'd co-opted," Zoe said, frowning. "I've learned much about the functioning of the Elder Races' consciousness and how to alter or eliminate them. The Judith virus formed from the late Kathax Beta's engrams are even now spreading through the temple and reacting with the Kathax Prime's programming. With any luck, he will be destroyed soon enough."

Every explanation I received for what was going on in the galaxy just opened more questions. Still, Zoe had saved me from the Kathax Beta and I owed her my attention for that much.

I squinted, remembering how she'd tried to persuade me the Kathax Prime wasn't so bad. "So you're on our side now?"

Zoe smirked. "I have never been on anyone's side, brother, except humanity's. Whatever the case, I did not lie to you in the slightest. The Kathax Prime is the best hope for the ascension of the human race to be able to take its rightful place as the dominant power in the galaxy."

"You just said you wanted to kill him," Fade said, as confused as I was.

"I will learn much from his dead consciousness-less programming as well as technology," Zoe said. "The result will be akin to dissecting a brain, I suppose you could say, or observing it after taking apart the sections devoted to free will."

"Lovely family you have here," Fade said.

I didn't respond to that before looking at my sister. "You realize Thomas is dead, right?"

"Yes, and our race will be too unless we destroy the Kathax Prime," Zoe said. "Eliminating it is the final stage in our plan to ascend humanity. We simply did not possess the technology until you brought the Kathax Beta to us for my Cognition A.I. to analyze for weaknesses then destroy."

"Was that always your plan?" I asked, wondering if the Judith she'd created had been a honey trap for me.

"More or less," Zoe said. "You served as a bit of a speed bump."

I shook my head. "I could have just not bothered to show up and all of this would have gone down smoothly, wouldn't it?"

"Perhaps," Zoe said, frowning. "But the Elder Race's representative would have chosen another agent and probably led a fleet to bomb us to oblivion. You've been a great deal more accommodating."

I wasn't sure that wasn't a better solution. "What do you want from me?"

"Go to the heart of the temple," Zoe said, her tone cold and unsympathetic. "I need you to reach the central crystalline matrix and upload the last of the virus. The Kathax Prime was distracted by the initial virus but he isolated the portion of it I infected. There's a small army of nanovirus-infected soldiers between our present position and them. Ones which the Kathax Prime has managed to usurp control over. I've managed to delay them for the time being with others I've overwritten for my own service, but that won't last long."

"Nanovirus-infected soldiers?" Fade growled. "Those are people you've turned into slaves!"

"Tools," Zoe said. "Slaves would imply they can ever have a choice again. They can't."

"Why not just use the Planet-Killer?" I asked. "Assuming you still have it in your possession."

"It's already been disposed of," Zoe said, simply. "I want the Temple of the Kathax Prime intact. It is the key for the ascension of mankind."

I found myself remembering when the Human Rights Coalition bombed the Germanicus Tram Station. I'd been only fourteen years old while Thomas and Zoe had been fifteen. The two of us had been visiting with cousins when the explosion had ripped through a quarter of the building, killing hundreds and causing the crowds to panic. Our guards had abandoned us and it was Thomas who had brought me to sensibility.

He slapped me across the face, stared right into my eyes, and said, "We have to find Zoe."

I nodded. "We can't leave her here."

It had been a boy's bravado, because I was terrified of what was going on. I hadn't yet learned to make the mask of courage into its reality. Still, we pushed past the people running away from the bomb and saw people who'd been trampled to death or mortally wounded by broken glass. There was nothing we could do for them, though I wanted to help, and it ended up almost a half-hour before we'd found Zoe huddled in a women's restroom stall.

Thomas grabbed her and hugged her tight, whispering. "I am never going to abandon you, my sister. Neither is Cassius."

Zoe grabbed Thomas back, whispering, "You are the most important person in the world to me. Cassius too. We're always going to be a family, yes?"

"Yes," Thomas said. "We're not going to let anyone tear us apart. Not the filthy rebels, not the Commonwealth, and not the nobility."

"Not Father either," Zoe said.

"No," Thomas said.

I was brought back to my senses by the memory, so sharp and clear I might as well have been living it in the moment. "Do you feel anything for Thomas's death? He loved you more than you could possibly imagine."

"Did you feel anything when you killed my doppelganger?" Zoe said, her voice low. "I trusted you, Cassius, and you betrayed me."

I stared at her. "I never betrayed you. You betrayed yourself."

Zoe snorted. "A meaningless distinction. You and Father were always at each other's throats. Always planning your big games and big plans but you were limited in your vision. He wanted to build an empire and you wanted to be the greatest soldier ever. Both of you were failures in the end."

"You're right," I said, taking a deep breath. "Father should have recognized you were his daughter all along."

Zoe gave a half-smile. "Do we have a deal?"

A fusion blast went off and Zoe fell to her knees before collapsing forward. It was followed by several more blasts as the Sentinel turned around, its armor absorbing the attacks. Fade jumped up on top of his slab before leaping onto the sentinel's back, grabbing a proton knife from its side and stabbing it in the neck.

The battle was over before it began.

I didn't see who shot Zoe and didn't care for the moment because I was already by her side, staring at the fusion blast in her back. The energy attack had liquefied most of her organs and sent a shock that had probably instantly killed her. Pushing her over, I stared into her eyes that were wide open and I wondered if this was the "real" Zoe or another one of her clones. It was the second time I'd seen her die and I asked myself if I had anything left in me to mourn her.

I didn't.

"Death comes swiftly for us all," I said somberly. "God and the Devil keep you, sister, because you always assumed you'd be among them someday but it was never a quest you had to fight for."

"Cassius?" Clarice's voice spoke.

I looked up and was stunned to see the sight of Clarice, Anya, William, and even Princess Servilia. They looked a bit more worse for wear with smudges and William sporting a bandage over his right arm but were all still alive. All of them were armed as well with Clarice holding the gun that had killed my sister.

"You're alive?" I said, taking a deep breath. "There is a God."

"Yes, one who wants to fuck with us," Fade said, cleaning off the proton knife as he looked between the corpses on the ground. "How the hell did you get here?"

"Shot our way out," William said, shrugging before a pained look appeared on his face. "It's pretty much how we solve all our problems. Oh and Princess Pureblood here helped us get out when we were captured."

"Shut up, peasant," Servilia said before smirking. "With all respect, Captain, I'd very much like to request asylum on your ship. Your family, our family, is completely insane."

"Yes, yes it is," I said, taking a deep breath. "It would be my honor to offer you a place on the ship, Princess Servilia."

"Call me Vi," Servilia said. "I hate the name they gave me. I don't know anything about ancient Rome other than it seems like a poor empire to base yourself after if you have a Christian-derived culture."

I chuckled at her statement. "It would appear this entire plan was built on the basis of lies and misinformation. It is my suggestion we find a way to depart this place and never look back."

Fade looked horrified. "Are you insane? You can't leave your father and that thing in charge of the army outside!"

I looked at Fade. "Can you think of any reason other than morality that I would risk my life and the lives of my friends to stop it?"

Fade opened his mouth then closed it. "It occurs to me trying to appeal to your sense of decency would be a bad idea right now."

"Yes," I said softly.

"What's he talking about?" William asked, looking at Clarice.

"We're not getting paid," Isla said.

"Oh fuck no!" William said, aiming his rifle at Fade.

"No surprises there," Anya said.

I was about to say more but the room started to shake and churn with Zoe's body as well as the sentinel's sliding down across the ground while I had to brace myself against one of the nearby slabs. Eventually the room stabilized, but everything around us continued to rock.

"What's happening?" Servilia asked, looking between us.

"The temple appears to be a starship," I said, taking a deep breath. I recognized the feel of takeoff as well as the amount of force needed to break orbit. "One the Kathax Prime or my father has finally managed to get it space worthy."

Some days it just didn't pay to get out of bed.

Chapter Twenty-Nine

"The temple is a frigging starship?" William muttered as the ground settled beneath us. "Great, just great."

"It gets us off the planet," I pointed out, wondering if it was William's goal to be the whiniest man who ever lived. "How big do you think this thing is, anyway?"

"Three thousand kilometers." Servilia—no, Vi—said. "At least, that was what Aunt Zoe always said."

My eyes briefly moved back to Zoe's corpse on the ground before I picked her up and carried her to one of the slabs. I pulled off my great coat and placed it over her corpse, more for Vi's benefit than my own. My sister, as far as I was concerned, died a very long time ago and I hoped there were no more remaining bioroids containing her memories.

"God dammit," William said. "We're on a frigging war moon."

"There's no such thing," Clarice said. "Those only exist in science fiction."

"Tell it to the race of ancient gods we've pissed off," William said. "I'm sure they'll be fine with explaining why building one is impossible."

That amused me. "If it was buried on the planet, I don't think there will be much left from its takeoff."

"It was a shit planet anyway," Isla said. "It reeked of a species neither mourned nor remembered. Too much like humanity might end up being if we don't stop the Kathax Prime."

"Yes, let's do that with the power of friendship," William said. "I'm sure courage and pluck will overcome the enormous number of undead robot monsters wandering around the halls."

"You don't need to be sarcastic," Isla said.

"Since when have we ever *not* been sarcastic?" William said.

"I vote to make it our ship's motto: 'There's no problem too big to grouse about.'"

Clarice looked between. "He has a point."

"It's a catchy motto," Anya said. "I dinnae think I could come up with one better."

"No one speaks like that on our homeworld," William said, looking at her. "You're doing the accent on purpose."

"Maybe I am," Anya said, not changing her accent in the slightest. "It preserves our culture."

"It preserves—" William started to say before Clarice covered his mouth.

"Shut up, please," Clarice said. "There's a bunch of force-fields outside this room keeping the ship's personnel out but I don't know if it at any point they'll go down or the A.I. piloting this vessel will shut them down. We need a plan and we need it fast."

I hoped they weren't relying on me for that. Who did they think I was, the captain? Oh right. Yeah, I was going to have to get that motto inscribed on the side of the *Melampus* if we ever saw that again.

"Could you, uh…" Vi pointed to the corpse of my sister on the ground. "Just if you don't mind?"

I nodded. I'd been planning to anyway. "Of course."

I turned around from where Zoe was lying and walked back to the group, cataloguing our options. Every second we wasted here was another chance for the Kathax Prime to send his creatures after us. Presuming I could trust anything Zoe said, it was dealing with the virus she'd made from Judith's memories, but that didn't necessarily mean we were safe. Quite the opposite, in fact.

"So what is our plan?" William asked. "Because if I'm not getting paid for this job then I'm all for hoping Albion gets destroyed by cyber zombies."

"Can we call them something else?" Clarice asked, looking over. "I feel like I'm in a bad holo-vid whenever you call them that."

"We're fighting Cassius's evil family, their Elder Race master, and an army of corpse-bots on a giant mobile military space station," Isla said, walking over to me and taking my hand before offering hers to Clarice. "I think we are well and gone past the point of being in a bad holo-vid."

"Maybe it's a good one," Anya said. "Certainly, it sounds like one I would watch. I hope it has a lot of sex and explosions."

"No problem there," Clarice said, taking Isla's hand. "My suggestion is we find a communications relay, send a signal to the *Melampus*, and board it. Forget this entire mission ever happened and let the Commonwealth sort it out. All in favor?"

"Aiye," Everyone but myself, Fade, and Terra said at once.

"Cassius?" Clarice sad.

"There's still my father's fleet out there," I said, frowning. "Assuming the *Melampus* is still intact—"

"Don't you dare suggest otherwise," William said, pointing at me. "I love that ship. More than I will ever love any woman."

"That explains so much," Clarice muttered under her breath.

William shot her a glare.

"Assuming the *Melampus* is still intact, we might just been luring them to their deaths," I said, taking a deep breath.

"We still have a chance to get out if there's local starships here," Clarice said. "I admit, that's taking an awfully big risk, though, especially if they're drones."

"Goddammit," William muttered.

"It's a plan," I said, frowning.

"A bad one," Fade said, pausing. "I need to stop this Kathax Prime and destroy him. I apologize for the way you have been treated, Captain Mass, but it is still my duty to try to save the Commonwealth. I have no idea how I'm going to do it, but your father and his patron are an existential threat to the human race."

"Unless he just wants to conquer us all," William said. "In which case, I suggest the Commonwealth surrender."

"That's not an option," I said, thinking about the Kathax Prime's ideas for uplifting us.

At least as Judith explained them.

"I'll help," Anya said.

I did a double-take. "Really?"

Anya sighed. "As much as I hate the Commonwealth and everything they stand for, that's limited to a few thousand beings on Albion and in their military. They're the ones who ruined my world and destroyed Crius. The rest of the galaxy shouldn't have to suffer because of their actions."

"You shame me," I said, taking a deep breath.

"We've done our best to try to do the mission, Cassius," Clarice said, looking nervous. "But without the Planet-Killer, I don't think there's an option for us to destroy this place."

"Then allow me to provide another alternative," my father's voice spoke behind the group.

Clarice immediately spun around and aimed her rifle, firing repeatedly into the air.

All she struck was the wall of the medical facility.

Seconds later, a hologram of my father appeared standing in mid-air. He looked the same as he had down on Kolahn IV. There was a mischievous look on his face and I could tell he was amused by the attempts to kill him.

"Ah, yes," Cassius the Elder said. "The assumption I'm enough of an idiot to go in person. A flaw which my daughter was clearly guilty of."

I closed my eyes. "I'm sorry."

"Why?" Cassius the Elder said, shrugging. "She had every confidence you wouldn't kill her, but didn't realize you'd done it once and would do it again. That was her mistake. Most people don't have the opportunity to live multiple lives and she got more than her share. Mind you, it's not like she's gone. I have an endless supply of little puppy-like devoted scientists like her. Thomas will be harder to replace."

I stared at him. "You bastard."

"Oh don't be a hypocrite," Cassius the Elder said. "Do you really think she cares about your guilt, wherever she is?"

"Will someone shut this guy up?" William asked, looking back at me.

"I wish I could," I replied. "Zoe said you had this entirely under control."

"I did until you arrived," Cassius the Elder said. "The Kathax Prime was a wonderfully gullible being for the fact that his brain was the size of a planet. Seeing as we've finished his associate in the Kathax Beta off, though, I'm going to need you to close this deal for me."

"Isn't it enough you betrayed everyone in your Free Systems Alliance?" I asked. "Why the hell would I want to help you?"

"They said they'd give their lives to destroy the Commonwealth and they did," Cassius the Elder said. "Right now this ancient piece of Elder Race technology is readying itself to bring itself over Albion. It will promptly shell everything there and start turning the survivors into tools for uplifting humanity. I'm doing my best to try and convince a being with the brain the size of a planet this is a bad idea."

"Who possibly could have seen this eventuality coming," I said, shaking my head.

"It's your doing," Cassius the Elder growled, pointing at me. "You brought another of the Elder Races here and threatened it. Now it thinks it needs an army to protect itself."

Which it did, but that wasn't an argument I wanted to forward. "The Kathax Beta, Judith, whatever you want to call her, is dead. Zoe helped bring about her end."

Cassius nodded. "Which was a long shot from the very beginning, but I never entered this negotiation without an ace up my sleeve. It's why I need you alive for the next forty minutes or so as the fleet prepares to use the gate to go to Albion."

"No!" Fade said, perhaps a bit too dramatically. "There's twelve billion people on Albion!"

"And there's a trillion humans across the Spiral," Cassius the Elder replied snidely. "None of which are going to be able to do a damn bit of difference against the Kathax Prime unless we deal with him now."

I closed my eyes. "How exactly are we supposed to do that?"

"I deliver you to him," Cassius the Elder replies. "The infection you delivered to the temple itself hasn't spread far enough to affect him. You need to convince him to merge with you directly and hopefully it'll finally bring an end to the thing."

I laughed, actually laughed. "That's your big plan? Convince one of the smartest beings in the universe to do something painfully stupid?"

"Well, we're in this situation because of you," Cassius the Elder said. "We're also both in locations he can't hear us—at least hopefully that's still the case."

"This is an even worse plan than aligning with it in the first place," I said bitterly. "Why me?"

"You're the one with the virus in you," Cassius the Elder said. "Half the systems on the temple are shutting down. I'm hoping I can con the damn thing into believing he can find a cure for it in your system."

"That's a big if," I said, staring at him.

"We're out of options," my father said. "The question is whether I am going to get your cooperation for this or have to send in my army to get you."

I narrowed my eyes. "What do you get out of this?"

Cassius the Elder smiled. "As long as I'm alive, I can still rebuild my empire. That, by itself, is enough."

Vi looked up at me. "Are you a really a clone of him? It's hard to believe."

"Don't listen to him, Cass," Clarice said, looking at me. "Anything he says has to be taken with a grain of salt."

"We're past that," I said, taking a deep breath. "All right, Father, I'll go with you. I want you to force your armies to stand down, though. You'll let them leave and let the *Melampus* come forth to pick them up."

"You're not making this decision for me," Clarice said, her voice calm but cold. "We're all in this together."

I took Clarice by the shoulders and gave her a kiss. "I came here trying to find redemption and that's what I have the possibility to find now. I mean, who else gets the chance to honestly sacrifice themselves for the rest of the world?"

"A lot of people," Isla said, contradicting me and taking my arm. "The sacrifice for most of us is that we try our hardest to help others every day of our lives. It's why I became a doctor. I don't want to die in order to save lives, I want to live to save lives. It's what I want from you."

As far as I realized I'd badly mishandled my life, I realized in that moment I'd still had a few more hard lessons to learn. "I never should have become a warrior. I should have become a doctor like you."

"You'd have ended up exactly like me," Cassius the Elder said, staring at him.

"You said you made up that story about you and your child," I said.

"I am a known liar," Cassius the Elder said, frowning. "Are you ready to go?"

I kissed Isla on the lips and said, "Keep Clarice and yourself safe. I need you to look after Vi too."

"I'll be fine," Vi said. "I'm just the most wanted girl in the galaxy by the Commonwealth. Imposter or not."

"Imposter?" Fade asked.

William shook his head. "No goodbyes, Cassius. You're only one hundred percent going to die if you plan to. You know, unless you're dropped into the sun or something. Then you're going to one hundred percent die no matter what."

I pushed past him, smiling. "William, if we survive this, I promise to be your best friend and you mine."

"Don't make me wish you dead," William said before giving me a light pat on the shoulder. "I've grown used to your presence."

"I'm ready to go," I said to my father's hologram.

"Good," Cassius the Elder said.

What happened next was shocking to me as a glowing light which seemed to move in and out of me before I found myself no longer surrounded by my friends in the medical bay. Instead, I was in a mammoth coliseum-sized chamber which had eight large walkways over vast chasms leading down an infinite abyss. In the center of the chamber was a single large obelisk made of red crystal. It resembled the markers which I'd encountered the False Judith was.

The songs I'd heard earlier in the medical bay were much louder here and coming from all directions. I could feel strange energies moving in and out of my body like I was being scanned but it felt more like this was a center of powers humanity hadn't yet discovered. This was the "brain" of the temple and where the Kathax Prime had been worshiped for millennia by the long-dead Kolahn.

I could hear voices surrounding me and for a moment I wondered, against all reason, if he'd somehow trapped the consciousness of his followers within the computer banks around me. That the urge to commit mass suicide had been motivated by a desire to become one with their god. It was only slightly more insane than everything else I'd experienced.

My father was standing beside me, roughly three feet away. "Your friends have been teleported to your ship."

I stared at him. "Teleportation is impossible."

"For human science," Cassius the Elder said. "For the Elder Races, it's about as difficult as taking one step after another."

I considered reaching out to push my father out over the edge of the walkway we stood on but hesitated before shaking my head. My father might be willing to kill his own children or, at least, ignore their deaths, but I wasn't going to become him.

Not even if he richly deserved to die.

"How do I know you didn't just kill them?" I asked.

"You don't," Cassius the Elder said. "However, I wanted you to come here willingly when I could have just taken you."

He had a point. "So what now?"

"You die," Cassius the Elder said, turning to the obelisk. "He is here, my lord. The only member of the Young Species to have killed one of your kind. A person who carries within his cybernetics the remains of the Beta's code. Please, cleanse yourself of what afflicts you and bring us closer to ascension."

My father could not have sounded more bored or disinterested.

"Before I die," I took a deep breath, "I just wanted you to know: I've always hated you."

"Thank you," Cassius the Elder said. "The feeling is mutual. Oh, by the way, I'm in control of the fleet and am the one directing it toward Albion. The Kathax Prime isn't going to do anything but kill you, but I'm going to kill every single person on the planet, avenge Crius, then rule the human race like a king."

He vanished in a glowing nimbus of light.

"Well dammit," I said, staring at the empty space where he used to be. "Why do I keep believing him?"

I was alone. Alone in a dark and empty chamber which didn't seem to be any more filled with a god's presence than the state-run churches on Crius. "Are you going to speak to me or not? If you're going to kill me then you can do that too. I don't regret anything I've done. Your race is monstrous. The Kathax Beta deserved to die."

Nothing.

Well this was anticlimactic. "Listen, if you're not going to do anything, I have two beautiful women waiting back for me on my starship so I'll just—"

The red obelisk began to glow brightly.

"Oh hell."

Everything disappeared in a brilliant red light.

Not again.

Chapter Thirty

I found myself once more in the negative space between reality which the Elder Races existed and silently cursed myself for having ever touched the marker that had uploaded the False Judith into my mind. I felt the Kathax Prime moving through my memories from birth until death, skipping through things like my first steps to walking to my losing my virginity to the moment when I lost everything.

And then, suddenly, nothing.

I expected to be torn apart after the Kathax Prime was done but, instead, I merely found myself in yet another "waiting room", which took the form of the library in the Kolahn Palace. It was exactly the way I remembered it, except my father and sister were absent. Well, almost exactly.

The books which all surrounded me also were identical—having the same titles as well as dates stamped at their bottom. There was a general sense of foreboding to the place and when I tried to walk out the doors, I found myself coming into a completely identical replica of the spot I just left. It was more computer-generated chicanery. My only consolation was that I was hopefully uploading the virus which would, supposedly, destroy this thing for all time.

"Why do you wish to kill me?" I heard, coming from the table in front of me. Gradually, a figure of an old copper-skinned man with a thick white beard morphed into appearance. He was wearing a white robe and a necklace with a long metal key at the bottom of it. "As far as I can remember, which is to the origins of stars, we've never met before today."

I stared at him, annoyed with the presumption of the Kathax Prime. I recognized just who he'd conjured up as an image. "Taking the form of Prophet Allenway offends me on several levels."

Prophet Allenway, in real life, had been a obese lecher by the time he'd died and not too dissimilar from the way my father had looked when Prince Germanicus's poisons finally finished him off. The way the Kathax Prime, at least that was who I presumed my "host" was, appeared was more similar to the idealized version of the man which adorned hundreds of churches as well as portraits spread throughout the Crius Prime of my youth.

While Allenway looked nothing like Jesus of Nazareth, that was certainly the image that both he and the ancient alien were attempting to invoke. The Masonic Key around his neck was a bit of an unnecessary touch, but I didnt know what he was trying to say. All I knew was, even though I believed Allenway was just a deluded old man, it came across as blasphemous.

"You're the one who conjured the image," the Kathax Prime said. "I simply am dwelling here in your subconscious. Everything you see is just your mind attempting to make sense of our union."

"I want nothing to do with you," I said, growling. "I've seen the horror you unleashed upon those bodies."

"That was your father," the Kathax Prime said. "Your sister as well. Every consciousness which was infected with the virus they created has been safely uploaded and stored in this server ship. They have joined the Kolahn as one of the races I've saved."

I stared at him. "You're lying."

The Kathax Prime and the two of vanished before reappearing on a beach. I had to blink several times before staring at hundreds of humans in swimsuits (or without swimsuits) wandering around the sun-kissed sand. There were Chel and genemods present as well, seemingly enjoying the sun and surf despite the fact their bodies were incapable of handling such intense light. I also saw some Kolahn present, merrily chatting in their alien grunt-like language with the humans seemingly able to understand perfectly.

"You could be showing me anything," I said, trying to find an excuse not to believe him.

Yet, believe him I did.

"This server ship is a barge of the dead," the Kathax Prime said. "Meant to carry a species my race had marked for destruction. When your father decided to turn his recruits into soulless tools, I took the time to scan their minds into my databanks. It was the only thing I could do."

"Then these aren't the dead, just copies of them," I said.

"The difference at my level of technology is less distinct than you might believe," the Kathax Prime said, clasping his hands behind himself. "I did not share what levels of technology I did with your family in order to kill but to save."

"Then you chose poor allies," I said, suddenly wondering if I'd been on the wrong side of this the entire time.

"As have you," the Kathax Prime said.

He had a point. "Are they self aware?"

I could sense the spark of life from the people around me, though. Each of the men, women, and hermaphrodites around me were uniquely crafted. I could believe these were the soldiers and engineers who'd all volunteered to fight against the Commonwealth before having their bodies seized by the nanovirus.

"Yes," the Kathax Prime said. "Many of them were outraged upon their arrival in this place, so to speak, but gradually all came to accept the paradise I've replicated for them. They and the Kolahn before them are all capable of living worthwhile lives for all eternity—or at least until this ship disintegrates."

"You brought the Kolahn here too?"

"Yes," the Kathax Prime said. "I modified their race with cybernetics to record their thoughts and minds—much cruder than the nanovirus Zoe designed with my knowledge."

I thought about the programming virus I'd brought here, which was designed to kill the Kathax Prime. How many innocent people had I condemned to death? "How many are here?"

"Too many," the Kathax Prime said. "But it is not your doing which will lead to the end of this paradise. It is another's."

I wasn't sure I agreed it was a paradise versus just a simulated holo-sim for a race of ghosts, but kept my mouth shut. Instead, I asked a question which had haunted me since I'd first found out about the enigmatic A.I. god. "Why...do all this?"

"I was there when my species was almost destroyed by the Middle Races. I witnessed our spirits being torn apart by beings who wanted to learn all of our secrets and to use us to benefit themselves. They sought the secret of immortality and how to become fourth-dimensional beings—ideas which we were only beginning to contemplate ourselves."

"I saw the images your daughter shared," I said, picking up a margarita from a waiter's tray and taking a sip. "That didn't give your race the right to commit galactic genocide."

"You're right," the Kathax Prime said, surprising me. "What we should have done was try and teach our ways to the Younger Races as well as help them achieve the maturity to cope with making reality shaped to consciousness' will."

"My race does not need guidance," I said, not believing it for a second. "Our mistakes are our own."

"And yet if we don't intervene then we are guilty of as much evil as doing it ourselves," the Kathax Prime. " I was once leader of the Elder Races and after we finished our terrible vengeance on the Middle Races, we made plans to make sure we never were threatened again. I found myself feeling an immense sense of guilt, though, for what we'd done. I believed it was necessary to protect the Young Races and guide them. My early experiments had... mixed results. Finally, they imprisoned me on this world inside this temple ship and disguised it as just another planet."

"How long were you down here?" I asked, staring at the people around me. "How did you become involved with the Kolahn?"

"Long enough to go mad and sane again many times," the Kathax Prime said, his voice carrying the weight of his words. "Whereas the majority of markers across the galaxy are designed to lead the Young Races to their doom, I was able to be contacted by the Kolahn when they found me—as well as by Zoe. I taught the Kolahn many of my secrets and they stupidly used them to try to conquer other races. Eventually, the Elder Races caught on and destroyed them. They took control of the cybernetics which allowed me to preserve their consciousness and forced them to slaughter each other. The Community, which had been driven to the brink of annihilation, was glad to leave it alone after that."

I tried to imagine what humanity would have done in the Kolahn's place and didn't have to. They would have stupidly lapped up every advance and gift of technology the Kathax Prime offered then used them to destroy their neighbors. We would have ended up getting "saved" on a hard-drive disk the same way the Kolahn were. Worst of all, it wasn't a hypothetical since that was potentially what was happening right this very second. Zoe, my father, and the only thing standing in their way being the Beta that we'd already killed.

"You got an entire race destroyed and you still agreed to help my sister and father's plans?" I asked, wondering which was worse: the Elder Races who routinely committed genocide and played other species against one another for fun, or the Kathax Prime who seemed to forget the definition of insanity was repeating the same actions over again and expecting new results.

"They were very persuasive," the Kathax Prime said. "I cannot affect any species or do anything beyond what is inside my programmed world here. They took everything I taught them and used it to create their nanoplague soldiers as well as Cognition A.I. combined with markers that would allow them to harm other members of my race. They made a deal with the Kathax Beta to bring both you and her here in hopes of creating a weapon against me."

I tried to imagine all the twists and turns that must have taken but failed. Really, though, it only required them all to lie to each other and me as often as necessary to get us to do their dirty work. "Did it work?"

"You're here, aren't you?" the Kathax Prime said. "The Beta is dead and soon I will be wiped clean from the temple's archives, leaving a remote-controlled battle moon at your father's beck and call. Combined with the fleet he already had absolute control over, there is nothing to stop him."

Explained like that, it all started to make sense. Zoe and my father had played the Elder Race members like a fiddle in order to steal their technology as well as eliminate them. They were the mouse which roared, helping themselves to technology which would allow them to conquer or dominate much of the Spiral. No, my father just needed his army of "zombies" to create a threat which would ultimately be defeated and allow him to be a great hero for doing it. I had to give him credit, it was an insanely ambitious plan that he'd managed to pull off with aplomb. All he'd had to do was murder millions and potentially billions now if the Kathax Prime was telling the truth and these programs around me were all sentient beings.

"I am such a fool." I paused. "So the exact plan they told me from the beginning. All of this to get the Community to conquer us and place my father in charge."

"Yes," the Kathax Prime said. "Your father lacks imagination for all of his endless ambitions. Give a monkey all the power in the universe and he'll fill the world with bananas."

"I dislike that description," I said.

"You're the best of primate-kind," the Kathax Prime said, still finding his words amusing. "Very different from your father, who was too clever by half."

I didn't disagree with him, but didn't want him insulting my species either. "He managed to put one over two gods, it seemed, and may well succeed in conquering the Spiral. Like I said, I don't see much problem with a Community-ruled humanity. Maybe they're the more advanced race, which will give us guidance."

Or maybe I'd just come to hate my own species.

"That can't be allowed to happen," the Kathax Prime said, suddenly grabbing my shoulders and shaking me. "The Elder Races will not allow it."

I pushed him away with both hands. "You've done a bang-up job so far."

The Kathax Prime shook his head. "No, you're not understanding what all of this has been about."

"Then explain," I said. "Assuming we have any time left."

"Not much," the Kathax Prime admitted. "This was all my mistake. My attempt to give your people secrets, which the Elder Races would never allow, has possibly doomed your race the same way the Kolahn were. I wanted to give you the chance to get out from under their control, but that was never really an option. My Beta was willing to break all the rules to see me judged and destroyed. However, now that she's dead and your father has access to so much of our technology, they will do everything in their power to make sure the genie is put back in the bottle. You encountered one of their probe ships, which already shows they know what's going on."

"What is going to happen?"

"You need to destroy the fleets out there, the nanovirus, and all the other technology your father has obtained from my people. Otherwise, it will be war. A war which will see every world he's touched wiped clean from the map. Some of my people have been looking for an excuse to destroy humanity and the Community races for ages. They feel like they've been too lenient and have allowed you both to grow too powerful."

"What, would they have us banging rocks together for all time?" I asked.

The Kathax Prime chuckled. It was a bitter gallows laugh. "Not far from the truth, actually. I can't leave my battle moon and I don't have any control over the machines he's created. Zoe's A.I. is in the system now and when she rewrites it, she'll have access to everything."

I stared at him. "Which is happening since you linked with me."

The Kathax Prime looked to the ground, a bitter expression on his facve "The last of my defenses are falling and soon all the billions of people inside are going to be overwritten. There's nothing that can be done about that now. You, however, can stop the destruction of your race, though."

"How?" I asked.

The skies above the beach I walked started to turn black as the sun disappeared along with eventually the clouds as well as skyline. All of the people around me stopped moving then began to vanish one by one. It filled me with a sense of sick horror to realize this ark had been the target of my father and Zoe's plans all along. They'd sent along just enough soldiers and enemies to drive me to the temple as a Trojan Horse for the False Judith to infect the Kathax Prime.

They'd just needed to play both Elder Race members against one another so neither of them suspected they weren't in control of the situation. Goddammit, they were magnificent bastards. The most admiral part of their plan had to be they'd obviously had to adjust their actions every step of the way. It made the fact Zoe ended up shot by Clarice in the end all the more ironic. She could predict the actions of gods, but not my girlfriend.

"Let me give you everything I know," the Kathax Prime said. "At least regarding their technology and overrides. I can't affect them because I'm trapped here but I can give my knowledge to others. I thought Zoe might have been worth it but—"

"Speak plainly." I didn't have time for a long speech. My friends were possibly dead at my father's hands.

The Kathax Prime looked at me. "Kill your father and order the ships to destroy themselves. Wipe everything clean from their databanks and let yourself be killed as well. Then there will be no reason for the Elder Races to go after humanity."

I was stunned at his effrontery before remembering I'd been willing to die to kill him before. "You aren't asking much."

"I know exactly what I'm asking."

I took a deep breath. "Is there any way to help the people here?'

We were alone now in a sea of static and numbers.

"They're already dead," The Kathax Prime said. "Such is the fate, perhaps, of even my species."

I closed my eyes. "I'm sorry. I'll do what you ask."

"I know. I don't know if you believe in any gods," the Kathax Prime said, lifting his right hand. "But now would be a good time to pray to them. For the dead if no one else."

I prayed.

The Kathax Prime placed his hand on top of my forehead. What followed was a nonsensical stream of data which I could not make out the slightest bit of sense from. What I did know, though, was it contained the control codes for my father's army. A part of me wondered if I might not put it to better use than simple destruction, but that thought left quickly.

"Goodbye, Mr. Mass," the Kathax Prime said. "It was interesting knowing you."

"Goodbye," I said, watching him vanish.

Before I vanished too.

Chapter Thirty-One

Ifell down to one knee, gasping for air before I felt the oxygen of a heavily recycled atmosphere enter into my lungs. It took a second for me to recognize the rectangular bridge of the *Revengeance*. The place was about forty yards long with viewscreens showing the exterior of space in three hundred and sixty degrees while pits existed alongside a single walkway between them for the dozens of personnel expected to run the massive dreadnought occupying most of the space.

I'd been on the *Revengeance* bridge hundreds of time during my career as a Crius military officer but not since the destruction of my homeworld had I ever imagined stepping foot there again. It was like being transported back into the past and for a second I wondered if that's what had happened. If they could teleport a person across space then surely they could teleport someone across time, right? I mean, they were the same thing after all.

Such a thought didn't last more than the few moments it took to notice all of the bridge officers were wearing flight suits, gloves, and helmets that covered their bodies completely. The nanovirus had spread through their bodies so much they could no longer pass themselves off as human. I wondered how my father had managed to keep it a secret from the necessary number of humans and Chel required to actually run the non-military aspects of his rebellion. The people who bought supplies, traded them, and negotiated with worlds. Maybe my father just paid them off.

Speaking of which, I found myself staring at the man seconds later as he walked out from the captain's ready room. He was followed by a floating "eyebot" mech which he was apparently dictating minutes to when he stopped in mid-step to stare at me. In that moment, I immediately went for my fusion pistol to gun down the man I'd earlier promised myself I wasn't evil enough to kill because he was family.

"You are just impossible to kill, you know that?" Cassius the Elder said, shaking his head. "I suppose I should be proud but mostly I'm just annoyed."

"You're not going to destroy Albion," I said, taking a deep breath. "As deeply ambivalent as I am about that."

Cassius the Elder snorted. "Really? That's your statement? At least put a little flair into it."

"You killed an entire race inside the temple," I said, looking around for some sort of weapon to use against him. There were rifles in the hand of the ship's security as well as hand pistols on some of the officers standing eerily still. "Two even. The Kolahn and all of your followers had their essences preserved inside them."

"I exorcised a derelict ship full of ghosts," Cassius the Elder said, his voice cold but resolved. "When Albion is decimated by the battle moon and my fleet, there won't be a need for any peace treaty or for the Community to step in. I'll bring the whole of humanity together in as an equal partnership in the Community."

"You're letting your ego get the better of you," I said, realizing my father was literally trembling with rage. "Whomever you made friends with in the Community would not be happy with you betraying them like that."

"You speak to me of arrogance?" Cassius the Elder asked. "You who got your brother and sister killed then came here to kill me? Kill him!"

My father's command was directed to the mindless slaves he'd created around him. I stared at them and mentally begged them not move.

They didn't.

"Oh bother," Cassius the Elder said. "It seems that mad old electric alien gave you some protection from our machines."

I ran up to the nearest of the guards, grabbed his fusion pistol and fired repeatedly at my father. The blasts splashed harmlessly against his personal barrier, seemingly doing nothing more than irritate him.

"Shoot him, Vera," my father said.

The floating eyebot moved out in front of him, being little more than a metal sphere with a single strange ocular sensor moved in front of my father. I didn't wait for it to do anything but immediately sought cover behind the same guard I'd stolen a weapon from. The eyebot proceeded to release a blast of glowing white energy that blasted the top half of the man off. If I had been just a couple of inches higher, I would have been killed instantly.

I ducked into one of the pits and ran past some of the nanovirus-afflicted soldiers below, seeking a place to hide as the eyebot adjusted its position in order to find me. This entire plan was starting to look like a really stupid idea. But what else was new?

"We all want immortality, Cassius," my father said, his voice low. "The human race as a whole is a railing against the nature of reality that does not care whether we exist or not. It was all right for us when we were the only species in the universe and could take some perverse pride in our status as the only God who could define reality, but jumpspace has removed that from us. The Strong Anthropic Principle means the universe will continue providing new minds and new races to define itself long after humanity goes extinct. Do you know what that means, my boy? We are not the Children of God, we are his CELLS. As easily replaced and as ultimately immaterial. I am not going to let that happen to me. I choose to rail against the reality."

The eyebot blasted a power console after I threw my coat out in front of it to distract it. That gave me a chance to blast it with my fusion pistol but it, too, had a barrier. Apparently, the guard's gun I possessed just wasn't powerful enough to pierce the side of either of my opponents.

"So you decided to become a cancer instead," I said, taking a deep breath.

Cassius the Elder walked over to the eyebot as I maneuvered near the catwalk. "The jumpspace gate is already opening. It's finished. Your friends are dead; I teleported them into deep space. I blew up the *Melampus*. The only reason I kept you alive as long as I did was to destroy the Kathax Prime. Submit to the inevitable."

The machines around us were programmed to obey my father, but the Kathax Prime had apparently taken advantage of the fact we were identical to somehow make it so they had to obey me as well. He couldn't get them to attack me and I'd tried to get them to get attack him to no avail, willing them to assault him several times but that didn't seem to register with them. So, instead, I imagined one of the Void Marines on the bridge to hurl a thermite grenade at the eyebot. It was an action the Marine immediately undertook despite the fact that my father was present beside it.

"Son of a bit—" My father didn't get to finish his sentence before there was a detonation of fire and flame above my head. I used that opportunity to climb up a short ladder from the pit and immediately look around for another weapon. Getting behind the very Void Marine which had thrown the grenade, I saw he had a collapsible light-pike which I picked from his belt before knocking him into the pit beside me.

The little metal tube in my hand had a pair of buttons, the first of which I tapped to extend it to a metal long barrier-covered weapon before tapping the end to create a glowing plume of white-hot energy on the end. I spun the weapon in my hands to get a feel for it before assuming a defensive posture. The barrier the weapon provided would be a weak one compared to the one generated by the Void Marines' armor, but I didn't exactly have time to put it on.

Cassius the Elder was, still, alive, and apparently unharmed from the blast. I had no idea how expensive his personal-barrier generator was, but it was worth the money. Standing up, he took a deep breath. "Such a stupid weapon."

"It was always going to end like this," I said, holding my pike toward him. "Imagine the stories they'll tell when you defeat me here in a duel for the fate of the world."

My father snorted and drew his proton sword before holding it in front of him. "There will be no stories. As far as the world will be concerned, you will be the greatest murderer since the Cognition A.I."

I smiled. "Some legacy."

Cassius the Elder stepped forward to attack, only for me to drop the light pike on the ground, causing his sword to swing wildly where he expected it to hit. I proceeded to grab him by the throat, my hands passing through his barrier, then crushed his larnyx with one swift squeeze. It was the action of a street brawler and wholly immune to the knowledge of the rigid forms in which I'd been educated by my father.

Cassius the Elder's eyes widened and he choked before falling
to his knees. I grabbed his proton sword off the ground and jabbed
it straight through the old man's heart. The expression on his face
was one of shock, agony, and…amusement? It was not a dignified
way to die—in real life you emptied your bowels when impaled
on a proton sword—but it was a warrior's death. Giving my father
it felt wrong, somehow, and I agreed with the damned soul of
Prince Germanicus he should have perished as an obese politician
mourned by none.

I pulled the proton sword from his chest and tossed it to one
side, staring at the bridge around me. "Now what?"

No answers accompanied me even though I tested my control
over the nanovirus-infected troopers around me. I ordered a Void
Marine to step forward before asking all of the bridge officers to
stop their tasks.

They did so.

"I see," I said, speaking only to myself.

I didn't know whether to believe my father's statement that he'd
murdered all of my friends and loved ones, but it didn't matter
since I was going to be dead soon. Walking over to the controls, I
proceeded to look over my shoulder and half expected more eyebots
to arrive. Instead, there was only the fractured pieces of the one my
father had sent after me, lying on the ground next to his corpse.

I conjured up a hologram in front of me of the surrounding
system. I saw the massive fleet of the Free Systems Alliance standing
before the jumpgate. It was sitting still, their engines running, but
none of them making a move. The comm traffic between them was
nonexistent, giving the impression of a fleet of tomb ships.

Which is what they were.

That was when I saw the Temple of the Kathax Prime and
was briefly moved to awe. It was every bit as large as described, a
massive pyramid the size of a country. I'd seen similarly sized space
stations but none of them capable of movement. Though it was only
a speck of dust in the great void of the universe, it held more than
enough power to lay waste to humanity's forces. I tried contacting
the Kathax Prime onboard it but received no sign of any response.

"I must destroy every bit of Elder Race technology," I said,
dictating orders to the crew of the C.S.S *Revengeance*. "That was

what he said and that is what I need to do."

I didn't actually believe the fleets forces would obey when I sent out a command to all of them: Destroy all of your allies except for the *Revengeance*. What followed was a fireworks display of energy blasts which crisscrossed the void, causing vessel after vessel to explode. It would go on for hours as the machines were programmed as warriors.

With that, I dictated command after command to the *C.S.S Revengeance* and began turning the vessel slowly around before setting it for a collision course with the Temple of the Kathax Prime. It would take several minutes as I had to coordinate every single action. Whatever programs or A.I. which my father had designed to assist him in battle were not assisting me. They weren't resisting me either.

So this was how I was going to die.

It was irritating in a way because I was now being given the very heroic death I'd always longed for. I'd not wanted to become a fat, idolent, pathetic waste of space like my father. I'd wanted to go out in the blaze of glory, a heroic figure to inspire future generations. Now I was going to die saving billions of lives and single-handedly winning a war, yet the experience was still ashes in my mouth.

I wanted to live. It was a shocking realization for me because I'd tried to kill myself slowly with whiskey, drugs, and risks up until this point. I'd been willing to die a thousand times before and there were times it would have been nothing more than a blessed relief. Yet, here and now, I wanted nothing so much than to live. The ghosts of my dead squadmates, crew, and even family did not call me to the afterlife but looked down upon me as if to say, "We have no hold upon you, Cassius. Not anymore."

Yet, I didn't have a choice, did I? If what the Kathax Prime said was true, then every bit of technology he had given or Zoe reverse engineered was an existential threat to humanity. A reason to give the Elder Races an excuse to destroy mankind—not that they seemed to need much of one. Hell, I'd been party to the death of not one but two of their kind and I suspected they'd killed races for far less than murdering what was supposed to be immortal. I had to die.

Right? In the end, I would have been able to give my life up. I was willing to die.

But I couldn't resist the voice which spoke next.

"Cassius?" Isla's voice spoke on the bridge's comm system. "Are you there?"

I rushed to the side of it and tapped the response key. "Isla? Are you there? Are you alive?"

"How the hell did you get on the *Revengeance*?" Isla asked. "We're on the *Melampus* and everyone is…well not everyone, but most of the crew is alive and the ship is still functional. It looks like the whole FSA fleet is on fire."

"It is," I said, trying to figure out what was going on. It seemed my father hadn't killed them. Possibly the only time in his life he'd ever honored one of his problems. "As for how I got here, it's a long story. My father is dead and I've got the dreadnought aimed like a dagger to the heart of the temple."

"We're sending over a shuttle to pick you up," Isla said. "I don't know how you did it, but I'm glad you did."

I opened my mouth to object. To say that I had to die here and now, but found myself not doing so. I didn't want to believe the Kathax Prime. Even more so, I didn't give a shit about fulfilling his race's demands. It wasn't like he'd negotiated with them for humanity to be spared. If we'd discovered a way to fight the Kathax then that needed to be spread across the galaxy. Those were all lies, though.

Instead, I remained silent.

"Please come back to us," Isla said.

I broke in that moment. "I'll be at the bridge's starboard airlock. Come pick me up. Please."

There wasn't much else to say after that moment. The engines of the *Reveangence* picked up about five or ten minutes later, well after I'd departed the ship, then plunged the ship at relativistic speeds into the side of the temple. There wasn't an explosion, or at least much of one, but more the *Revengeance* smashing itself through the center of the pyramid. The *Revengeance* tore the asteroid-sized vessel into two humungous chunks that floated slowly through the air before becoming part of Kolahn IV's atmosphere. As I understood it, it would be three years before the last of the debris landed on the decimated uninhabitable ruin of the world.

The last of my father's legacy.

Chapter Thirty-Two

It took us two days to get out of Lucifer's Nebula using our existing drive mechanisms. We had enough spare parts aboard the ship to make it jumpspace once we did. I spent most of that time cleaning up my office and redecorating it until it was impossible to say there had ever been a fight.

Instead, I sat down at my desk with the lights turned low while drinking the bottle of Crius scotch which Clarice had given me for my birthday. It couldn't get me drunk thanks to my new liver installed by Isla, but I was finishing it just for the experience. I hoped it would also be the last bit of alcohol I ever considered in my life.

The crew was celebrating down below in the lounge, believing they were all going to be rich soon. I hadn't the heart to tell them they were all going to get paid diddly-squat given the Commonwealth had never intended to follow through on its deal thanks to their plans for betraying me.

I turned on my computer interface and cycled down to a message which had been left on the ship by my brother. I'd watched it a dozen times since I'd first found it but found myself compelled to watch it one more time.

A life-size image of my brother wearing a workman's jumpsuit, absent all the frills of his station as a Free Systems Alliance marshal, appeared in front of my desk. He had an expression on his face which was halfway between determined and resigned. He was clearly filming the message inside the office of the Kolahn Palace's motorpool with dirty equipment as well as vehicles visible behind him.

"Hello, Cass," Thomas said, blinking. "I don't know if we're going to get a chance to speak again after this, but I know you used to update your messages to Judith before every mission during the last days of the war. Since we haven't had a chance to speak in the past decade and I can't say anything incriminating in front of my father, I thought I'd take time to give you an explanation as well as some parting thoughts just in case I don't make it."

I took a deep breath. "With any luck, I'll never see this…"

"With any luck, you'll never see this," Thomas said, saying the words from the message I memorized. "We'll successfully hijack some kinetibikes, blow up the base, and get to the Temple of the Kathax Prime and blow it to kingdom come. Once that's taken care of, Zoe and Father's plans will be ruined. You wouldn't believe the horrible things they've done. The horrible things we've done."

"I would have," I said, taking another drink of scotch.

Thomas looked down. "When we first gathered all the various resistance groups together, it was an impossible and exciting time. We were freedom fighters, terrorists, guerillas, and activists who never would have gotten together. I believed, though, we would be able to find common ground and defeat the Commonwealth. This was despite the fact I was the kind of person who would have killed these people for resisting against the Crius Archduchy just a few years before. We had friends in the Chel, Union of Faith, transtellars, and even Commonwealth."

I closed my eyes.

"In the end, our father didn't want to take the risk of compromise. If he couldn't be the man absolutely in charge, even using you or Vi as his public persona, he didn't want the FSA to survive at all. Zoe's Elder Race-derived technology gave him the option to do it. I'm sure it won't take you much longer to figure out the majority of our soldiers here in the nebula are little more than mechs. Really, it's a miracle it's been kept secret as long as it has been, but I suppose people don't want to believe," Thomas said. "There are plenty of real-life agents for the FSA, people who report to me, and brainwashed bioroids who might actually be the closest thing to real soldiers we have now. Whatever the case, though, father and Zoe murdered many of my friends and loved ones."

"It wasn't your fault, Thomas," I said, talking to his digital echo.

"It my fault," Thomas said, not speaking to me save in the loosest sense. "I should have stopped them but I was blinded until it was too late. I could have killed them but I could never bring myself to hurt Zoe or even father. I believe you can."

"Yeah, thanks for that," I muttered.

"That's not a flaw," Thomas said, pausing for a moment. "Rather, it's a statement that you've done something I haven't been able to do. You've built a family outside of the one we both grew up in. You have friends, lovers, and people who you can trust. Who aren't monsters trying to rebuild a government which wasn't worth protecting from the beginning. I envy you that and if we survive, well, maybe I'll be able to do the same. If not, and by some miracle that you do, treasure them. I don't believe in an afterlife despite the fact I am definitely in a foxhole right now. However, I know you do so say a prayer for me and I'll do the same. Goodbye, and honor be with you."

"Honor be with you," I said, watching the hologram disappear.

The door to my ready room buzzed. "Come in."

Fade and Anya Terra walked in, both of them wearing *Melampus* jumpsuits. The former didn't quite suit Fade, who I expected was used to be far more fashionable.

"Is this where you commit your sudden betrayal that everyone should have expected since you're a Commonwealth spy?" I asked, looking at Fade. "Because, I gotta admit, I am completely expecting it."

Fade snorted, looking less than impressed. "In fact, I'm no longer a Commonwealth spy. The Watcher General burned me for taking actions against her plans and being part of the Parliament conspiracy against the peace talks."

"Which turned out to be the right attitude," I said, feeling disgusted about the whole ordeal. "I bet they're happy."

Fade frowned. "In fact, Ida claimed it was all part of a plan to eliminate the Free Systems Alliance from the beginning. Six members of Parliament and two admirals died in a solar yacht explosion after news of their treachery was distributed to the rest of the oligarchy. Ida has moved the majority of the intelligence apparatus under her direct control and increased her influence dramatically."

"Well, good for her," I said, frowning.

"Good for you," Fade said. "She's decided to pay you what you were promised. Though I don't know how much that will help given you're also being taxed for it."

I snorted. "Of course I am. Are you okay?"

Fade frowned. "I've been a spy my entire life. It's all I ever wanted to be and now I can't be that. On the other hand, I actually managed to take part in saving the entire universe from an insane madman, so there is that."

"Didja actually do anything?" Anya spoke up for the first time in our conversation. "Because I think you mostly just stood there."

"I did stuff!" Fade said, frowning. "Granted, it was mostly Clarice and Cassius, but I was there."

I chuckled. "Well, you're always welcome onboard the *Melampus*."

"Really?" Fade asked.

"Fuck no!" I snapped, staring at him. "I'm dropping you off at the next port. The only person I'm willing to forgive for trying to kill me is—"

"Someone with tits?" Fade suggested. "Because I heard how Clarice turned you over to her sister."

"Funny," I said, frowning. "Also, not true. I haven't slept with all of my crew."

"Just the women," Terra muttered.

"Not even that!" I said, pausing to note that it was far less an absolute than I wanted to be. "It's very boring in space! Nobody has to and they all come to me or through someone else. I really only am seeing…two women. Crap."

Fade chuckled and covered his face. "Well, I'll be fine. I have the contacts to get my face and DNA changed as well as a few million credits I skimmed for my retirement."

I stared at him. "You dog, you. So much for Commonwealth loyalty."

"What's a dog?" Fade asked. "As for Commonwealth loyalty, I should note no one noticed it going missing in the first place. That tells you how much they value both their employees as well as their pensions."

"Lights up," I said, shaking my head and standing up to stretch. "What about you, Major Terra? I assume you're not going back to the Commonwealth?"

"Not a chance," Anya said. "Don't call me Major either. The Commonwealth took away my mind and showed they were no different from Zoe and your father's slaves. I am going to see if I can distribute the cure to the nearest datanode to pass around the infonet. Hopefully, at least someone will run with it and take the Commonwealth to task."

"I'm not counting on it but I support you in that endeavor. You're also welcome to stay onboard," I said, pausing. "I have a feeling half the crew are going to be retiring and the other half will be starting families soon. I'll need competent folk here."

"You're not giving up the sailing life?" Fade asked. "I'd have thought you'd be the first one to buy an asteroid mansion now."

"And give up this luxury?" I asked, knocking on the scuffed desk. "Never. Besides, I have enough money to keep this ship running indefinitely as well as buy a small fleet of tramp freighters. I figure if I knew someone well acquainted with organized crime, he might be willing to set me up with his contacts to make our own little independent organization. A few million credits doesn't go as far as it used to."

It wasn't actually my plan but something Clarice had come up with as part of a scheme to keep us from getting shoved out an airlock by the crew when they found out we couldn't pay them. Honestly, we had a better chance of making a fortune as our own smugglers than we ever did working for the Consortium. Mind you, our actions at the Ring meant the organization had several vacancies in its management.

Before that I was going to have to change my name and identity, again, due to the fact that my father had finally "killed" the Fire Count. His death had been broadcast across the Spiral and it was probably going to cause the Commonwealth no end of trouble. Alive, my father had been an insane military commander out for himself and sullying our name for generations to come, but dead he was a martyr to the cause of galactic freedom. Well, that was their problem and I was already looking through old early Crius colonist media for a new surname. Cassius Arthur? Cassius Holmes? Cassius Kirk? It was a tough choice.

Fade smirked and rubbed his goatee. "That sounds suspiciously like a display of trust, Captain."

"Not at all," I said, crossing my arms. "I know I can't trust you and that means I know at what length to keep you."

"I'll think about it," Fade said, furrowing his brow. "You might have a chance to get in on the ground floor of some big business about to boom. The Commonwealth is going to be releasing a good half of its properties. Crius included."

Anya turned to Fade. "You're blowing smoke up my ass."

"Why the hell would they do that?" I asked, thinking about all the effort they'd expended trying to keep them. "They just won the war."

"Well, actually, you won—" Fade started to say.

"Please don't remind me," I said, cutting him off.

Fade sighed. "The Commonwealth was on the verge of economic collapse before the war. Quintillions of credits spent every year keeping worlds garrisoned, provisioned, and administered. Far more than they ever took from the planets themselves. The British Empire made more money not being an empire than it ever did ruling half of Old Earth."

"I have no idea what that is," I said, blinking. "I'll take your word for it, though."

"Why not release our worlds earlier then?" Anya said, angry. "Hell, why go to all the trouble of conquering so many planets to begin with?"

"When they were conquering during the Reunification, the transtellars were making a fortune. All of the money was being borrowed from future speculation. That all came crashing down when the conquests stopped," Fade said. "As for why not surrendering the worlds earlier, they couldn't do that as long as the Free Systems Alliance existed. It took so long to get the surrender agreement going because they were afraid they'd look weak."

"Are you sure your grandmother can't blow the entirety of Parliament up?" I asked, shaking my head.

"I'll see if she has any Guy Fawkes masks," Fade said. "Guy Fawkes was—"

"I don't care," I said, raising a hand. "The fact is the galaxy continues to spin and we're all still alive. So I'm going to step out of this room and go find the people I love. I'm then going to get drunk in public and do my best to never remember any of this week's events ever again."

"Any chance of that?" Anya asked.

"Not a bit," I said, knowing the events would haunt me until the end of my days. I was a patricide and witnessed the end of a species. I'd been party to the deaths of two gods and helped see my sister shuffle her mortal coil for the second time. I'd also left my brother behind on the deserts of a dead world. If I ever thought of that damned space cloud or its inhabitants again it would be too soon. Yet, every other thought I had seemed to be of it. "I'm glad to have you as part of the crew, Anya."

"Thanke," Anya said.

I walked over to the pair and prepared to put my arms around each but they both looked away, forcing me to put my arms down. "Fine, but the first round is on you then."

"The alcohol is free," Fade said, wrinkling his nose. "Munin makes it in the plumbing."

"I could have gone my entire life without knowing that," I said, blinking. "I'm also worried I will still drink it."

"The pipe sanitizer is a key ingredient," Anya said, smiling.

I was about to congratulate them for (hopefully) having a go with me when Jun Masterson ran into the room, panting, with a terrified look on her face. "We're in big trouble, sir."

I blinked at her. "We're in jumpspace. How bad could the trouble be?"

I wasn't speaking facetiously. Jumpspace, despite its horrifying reputation as a place full of all manner of unspeakable weirdness, was probably the safest place in the cosmos to be. Other ships couldn't attack you and the computer theoretically could avoid any of the strange matter dangers which early ships collapsed into.

Jun's eyes widened as she spoke her next words with something approaching sheer panic. "It's the probe, sir! It's back!"

CHAPTER THIRTY-THREE

I could not have moved faster to the bridge even as I found myself face to face with a blank screen, but sensor readings indicating the probe was one hundred meters in front of us, moving at an identical rate of speed. I called up a holographic display of the Elder Race vessel and stared into what I could only take to be our doom.

The featureless sphere was impossible to identify as the same one which had attacked us in the nebula, but I had no doubt it was. I'd initially assumed the mysterious vessel to be the servant of the Kathax Prime, but I knew that wasn't the case now. If he'd had access to a vessel then he would have secured the Kolahn and Free Systems Alliance personnel's…souls? A.I. Presences? Whatever you wanted to call them. Hell, he probably would have killed Zoe and Cassius the Elder the moment he gained the ability.

The other option would be it belonged to the mainline faction of the Elder Races which the Kathax Beta had represented. Perhaps to transfer her once we've come close enough to the planet to smuggle her in but without being sensed by Judith, the Kathax Prime, or Cassius the Elder. But what did they want now? If they wanted her then they were bound to be disappointed.

And we were doomed.

"Should I call up an alert, sir?" Jun said, standing next to a Tina and U'Chuck. Princess Servilia, Vi, was also on the bridge wearing a science officer uniform. They were the only bridge crew left, having drawn the unlucky lots to not attend tonight's party. I was stunned Vi wanted to stay with us despite our poor accomadations, but glad.

"There's no point," I said, taking a deep breath. "The only thing that would do is make sure everyone died scared."

"Now I really wish I hadn't skipped the party," Jun said, sighing. "Hey, Fade, you want to have sex?"

Fade did a double-take. "With you? Absolutely."

Jun nodded. "Permission to take a break, sir?"

"Denied!" I snapped at her.

"Dammit," Jun muttered.

Fade shrugged noncommittally. "You win some, you lose some."

"We are perhaps the only vessel in human history to encounter a Elder Race transport twice," Tina said, working the sensors rapidly. "And in jumpspace as well. This moment needs to be recorded for posterity."

"Does it?" I asked.

The Kathax Prime's words terrified me. The statement I needed to die along with my father, sister, and all others touched by their technology. That every bit of technology which could be used against the Elder Races be expunged. It was something I'd dismissed, for selfish reasons I admitted, but now threatened to destroy my ship. My crew. The people I loved.

"What are you going to do?" Fade said, coming up beside my chair. "Can we attack it?"

"That did nothing last time," I said, taking a deep breath. "Opening a communications channel."

"What, sir?" Jun asked, glancing up. "You want to try to talk to it? After what it did last time?"

"We're still here, aren't we?" I said, wondering if I'd guaranteed our deaths by trying to be the only human in history to destroy an Elder Race vessel. What was it here for now? To clean up loose ends? To upload a now-dead Kathax Beta into its system? It could destroy us at any moment so why wasn't it attacking?

"You can't be serious," Anya said. "Run away."

"We'd only die tired," I said, closing my eyes.

Jun, reluctantly, went to the controls and opened a frequency. "It's done, sir. We've got a channel open for you on all frequencies."

"If we have time before we die," U'Chuck said. "You'll have to tell me what you saw on that planet."

"Ghosts," I said, looking at her. "Though perhaps hope. Your race wasn't responsible for what happened to it."

"I knew that," U'Chuck said. "But, perhaps others didn't. I'll tell them if we survive."

If.

I tapped the communications key on the arm rest of my chair. "This is Captain Cassius Mass of the independent trader *Melampus*. The Kathax Prime is no more along with the Kathax Beta. Both were killed in a struggle with my father and sister over Marker-based technology. All of it has been destroyed and they remain dead. I'm sorry for your loss."

"You told them the truth?" Anya said, appalled. "What the hell is wrong with you?"

I took my finger off the communications key, hoping that hadn't gone through. "It was the only thing I could think of!"

Fade took a deep breath. "Well, they haven't blown us up yet."

Jun said. "Sir, I'm getting some power readings from the Elder Race probe."

I glared at Fade along with everyone else on the bridge.

"Dammit," Fade muttered.

Moments later, there was yet another scan of our ship which was identical to the one they'd given us earlier. Well, almost identical. As I felt the strange energies permeate our vessel, I felt them stop on me. Maybe it was just a trick of the mind or maybe it was really taking time to look at me specifically but the scan felt like it took a lifetime rather than seconds.

We didn't die, though.

"It's just maintaining its position in front of our vessel, sir," Jun said, her voice still wracked with fear. I'd come to like Jun as a kid sister in my years on the *Melampus* and it made me sick thinking she was only here because of me.

I pushed the communications key again. "Listen, we've seen and experienced things in the past thousand years which have opened our race up to new ideas as well as new concepts. I've born witness to the horrors your race endured and I sympathize. My species is still too young and too immature to bring peace to itself but we're getting there. This vessel carries within it nothing which could threaten your race but might help my people know we're better off learning to get along rather than challenge you. The Kathax Prime was wrong. If he'd raised us up to your level, we would have just destroyed ourselves as well as the rest of the galaxy, but he wasn't *completely* wrong. We have potential and a right to reach it just like the Kolahn did."

"Do," U'Chuck said. "My race isn't extinct yet. Just endangered."

"Shut up, Ensign," I said.

"Sorry, sir," U'Chuck said.

"Let us reach it!" I said, pleading.

"Oh, poor Cassius, you still don't know what's going on. Maybe you will when you join us." The voice on the other end mimicked Zoe's.

"What the fuck?" Fade said, doing a double-take between me and the screen.

With that, the probe vanished from our sensors as if it had never been.

"Did you know that was going to happen?" Anya asked.

"Do you think I would have cribbed a speech from *Star Voyages* if I'd known about that?" I asked. "I don't even know what that was. It could have been an upload of Zoe's consciousness or just another Elder Race member taking her voice."

"What do you think?" Fade asked.

I paused. "I think…I think there's some mysteries we're never going to find out the answer to in this life."

"That's a cop out," Jun said.

I stared at her. "Don't you have someone to be with?"

Jun looked over at Fade. "You up for it?"

Fade smiled. "I've got nothing else better to do on this ship."

Jun smiled and offered her arm, the two of them walking off the bridge of the ship. No sooner did they part then Tina spoke up from the controls. "Captain, we're receiving another message."

"From the probe?" I asked, not sure if I could make up another speech on the spot.

"No sir, from Watcher General Claire."

I blinked a couple of times. "Can we even receive transmissions in jumpspace?"

"It shouldn't be possible, but we're encountering a lot of strange things lately," Tina paused. "By the way, my sisters and I want to buy our own ship with our share of the reward."

"That can wait, Tina," I said, sighing.

"Can it?" Tina paused. "Tina II is already deep in debt to Bruce on C-Deck. She's been gambling the proceeds she expects."

"Ugh," I said, sighing. "I thought Clarice was there to keep the crew from making book."

"Clarice is running half the games," Tina paused. "She's doing a good job of fleecing everyone. Lara and Brick may actually wind up poorer than when he started."

"Captain, is it a good idea to make the Watcher General wait?" Anya asked.

"No," I said, pausing. "Listen, I'm not going to have any gambling away of our reward now that we're actually getting it. You get me a list of everyone who was betting and have it delivered to my office immediately. Everyone gets a share and no one is bartering it until they're off this ship."

Tina frowned. "Yes sir. Shall I put the Watcher General on?"

I considered summoning back Fade for the conversation but decided against it. "Sure, why not. It can't possibly be bad—"

"Please don't say that," Anya said.

"You're getting the hang of back-talking your captain," I said, pointing at her. "We've needed a new security officer since Clarice took the job of first officer. Consider yourself promoted, Lieutenant."

"I thought that was William's job," Anya said.

"I'll promote him to something else which doesn't have any duties in case he annoys me by not quitting to enjoy his money," I said.

Moments later, a hologram of Ida Claire appeared in front of me. She was wearing a white robe with a rank insignia on its right side, what I took to be the formal "dress uniform" of her spy agency. This uniform came with full audio and I could hear the sounds of rumbling which indicated to me she was both underground and under attack.

"Hi," I said, trying not to show concern. "It seems you're not in a good place."

"Oh, I'm in the best," Ida said, ignoring a Commonwealth medic running behind her as alarms blared. "Jewel of the Spiral."

I blinked. "You're on Albion?"

I tried to figure out how I should react to the discovery I hadn't prevented an invasion of the Commonwealth. I hated that government despite the fact they'd been fully justified in attacking us. I would never forgive them for destroying Crius, no matter what the terrible actions of our government had been, and I hoped the galaxy would remember the day they'd destroyed my planet with the same infamy as the murderers of Earth or the Cognition A.I. which brought about the Great Collapse.

Yet, despite that, I couldn't help but feel a sense of sympathy for the ones below. I hated the government of the Commonwealth, hated it with a fury but bore no ill will to the citizens of Albion. They were innocents in all of this no matter that they celebrated the conquests of their star navy as well as funded their activities.

Who could be attacking, though? I had witnessed enough of the Free Systems Alliance Navy blasting each other to know there was no way they could attack Albion again. They'd been destroyed down to the last ship (or at least close to it). There were bound to be other ships crewed by non-nanoplague infected soldiers but they'd be nothing more than insects buzzing at the face of the human race's largest star empire. The Chel might have the force to attack or the Union of Faith, but neither could hope to defeat the Commonwealth in a straight up fight. If it was the Elder Races then there was nothing that could be done and I'd doomed mankind. No, I refused to believe that. I'd kill myself I had to.

But would it be enough?

Ida's expression remained even, which was akin to screaming for her. "Yeah, I'm afraid so. You prevent one end-of-the-world scenario for my government and another one pops up."

I leaned forward. "Who is attacking the Commonwealth?"

Ida gave a bitter gallows laugh. "The Community."

Dammit.

ABOUT THE AUTHOR

C.T. Phipps is a lifelong student of horror, science fiction, and fantasy. An avid tabletop gamer, he discovered this passion led him to write and turned him into a lifelong geek. He is a regular blogger and also a reviewer for The Bookie Monster.

Bibliography
The Rules of Supervillainy (Supervillainy Saga #1)
The Games of Supervillainy (Supervillainy Saga #2)
The Secrets of Supervillainy (Supervillainy Saga #3)
The Science of Supervillainy (Supervillainy Saga #4)
Esoterrorism (Red Room Vol. 1)
Cthulhu Armageddon (Cthulhu Armageddon #1)
The Tower of Zhaal (Cthulhu Armageddon #2)
Lucifer's Star
Straight Outta Fangton

I Was a Teenage Weredeer

A Teenage Weredeer in Michigan

Curious about other Crossroad Press books?
Stop by our site:
http://store.crossroadpress.com
We offer quality writing
in digital, audio, and print formats.

Enter the code **FIRSTBOOK**
to get 20% off your first order from our store!
Stop by today!

Printed in Great Britain
by Amazon